Clubs

KYRA IRENE

Book Cover Design and Formatting by Books and Moods

Editing by Bryony Leah

For Ana, may your nightly visions come true.

Content Warning

Your mental health is *very* important to me. If you find any of the following to be triggering, please put yourself first.

Sexual assault, loss of a parent and sibling, death, murder, violence, and trauma.

Playlist

"Mockingbird" — Eminem
"Dreams" — The Cranberries
"Me and Your Mama" — Childish Gambino
"Everything I Wanted" — Billie Eilish
"Superstar" — Sonic Youth
"It's All in Vein" — Wet
"Fly Me to the Moon" — Frank Sinatra
"Elastic Heart" — Sia
"Oblivion" — Labrinth
"Reflections" — The Neighbourhood
"Let You Scream" — St. Loreto
"Home" — Edward Sharpe & The Magnetic Zeros
"Feeling Good" — Michael Bublé
"West Coast" — Lana Del Rey
"Sway" — Michael Bublé
"Leadlight" — Julia Jacklin

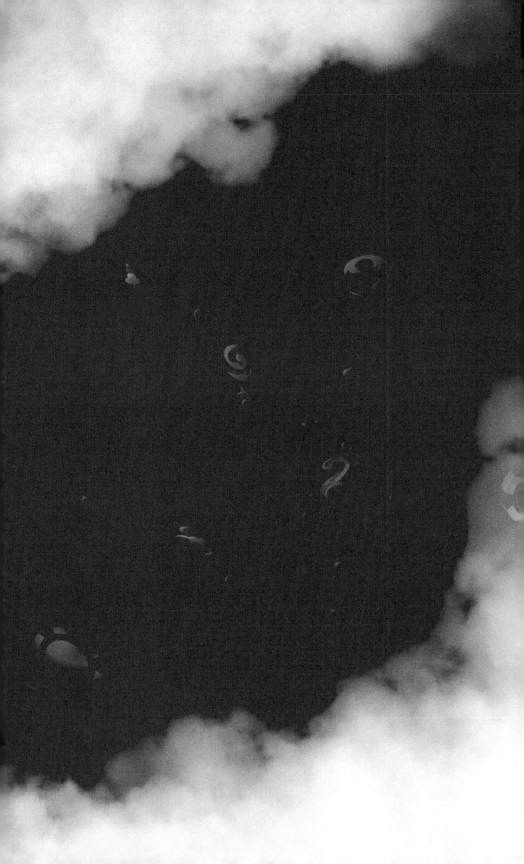

Chapter 1

Mikhail

I watch the way his hands curl around the sweating glass of vodka. He sits at the bar like he owns it. He could. By the way his suit clings to his body, it looks as if it was tailored to fit his every curve perfectly. Everything about him screams money.

I look down at myself. I look nothing like him. My clothes are ripped to shreds and my shoes are on their last life. The rubber is falling off, the seams frayed beyond repair.

"Mikhail." Kirill mutters my name. "You need to do it this time." His pale skin is far more bruised than mine.

"Okay."

His gaze his cold, though I'm not surprised. It has been for a long time. There was once life in those spotted amber eyes of his. It doesn't matter how long you stare into them—there is nothing left. They're dark. Deadly.

Just as I'm about to take a step toward the bar, he wraps his fingers around my wrist, pulling me back to him. "You need to be strong if you want to eat."

"Okay," I tell him again.

Sometimes this way of life is illegal, but no one cares to acknowledge that.

Money is paper, and yet people go feral over it—myself included.

But here's the thing about money: it doesn't matter how much someone makes, they will always live paycheck to paycheck. The more buck they make, the more their standards for living increase. I could have a very high-paying job, but would I pocket anything? *No.* Because once I get to that point, I'd want a house with ten bedrooms I'd never use and a six-car garage for the cars I'd never drive.

Money is the most fucked-up thing mankind relies on, yet here I am stealing it.

I know how wrong stealing is, but it's our way of life. Going back home isn't an option for us anymore.

"Home" isn't the right word for that place. It's a hole-in-the-wall filled with my father's things. Empty bottles cover the table. Every passing hour he adds three more. The couch is stained with his urine. Maggots crawl over the half-finished meals he spends all our money on. The house never sees the light of day. The TV's on for hours on end while my father sits on the couch with his mouth gaping open attracting flies. His teeth are rotting, and he never does anything to fix them. He eats like a king while Kirill and I only get an uncooked box of noodles for dinner every night. My body screams for nutrition, but I'm not able to get any.

Every time I come home to see him shoving mounds of food into his mouth, I cling to the hope that one day ... one day I will be able to eat like him. There is a thing about hope that no one cares to acknowledge: it only answers the people who already have everything in life.

People who have money don't have the worries I have. Their vision isn't clouded by the foul play life constantly throws in my face.

I hate the life I have. While I am thankful to have a roof over my head, I can't help but wonder how grand my life could have been if I had a parent who actually cared about me.

No child my age should have to worry about when their next meal will be or if they will even get it. *Is a warm meal really that much to ask for?*

The kids at school have it. Most of their parents even write notes in their lunchboxes wishing them a good day.

My mouth salivates when I see their lunches. If their midday meals are that good, I can't even begin to imagine what their dinners look like. Their parents probably tuck them in at night and wish all the bad dreams away before they shut their eyes.

I will never have that.

All my life I've been called "responsible for my age" as if it's the biggest compliment I'll ever receive, but it never was and never will be.

It's the most backhanded excuse of a compliment I have come to know. I was forced to take on a parental role for myself as if I know how to parent. My peers get praise when they did something right. They get a C? That's *life-changing* for them. But what do I get when I run home with excitement pumping through my bloodstream to tell Father I got the best grade in class?

I get nothing.

Receiving a common education is like finding a gold mine, but my work is worth nothing. It's a standard that I'm meant to uphold.

Most of the time, people like me don't even realize they're neglected. Neglect doesn't transfer as an act of trauma, although it should. I am never noticed in a positive light.

But hey, I have a shirt on my back and a crumpled-up pillow to lay my head on at night, so all is well in the world.

Sue me—I want more.

I force down a sickening feeling I've been holding onto for days on end. The built-up shame rolls down my cheeks as my throat thickens with sobs. My cries for help will never be answered. No one cares, and I'm not even sure if I do at this point.

All I want is for something to point me in the right direction. The thought of doing this for my whole life opens an endless pit of dread in my stomach.

I bring my hand up to my warm, wet face only to notice how much I've been drowning in my own grief. I've suppressed so many emotions, and the bubble finally popped. I use my dry sleeve to wipe away the tears that fall effortlessly down my face.

I'm not crying out of weakness; I'm crying because I'm fucking angry at the world for

giving me nothing.

"Mikhail." My brother whispers my name. I don't dare to look back at him. If he sees that I'm crying he'll call me weak. I don't want to be weak. "You've got this," he says with a strong voice.

With my back still to him, I nod.

A woman bumps into my shoulder as she walks past me wearing clothes that scream "Daddy's money" while I walk off with a twenty I slipped from her purse. She looks like the kind of girl who'd spend thousands of dollars on a bag just to hold more of her dollars.

It doesn't matter how bitchy she is to her family. One of the many privileges of having a lot of money: being snobby is a given. In fact, it's considered classy if you have enough of it. Her father must show his love by providing the materialistic items she begs for.

My father has never shown me a sliver of love. Not that I think it exists anyhow. The only thing that can truly connect one person to another is commitment. That's what Kirill has shown me.

If he can stick by my side, I can stick by his.

I force my eyes shut as I try to gather the strength to do what needs to be done. When I slowly open them back up, my vision is blurred, but I can still see where I need to go.

The man's suit jacket hangs off the back of the chair. I crane my neck to see around the corner and watch him make his way toward a door at the end of a long, narrow hallway. Only men with money and power are allowed past those doors.

I glance back at Kirill, who stands behind me as if he wants to do it instead. He'll never stop trying to protect me, but I want to show him I can help. I can be the one who sticks by his side to protect him.

I straighten my back as I walk confidently toward the jacket, exchanging a nod with the bartender as I go. He looks at me strangely, probably wondering what someone as young as me is doing at the bar.

"Do you want water? I have orange juice too," he tells me in Russian.

"Water, please." I smile, grateful for his kindness. "Two, if that's okay?"

"Of course."

He turns around to make the drinks, his back facing me as my hand slowly reaches into his pocket. I feel bad for stealing in general, but it feels worse now that I'm doing it in the presence of someone who doesn't share my greed. He doesn't understand. No one ever will.

The moment I feel the leather wallet in my hands, I want to make a run for it. Instead, I put it in my back pocket and wait for the water.

The bartender places two Styrofoam cups on the counter with lids and straws.

"Thank you," I tell him. I walk toward the door with a casual pace so I won't draw any attention. When I meet Kirill there, I hand him one of the waters.

"Did you get it?" he asks as he puts the straw in the cup.

"I did."

"Then let's go."

I follow my older brother outside, but my body slams into his when he comes to an abrupt stop.

"Vor." Thief.

I look past Kirill. My eyes widen and fear floods my stomach as one of the men pulls a gun out of his jacket. Kirill shoves me in the arm, telling me to run. I take the opportunity to dive through the man's legs and make my escape.

I laugh with Kirill as we run side by side as fast as we can. There's a jump in his step while he runs. "You fucking did it!" he shouts at the top of his lungs. He's proud of me.

Holy fuck. I did do it.

A large smile tugs at the corner of my lips, and I allow it to take over. In this moment, I'm not scared to let this overwhelming feeling of success take over my thoughts.

My legs move faster than I ever thought they were capable of. I turn my head to look behind me and see the men trying to catch up to us, but they're not fast enough.

None of that matters once we reach the dead end of an alley and I stare into the face of a man who doesn't look like someone we want to mess with.

My face numbs at the glare he gives to me and my brother. He doesn't appear to be pissed; if anything he looks intrigued, and I'm not sure what to make of that. The man's eyes are hooded and have the color of the dark moss that grows on the bottom of aged trees.

Kirill stands with his legs lined up with his shoulders. He doesn't look as nervous as I am. But then again, he never is. He's always been the man to be strong.

While my spirits fall, I see his interest spike.

I can feel my heart racing as if it's about to pound out of my chest. I bite down on the inside of my cheek to refrain from saying something I'll regret.

"You stole from one of my people," the man in a light gray tux says to us in Russian. He laughs at my silence. The sound doesn't bring joy but fear, the vibrations that fall from his throat are coated with power. The sound of his voice alone could make a grown man question everything about himself. "If you steal from a man, you own up to it."

"I was just trying to feed my brother," Kirill says, taking the blame for the wallet I stole.

He looks me up and down with his dark eyes. "Your hands and face—what happened?"

"Our father," Kirill starts.

"I asked the kid. I'm sure he can answer for himself."

A noise escapes Kirill. I glance at him with a hope that's quick to wash away. The man I've always looked up to seems to be drowning in shame all of a sudden. I pull at his arm, begging for his attention, but he refuses to look at me.

Is he ashamed?

Terrified to speak up, I gulp down my fear. "As he said, it was our father."

"He beats you two?"

My brother and I nod slowly in response.

The person we stole from walks up behind us, screaming to the world that we're thieves.

"If it's that big of an issue, do something about it," Mr. Gray tells him. His words come out almost as a threat—not to me or Kirill, but to the man.

"I'll fucking kill you," he says, kicking me in the stomach, only worsening the pain of my already cracked rib—the rib my father cracked just this morning.

Mr. Gray takes a gun out from his waistband and places a bullet in the center of the man's forehead. He gives it no second thought; shows no sign of mercy. He shows no emotion at all.

My heart drops and I shudder at the loud gunfire. A high-pitched ringing fills my ears and makes everything around me sound muffled. I had no idea they could be so loud.

The man falls to the ground, and I watch the endless stream of blood flow from his skull. I stare at the dead man as if I've seen many bodies drop to the floor. It doesn't shock me as much as I thought it would. Seeing the man fall to the ground isn't what scares me—it's the sound of him choking on his own blood. It gurgles through his closing throat while he fights for his final breath of air.

Mr. Gray walks up to the dead man and mutters something under his breath. He's calm and collected. That should terrify me, but it doesn't. In fact, I admire it. Even at the age of thirteen, I'm not ignorant to the idea the man who hit me deserved to die.

"Never speak empty threats. If you have a purpose, you stay true to it." Mr. Gray looks directly at me. His hair is slicked back and his eyes have dark shadows. I look up at my brother and notice he's just as in awe of him as I am. "Never let a man beat you when you're already down, kid." His words are aimed at me. Then he demands, "Your names?"

I normally refrain from telling anyone anything about me, but there's something different about Mr. Gray. I feel obliged to tell him everything.

"I'm Mikhail. This is Kirill."

"Did you two deserve the beating you got?"

I ponder his question. Do we deserve to be beaten for stealing something from another person? *Yes.* But does anyone ever deserve a beating if they haven't done anything wrong? Father hit me because I started to clean up his mess—at least, I tried to. I started by sweeping the bugs off the ground and gathering his trash. He didn't like that. He grabbed me and beat me until I was choking on my own breath.

"No."

"Does he deserve the same beating you got?"

I nod in response because my own voice fails me.

The man walks a circle around me and my brother, looking us up and down as if he's inspecting us. "I've heard about the both of you. I don't think you realize how fast word can travel."

"It took you long enough," Kirill says with determination.

My mouth falls open and I look back up at Kirill. There isn't any shame in his glare. It's as if he's wanted to get this man's attention for some time, but why would he want that?

The stranger tilts his head, welcoming the idea Kirill has been committing crimes to get his attention. Almost ... *proud*.

A wicked smile takes over his lips. "Okay."

I turn and pull at my brother's arm, begging to get out of this situation. We shouldn't be standing near a dead body asking for problems. He said I needed to steal so we can eat, but I'm starting to think he did all this on purpose.

We stole from the wrong person, and that's exactly what Kirill wanted. *Does he think he and I can't conquer the world by ourselves?*

"All right, get in the car." Mr. Gray turns on his heels and begins to walk out of the alley, leaving the dead man to rot.

"Us?" Kirill asks as if he expects anything less.

Mr. Gray stops and turns around slowly. "Unless you'd like to go back to what you were doing."

I race after him, afraid he'll leave. He has a long stride to his walk, and I struggle to keep up with him. Kirill and I must look like little ducklings following their mother. The thought alone is kind of embarrassing, but I'll own up to it. The man is direct with his words and holds a strong sense of purpose. I fear him a million times over, but it's not the fear that I've come to know. In a strange way, I want to follow every step he takes.

A black Mercedes pulls up to the edge of the sidewalk. Mr. Gray opens the door and motions for us to get in. I've never been in a car before, and I'm sure it shows. I stare at the shiny leather cushions as I scoot to the other side to make room for my brother.

"Where do you two live?"

"Just around the corner. It's the gray building with bikes in the yard."

The man is strong and apathetic. I can tell by the lack of worry lines on his forehead that he doesn't carry concern on his shoulders. To be a man like him means to expect everyone around you will be just as tough. *But what happens if I share my pity for others?* No one should ever want to be like him, but a tug at my heart tells me to take note of everything he does.

"Idi k nim domoy."

Kirill grabs onto my hand and holds it tight to his chest, his heart beating fast. *Is he scared?* This is what he wanted all along—he should be thrilled about this. My eyes fall to my lap and my mind races in circles. Kirill is a very private person, and I shouldn't be upset with him for trying to help us, but anger crashes through me when I realize he should have told me about his plan. That's the least he could have done.

"Kirill," I whisper as quietly as I can.

The muscles in his neck tense when he leans down to hear me. "Who is this man?"

He licks the bottom of his lip and looks around us to make sure no one's listening. "He's Bratva," he says in a low growl.

Bratva. We shouldn't be involved with them—I know that much. The crimes my brother and I commit are child's play compared to what the Bratva does. If Kirill means to work for them, stealing is the last thing we'll be doing.

The car comes to a short stop, and Mr. Gray opens the door. "Out," he demands.

I scramble to get out and stand on the sidewalk. I don't want to go back into that building. I never want to see it again.

"Which door?" I look up at the man whose eyes are filled with purpose.

He looks pissed, but not at me or my brother. Lifting my head, I survey the buildings that surround us. They all look exactly the same, built with cheap material, the stone walls threatening to crumble from a single touch. Trash is placed where bushes should be growing. The lights that hang from the walls flicker on and off, hardly guiding the walkway.

I grab onto his hand and lead him to the rusted yellow door that separates me from my failed excuse of a father. Mr. Gray sniffles and kicks the door down as if it's made of paper. He steps over the trash and wrinkles his nose at the rancid smell.

I follow behind him while my brother waits outside. I don't blame Kirill for not wanting to come in. He's suffered at the hands of our father much longer than I have.

My father stands up from the couch, bags of chips and beer cans falling off his lap. "Mikhail," he grumbles in Russian, "who is this?"

"Kirill, do you need anything from inside here?" Mr. Gray asks, looking back at him.

"No."

"Mikhail, do you?"

I try to remember the items I own. I don't have much of anything. I don't even have a bedroom; I sleep in the hallway in a sleeping bag or in the lobbies of cheap hotels. "Yes," I tell him when I remember the notebook I want to grab.

"Get it quick and come back."

I rush past the filth, stepping over things that make me want to hurl. Once in the hallway, I reach under my sleeping bag and grab the notebook.

Scampering back to the main room, I see my father staring at Mr. Gray. It's strange—I've never seen my father show fear, but he is now. He grabs me by the hair and pulls me close.

"Mikhail, remember what I told you?" Mr. Gray asks, pulling me toward him. It's as if these men are fighting over whose side I'm on.

"Never let a man beat you when you're already down," I repeat the words he spoke to me only a moment ago.

"That's right," he says, placing a gun in my hand.

I stare down at it and feel its power taking control of my thoughts. The bullet that rests in this chamber could end a life. It could end mine, but I hold its power.

"If you choose to be a part of this, you simply point this at him and press the trigger under your index finger."

If I choose to be a part of this.

"Mikhail wouldn't kill his own blood—he knows better than that. You shouldn't bite the hand that feeds you," my father says.

"Do you?" Mr. Gray argues in Russian. "Do you feed him? The boy is nothing but bone." He steps behind me and places his hands on my shoulders.

I hold up the gun and watch my father stare into the eye of the pistol.

"Close your eyes if you must."

No. I want to see the life in his body die. I want to hear the last and final breath he ever takes. *I want him gone.*

I hold my finger down on the trigger and watch the bullet go into my father's chest. My body jolts back into Mr. Gray and my ears ring. My father's hands fly to the wound and he falls back into his chair, choking on his blood. It's poetic really. He lived his life until his death in that very chair.

"*Ya gorzhus*, Mikhail."

He is proud of me. I just killed my father, and I don't feel anything ... nothing at all. I watched his face turn red and his mouth gape open. I watched him process that his own son just shot him and he couldn't do anything about it. And I feel *nothing*.

"Right. You two will come with me now."

We walk to the car and sit in silence the entire ride. I don't think Kirill agrees with what I did, but a part of me doesn't care. I can be the one to stand up for us. He needs me to be.

The driver pulls the car into a long, narrow driveway. I lift my head to look out the window at the beautiful land that surrounds us. Tall cypress trees line the concrete. The house looks *huge*. Snow dusts the black roof, making it appear a faded gray. Tall windows cover the entire side of the house. A fountain rests in the middle of a small island at the end of the driveway.

"This is your new home. Does it suffice?" Mr. Gray asks with a subtle smile.

I can hardly contain my excitement as I nod over and over again.

"My name is Pavel Stepanov. You will take my last name, and I will take you in as my own. I will raise you as my sons. Be sure not to come into my office. That is where I work and must not be bothered. Kirill, you still need to prove yourself, but we will talk about that later." He gets out of the car and leads my brother and me to the front door.

"This is insane," Kirill mutters.

A young woman walks down the stairs with a toddler in her arms. She looks at Mr. Stepanov with curiosity written on her face.

He motions for her to come to us. "See this little one? Her name is Anya. She is your sister, and you will not let harm touch her."

"Can I hold her?" I ask the woman with long brown hair. She has kind eyes. I almost never come across eyes like hers.

The woman kneels to the floor so I'm level with Anya. Her face looks smooth, and her lips pout. She has big eyes and dark hair. Her fingers move to try and wave at me. I wave back.

"Galina, once they are ready, show them around and let them pick their rooms."

A wide smile spreads across my face as I hold my sister in my arms. I try to wrap my mind around everything that happened today. I can't think of a single thing that went wrong.

In fact, I don't think I've ever been happier.

Chapter 2

Mikhail

TWO YEARS AGO ...

My father's men flood the door to his bedroom. He can't have a moment of goddamn peace. There isn't a single thing that makes them different from one another. Not even their morals.

Even I can understand why a man lying on his death bed might beg for a moment of peace, but they don't show my father the decency.

They take their turns saying their goodbyes, but I know they're all full of shit. They don't care about him. They have no reason to. He's used them for the entire time they've worked for him.

To Pavel, his men are his shield. They protect him from a tragic end. He doesn't care if they live or die. That's what makes him capable of doing what he does.

His tragic end: cancer. Fucking cancer.

A strong man like Pavel was meant to die defending his kingdom, to remain strong until his last and final breath, but the devil had other plans.

Tumors are spreading through his brain like wildfire, threatening to kill him in less than a month. It's almost as if they feed off one another.

There are times when he'll look me in the eye and not recognize me. I know in these moments hope was created as some inspirational bullshit to keep people from facing the harsh reality of life.

Hope rests in the hands of the devil. Every waking hour you think there's something out there to grant you your wishes, the devil claps his hands and shatters your hopes as if they were nothing.

This is my harsh reality. The man who took me under his wing as his own is leaving me in this world to fend for myself.

He taught me everything I know, and yet I feel as if I only know the tip of the iceberg. I was supposed to have years with him.

I lift my attention away from the ground and watch my father cough into his pale, veiny hands. He's weak, but he tries to cover his pain with a soulful smile.

"Misha." He calls my name.

I brush into his men's shoulders to get them out of my way. These men will never be anything. There's no doubt in my mind each of them tried to convince him to pass his power over to them. Their faces all lack emotion, which seems disrespectful to my father in a strange way.

"Give us the room," my father demands.

Turning their hunched backs, they mope out of the room swearing under their breath.

I watch the door until I hear it click closed. Then, pulling up a padded stool, I take a seat next to my father.

He turns his head to me slowly as if it takes every muscle in his body to accomplish such a simple task. I grab his hand and pull it to my chest.

"Still beating strong," he says.

"Still beating for you."

"Mikhail," he starts.

Barely able to keep my emotions under control, I hold his hands to my face, allowing a tear to fall down his wrist.

"You cut that shit off right now." He uses humor as a coping mechanism.

I laugh through the tears and shake my head. "You're leaving me soon."

The machine that beeps to the sound of his heart only continues to slow. It's a matter of minutes. I can feel an ache in my chest—a kind of pain I've never felt before in my life, and that says a lot. It feels as if my heart is rising into my throat.

Life is a fucking joke. Nothing can ever be enjoyed because the second I allow myself to feel joy, nothing but hatred takes over.

I *hate* this.

I let the hate consume my thoughts as if I'm never supposed to feel anything else, because I don't want to. I don't deserve to. I've enjoyed many things in my life, but this moment proves to me that I was weak.

I cared for my brother in a way most can't even begin to understand. I loved him more than I hated him, and look where that got me.

He left me too.

I'm all alone in this world, and there is nothing I can do about it except face the harsh reality.

If I never allow myself to feel love—to feel overwhelmed by the happiness others can give me—nothing will hurt me.

"Mia has an envelope that you need to open. It includes everything I have planned for you."

"This is wrong," I tell him.

I know deep in my heart that my father never meant for me to take over. I could see it in his eyes—he never looked at me like I was worth what he is about to give me. He thought I was less than Kirill because I had a softer heart than him. I was the person to take care of Anya. The little girl she once was had my heart on a leash, and I didn't have a problem with that.

I hold my breath in a weak attempt to tell my body to get its shit together. I don't want Pavel to see me crying while he's on his death bed, getting ready to hand over his legacy to me with open arms.

"No. It is right. I raised you as my own from the moment I saw you. All these years I've known it's you who will take over. I trust you will do exactly what needs to be done. Take back, Mikhail. Do not give. Be ruthless if you must, and never—"

"Never let a man beat you when you're already down."

"Take back New York," he mutters, his voice so clumsy I can hardly understand him.

I listen to every beat of his words as if each one is about to be his last. He tells me that he always knew it would be me, but I know he's just saying that so I have faith in myself.

His eyes flutter with each word I say. His body is failing him, and I can do nothing but watch the strongest man I know become the weakest. Become nothing.

The monitor that was once beeping to the sound of his weak heart becomes flat. Lifting my eyes, I watch the line on the screen run to the edge, not once rising to his regular heartbeat. I stare at it as if it's going to change, but it won't. It just sings the devil's wrath. That one tone over and over again, screaming to me that he is gone.

I let go of his hand gently and place it beside his body, wiping the tears from my eyes. I lift myself off the chair and bring my ear to his mouth.

I hear no snarky remark fall from his lips. I don't hear his breath. I don't hear the sound of his laughter, a signal he's about to rise from the bed and tell me it was all just a joke.

I yank the cord out of the wall and listen to the room fall silent. I never knew silence could be a fucking joke.

A cruel laugh escapes me, and I force my eyes shut, pressing down on them as hard as I can. I'll only give myself a moment to grieve; after that I won't allow myself to feel anything else. No love, no remorse ... nothing.

I walk to the door and swing it open.

Leaning against the wall with one of his legs crossed over the other and his arms folded across his chest, he looks at me as if he already knows what I'm thinking.

Lev has been one of my right-hand men for a long time now. He'll stay by my side no matter what I do.

"I want a moment with him," a man says, walking up to me until his face is only inches from mine. His attitude makes up for something I'm sure he lacks. He has no reason to be challenging me right now.

My father never hired ignorant men, only men with the urge to fight for a power they'll never have.

"You can have your moment at his funeral." I walk past him to Lev. "I want it arranged for today. I don't care who can make it—I want him buried properly, and I will not wait for the convenience of others."

"Yes, boss."

I feel the man's eyes drilling a hole in the back of my head. He's envious of the power I hold. He speaks up to challenge me, but I quickly shut him down.

"I buried my brother, and now I will bury my father. It would be an inconvenience to have to bury you as well." I gulp down my frustration and realize I don't want these blood-sucking vultures in my house any longer.

Reaching for my gun in the waistband of my pants, I try to think about what my father would want. Would he sacrifice his mental being for the feeling of security, or would he place a bullet in the center of his skull for the bother he's causing? I guess I'll never know.

Before I can stop myself from speaking my irrational thoughts aloud, I say, "I want everyone out of this fucking house besides Lev, Adrian, and Dimitri. Until the rest of you can prove to me that you will respect me, you are dead to me."

Men who aren't on my side don't benefit me in any way. The ones who live in this house will continue to get in the way of my business. With Father gone, I can finally avenge my brother. I don't care whose blood I have to spill in the process.

They swallow the little pride they have left and walk down the dark hallway with their heads bobbing between their hunched shoulders. If their steps were any heavier, I'd call them out for acting like children who didn't get their way. They're adults and shouldn't act as if my father's death is inconvenient for them. Hell, if it weren't for Pavel, they'd be sitting in some alleyway holding out a metal can asking for spare change.

Once they disappear around the sharp corner, I stop and look at Lev. "I don't need to talk to Mia to understand Pavel already started his plans in New York. Tell the man to pack their shit—we are leaving tonight." With my hands held by my side, I brush past him and swear under my breath. "And don't forget to gather everything Kirill had on *Koldunya*. I'm sure Ludis is hiding her out in New York."

With a final glance at the wooden door keeping my father hidden from the world, I realize I'll never be able to set foot in this house without feeling like the good memories are now tainted. Anya's loud, high-pitched snickers echo through the halls as if they were always a dream and nothing more.

These walls will never hold another happy memory now that both Kirill and Pavel are gone. They made this house a home. Without them, it's just four concrete slabs holding up a roof. Nothing here will ever be enjoyed again. The sheets will never be slept in. The coffee machine won't run at an ungodly hour anymore. The piano keys will never sound again.

Nature might as well take over this land because I want nothing more to do with it. A part of me died with this house and my family members. A part of me I don't wish to ever get back.

Chapter 3

Sloane

I've memorized the number of steps it'll take him to get to my room just from the sound of his heavy boots slamming into the wooden floor.

My heart beats rapidly as I rush to look outside. Kneeling to the floor, my fingers hold up my weight. Through the blinds, I see three blacked-out cars pull up in the driveway. The headlights shine through the window, making my pitch-black room bright with a warm yellow glow. Men step out and look at the house. They're all wearing fancy suits that look expensive enough to cover our mortgage. They scan the house as if they've never been here before, but they have.

They come here all the time. What makes this time any different?

When their attention drifts to the side of the house where my bedroom is, I duck down quickly to make sure they don't see me. I was only ever allowed to see *one* person, but not the rest. My hands curl and I place them across my chest, and my breath shakes while I maintain my focus on the silver doorknob.

Dad walks in with my brother, Alek. He starts talking in Russian, but my dad yells at him. I watch them exchange angry looks.

"Sloane, you know the drill. Do not make a sound, and do not leave this room."

I've memorized the drill. Ever since I was little, those three cars have come to our home once a month. I know what my dad does. I may be sheltered, but I'm not an idiot.

"I know."

He kisses the top of my head and closes the door softly.

I crouch to the floor and place my ear to the small gap along the bottom. On the off chance one of them will speak loudly enough, I want to be able to hear it. I'm a nosy son of a bitch. I just can't help myself.

Their voices are deep. They don't sound like the men who normally come by here. The way they speak to one another makes it sound as if they're arguing.

I lie like this for so long I start drifting off to sleep, but the door that slams right into my head wakes me up instantly.

"Shit, I'm sorry," Ruslan says, helping me up from the ground. He wears a different expression from the one I've been accustomed to. It's almost as if worry is gnawing at him. His slicked-back blond hair is tousled, and his cheek bones are more prominent than usual due to the lack of a smile on his face.

"It's all right." I smile brightly at him.

"It's Friday. Why aren't you dressed?"

Friday. Family dinner. I don't know how I forgot. "It must have slipped my mind."

He shoots me a questioning look and mumbles under his breath, "I'll send Ingret up. And don't forget my fight is tonight if you still want to tag along."

I nod, trying to keep my excitement at bay. Ruslan is the only one who lets me leave the house. If Dad ever found out, I'm sure he'd have a heart attack.

Ingret shoves past him through the doorway, shooing him out of the room.

"Guess she's already here. I'll leave you guys to it," he mutters, finally showing me his usual smile.

She holds a black silk dress and places it against my body. "Perfect. Change into this."

I smile and take the dress from her. It is perfect. It shimmers, but it's subtle.

"I don't want you to overthink tonight," she sighs, looking through the jewelry on my dresser.

"I don't want to either, but all they do is argue, and I hate it."

She ignores me and ransacks my closet for shoes as if I'm not capable of picking them out myself.

"Why am I dressing differently tonight?" I ask her. Our dinners are always formal, but never *this* formal.

"He has men coming tonight. Not the ones who just left, but others."

"And he's letting me downstairs?" My stomach twists with nerves. He never lets me see anyone from outside the family. *What changed?*

"I was thinking the same thing." She shrugs and holds out some gold jewelry for me to take, placing the heels on the floor.

I change into the dress and everything else she picked out for me.

While I may not be allowed to see anyone besides family, Dad has taught me a lot. I'll never forget something he told me when I was in my mid-teens: "Similar to the phrase 'poison is a woman's weapon,' words are a woman's venom."

Through *years* of experimenting, I've found Ruslan hates my sarcasm and Alek hates when I talk about how great Ruslan is. As if he's competing to be better than his brother. As fucked up as it is, I do it anyway. Brothers are ruthless sometimes, and I refuse to let them walk all over me.

I blame Ruslan for all my snarky remarks. If he'd acted like they didn't bother him, I'd stop completely. But I feel it's my duty as his sister to be a royal pain in his ass. Plus, I will always welcome a good laugh with open arms.

Ingret has always been my favorite person in this house. I'll never admit it to her, but she is. She's been a part of this family for as long as I can remember. She's my father's age, mid-fifties. I'm honestly shocked they never formed a romantic connection.

I know my dad will never move on from my mother, but he has to try. Despair drags me down when I see how closed-off he is. I'm sure there's a woman out there for him who would be able to heal the cracks in his heart. Maybe then he'd stop keeping me locked up in this house like Rapunzel. The time will come eventually—I'm just waiting for it. I've been waiting for two years.

Dad rarely talks about my mother, but I don't think that's a bad thing. If he can't even bring himself to speak about her, perhaps she should be forgotten altogether. Why live with numbness infusing your body when there are so many wonderful things life has to offer?

As if I'd know about the wonders of the world. I roll my eyes at the thought. I'll never be allowed to leave this house. I crave adventure more and more as the days pass by, and there is nothing I can do besides crush my own dreams.

Ingret's curly blonde hair sways over her shoulders with each step she takes. "There is a lot you don't know, but you need to keep it that way." Her emerald eyes are coated in worry.

"I know." Another lie. I don't want to keep it that way; I want to know everything. I don't hold my ear against the door for hours on end for fun.

"I will be there with you, and if things get too much, you can leave, and I will keep your father under control."

I can't help but laugh. "Yeah, you're the only one who can do that."

Her hands find her curvy hips and she does a short, quirky dance. "I know." She laughs. "Don't you ever tell him I said that!" She makes a fist and punches my arm softly. "Now go."

I leave my room and sneak down the long hallway, peeking my head around the corner into the formal dining room. Light blue panels with white trim line the walls. The table is centered in the middle of the room with a chandelier hanging above it.

It's strange to see other people sitting at our table. Sitting in the room

I've seen once a week for my entire life. The room I know like the back of my hand, yet I know nothing about the people in it.

"Sloane, come take a seat," Dad says as if he can see through the walls.

I clear my throat and enter the room. There's a seat right by my brother, Alek, that I slowly walk toward.

The walls start to close in as I feel my anxiety getting the better of me. I sit down in the chair in front of the window. The seals are aged, allowing the warm breeze to drift past me.

The strange men sit across from me. I try to get a good look at them, but I force my eyes down when I see the man sitting in the middle staring at me as if I'm a mirror showing his reflection.

These dinners are always the worst. Alek picking a fight with Dad is inevitable.

I know my place in this family, but sometimes I can't help but want to stand up for my dad.

But then I remember Dad handles Alek just fine on his own. I've come to the conclusion he only lets Alek talk to him like that to prepare him.

"You okay?" Ruslan nudges me.

"I—yes, why?"

"You just look worried." His brow furrows as he looks at me strangely. His blond hair is messy, but it suits him.

I shake my head quickly, not breaking eye contact. I've just been playing the waiting game for years, and I'm ready.

Ingret sits down next to my father and nods for us to begin our dinner. The food she cooks is the kind I'll never tire of. She uses seasoning in a way I'll never understand.

I cut into the steak and taste each flavor on every part of my tongue.

"Allow me to skip past the bullshit," one of the strangers says to my family.

I drop my fork loudly. Dad looks in my direction, curiosity written all over his face. He's probably wondering what sort of scene I'll cause today.

"They're coming, and you know that. You need to kill him if you want full control," the strange man continues, his eyes stern.

"He said not to," Dad says.

"Who's coming?" I manage to get out, eager to grab onto everything I can.

"Oh, Sloane, allow me to introduce myself and my men."

Four men stand up out of their seats.

"My name is Vladimir. This is Stepan, Ilya, and Volo."

"This was a mistake," Dad says to the men.

Confusion and worry only heighten my anxiety as I try to concentrate. They start to argue in Russian, their voices flooding my ears.

"Sloane, come with me," Ruslan says from across the table.

As soon as the men sit back down, I notice they all have guns placed in the waistbands of their pants.

I get out of my seat and follow Ruslan out of the room. He stops at the stairs and pulls me toward him.

"I don't want you to worry."

"What's happened?"

"I don't know why he brought them here. Listen, go upstairs and get your insulin pen just in case. I'm about to head out."

I search his eyes for the answer his words won't tell me, but it's useless. I think he's just as clueless as I am. "Okay," I tell him and rush upstairs.

What was the point of the dinner if he and I are leaving?

I tuck the insulin pen inside my bra. Before rushing downstairs, I arrange my pillows to make it look as if I'm in bed.

When I meet Ruslan downstairs, we make our way out to the car in silence. He drives us down the long, narrow driveway. The window rolls down, and he scans his card so the gates will open.

"Thank you for bringing me with you," I tell him.

He takes his eyes off the road for a moment to smile at me. "Of course. I wouldn't want to leave without you."

The ride to town doesn't take long, but the entire time I can't stop thinking about what everyone was yelling about. If there's a problem, Ruslan will take care of it easily. He's been a hitman for years. He's the one who takes out our father's enemies. He goes after the men who want the power

Dad has and takes away their greed. He's like a ghost, always lurking in the shadows, removing threats one by one.

Alek doesn't know about this. He thinks Dad isn't doing much, but that's because Ruslan's taking care of business for him.

I follow Ruslan down the sidewalk when we arrive. The dark street is filled with the city's nightlife, everyone drinking and laughing. At some point in my life, I hope I'll be able to go out and enjoy myself like them.

"Sloane," he calls, gesturing for me to catch up. He throws his gym bag over his shoulder and walks down a dark alley.

I grab onto the metal railing and step down a short flight of stairs.

A man stands in front of the door at the bottom of the stairs blocking my entrance. He eyes me as if he could break me with his bare hands. But when he sees Ruslan, he steps to one side.

It took me a while to come to terms with the fact Ruslan does this for fun. It's not even about the money.

And there's *a lot* of money.

The second I step through the door I'm overwhelmed by the smell in the air. It's putrid.

"Remember what I told you?" my brother asks as he wraps some kind of bandage over the skin on his wrist.

I nod. "Don't talk to anyone. Don't look at anyone but you." I repeat his rules.

I don't like how rules are constantly laid out for me, but I understand they're for my benefit. I'll listen because the second I go against the rules, Ruslan won't take me with him anymore. And I love coming to these matches. They interest me.

It's not necessarily the fighting I find interesting, but the emotion on the men's faces. I can often tell if they're fighting for something or if they just want to fight *someone*.

If my brother took the money he won, he'd be able to live off his savings. But he doesn't take the money. He donates it.

I'd love to be able to donate someday, but it's not my place. I don't even have any money. Everything I have is my family's.

Ruslan puts a mouth guard over his teeth and taps his knuckles on top of my head. "I'm going to practice," he says, walking toward a red bag that hangs from the industrial ceiling.

I find a bench and move over heavy bags that smell like shit, but something grabs my attention.

A silver chain with what looks like diamonds on it.

Real diamonds.

I look around to see if anyone's watching me, but they're all too busy punching each other.

I shouldn't take it. Men come here to make money. Most of them need the money.

I intertwine my fingers to keep myself from reaching into the bag. I can't stand this feeling. It's as if the chain has eyes and is staring at me, begging me to take it.

I shake my head. *That's ridiculous.*

While I wait on Ruslan's fight, I think about all the things I could do with the chain if I sold it. I could start a life for myself and get the hell out of here. Not that I'd particularly want to sell it, but I do want to have my own life. Constantly sitting in my room for years on end is proving to be a waste of time. I'd rather die out in the world doing something dangerous, something fulfilling, than rot in my bed for safety.

More people flood the small underground room, and my skin crawls. Being around this many people makes me nervous. I'm afraid I'll mess something up.

Ruslan walks over to me, sweat dripping down his face. "You good?" he asks as his eyes search mine.

I smile through the uncomfortable feeling and wave him off.

Everyone gathers in a circle surrounding the ring. My brother steps up and stares at his opponent.

I watch everyone fight, but I don't watch him. He's the one person in my life who never loses anything. But it hurts me to see him get punched over and over. Even though I know he'll win, it's a strange feeling watching the strongest people you know take a beating.

I clear my throat when I hear everyone chanting for Ruslan.

Standing up, I reach into the bag and grab the chain. Black clothes fall out, and I bend down to pick them up, but I stop when I notice the entire bag is full of stacks of money.

My eyes widen. *That's so much fucking money.*

Focusing on the money and the chain, I'm left with a feeling of greed. I have to take it. I can't help myself. It's right there.

A large hand grabs onto my wrist and twists. I screech from the pain and try to pull my hand away. The tall man looking down at me hits me across the face.

With the chain still in my hand, I rush to the door and make a run for it. Kicking the heels off my feet, I race down the sidewalk, passing by everyone.

Why the hell am I running? Oh my God, what am I doing?

I turn my head behind me quickly to see if he's still running after me and find his face flashing with anger. I can't help the laugh that escapes my lips.

This feeling is incredible. Adrenaline spikes through my blood, a euphoric sensation. My feet slam onto the rough stone, bound to leave cuts on the bottom of them, but I couldn't care less. I can't feel anything besides the beat of my heart crashing into my ribs. I've never felt like this before. *I love it.*

"Vorovka!" he shouts after me. *Thief.*

An alarm rings in my head when I hear the Russian in his voice.

I turn back around, and a man steps right into me. I slam into his back and fall to the ground, scraping my knees.

"Vorovka!" the man huffs, trying to catch his breath. *"Vorovka."*

Standing around me in a circle, four men stare down at me. Three of them laugh at the guy who was trying to get me, but one just stands there staring me down. He's wearing a suit tailored to fit him perfectly.

I mutter under my breath as I try to get myself off the ground. The man in all-black offers his hand.

"Ne tron' yeyo. Koldunya," a bald man says. The man who stands out from the rest takes his hand back just as I was about to grab it. Tattoos in an

abstract pattern line his entire neck up to his hairline. *"Vashe imya?" Your name?*

When his eyes find mine, I can't help but stare.

"I see. English?" he asks. His voice is deep and his Russian accent barely noticeable.

"Yeah," I answer without giving it any thought.

He offers his hand again, this time not taking it back. When I grab onto him, he lifts me off the ground.

"Your name?"

"Sloane," I tell him. *Does he know me?* He should.

His jaw clenches, and he fights a smile as he looks at his friends. "Sloane, I'm Mikhail. Is this man bothering you?" He narrows his deep blue eyes on the man I stole from.

Mikhail.

I turn to look back at him, and he steps closer to me. Mikhail holds up his hand. The man looks like he's about to piss himself, and rightfully so; Mikhail looks fucking terrifying.

"No," I answer honestly. *I'm the one who's bothering him.*

"He calls you a thief—are you?"

"No." *That was a lie.*

"Mm-hmm." He takes the chain from my hand and holds it up. "No, I know a thief when I see one."

There's a lump in my throat as I process his precise accusations. The way his eyes roam freely over my body leaves me feeling uneasy. He can see straight past my lies as if he knows everything in the world. It's strange. Lying has proved to be an easy task in my household, but this stranger is able to see right through me, and I don't like it. I never thought I was this easy to read.

"I wasn't stealing from him. His bag fell and I was putting it back," I say, trying to lie again when I know I shouldn't.

The man behind me yells in frustration. "Sloane, if you're going to steal from me, you'd better own up to it."

"From you?" My eyes widen.

"Stealing from me is wrong, but stealing from him isn't?" He holds up the chain in front of my face. He knows I stole something from him, and instead of taking it back, he's dangling it in front of me as if I'm a child begging for a piece of candy. "You want it?" he asks. "Take it."

My frustration builds as I try to step away, accepting the chain as a loss, but he doesn't move. He doesn't move an inch. His tall frame overpowers mine.

"What do you want?" I ask.

"What makes you think I want anything from you? If you want the chain, take it." His looks are serious, and his words make me question everything around me.

If he isn't upset with me stealing, then he shouldn't have stopped me.

He waves it in front of me. It's humiliating. I never beg for anything. *"Ostavlyat'."* *Leave.* Well, he's not making me beg, but it feels like it in an odd way.

I take in a deep breath and reach for the chain.

Mikhail looks at the man, his face clear of any emotion. He slicks his hair back and walks around me in a circle. My breathing picks up when he pulls on my hair. *"Sloane,"* he says my name, annunciating the vowels slowly.

"I should really get back—" I start, but he stops me.

"And where exactly will you be going?"

For the first time in a while, I'm at a loss for words.

"What happened to your words? You had so many of them only a moment ago." He stops right in front of me, but I force myself to look at the ground. I wouldn't be here if I listened to my brother. Hell, he's right around the corner—I could still go to him, but there isn't a doubt in my mind these men would follow me.

It seems the predators finally found their prey.

Mikhail grabs onto my shoulders and turns my body toward the road. "Get in the car, Sloane."

Fuck.

Fuck.

Fuck.

I raise my gaze to his. His blue eyes turn dark, piercing mine.

"I don't want to," I tell him.

His head falls back, making his neck appear thicker. His teeth graze his bottom lip. "Oh, I don't care what you want."

We battle one another with our eyes until he looks at one of the men behind him.

"Lev, posadi yeyo v mashinu." Lev, go put her in the car.

Lev, the man Mikhail was speaking to, steps up, grabbing my arm. "Sleep tight."

I hardly have a second to react when I feel a sharp pain—a pain I know all too well—stab my arm. Mikhail's lips form a smug smile.

"What did you—?"

Black.

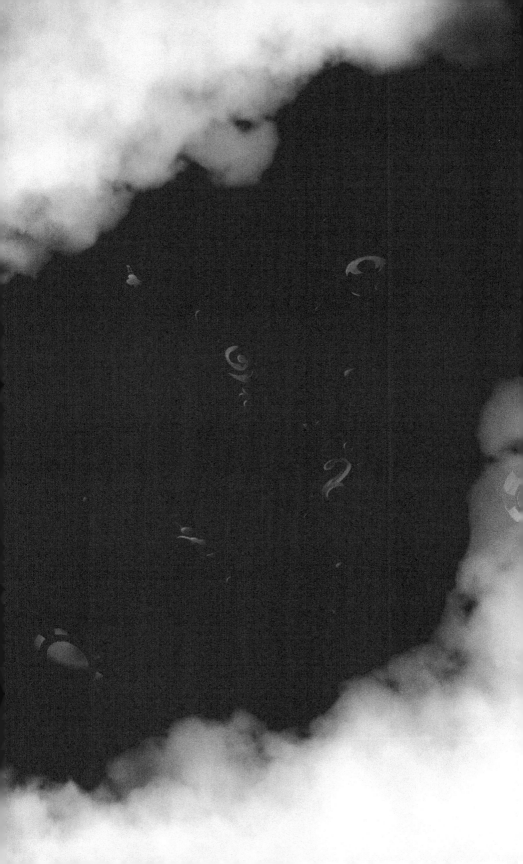

Chapter 4

Sloane

My eyes flutter open, and I kick the soft cushions off me. I push myself up, resting my weight on my arms.

My head throbs with pain. My body begs to lie back down, but my mind is running a marathon.

"You've got to be kidding me," I mutter to myself as I remember what happened. *He fucking drugged me, and for what?* All he had to do was ask for the stupid chain back and I would have given it to him. Leave it to the sarcastic, shrewd asshole to drug me and drop me off God knows where.

I pull my arms and legs from the ropes, but it's useless. My face scrunches together in frustration. Whoever tied these knots must've been a boy scout—they're so tight they'll leave marks on my wrists.

"Great," I mutter and fall back onto the bed.

My arms may be tied, but I can still move them, thank God.

My eyes open all the way as I glance across the room. My vision is blurry, and the moon casting small rays of light doesn't help much. I can hardly see anything besides a bathroom to the right of the room. My body feels like it's sweating out of every pore, and yet I'm shivering.

My pen.

I need my insulin pen.

Quickly, I bring my arm close to my core and start to pull at the knot. After several attempts, I get one arm out and then work on the other.

I need some water. I hate this feeling.

I lift my arm to reach into my bra, grabbing the pen and adjusting the unit before I shove it into my arm. I wait a couple of seconds before taking it out. Then I take in a deep breath and hide it in the cushions.

I'll be all right for twenty days if I can take the units accurately. I have to. The last thing I need is for them to use this against me in a sick way.

Once I get my other hand free, I push myself off the large bed. Holding my hands in front of me, I trace the outline of the room. My balance seems off. It could have been from the shit they injected into me, or the poor structure of the building I'm in.

"She's up." A deep voice comes from the corner of the room, where a large figure leans against the doorframe.

I jump at first, but then I grow curious. *How did I not notice the door opening?* My chin lifts quickly as I try to scan the man's face. He walks up to the side of the bed and flips on a light. It takes a moment for my eyes to adjust, but as soon as I see him I want him to turn the lights back off.

He flashes me a cunning smile as he takes a seat on the ottoman, throwing one leg over the other. His hair is shaved, revealing a deep scar in the center of his skull. This is Lev, if I remember correctly. He's the one who drugged me. His face is on the longer side, and so is his nose. He stares at me, and I do the same, both of us challenging one another. Lev swirls a dark scotch in his hand.

I watch his demanding expression become curious. The thick hair above his eyes looks like two caterpillars inching toward each other on his broad forehead. Nothing about his appearance is welcoming.

"Why am I here?" I ask even though I know I won't get an answer.

He looks down and smiles.

God, what a dick. He probably gets off on this.

"Take a wild guess," he says after a pause.

My face falls flat. "Hmm … You can't get a woman, so you've kidnapped one." I've never felt my body lock up with rage like this.

His tongue rolls over his teeth as he makes his way over to me. "You're lucky you're not mine to touch." A low chuckle escapes his chest.

"Yes. I'm so lucky." I smile at him, drawing out my response.

"You should get more sleep. You may need it." He smirks.

I cringe. It doesn't take a genius to comprehend the meaning behind his words. Ruslan was right: men are fucking pigs.

"He'll be here soon. Care to pass the time?" He gets up and looks me up and down. He smells like alcohol mixed with a hint of chlorine—a smell I definitely don't like. The chlorine most likely killed the last few brain cells he has, which is why he doesn't understand what common decency is.

Just as I'm about to respond to him, the door swings open, and my head darts to the man who walks in.

"Proch." Out.

"Ona derzkaya." She is feisty.

Lev leaves the room and Mikhail shuts the door. He's dressed the same. Nothing has changed besides his expression. He walks to the floor-to-ceiling windows, the muscles in his back filling his suit as he moves the curtains all the way open.

I inch toward him so I can look out the window. I make a sound and my eyes open so wide it feels like they could fall out of their sockets. There's nothing out there besides a black ocean. The current is still, leaving a clear reflection of the bright moon on the surface of the water.

My mouth runs dry as it hangs open in shock. Horror settles in my throat as I feel a panic attack ready to hit me at any moment.

The psycho man seems content with my reaction as he turns his head back to look at me. The corner of his mouth lifts in a satisfied smile.

I'm in the middle of nowhere. There's no way Dad will find me. I know for a fact this was not the plan.

As much as I want to keep a relaxed composure, fear smacks me right in the face. "Oh God," I mutter as I pace around the room with unsteady breaths.

Based on Mikhail's reaction, I might as well give him a bowl of popcorn to enjoy the show.

This is absolutely fucking insane. Who the hell does this?

An nervous laugh slips past my lips. I mean, it's brilliant, really. Even in my position I can admire the brains behind his devious plan—whatever this *plan* is.

I stop marching around the room when I begin to feel lightheaded. My head falls back when Mikhail takes this as an invitation to approach me.

"Arms up," he says just as he stops right in front of me.

My mouth falls open slightly as I register his demand. *What the fuck is wrong with these men?* "I'm not your whore." I glance at him with pure disgust. "Fuck off."

"Arms. Up. I will not ask nicely again."

My words mean nothing to him. It wouldn't shock me if he didn't even register what I said to him. He saw I didn't act on his demand, and in his messed-up mind that translated to giving me another command.

I can already tell he's the kind of man who never hears the word "no." Mikhail won't stop until he gets his way.

He looks at me as if I'm a bother when he's the one who kidnapped me and trapped me on a fucking boat. If he doesn't want to look at me, he can take me back where he found me.

The only hope I can cling to is that I'll find out what he wants. After all, I'll never be able to get out of this if I don't know how to work his mind. I need to do exactly what my dad once told me: "Find their weak point and don't stop digging."

All my life he's told me there are men who'd love nothing more than to see my head on a stick. I violated some treaty, and now I'm what everyone wants. Dad's lifelong goal is to keep me sheltered forever. Of course, his boss has other goals in mind. Though I didn't think it would happen like this. I understand everything now in a way I couldn't before.

Mikhail looks satisfied with being the one to find me first.

"I will not tell you nicely again. Fuck off," I say once more, growing agitated.

This gets his attention quickly. His neck thickens when his head falls back as he looks at me with irritation. He grabs me by the hip and throws me onto the bed as if I'm as light as a feather. Before I can scurry away, he pulls on my right leg, dragging me to the edge of the bed so I'm closer to him.

"This mouth of yours," he says as he reaches toward my lips, "is so foul."

If I allow the rage to take over any more I'll spit on his face, but I'm smarter than that. I try to turn my head away from him, but his grip keeps me still. His body hovers over mine, making me feel incapable. It'd be useless to fight him; he's nearly double my size.

His arm snakes around my waist as he lifts me off the bed. I raise my arms up no matter how much I don't want to. Tugging on the bottom of my dress, Mikhail brings it up past my waist. I shoot him a glare before he lifts the dress off my body completely, and he returns it. His cheeks look sunken, defining the structure of his face. He's beautiful in a sick way. He has full lips, a razor-sharp jaw, and a narrow nose. Underneath his black suit I know there's muscle, and that thought alone makes me want to run for my life. He doesn't seem like the kind of man to make small talk. He's demanding and cruel. People like him never talk—which only makes this harder for me.

He doesn't look like the man in the picture I saw years ago.

My head levels with his chest and my gaze falls down his torso, catching sight of a knife and gun placed in the waistband of his pants. He wears them exactly like the men in my family do.

In an odd way, I find comfort in the thought. I've dealt with men like him so many times it might give me a fighting chance.

I look up at him with my jaw clenched and reach quickly for his knife. He grabs my hand before I can get the weapon and twists me around so my back is against him. I'm winded from the way his hands dig into my breastbone.

He leans into me, bringing his lips close to my ear. "That won't get you anywhere, *kroshka*."

Crumb. He just called me a fucking crumb.

"What do you want?" I grit, turning back around.

He shakes his head slowly with a small grin. Then he lifts the dress over my head.

I try to focus on my breathing as he places my dress down on the bed. I feel vulnerable. This man is disgusting.

He walks over to the dresser and pulls out a crewneck and a pair of shorts.

My shorts.

My eyes can't focus on a single thing as I try my hardest to process what's happening. Nothing around me feels real. It's like a fever dream.

"Who are you?" I finally ask.

"Don't ask questions if you already know the answer."

"Not your name. *Who* are you?" *Is he in charge now?*

"You really want to know?" He comes back over to me and kneels on the floor. By the look on his face, I can tell he wants me to listen. When he speaks, my chest tightens in an attempt to prepare myself for his cruel words, but not even an iron shield could protect me from his deep, grim voice. He taps my leg to lift it up.

Thinking this was going in a different direction, I grab onto his shoulder to steady myself as I put my feet through the shorts. While he may be an asshole, at least he has the decency not to demand my body as his.

He pulls the shorts up past my waist, his large hands grabbing onto my hips to move me closer to him.

"I do."

"How oblivious are you?"

His words hit me like a dull knife, but I guess that's something I'll just have to get used to.

He doesn't seem to understand the meaning behind my question, and that doesn't surprise me.

"Guess your father doesn't fill you in on as much as I thought."

His words make me question myself. My father tells me everything I need to know. Which is why this isn't making sense.

"Up." He jerks his head in an upward motion.

I do as he says, and he puts the crewneck on me. It's much larger than anything I own, so it has to be his. It even smells like him. Aftershave and vanilla. He gathers my hair and lifts it out from under the shirt then moves it to the side of my face.

"Go back to sleep. Someone will be here to wake you up in the morning."

His hands trail down the length of my arm before he steps away from me.

Glancing to the bed that has four ropes attached to its corners, I wonder why they're there in the first place. If I'm in the middle of the ocean—which I probably am—there is no way I'll be able to leave this ship. There's no telling how far offshore we are. Even if we're only a mile away from land, I won't be able to leave because I can't swim.

I've spent my entire life in a house. I never thought I'd need to know how to swim.

I'm standing in the center of the room with my arms folded across my chest when I feel a cold breeze pass by my bare feet. Turning around to face the door, I see Mikhail's head lower between his shoulders. Just as he's about to leave, I ask hesitantly, "Can you ... um, can you leave the door open?"

I know I just revealed one of my weaknesses, but I'd rather him know I hate locked doors than suffer the feeling of being trapped.

This might be a mistake. I'm not sure why I even bothered. I'm his captive; a locked door is almost a given. Men like him grab onto every weak point they can find. I have no idea what his intentions are, and that doesn't help my situation.

The cruel smile that seems to be a common occurrence tugs at his lips once again as he takes slow steps toward me. Seeing a man with dreadful eyes and a calculating smile makes you wonder if there's even a soul in his body.

"I'm curious," he says as he pulls down on one of my curls. "Is the child of the Bratva scared of being alone?"

Disgust floods my vision. *He does know my father.* "Who the fuck are you?" I ask again. This is an act of war. He doesn't even realize what he's doing right now.

A wave of nausea hits me when the tip of his finger lifts my chin up so I'm forced to look him directly in the eye.

"I'm your worst fucking nightmare, *Koldunya.*"

Chapter 5

Mikhail

She hides her fear well, but not well enough. I know every pretty thought that runs through her mind. The way she breathes—it's not stable. The way her eyes roam the room instead of looking me in the eye. She wears her thoughts on her face as clear as day

I used to be exactly like her. She even steals like I used to.

I never thought my father's passing would bring such good luck. She fell right into my arms, right where she belongs.

Sitting at the large table on the middle deck, I look up at Mia. "Is she up?" I ask.

Mia never looks me in the eye. I've never done anything to her, but she's always feared me. "She is, sir. She's getting ready in the dress you told me to lay out for her." She blinks rapidly.

"Good. I expect her in five."

Leaning back in the white padded chair, I readjust myself. This isn't exactly what I had in mind, but the property my father bought before he passed wasn't far enough. I want to make sure the Romanos have no clue where she is. I prefer the cold in Russia over the direct sun constantly burning my skin, but there are pros and cons to every situation, I suppose.

Adrian sits across from me, Dimitri right next to him, and Lev at my side. They stay quiet, staring at the white plates in front of them while patiently waiting to eat.

Waves crash against the sides of the boat, and the warm wind gently blows the leaves of the plant in the center of the table.

"They're looking for her," Lev speaks up, breaking my moment of peace.

"I'd be shocked if they weren't. Do they know you're working with me?" I ask.

"No. I'm not going back either. I'm with you."

I give him a strange look. He phrased that in a way that's off-putting.

I had Lev sort out a lot of the transactions with the men who work for me. This was my way of getting Sloane. If I were the one to go out and get her, there would've been a bright spotlight on me.

"Yeah, well, it's not like you have much of a choice, Lev." I reach for the juice and pour myself a glass.

All my life I've known exactly where Sloane was. Everyone in the Bratva did. When Kirill told Giovanni Genovese he had a sister, everyone was ready to kill my brother themselves. The alliances we had with other families were torn when they found out about Sloane's father's infidelity. A cheating woman is a dead one.

We all agreed to keep our mouths shut about the truth as it could work in our favor in the future. If Sloane were never born, there was a chance we could all get passed the issue, but Kirill had other plans in mind. It was a premature move on his part. It was supposed to remain a secret, but I understand why he played that as his last card. He stirred up so much shit with another family there was no going back at that point.

My father allowed me to become more involved once I turned eighteen. Growing up with the Bratva, Sloane was known as the witch. People talked about her all over as if she were a myth, never seen before. They said her looks alone would leave you questioning what was real. Some of the men would volunteer to handle business with Ludis on the off chance they could see Sloane with their own eyes—to put the myth to rest.

The few who have seen her agree with the tale. Now that I've seen her, I'm finally able to form my own opinion on the matter. I believe it in a sense. She is beautiful, but I'm seeing reality just fine.

"She's a pretty little thing—Sloane," Adrian says as if he can hear my thoughts.

I scowl at him, suddenly nervous he'll believe in the stupid myth. If Sloane is able to manipulate my men, I may as well call my efforts a loss. "She is. You put a fucking hand on her, and your thumbs will be missing."

"And who says she's yours?"

"I do. And if I need to repeat myself one more time, your tongue will be missing as well."

Dimitri covers his laugh as he reaches for a slice of toast.

"You think something's funny, brother?"

He clears his throat and takes a bite. "No. This girl is just going to cause a lot of problems."

"They're problems I will deal with."

Dimitri scoots his chair toward the table. "I don't know about you guys, but I don't think this plan is even going to work."

"Did I ask for your opinion? You're welcome to walk out the door if you don't want to be a part of this."

He looks down at the table, shaking his head. It's good that he's aware I wouldn't let him leave alive. "Giovanni doesn't even know you have her," he says.

Agitation overwhelms me as I take in a deep, exhausted breath. "I'm sorry, do you want to take over, Dimitri?"

My attention is stolen by Sloane as she takes small steps toward the table, her hands clasped in front of her. She isn't wearing the dress I told Mia to lay out for her; she's still wearing my crewneck and a pair of shorts. Her long, natural curls flow with each step she takes. Her face is pale, lacking any color. Her hair is so blonde it looks bleached.

I get up and pull a chair out for her. She looks up at me and smiles softly. "Thank you," she says.

Her words run through my mind on repeat. Whether she realizes it or not, there's a kind melody attached to her voice. I've never felt any reservations about what I do, and that won't change just because she thanked me for my ingenuine actions.

I reach for my knife and grab a chunk of her hair, cutting it right off. "No, thank you," I say, returning to my seat and taking another sip of my drink.

Her mouth falls open as she reaches to grab the strands of hair that are shorter than the rest.

"You're not going to find the missing hair there, sunshine. He has it," Dimitri chortles, pointing over to me. His childish attitude only puts me in a sour mood.

"And what was the purpose of that?" she asks, her voice stern but not intimidating by any means.

"Just eat your fruit, *Koldunya*." I push the plate closer to her. "Adrian, package this up and deliver it."

"I—"

"Yeah, we've done the stuttering game enough," I say, looking right at her for a moment. She's fragile. I can see the veins in her thin skin. "Here, cheers."

She doesn't pick up the glass.

Mia walks over to us, placing our meals on the table.

"Thank you, Mia."

"Of course." She nods and walks out.

I address my men next. *"Ostavte nas." Leave us.*

They all nod and follow behind Mia.

Sitting back in my chair, I look at Sloane. Her oval face drops with disappointment. She won't look at me, just like Mia won't. I can't blame her—I just humiliated her in front of my men.

"You're going to need sunscreen," I tell her while I admire how smooth her skin is.

"I think that's the least of my concerns." Her eyes go squint as she gives me a mocking smile.

I ditch the juice and grab my glass of vodka. "You're right about that."

"Just tell me what you want. Where are we even at?"

I lean around the table, grabbing onto the handle of her chair and pulling her close to me until her legs are touching mine. "You're going to help me get what I want." I trail a hand along her thigh. It feels smooth, as if she has body oil on her skin. "As for where we are ..." I look around us and smirk. "Looks like your own personal hell to me."

I understand why men want her. She is gorgeous. Her full, rosy lips, button nose, and long eyelashes make her look innocent—and she probably is. In her sweet mind, there isn't any darkness.

"You like it here, Sloane?"

"No."

"That's unfortunate." I take another sip of vodka and click my tongue. "You might be here for a while."

"You're a piece of shit," she says as she grabs a banana from the bowl in the center of the table, along with a slice of toast.

She's feisty, I'll give her that. I expected her to obey my every command, but she fights back. Which means this will be fun, no doubt—but she'll also be a pain in my ass. No one has fought me since Kirill died.

"I'm many things."

She reaches for the butter and spreads it over her toast. Her bright doe eyes look at me and then dart back down, her emotions written all over her face. When her grip tightens around the knife, I don't stop her. I can read her actions from a mile off and know before she moves that she's going to try to stab me with it. I can take the hit. It's a butter knife after all—it won't do anything. I've had a sharp knife plunged into my palm before, and this is nothing compared to that.

"That was a perfect way to ruin breakfast," I say, turning the knife back on her.

Her body stiffens under my touch. She looks at me in pure disgust. I don't feel guilty or ashamed of my actions, but it seems she does. She can't even attack me with confidence. Her words are the only weapon she has, and they won't get her far at all.

With the knife to her throat, Sloane grips the edge of her seat.

"There are rules, *Koldunya*." I dig the knife deeper into her skin. "If you try to leave, you will be punished. If you refuse to care for yourself, you will be punished. If you defy me in any way, you will be punished."

"Your rules don't mean anything."

"They do. And on the off chance you withstand my punishment and continue to defy me, I'll pay your family a visit."

Her breathing halts and she shuts her eyes. See, now, that's the reaction I wanted. It's as if she doesn't care what happens to her, but if anything happens to her family it's a different story.

"No," she whispers.

I lean back in my chair and readjust myself. "You can leave."

She opens her eyes and pushes her chair back quickly. I don't bother looking up at her no matter how priceless her reaction may be.

Getting to know Sloane will be a lot more fun than I imagined.

Leaving Lev with Sloane, I only hope he can handle her. The ship is a couple miles off the shore of Long Island, making my trip to the city a hassle. On the way there, I went through everything my brother has on Sloane.

Kirill didn't do his research correctly; most of the information he has on her is wrong. He wasn't as connected with the Bratva as I thought. A part of me isn't even surprised because he never thinks his plans through. If you hand him a gun, he'll ask who he needs to shoot. He doesn't care for reason or motive. He thought Sloane once lived in an orphanage, but she didn't. Her father, Ludis Koziov, swept her away as soon as he found out she was in the NICU.

Ludis has tried to keep her hidden from the other families her entire life. He's done a good job for the most part, but it seems Sloane doesn't quite understand she was supposed to *stay* hidden. Seeing her running through the streets of the city was the last thing I expected. I thought I'd have to take out her brother to get to her.

Men want her dead, myself included, but that wouldn't have stopped me from showing up to her house and taking her from there. How lucky I was to have her fall directly in my arms instead. This small, pitiful girl is the reason all our alliances are now void, and she should've listened to her father. Ludis's actions alone should have gotten him killed years ago, but my father didn't think it was necessary.

Ludis may be getting weaker as time goes by, but underneath all his hurt is a man like me. A man who wants nothing but revenge for his family.

Unfortunately, we're avenging two different families, and he's on the wrong side.

I never thought Ludis would be the man to break the alliance, but some people just have no mercy. Neither did Kirill. There wasn't a drop of remorse in his heart the day he killed Sloane's birth mother. It used to be difficult for me to understand how he could be so detached. My brother didn't ever think about the consequences. He didn't blend in well with our lifestyle after we were adopted and was the kind of man who handled everything with purpose. He wanted to keep us safe, but all that changed once he understood we had power through Pavel. He became reckless. He went behind our father's back all the time, and I couldn't do anything about it.

It took a while, but his mistakes caught up to him. Of course, I was thrown into the crossfire, always having to do his dirty work. That's why the Romanos hate me. Because the older I got, the more I knew I was the one who had to take care of Kirill. He needed me by his side. He'd call me all the time and demand I help him. I couldn't say no.

He was supposed to be my big brother, my protector, but everything changed after he realized he didn't need to take care of me anymore.

Kirill wanted to marry Nina to form an alliance with the Cosa Nostra. He never told anyone what his plan was or even why he wanted to—he just went ahead with it. He had a strange obsession with Nina. I understand why she wanted nothing to do with him; Kirill wasn't much of a person at that point. He depended on drugs that made his body age far beyond his years.

He never would have been able to give her a future. If Giovanni didn't kill him, the drugs would have done so soon enough.

My brother had many years ahead of him, but he welcomed death with open arms. The devil's dark shadows didn't fall through his grasp—he was able to grab onto it.

I don't want to take Nina away from Giovanni. No, falling in love was the stupidest thing he could have done, and I'd rather he live with his mistake his entire life. She's his biggest baggage. A weakness.

For killing my brother, Giovanni Genovese will get what's coming to him.

Through the years, being shot twice and almost getting my ear cut off, I grew sick and tired of playing my brother's games. While I was always trying to help him, my life was constantly on the line.

Now he's not here to finish what he started, but I still can.

The second I set foot in the VIP room of the club, three women surround me. The lights in the room shift from a dark red to blue. Adrian sits on the bench in the corner with a woman's breasts in his face. I shake my head and try to cover my laugh with my hand.

"You're spending your free time wisely, cousin," I tell him in Russian.

He takes his head away from her and glares up at me. "Damn, you're finally here."

In the corner of the room is a small bar full of my favorite drinks, which I have one of the bartenders restock before every meeting. Some of the idiots I'm meeting with today drive me to the point of thinking alcoholism is the least of my concerns.

I pour myself a glass of vodka and swirl it, droplets falling down the outside of the glass. "Where are they?" I ask, just as Dimitri walks in with the pests I need to deal with. "Perfect," I grumble. Setting the glass on the table, I take a seat.

One of the women tries to straddle my lap, but I brush her away. I didn't hire them for me—I hoped they'd be able to distract the other men and get them to lower their guards. I need to know where they fucked up.

They walk toward the table with caution.

"So, what happened?" I finally ask.

Aaron is the younger one. He hasn't been working for me all that long—

I'd say it's been about three weeks—and he's already fucked up. His eyes are exhausted, and his hair is cut short. "It's gone," he says in a shaky voice.

"Well ... what do you want me to do about it?"

He shakes his head. I don't think I've ever seen a young man look so scared. He's got to be nineteen at least. He's a tall boy, lacking in muscle.

"Are you going to kill me?" he asks.

I contemplate this for a moment, but that wouldn't achieve anything. He knows where the money went, and now he needs to fix it.

"I could take a finger," I scoff. "But I want my money, Aaron."

"Boss, I don't have it, I told you. Just let me pay the price."

I take a large sip of my drink and slam it down on the table. "A finger won't get me my money back, will it?"

He stares at me, confused. That's two people who've stolen from me in the past twenty-four hours. Any other day I'd cut the loss, but he needs to prove himself.

"No, boss." He looks down, embarrassment tormenting him.

"So what'd you get with it, man? New PlayStation? Maybe you got yourself a car."

He looks straight to the ground, his cheeks flooding with humiliation.

"No? Was it a house? That was a hundred thousand."

The poor man looks like he wants to die on the spot. I can't be the one to coddle him like a fucking child—my father didn't coddle me, and I turned out just fine.

With the lack of a response, I get up from my chair and walk to the door. "Better find some way to make back my money." I take a step out into a sea of hundreds of bodies dancing to the music and glance back over at Aaron and his buddy—I can't remember his name. "You have a day to return it," I tell him.

"I can't get that kind of money to you in a day."

"You have twenty-four hours," I say, closing the door behind me.

Truth is, I don't need the money from Aaron, but if he wants to join me, he needs to prove himself. And if he doesn't—as I guess will be the case— he'll lose a finger and I'll throw him out.

Men never fucking fail to surprise me.

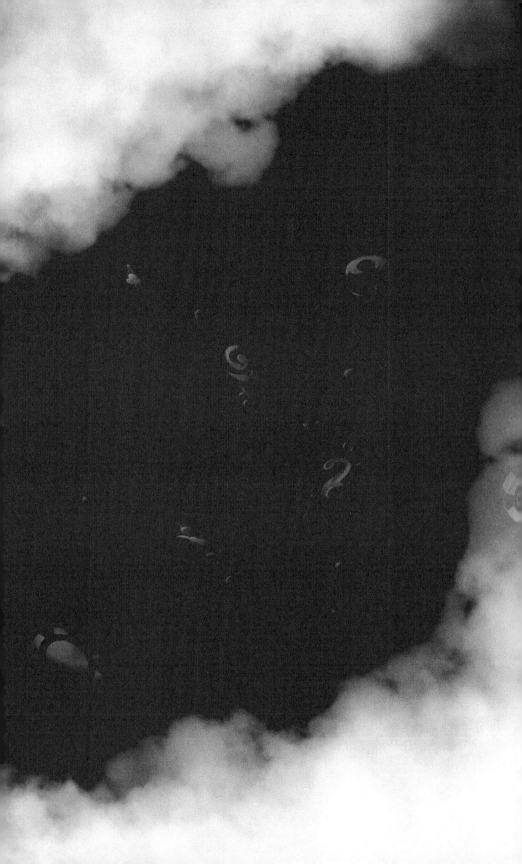

Chapter 6

Sloane

I t's been two days. Two whole fucking days I've been locked in this room. The minute I got back here he sent someone to lock the door. I banged my fists against the solid wood for a while before tiring myself out.

I'm used to being kept in a room for days on end after all—the only difference is I have no choice but to stay in this room. Back home, my door's never locked. My family trust me to listen to them.

Mikhail has no reason to trust me, but that doesn't make me like this any more.

I've tried to come up with a plan to get out of here, but my ideas are worth nothing, and neither is my effort. I'm just worried about my family. Mikhail threatened them as if their lives were worth less than the gum on the bottom of his shoe, which only confirms my worries: he has no idea what his father planned.

If Mikhail isn't aware—and I'm sure he isn't—then I may as well be dead. There will be no mercy shown, no communication, and no empathy. He breathes in anger and breathes out insults.

I'm not meant to be his nemesis. If I knew what his issue was, I could tell him what he wants to hear and maybe he'd let me go. But I don't know anything. I'm clueless, and that's exactly what he wants.

Killing him won't work. He can predict my moves from a mile off, and my strength is nothing compared to his. I think I just need to lie low, not cause any issues. I need to make it look like I have no problem being here. I have no idea how long I'll be stuck here for, so I may as well live up to my full potential.

Pushing myself up, I stare ahead of me. While I may be a hostage, I have to admit the accommodations could be worse. I could be locked in a cold, dirty cell with metal chains around my legs. Instead, I'm in a room that's rather modern. The large white bed faces the wall of windows with a view I'll never tire of. I've never seen the ocean before now—only in movies, but they don't do this view justice. Each morning I'm woken up by the comfort of the warm sun against my skin and the chants of seagulls. The sun alone beats the dark, colorless room I have at home.

The best part about this room is the button on the nightstand that controls the windows. I can have them open at night and listen to the water crash against the boat. I've never slept better. Ironic, considering I'm being held hostage.

With how fancy the yacht is, I can only wonder if he bought it just to trap me here. If that's the case, I've never felt more exceptional in my entire life.

But what will he do with me when he doesn't need me anymore? Kill me?

I'm sure kidnapping is one of his favorite daily activities. I bet if I were to look at his hands, I'd see dried blood under his nails.

I shake my head to rid the negative thoughts and grab the remote from the nightstand. When I press the power button to turn on the TV, however, the screen remains black. Turning the remote over, I open the back and laugh. Of course he'd take out the batteries.

Asshole.

Letting out a harsh breath, I turn to the bedroom door as I hear it unlock. I watch the knob closely as the seconds pass and yet no one steps through. I grow impatient and scoot out of the bed. My hand touches the cold handle, opening it only to see no one on the other side.

Why would they finally give me the option to leave and not tell me?

The second I step out of the room, my hair blows in the strong current of the wind. I know we're not moving because I can't hear the hum of the engine. The wind must be strong because there's nothing blocking its path. No mountains, skyscrapers, or trees—just the lonely, open ocean.

I've only been out of my room once, and at the time I couldn't admire anything about the ship because I was nervous about seeing Mikhail.

My hand glides across the white railing that separates me from the water. The windows I pass by are dark black and reflective. At the end of the pathway, I see a narrow set of stairs. I walk up with a quiet step, careful not to draw attention to myself. If I can avoid Mikhail like the plague, I will.

Once I reach the top, I see Dimitri—I think that's his name—through the windows. These ones are clear. If I saw anyone else in the room, I would've turned back around and acted as if I never saw them, but I think I can work with Dimitri. He reminds me a lot of my brother, Ruslan. I've only spoken to him once, but the first thing he said to me was snarky. While I might have been annoyed in the moment, I can laugh about it now.

I watch him closely from a distance. He sits on a long white sofa facing the wheel. His elbows dig into his knees as he stares at a large sheet of paper. Before he catches me staring at him, I decide to knock on the door.

Lifting his eyes, he squints at me before he jerks his head to the side, telling me to come in.

I open the door, proceeding into the room as if there's yellow caution tape attached to the frame. My attention goes straight to the panels that control the boat. Five large screens are placed below the slanted window, giving a view of the entire ship. There are so many red buttons I'm afraid to even be in this room.

"Are you thinking about taking control of the boat, *matros?*" he asks, flashing me an infectious smile. *Sailor.*

Dimitri's face is on the rounder side and his beard looks prickly. His eyes are hooded, almost welcoming.

I smile weakly and say, "Not like I could."

He takes off his glasses and hooks them on his shirt so they hang above his chest. "No, you couldn't." His eyes fall down, tracing the outline of my body. "But what can I do for you?"

His words aren't coated with irritation toward me like Mikhail's are. "I'm bored," I admit as I step toward the table and take a seat on the cushions next to him.

He narrows his hooded honey-colored eyes. "I unlocked your door so you'd have the opportunity to look around before Mikhail comes back," he says almost hesitantly. "And he will be here very soon."

I give him a strange glare with my eyebrows raised. One of Mikhail's men shouldn't be going against him for my benefit, but I'll gladly take it. "How long have you been on this ship?" I ask, growing curious.

Dimitri doesn't show any anger toward me, and in the position I'm in, that's like finding a diamond at the bottom of the sea.

He looks up while he loses himself in thought. He must have been here for a while if he has to take a moment to think about how long it's been.

"I'd say about a year. Don't quote me on that though."

"I see," I mutter, lifting myself off the couch and walking to the door. "What should I explore?"

His fingers comb through his hair as he clears his throat. "The bar. But you'd enjoy the small office on the second deck." He winks at me, moving his arms behind his head, and I notice a gold ring on his finger.

Most men in the Bratva only marry for title, but Dimitri seems like the kind of man who'd marry someone for love. His personality doesn't scream "business."

"I'll check it out," I say to him with a smile.

"Sloane," he calls for me just as I'm about to step out of the room. When I turn to look back at him, he speaks before I can ask him what he needs. "Mikhail has a dinner planned for the both of you. He has a dress he'd like you to *actually* wear this time. I'll hang it on the back of your door, and I suggest you do as he says."

I may have spoken up too soon about Dimitri. He was the one who didn't demand things from me, although that has changed quickly.

"Sure thing," I say, walking out of the room.

Skipping past the stairway that I took to get up here, I decide to go down on the opposite side of the boat. The longer I take with each step, the hotter I feel the sun burning the soles of my feet. Keeping myself steady by holding onto the rails, I race to the covered center of the boat. There are no walls, only a ceiling held up by two rounded pillars in the center. A huge gray couch with white, fluffy pillows sits in the middle of the area facing a TV. A couple of snake plants in light blue pots are scattered around, giving the deck the perfect amount of color.

A feeling of bliss fills my mind when a strong draft passes by me, smelling like fresh summer. I never thought a smell could feel so welcoming.

It's a terrifying thought, feeling comfortable in a place where I should be fearing for my life. I'm not sure what Mikhail was expecting on my part, but he won't be getting a damsel in distress. If that's what he had in mind, he wouldn't have put me on a floating sanctuary.

Mikhail doesn't seem like the kind of man to go into a plan prematurely. If he did his research on me, he'd know I haven't seen much of the world. *Did he think bringing me here would terrify me?* I suppose it did at first, but that was before I was able to explore, even if I have only done a little snooping around.

The quiet bliss is snatched away from me when I hear a thudding noise. I follow the noise past the entertainment system. There's a large kitchen connected to the living room. The walls are made up of windows, which seems to be a common design concept of the yacht. I love it because I've lived in the shadows my entire life.

My feet don't make the floorboards creak with each step I take. That will take some getting used to. A woman with short black hair tied into a knot on her head with a hair net has her back to me while she washes pots and pans. Mia. She must be the cook.

I stand for a moment and appreciate how beautiful the room is. White marble countertops with oak lining. The ceiling is a skylight—there's no need for a light to be on during the day, especially since the room is open to the deck. Two bamboo chairs sit in front of the bar. A wicker bowl is placed by the sink on the island, giving the kitchen a pop of color.

I'd love to talk to Mia, but she gives off the impression she's only here to work and wouldn't humor my small talk.

Crossing my arms over my chest, I back out of the room quietly, careful not to make too much noise and startle her. Placing my hand around the corner, I stumble over my feet as my back crashes into something strong, and I feel two large hands holding me up from my elbows.

My neck stiffens as turn, looking up at the man holding me steady. *Mikhail.*

His expression is cold, lacking any emotion, and that makes the palms of my hands sweat like they never have before. The bottom of his lip tucks into his mouth and his white, well-kept teeth graze over the surface gently. His neck thickens while he shakes his head at me.

"And who let you out?" he asks in a deep, steady voice that forces shame to corrode my insides.

"I did," I admit with a shaky breath that I try my damn hardest to control. Technically, Dimitri allowed me to walk out of my room, but I'm the one who let myself out.

It feels like a trap. Mikhail must expect me to be at his beck and call while I rest in the room he so graciously set up for me, but I won't.

He lets go of my arms and steps to the side. "I guess this boat isn't big enough," he says, not masking his disappointment at seeing me as he continues past me.

My eyes roam around while I try my hardest to bite back my next few words, but they come out anyway. "With your ego, definitely not."

He stops but doesn't turn around to address me. His muscles stretch out the back of his white button-down shirt. Clearing his throat, he says, "Be ready in an hour. I expect to see you at dinner."

With his hands in his pockets, he walks off around the corner, leaving me with an awful taste in my mouth. I plan on getting the answers I deserve at this dinner, and he'd better give them to me.

As I ransack the dresser, I'm only able to find clothes that are white and blue. While they're all my clothes, he forgot all the other colors as if they never existed. I do everything in my power to find something other than the dress hanging on the back of the door, but it's my only option. As tempting as it might be to show up to his dinner with a pair of sweatpants on, I'll listen to him *just* this once.

I take the dress off the hanger and hold it against my body. He's got taste, I'll give him that. The cerulean-colored dress looks faded, and the bottom of the material is ruffled. Sighing, I put it on and notice it fits smoothly against my skin. The fabric has a bohemian stitch around my waist and a subtle V down my chest. He knows my size for everything—even the heels I put on are the perfect fit.

I take a deep breath as I close the bedroom door behind me. The thought of seeing Mikhail again has me nervous. One look from him and I start to question if I'm in a nightmare I'll never wake up from. I really should watch my attitude when I'm near him, but my comments seem to slip out no matter how hard I try to hold them back.

Mikhail never mentioned where this dinner would be held, so I spend a good ten minutes looking around for him, only to find him sitting at a table on the opposite end of the ship where I shared breakfast with him a few days ago. The space is welcoming. The wooden table has white chairs surrounding one side and a bench on the other, but only one person is seated.

Mikhail sits at the end of the table with his eyes devouring every move I make. "Sloane." My name rolls sharply off his tongue. "Sit," he commands.

Ignoring his demand, I admire the space around me. The dining room has a perfect view of the open ocean, and the sky takes my breath away. With only a few clouds visible, the light takes over everything my eyes can see just before the ocean swallows the sun. Many shades of orange and yellow blend together seamlessly like a work of art. It looks unreal.

The warm breeze surrounds my skin like a soft, warm towel. The sound of trickling water overpowers the jazz playing in the background. Candles that smell of roses line the table.

This is a view I could never tire of, but I'd love to have different company.

Mikhail looks distressing, contradicting the feeling of calm the space gives off. But the candles—what is he doing? Walking up to the table, I take a seat on the bench so I'm sitting far away from him.

"What the hell is this?" I ask, lifting the flute of champagne and bringing it to my lips.

After I gulp down a couple of sips, I look at him. His eyes are fixed on mine. The candlelight creates a small sparkle in his pupils, giving him a look of innocence—everything he isn't.

"Eat."

"No 'how was your day?' Mine was good, thanks for asking." At a dinner as nice as this one, I'd expect to have some kind of conversation with humanity, but that might be asking too much of a person like him. He isn't a gentleman, and I don't expect him to be.

I look down at my plate and see a meal that looks and smells delicious. Potatoes, pork, and asparagus. He doesn't have to tell me twice to eat.

He places his elbows on the table, his white shirt rolled halfway up his arms. He wears silver rings on each hand, and tattoos take over his skin. "Eat," he demands again.

I was going to eat, but now he's demanding it of me, I'll take my time doing so. "Not that hungry," I lie and smile from ear to ear. Anything he tells me to do, I'm bound to do the opposite. *Does he think I care about what he does to me?* I don't. When I said I would rather die out in the world doing something dangerous than rot in my room back home, I wasn't lying.

"I could just skip past your punishment and move right to your family. But that's your decision."

This gets my attention. If he has something against my family, he has something against me. But what could they have done to him? My dad respected his till the end. I hate how he uses my family against me. How lovely it is to come to a dinner and have my family threatened because I refuse to take a bite of potato ... I could roll my eyes at the thought, but based on our few interactions, I already know that would piss him off. It doesn't take much to push his buttons.

"What is your problem?" The words spill freely from my mouth before

I can hold them back.

He taps his fingers on the table and says, "You're my problem. You got my brother killed."

I wince at his words. He says them like they mean nothing to him. I'm the reason his brother is dead, and he can't even show a drop of remorse for his bother? For some reason, he thinks I'm capable of getting someone killed. *Does he think I go on killing sprees?*

"I've never killed anyone," I argue.

The muscles in my face relax once I realize. I should have connected the dots before—I don't know how I didn't. This is a revenge plan. I'm collateral damage, and taking me is his way of getting back at them.

"I can't undo what they did," I say steadily.

My realization seems to please him. His brows crease together slightly as he fidgets with the ring on his finger. "No, and I don't expect you to."

I lean in closer to the table and pat the palms of my hands on the bottom of my dress as I grow anxious. "So how is this my fault? Why am I here if I didn't do anything to hurt you?"

He's placing his anger on me, and I didn't do anything wrong.

Mikhail brings a glass of vodka to his lips and takes a couple of sips. "What makes you think I'm hurt?"

I lift my eyes to his. Those blue eyes ... they pierce through any emotional shield I have. He doesn't look hurt, annoyed, or even angry. He looks defeated. I don't think he meant for me to see the shift in his energy. He says he's not hurt, but the way he fidgets with everything around him makes me believe otherwise. Maybe I'm reading into his movements too much, but I'll take whatever I can latch onto for answers.

"If you weren't hurt, you wouldn't be using me as blackmail."

"Who said you were blackmail?"

His questions frustrate me. I ask him something and he just flips it back to me.

"Why can't you just answer my questions?"

"Why can't you ask the right ones?"

I cross one leg over the other and readjust myself on the bench. I don't know what his game is, but I can't help but feel intrigued. He's already changing my mood, and not for the better, but I'll indulge him. "Right. What's your favorite color?" I ask.

"No."

"'No' isn't a color, Mikhail."

His tongue rolls over the inside of his cheek. "You want to get to know me?" he asks while he rolls his shoulders.

"And you me." I look at the glass of champagne placed next to my plate. Then I grab the flute and take a sip.

Mikhail looks curious, but only for a moment before he pulls away from the table. "Eat your food."

"I'll eat, but I want my door to remain unlocked," I say, challenging him. If Mikhail didn't need me alive, I wouldn't be here right now, and that gives me the upper hand. Murder might be at the end of my story, but at least it didn't start that way. There is no light at the end of the tunnel for me. I'm far away from home with a man who would love to see me dead. I might as well see if I can better my accommodation.

"What makes you think you can demand things of me? Do you think I care if you rot in your room? I don't."

My lips part in shock. This man is the devil's spawn. "What are you trying to prove to me? Why this dinner?"

"To show you I'm not all that bad."

"Oh, that's brilliant coming from you." *So he kidnaps me and then tries to convince me he isn't a bad person? I've got to say, that's a new one for me.*

"If you didn't want to come, why did you?"

As if he gave me a choice! If I didn't come to this dinner willingly, I'm sure he'd have gotten one of his men to drag me here. But I'll humor him. "I came for the drink. Don't get caught up in the meaning behind it."

"Oh, that's cute coming from you. Remember you willingly sat down in that chair to spend your time with me."

"I think you're forgetting you threatened me. I can't willingly do anything."

"Why the fuck do you talk so much?" he asks, running his fingers against his full lips.

My chest rises and falls in shock. I thought we were just having a conversation; I didn't think I was talking too much. *Was I?*

He reaches for his drink, downing the entire glass again.

"You asked me to have dinner with you," I snap. It's as if he got what he wanted and doesn't need to hear any more.

"I did. And if I were you, I wouldn't mistake my kindness for anything else. I would gladly choke you with the hand I feed you with."

It feels as if there's a lump in my throat. For the first time since I've been on this boat, I don't feel the need to say something smart back to him. He saw me getting too comfortable and shot that idea down real quick.

After swallowing my pride, I lean even closer to the table. "What was the point of this dinner? These questions were surface-level, and we didn't even get anywhere."

"Did you want this to go anywhere?" He leans into the table too. A grin tugs on his lips as he looks up and down my body.

Did I? Maybe deep down I thought I could get some kind of leverage out of this conversation, but that wasn't the case. If anything, we just pissed each other off. So I don't say anything. It's like feeding a stray animal I never want to see again; the more I give him, the more he'll come.

"Don't worry. That was rhetorical, my love."

It feels as if every atom in my body is about to explode. This man infuriates me, but I can't let my rage get the better of me—he feeds off that.

Mikhail stands from his chair and walks over to the ledge with built-in cabinets. He grabs something off the top and makes his way back to me. He kneels to the ground and grabs onto my ankle. A part of me wants to knee him in the face, but that would only make my situation a million times worse. Instead, I sit still while he straps a black piece of plastic around my ankle and presses a button. The red light blinks repeatedly.

He's going to track me. The ship isn't small, but I wouldn't deem a tracker a necessity unless he wants to know exactly where I am. That's most likely the case, after all, but does he really think I'll go anywhere if he's threatening my family?

"I expect you to eat every last crumb off the plate." He places his drink on the table and stands up to walk to the door. "Your door will be unlocked. You have fresh linen. Do you need anything else?"

"Wow, thanks so much for taking such great care of me. I'll be sure to leave you a fantastic review on Kidnap.com once my stay is over," I say, smiling at him.

He stops in his tracks and turns to walk toward me. His blinks are slow as he lowers himself over my body. As his hand lies flat against the table, I hear the beat of my heart echoing in my ear. His face is so close to mine I can feel his breath.

I shouldn't have been so reckless with my words.

"And what makes you think your stay will ever end?" He lifts a hand to tuck a strand of hair behind my ear. Then he brings his thumb to my bottom lip and traces along the curve. "Watch this pretty mouth of yours."

My hands clench around the soft, thin material of my dress. I try to ignore the feeling my body creates at his touch, but I can't. A warm sensation builds in my stomach, mixed with nausea.

Mikhail seems to notice how my body reacts to his touch.

I just made his job easier.

Chapter 7

Mikhail

The night I put a tracker on Sloane, she stayed in her room. She does the same thing the second day, the third ... and the fourth.

I'm giving her the freedom to roam as she pleases—as she *requested*—but she refuses for some reason. I hate people going through my things, but I kind of want her to. I want her to get to know me without me having to talk to her. She should know who I am and what I'm capable of. If she did, maybe she wouldn't fight me so much.

God, the fucking mouth on her. She never knows when to shut up. Every time she opens those lips some snide comment comes out. It's amusing—she always looks so shocked by her own words as if she never thought herself capable of being a little offensive. The girl is a glimmer of sunshine in a dark room. Eventually, though, the sun will go down and there'll be nothing but darkness—and that's when it'll get interesting.

I can tell being trapped in here isn't something she's scared of, and that pisses me off. For the first couple of days, she paced her room day and night—I could hear her light-footed stomps on the floorboards—but now she's content resting in bed. Something's changed. Was it the locked door?

"Did Adrian call you this morning? How did his encounter go?" Dimitri asks.

I let out a bitter noise when I remember the phone call I had with him. "Yeah. His finger is gone and his eye is still fucked up. He's watching the city right now."

When Adrian told me he wanted to deliver Sloane's hair to Giovanni in person, I let him because I thought the outcome would be funny. He told me about the endless stream of threats Giovanni gave him. It was all fun and games until he took his finger. That pissed me off, but I can't say I didn't expect it. Taking his ear would've been a typical move for Giovanni, but a finger is different.

Some things with Giovanni haven't changed. Once he has his heart and mind set on something, he goes for it. Which is exactly what I want him to do. Giovanni will take his men with him to Russia in the hope of finding Sloane. That's exactly what I want.

Little do they know, she's right under their noses. Only about ten miles offshore. She'd be easy to find if I stayed in the city, even at the beach property my father purchased. The Romano and Genovese families would see her, especially if they got the police involved.

But they don't have a single fucking clue where Sloane is. Three families with all the resources they could need at their disposal, and they can't even find her. It's laughable.

Giovanni has caused more fights than I can count, and he can't decide what his next move will be. The moment he's brought to me, I'll put him through hell and thrive on his empty threats. Or maybe I'll let him sweat for a little while longer.

"What, he can't handle her body or her attitude?"

"Probably both." I shrug. Adrian was the first of us to crack. He believes in the tale of *Koldunya* and claims the moment Sloane looked at him he forgot everything he was doing.

The tale is fucking stupid.

Dimitri laughs with me. "Do you know how long he's staying in the city?"

I shake my head. I've been wondering the same thing. I know there's another reason he doesn't want to come back, but I don't know what it is. He's probably tired of being tied up in all my shit, but it's not my actions that cause him issues—it's his strategy. He's fucking lucky Giovanni's turning softer than before.

"Do you want to target Nina too?" Dimitri asks.

I shake my head quickly. "No. She's pregnant."

His eyebrows rise. "Okay, that's a two-for-one."

His words irritate me. I know he craves a fight and has to be the first to spill blood, but this is where I draw the line. A thick fucking line. "I'm not taking his wife away."

"What the fuck happened to you, Mikhail?" He looks at me, his lips pressed tightly together.

"Nothing fucking happened," I snap. I can't have my men questioning me, but I don't want to lose sight of who I am. If I had a daughter on the way, I'd protect my wife with my life. One of the many reasons I don't form emotional attachments.

I never want to harm Nina, only Giovanni. But now I can use her against him to get what I want. He doesn't have to know I wouldn't ever do anything to hurt his family; he just needs to believe I'm capable of it.

That's something Kirill taught me: I need to be steps ahead of my enemies. I need to think like them. He always said that in order to generate concern, you need to use their weaknesses.

That's what I'm trying to do with Sloane. I'm sure she has more than one weakness. Her family is an obvious one, but I've yet to find another. I plan to tear her down till there's nothing left but bone. I'll know all her secrets, fears, hopes, and dreams ... everything.

Dimitri's hands find his face and he hides his expression from me. "Are you sure Sloane doesn't know anything?"

"That's exactly what I've been trying to figure out. She fights fire with fire."

"I told you,"—his face looks blank, just like mine—"the girl is Bratva too. She was raised by Ludis—of course she's going to find your spot. She's fucking ruthless. I like it." He smiles as his mind drifts off into oblivion. He stares at the ceiling, a small smile curving the corner of his lips.

"Dimitri." I snap my fingers in his face.

"Right. Um. Do you think if they see her, they'll make a deal?" he asks.

I stare down at my desk questioning my next move. I knew I wanted Sloane here, but I'm not as prepared as I'd like to be.

"No. They'll ambush, and I don't want to risk your lives. The Romano and Genovese men have an army now they're combined."

"We need to arrange a meeting with them eventually," Dimitri insists.

"It's only been a few days. I want to see them sweat a while longer. You can go," I tell him, and he exits the room and shuts the door behind him.

I spend the next couple of hours scrolling through tedious documents, planning on taking more from Giovanni than just Sloane.

Chapter 8

Sloane

The tips of my fingers graze the birch oak shelves. I've never seen a room like this before. The ceiling is curved with wooden columns that stabilize the roof, and paneled windows cover the entire wall. The room has three levels. While it's not a large room, it feels that way.

The steps are each lined with a warm yellow light, and so are the white bookcases, which are filled with books I recognize instantly. I've read almost every single one. Books have always been my escape. For years I've buried my head in thousands of words, losing all concept of time.

I kneel to the ground and pull out a book with a bright pink spine. Flipping through the pages, I notice red ink lining the margins—someone's handwriting.

Lifting my eyes, I glance around the room. It has a feminine touch to it, which is the opposite of the rest of the boat. I think that's why I like it so much. With curiosity getting the better of me, I begin to open drawers. Leave it to me to snoop through everything the day I finally decide to leave my room.

Shriveled and dried roses fill the top drawer below the stacks of books.

They've turned a brown color over time, but I know they were originally white.

That's odd.

I open the second drawer and see a notebook. Picking it up, I notice the edges of the paper are folded because it's been shoved into a small space with a bunch of other items.

"You're snooping," a voice says, breaking my thoughts.

I turn to the glass door and find Dimitri standing there with his arms crossed over his chest. "I—" I stutter. "Yeah, I was."

He smiles and takes a seat on the couch in front of me. "I'm not stopping you, sunshine."

Is this some kind of joke? It can't be though—not from Dimitri. He's the one who encouraged me to look around in the first place, but I'm curious as to why he's even helping me.

"Why not?" I ask.

"Mikhail doesn't give you much to work with. That, and you've mentioned you're getting bored." He plucks at the cuff on his shirt.

"Kind of." I half-smile and let the air out of my lungs with a sigh.

"What do you normally do? Like, before you came here."

I drop the book quietly in my lap. I never really did much at all. I was a house cat feeding off what others were able to provide for me. Even down to basic conversation. I craved human interaction. Ingret was always home with me, but she kept busy while my family were out.

Lonely isn't a good place to be. It creates anxious tendencies: nail biting, feet tapping, irrational fears, and obsessive thoughts. When something is kept in confinement, it's not able to grow. I was never given the opportunity to form connections with anyone else, and it eats away at me.

"I never really get out much," I say, trying to sound at bay. "Playing the piano and reading is how I pass the time, but I've read all these." I point to the shelves of books.

"You two have similar taste then."

"Who?" I ask, eager to find out if there's another woman who might have been trapped here before me.

"Anya, Mikhail's sister." He leans into me and takes the notebook from my hands. As he flips through it, he laughs. "Yeah, this is hers."

Anya ...

"Why are her things here?" I ask.

He taps his fingers against his lips. The one time I'd love some answers is when he begins to question if he should even be talking to me. *Perfect.*

"Anya and I stayed here for quite some time together before Mikhail wanted to take over," he finally says.

Take over. He just needed a remote place to keep me sheltered from anyone who might want to find me.

"Where is she?"

"Watching my babies and waiting for me to come home."

My hand flies to my mouth. "You married his sister? Isn't that like ... I don't know—"

"Wrong? Yes, on many levels." His laughter warms my heart. "But Mikhail would never say no to Anya no matter how much he hates me."

He smiles brightly. I knew the ring on his finger wasn't for a marriage he didn't care for. A woman who's able to make a man smile like Dimitri is right now is a woman who will be with that man forever.

"Why does he hate you?" I ask, still smiling.

"Oh, that's a long story. It all started with my absence from the meetings. I couldn't go anywhere once she started talking to me. She's very easy to talk to, just as you are."

I raise my eyebrows. "You should tell that to your boss."

"There's no telling him anything. That's why you interest me."

"What do you mean?"

"It's like you just say whatever you please. I admire it, but I hope it doesn't bite you in the ass one day."

"You and me both."

He gets up from the couch and walks toward the door. "There's a grand piano in the main room, just so you know."

Not long after Dimitri leaves, I take another look at the notebook and decide to grab it along with the novels and take them back to my room.

Many of them fall from my arms because of how many I grab at once.

My eyes strain as I read till the sun goes down. I don't even realize how long it's been until I can't see the words anymore. This is the first time I've been able to take my mind off the fact I'm trapped on a boat.

Starting to feel hungry, I make my way into the kitchen with the intention of grabbing an apple, but instead I find Mikhail. His back is bare of any clothing, but he's still wearing his suit pants.

"You should announce yourself when you walk into a room."

I know he's talking to me, and I can understand him, but I ignore him as I look at the marks on his back. At first I didn't notice them. I was too focused on his muscles and the tattoo covering his entire back, many pieces of art all connected into one. But the scars ... They're long slashes. Some of them are longer and thicker than the rest.

"What happened to your back?" I ask even though I know I should stay quiet and rush back to my room.

"You know what they say about the cat, don't you, Sloane?" He directs his attention away from the stove and brings it to me.

My head tilts as I try to understand. "The cat?"

He grabs the handle of the pot and pours the food into a bowl. "Curiosity killed it."

I hunch over and roll my eyes. "You're hilarious, truly."

"Don't be a cat. I'm not really in the mood to kill you right now."

I make an annoyed face and walk up to the counter to grab an apple out of the wicker basket. Does he expect me to be thankful for his words?

The energy in the room shifts when I feel how close he is to me. If I were to lift my elbow up slightly, his skin would be on mine. There's something about Mikhail that I find enticing when I shouldn't, but I can't help but want to know more about him.

I turn on my heel and face him. His attention is on the stove as he stirs the food. My eyes trace his body. He's tall, and his broad shoulders make his waist appear thinner than the rest of his body.

While I admire the sort of beauty the devil can create, I notice how orderly Mikhail is. It's beyond me how he can cook something messy and yet not leave a speck of mess anywhere on the white counter. The spoon even has a holder on the side of the stove, but he rinses it off before placing it down.

He gives me a sideways glare before he dips a spoon into the soup and brings it to my lips. "Try it," he demands.

I look at the spoon and question if it's poisoned. The idea doesn't shock me as much as it should. It's definitely something he'd do.

As if he can read my thoughts, Mikhail takes the spoon away from me and tastes it for himself. Then, dipping it back into the pot, he brings another spoonful to my lips. I push it away and watch in shock as the liquid sprays up over his face.

Fuck, I didn't mean to do that.

Every muscle in his face relaxes as he reaches down and pulls the hem of my shirt up to his face, wiping off the soup. "Your series of poor choices ends today, *moya malenkaya koldunya.*" *My little witch.*

Ignoring his thoughtless demands, I ask, "Was it someone in your family who did that to you?"

He slams the pot down on the stove and steps toward me. Every muscle in his jaw hardens as he grabs me by the neck. "What did you just say?"

My hands hold onto his as his fingers dig into my skin. I can breathe just fine, but he's cutting off my circulation.

When he realizes I'm struggling, he releases his grip. "Get out of my sight," he demands.

My hands replace his as I try to soothe the skin he grabbed. No one's ever grabbed me like that before.

Mikhail simply looks down at me in disgust.

I shake my head slowly and walk to the stairs to call it a night.

I thought I could do this. I thought I could handle him, but now I realize this man doesn't make empty threats.

Chapter 9

Sloane

t's nearly midnight, and I can't sleep because that's all I do to pass the time. I don't think I've ever gotten this much sleep in my life.

I take the comforter off the bed and move it to the open windows, where I wrap the blanket over my body and sit down. Just as I was starting to feel comfortable here, Mikhail made sure the feeling wouldn't settle. He's so heartless I can't even begin to understand what made him this way. Dimitri practically admitted Mikhail would do anything for his sister, but I can't see how that's possible. And those *scars*. Who the hell did that to him?

I pity him in a sense. Maybe if he didn't grow up in such a toxic environment, he'd be different. Able to show compassion and humility.

I stare down into oblivion while I think about my family. I miss them now more than ever. I wonder if they know Mikhail took me. Do they think I ran away? Hell, maybe they think I'm lying in a ditch somewhere.

"Jesus," I mutter to myself. I know for a fact Dad is losing his shit right now, flipping tables and demanding his men search for me. But thinking about that won't get me out of here. I need to find something on Mikhail. I need to be able to use something against him.

I throw the blanket off and walk down the side of the boat. Small lights line the bottom of the rails. This is the stupidest idea I think I've ever had, but it's my only chance.

I roll my shoulders to rid the nerves that crush my lungs with a death grip and continue down the lit pathway. I pass by many doors but come to a halt when I see one cracked open at the very end of the hallway. I walk slowly up to it, careful not to make any noise. Pushing the door open, I cover my mouth with my hand to quiet my breathing.

Mikhail.

He's asleep, lying on a large bed with dark sheets, his arm resting gently above his head, no sheets covering his torso. He's made of muscle, and this should terrify me, but right now it doesn't. I kind of see it as an opportunity. In a resting state, completely vulnerable, he almost looks sweet—the opposite of what I've come to know him as.

I look around the room to see if there's anything of his I can take to use against him, but there's nothing. His room is spotless. He doesn't even have a water bottle by the side of his bed. The carpet even has the lines from a vacuum. Nothing about his room defines his personality. There's no clutter that could show a sign of any hobbies he might have. It's just his bed—the stage for his dark and demented dreams.

With my hand still over my mouth, I turn to leave, but something stops me. There's a gun on the dresser. Which feels like a trap. A man like him wouldn't leave his weapon out in the open like this, would he? But if he feels safe in the comfort of his own space, why wouldn't he?

I walk up to it, considering my options. I could shoot him. But then his men would do the same to me. My hands begin to shake. Could I even do it? Could I kill someone? It contradicts everything I believe in.

"Pick it up," a deep voice mumbles directly in my ear, making me jump out of my skin.

I look up into the mirror to find Mikhail's big frame swallowing mine. My body covers his chest. His face is dead with no emotion.

"Pick. It. Up." His voice is so deep I feel my heart drop.

I stare at him, and he does the same. His head falls back, and I see the outline of his jaw. His mouth opens slightly as his tongue rolls over his teeth. I gulp down my fear as he presses the front of his body to my back. He could snap me in half like a stick.

I walked straight into the lion's den without thinking he'd wake up.

My hands fumble with the gun. Once it's in my hands, Mikhail grabs onto my waist and turns me toward him quickly. My skin flushes as his fingers dig into my sides, tightening his hold on me.

"Point it at me." His gaze narrows.

"I don—" I stammered.

He leans into me, his mouth right next to my ear. "Point. It. At. Me."

I do as he says and point the gun at him, my stomach flipping with nerves. Why is he doing this? Everything is happening so fast I feel like I can't breathe.

"Pull the trigger, Sloane."

I look down, but he lifts my face up with his thumb. "If you're going to kill me, you'd better fucking mean it. Look me in the eyes when you do."

Barely able to keep myself steady, my heart thunders inside my chest. I don't think I can do it. As much as I hate him, I don't think I'm capable of killing him.

"I can't," I admit. He doesn't need to know why.

He grabs my waist again, but this time he lifts me off the ground and sets me down on the dresser. His hands feel huge. He pushes my legs apart and steps between them. The gun is still placed against his chest. I'm scared to move it.

"You can't?" he repeats as his hand wraps around the back of my neck. He's softer with his hold on me here compared to his touch in the kitchen.

"No," I manage to get out.

"Tell me why."

I can't tell you. "It wouldn't change anything," I admit.

He leans his face close to mine. "It would change a lot, *Koldunya*," he whispers in my ear. Chills run through my body. "I would be dead." He lays his hands flat on my thighs and inches closer to my waist. "I won't give you another chance."

I shake my head, trying to come up with something to say, but nothing comes out. He lifts my silk gown from under me so it's bunched around my waist.

Then he pulls me closer to him. His muscular frame pushes right against mine. My head falls forward slightly when his lips hover over my neck. Goose bumps take over my skin. I lose control of my breathing as his hands roam my body freely.

"You're just as fucked-up as I am," he says as if he can read my mind.

His words don't even get to my head because I already know that. The want I have for risk is something I shouldn't touch with a ten-foot pole, but I *want* to. There is nothing welcoming about being here with Mikhail, and yet I can't think of a better way to spend my time away from home. Years of being locked in a house hasn't done me well. Mikhail intrigues me. Am I really as fucked-up as he is?

I don't know if I can't move because I'm terrified or because I want him to continue putting his hands on me.

His fingers trail closer to my inner thigh, and I suck in a sharp breath. When he reaches the seam of the lace, he pulls it to the side. I don't stop him because I want this as much as I don't want to admit to it. It feels as if my mind and body are screaming at each other. My body wants to pull him into me and crash my lips against his, and my mind wants to push him off me and tell him to go fuck himself.

But my body is winning.

His finger slides over my clit, and I drop the gun. His touch is soft—I begin to crave it. I've never hated someone so much yet wanted their skin on mine. I swallow the noises that threaten to fall from my lips.

"*Oni biliy pravi o tebe, Koldunya,*" he mumbles. *They were right about you, Witch.* He takes his hands off me and steps back.

"What are you—?" I breathe frantically.

He turns away from me, picks up the gun from the floor, and opens the bedroom door. Then he stands by it staring at me. "Out," he demands.

"I thought—"

"You thought what? That I'd fuck you?" His eyebrows rise slightly.

Thank God it's dark in here. What the fuck was I thinking—that he wanted me too? This is humiliating, but he doesn't need to know he just offended me.

"Can't please me, and I'll just find someone who can. Lev? That'll be interesting," I say with a sass that comes out of nowhere.

He walks over to me slowly, pulling me into him by my hair. My body stiffens when I feel the cold metal touch my inner thigh. I don't need to look down to realize he's holding the gun I threatened him with against my skin.

"Oh, yeah?" he asks as his grip on me tightens. "Tell me what his reaction is when you're screaming my name instead of his."

I tilt my head to the side and push Mikhail's chest to get him out of my way.

"Sloane," he mumbles.

I hesitate to walk out the door.

"I want you on your best behavior tomorrow. And if not, I'll just lock you up again."

And with that, I storm out of his room.

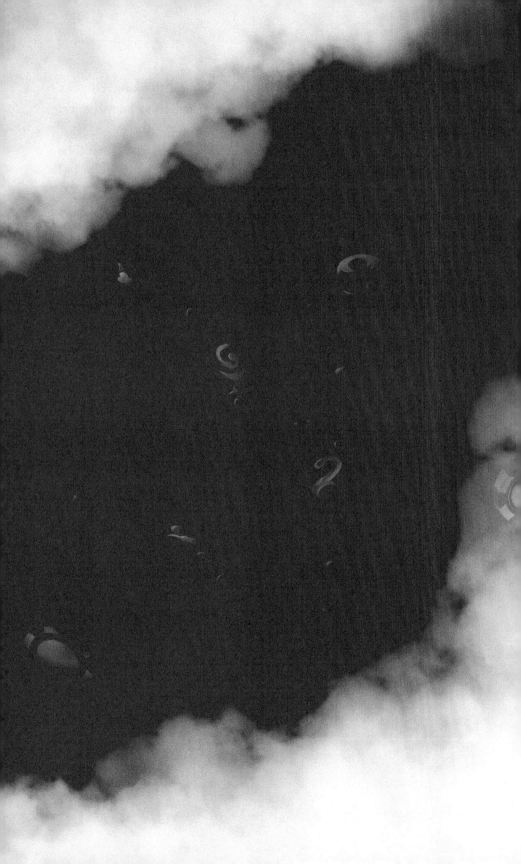

Chapter 10

Mikhail

I walk into the billiard room and grab a pole off the wall. Then I step up to the table and hit the cue ball, knocking a four in the hole.

"You're late," Lev says.

I continue my aim for the next hole while he scoffs. "By like five minutes," I counter.

"They seem to be hitting it off," Lev whispers, swirling a glass of scotch.

I look over at Mia and Adrian and find they're laughing with one another while they both sit on a small chair in the corner of the room. I knew it would happen eventually. It was just a matter of time.

"Finally." I wink at Adrian, and he rolls his eyes at me.

"Enough of the game—you need to look at these," Lev says, directing my attention to the files that cover the entire table. I just started playing, but he's right: I need to sort this shit out. I don't have Sloane on the boat for shits and giggles.

I take a file from the table and lay all the pictures out. "Which one is Giovanni after again?" I ask him.

"324 Parkway."

He's after the one building I want. The *one* building my father wanted me to take back. Giovanni might not even know about this, and if he does, I'll kill him twice over.

I read the paper and see a name I recognize.

Gabe.

At this point, it's just one bad thing after another. After losing two people who meant everything to me, life can't seem to give me a fucking pass.

"Why the fuck is Gabe's name on here?"

"I'd assume it's because he wants to get it before you do."

No kidding. Gabe has done shit like this my entire life. He goes after what I want every single time. He's my cousin and believes he deserves to rule instead of me. He'll never be able to comprehend that Pavel gave me his kingdom instead of him. He'll never be able to get that through his thick skull.

"A meeting will be arranged with him," I demand.

"Good. He's using Kirill's tactics," Dimitri says as if I'm not already aware of his scheming tendencies.

Acting innocent until proven guilty—that's his thing. I'm sure Gabe's plan is to make it look like he has my best interests in mind, but he never has. He's a snake who'll go against me if I show one sign of weakness. He's never gotten along with anyone in my family. I can't even begin to understand how the fuck he's still relevant.

"This is the building worth seven million."

"Yes, but I don't think Giovanni has the funds for it right now. You could take over his entire section of the city if you wanted to."

I shake my head. I don't want to take everything from him; I only want the buildings he hasn't gotten yet. I want what's mine.

"I don't want his parts of the city. I just need that building. It doesn't matter whether I have more money than Giovanni or not—it's controlled by investors. If the three brothers choose me, it will eventually go in my name. All I need is Parkway and a house. The rest will come easy after that."

"Many will see it as a threat."

"I don't give a fuck." I need 324 Parkway. If Giovanni takes it over, it's a roadblock.

I wasn't planning on going back to New York yet—not for a while. But then I found out Giovanni is bidding. It'll be nice to see Nina again.

I want everything in my name. I want the Stepanov name in New York. I'm tired of being seen as a threat an ocean away.

I reach for a cigarette from my pocket and light it.

"Reservations are planned for West 90—it's in the Upper East Side. Clarke's territory," Lev says.

"That's too close," I tell him. "I told you to stay clear of them. Get rid of West 90."

If I target the Clarke family, they'll come after me with their fucking pitchforks raised. They're ruthless and don't blink at the sight of blood—as a matter of fact, they're usually the first to spill it.

It's been years since we last heard from them, and I'd love nothing more than to keep it that way. West 90 isn't an option because it's on their land. The second I sign a contract for a building in their territory, they'll walk off with my head.

I could go the usual route, the way my family's always done their business—drug distribution, loan sharing, tax fraud, and extortion—but I want to do this a better way. Property management. I won't have to get my hands as dirty, and the feds won't be on my ass like they are now. I want to control the city and make a profit without them even realizing it. I have a feeling that's what my father wanted, but he never wrote it down. He made sure I would own the city again, but not in the way I figured. He must have known I enjoy management more.

"You could take over more this way."

"I'm not trying to start a war with the Irish, Lev. They've been doing their own thing for years, and I want them to keep it that way. I already have too much going on with Giovanni."

"I've got to hand it to you, man," Dimitri says, taking a sip from his glass, "I thought this was just about revenge."

"It is. But I also want what's best for this family. It's what my father wanted."

"And what's the plan with Sloane?"

I have many reasons for keeping her. Selfishly, I want to because of how my body reacts to her. I like how she always has something smart to say back to me, but if I keep this going, I might snap. I've never dealt with anyone like her. When people piss me off, I'm able to handle it—but I need Sloane alive.

There are two other reasons I have to keep in mind. One: if Giovanni takes a property I want, I'll trade her for it. Two: if everything works out and I claim my section, I'll use her for a contract. They can have her back if they agree to remain civil.

"It really all depends on how the event goes, doesn't it?" I say.

"Will Giovanni be there?"

I shrug. "Depends on how badly he wants it and whether people will invest their money in him or me."

"He has a wife and a daughter on the way. They'll invest in him because he looks better."

I'm aware of that. A family man is viewed in a better light than a single man. "That's what Dimitri was telling me."

"Sloane," Lev insists.

I put out the cigarette in the ashtray and fold my arms across my chest. "Yep. Don't ask me how I'll get her to agree. She's a wild horse who refuses to be ridden."

"Make a deal with her."

"Like what?" I ask, interested in his idea.

"If she does this for you, you'll let her go."

Let her go.

The thought of letting her go pisses me off. I'll never admit it to her, but I've been enjoying her company. She maddens me. She makes me feel things I haven't felt before. I fucking hate her. She never knows when to shut up and mind her own fucking business.

"She would believe you—you know that," Lev muses.

"I wouldn't lie to her. If that's what I tell her to convince her, then I'll stick to my end of the deal."

"A man of honor," he chuckles.

I toss my head back. "A man of honor."

It would leave me empty-handed, at risk of the families coming after me.

Grabbing the pool stick, I place it back on the rack. "Max is arriving tomorrow. And there will be no fucking fighting."

"He's with Giovanni. Fighting is bound to happen," Lev says, the veins in his neck standing out.

"He's with me."

I end my conversation with Lev and head back to my bedroom, where I take a shower and lie down on the firm mattress. I'd never be able to stay in New York without Sloane. She connects two strong families, and they'd do anything to get to her. But now I have to worry about her. I have to protect her from the people who want to steal her from me.

She doesn't know the truth about anything, and when she learns, it'll shatter her precious, fragile heart.

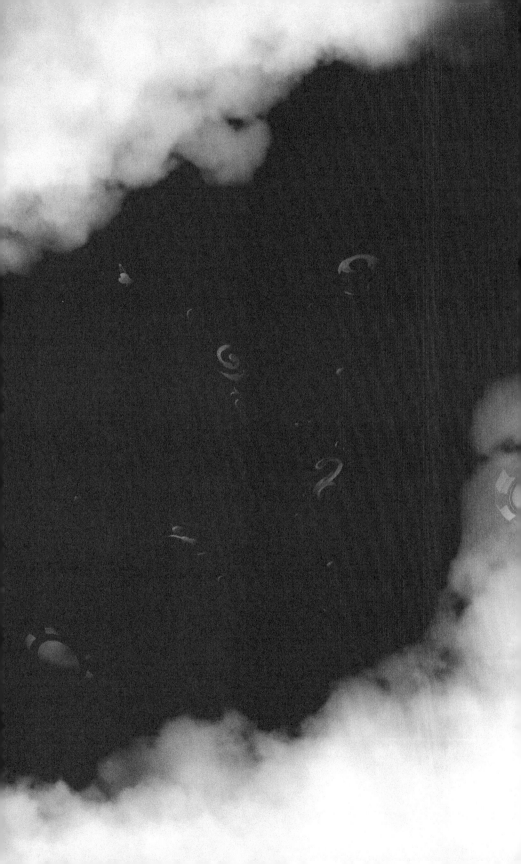

Chapter 11

Sloane

I spend the next day trying to familiarize myself with everyone on the boat.

Mia seems kind and has no business working for these assholes. I have a feeling she only works for Mikhail because of the money. She never talks unless she's speaking to Mikhail directly. She is the cook and nothing more.

Dimitri has a sense of humor. He laughs at my sarcasm, which is not something I'm used to. I find it easy to talk to him at times. It's hit or miss with him, but I've noticed something: whenever his shirt is buttoned, I shouldn't talk to him. His temper is at its highest and he's almost always busy on his computer or on the phone. But in the off chance his tie is off and his shirt unbuttoned, he smiles a lot. He jokes left and right, just trying to have a good time. I admire him for that. He's able to separate his work from his life. A part of me thinks he does that because he doesn't want to take his work home. He tells me he has three kids at home. It's obvious to me that Anya and his children mean everything and more to him.

Lev is just like Mikhail. They're always serious. I refrain from saying anything when I'm around them because they always manage to put me on the spot or make fun of me in a sickening way. Mikhail called him "brother" at one of our breakfasts, but they don't look related whatsoever.

Speak of the devil, I find him leaning the upper half of his body against the side of the boat with his phone up to his ear. Turning his head slightly toward me, he looks me up and down and rolls his tongue over the side of his cheek.

"One moment," he says to the person on the other end of the line. He watches me as I brush past him, but he grabs onto my hand.

His hand covers the bottom of the phone as he asks, "Where are you going?"

I glance down at the swimsuit I'm wearing and give him a look. "To the hot tub," I tell him with confidence.

"You're not going anywhere. I have places to be and I don't trust you alone, so you'll be coming with me."

"I have a tracker on me, and you most likely have cameras everywhere," I huff.

"Don't play," he mutters.

"I'm not going anywhere with you."

"I never gave you a choice, *Koldunya*." His hand wraps around mine. "Find a dress to wear. I'd prefer if it were blu—"

"I don't care what you prefer," I say, interrupting him.

"Did I say you could talk?" he asks.

"Did you say I couldn't?" I bite back.

"Go fucking change." He steps back and walks down the hallway, leaving me to deal with his sour mood. But what's new?

I walk back to my room with dread and take in a deep breath. I put on the blue dress I wore to Ingret's birthday dinner. Mikhail found a way to get all my things here, and it's fucking creepy.

He treats me like his doll, and that frustrates me. It's not difficult to treat someone like a human being. People have emotions, but Mikhail acts as if I don't. I don't like being pushed around and forced to obey his stupid commands, but I have no other choice.

Unless …

Spending time with Dimitri served me well because I found one of his burner phones on the counter this morning. I'm scared to use it because I don't want Dimitri to think I went behind his back. I care for him in a strange way, but I need to call my family.

Reaching for the phone, I dial my brother's number. It rings a couple of times before he finally picks up.

"Koziov," he mutters.

"Ruslan?" I ask.

There's a pause followed by a long, hopeful sigh. "Sloane?"

Hearing my brother's voice overwhelms me with comfort. "Yeah, it's me. Listen, I need your help."

He yells at someone in the background, probably telling them to shut up. "Where are you? Was it Giovanni?"

"Giovanni? No, it was Mikhail, but don't—" I try to continue, but he interrupts me at the worst of times.

"Sloane, please tell me you're just pronouncing that name wrong."

"What do you mean?"

"Mikhail Stepanov?"

"Yes," I admit, but then realize I can't say much else because he doesn't know anything. The plan was between three people.

"Fuck. Shit, okay."

"Listen, just tell Dad where I am, but don't—" I say, but he interrupts me *again*.

"He's the Bratva, Sloane."

Another knock sounds at the door, and I hang up the phone quickly, frustrated with the fact I wasn't able to tell Ruslan not to send anyone. I just need Dad to know where I am.

"Coming!" I rush to the door, opening it to find Mikhail leaning against the doorframe with his arms crossed.

"Are you ready?"

I look down at the dress and heels he's making me wear. "Yes. I would love it if you gave me dresses in other colors."

He looks me up and down and licks his lips. "Why would I want to do that?" he asks, stepping up to me and pulling on the dress strap. "No. You complement me this way."

I complement him. "The color blue complements you?"

He lifts my chin with his thumb. "Your innocence does."

I swallow, prepared to say something smart back to him, but I hold my tongue.

He leads the way and holds the bottom of my dress up so I don't trip. Once at the bottom, I notice an area of the ship I've never explored. It's kind of like a garage, but for a speedboat.

I could have tried to leave this entire time?

His hands grab onto my waist, and he lifts me onto the small boat. Something feels off. I don't know why he's being somewhat kind, but I'm not complaining.

Mikhail sits behind the wheel and starts the engine.

The wind is chilling, and Mikhail drives the boat like a maniac. I look back at the yacht as it grows smaller and smaller in the distance.

The ride onto the docks doesn't take as long as I expect it to. We get off the boat and switch over to a car. I give him a glare when he opens the door for me.

Mikhail gets into the driver's side and puts his hand on the back of my seat while he backs up.

"Where are we going?" I finally ask.

"To see an old friend of mine."

I nod.

The drive is long, but it's a straight shot to town. Does he even realize he's showing me the way back? He pulls the car up to the entry. Getting out, he tosses his keys to a man and tells him something in Russian. Then he comes over to my side and opens the door, holding out his hand for me to grab.

Reaching out, I take Mikhail's hand in mine. He leads me through the rotating doors into a huge building.

"Where's your friend?" I scream over the music.

He looks down at me with a smile—one I've never seen before. He looks like a decent person when he smiles. Small dimples form on his cheeks.

He looks *handsome*.

The crowd separates when everyone looks at Mikhail. They must know who he is, otherwise they wouldn't move.

We get to the side of the club where the booths are. They all look similar, but there's a man dancing on one of the tables singing to the song that's about to blow my eardrums. Mikhail lets go of my hand and grabs onto the stranger's. He grabs a glass filled with alcohol, and they dance together to "Pursuit of Happiness" by Kid Cudi as if no one's watching.

Mikhail's neck falls back while he laughs. The sound is like wind chimes on a windy day. *Magical.*

The other guy, who I assume is Mikhail's friend, offers me his hand. I shake my head, but he hops to the ground. He stands behind me and grabs onto my waist, making my body move with his. The man is a fucking giant—he's even taller than Mikhail.

I feel as if my limbs are on strings, the stranger manipulating the way I move. Even without alcohol, I'm beginning to enjoy my time. I turn to face him. My arms can't wrap around his shoulders, so I grab onto his hands instead, and he continues to move my body to the music.

"Just let everything go and feel it though your body," he whispers to me.

Letting myself get caught up in the moment, I smile. The man is obviously drunk off his ass, but I don't mind. I've never been out like this before. I feel a small wave of anxiety wash over me at how many people are here, but the stranger makes me forget. I feel every beat of the music in my body. The effect he has on me is dangerous. I'm able to forget my worries.

Then large arms snake around my waist and pull me back. I can tell by his smell it's Mikhail. He raises my arms out and hovers his own behind mine. When the stranger takes a large sip of his drink and offers me some, I take it without any worries. I'm having a great time even if I'm with a psycho and his friend.

Mikhail takes my body in his and twirls me in a circle. I laugh uncontrollably.

"Are you enjoying yourself?" he asks in my ear.

I nod in response. It would be hard not to.

I know he's enjoying himself just as much as I am. The moment he saw his friend, his demeanor shifted.

Mikhail leaves my side and whispers something to his friend. They both laugh and walk back to the table. "Sloane." He calls for me to follow.

And I do. I slide into the booth and wave my hands above my skin to try to cool down.

"We're going to need cards," the stranger says as he pulls some out of his pocket.

"Of course you would," Mikhail says with a smile.

"And your lady will need a drink."

Mikhail raises his hand, and a waitress comes over. She leans her entire body into him. She speaks to him in Russian, and it seems she's flirting with him. His hand lifts to her waist, and I look down. I don't know why it bothers me so much. I don't even feel anything for Mikhail. He can do whatever he wants, just not right in front of me.

The stranger pulls me closer to him and brings his mouth to my ear. "Do you know of any games?"

"No, I've never played cards."

He smiles. "We'll play something simple then." His voice sounds different from everyone else's. His complexion is darker, and he has an accent.

"Where are you from?" I ask.

"Italy, but I live here in New York."

"For Mikhail?" I ask.

He shrugs. "He's worth it."

I make a face at him. If it's this version of Mikhail, I understand. But the version I've been dealing with? I don't understand how he's worth anything.

Lifting my eyes to Mikhail, I see the waitress is still here, but with a drink. She must have left without me noticing.

I didn't want to notice.

"Is it true?" she asks me, her Russian accent strong.

My eyebrows knit together. "Is what true?"

"The tale of the witch. I want to find out."

Before I can ask her more, Mikhail waves her off. She slumps over with a saddened expression and walks away.

The tale of the witch.

"Everyone thinks you're—"

"Max, enough." Mikhail interrupts his friend.

I watch them both stare at each other. It doesn't take a genius to figure out what Max was about to say.

"Give me a number," Max says, looking at me.

"Five."

"Higher or lower, Sloane?" Max asks with a bright expression.

"Higher or lower than what?"

"You're supposed to guess if the card in my hand is higher or lower than the number you just told me."

"Higher?"

"Damn it," he says. And then he asks the same questions round after round. "You guys are really screwing the dealer."

Mikhail laughs and motions his head for me to move closer. He pulls my legs into his lap and reaches for his drink.

Max downs shot after shot without a care in the world.

"How did you guys meet?" I ask.

They both look at each other and burst out laughing.

What the hell is so funny?

"I met him while he was trying to kill my brother-in-law," Max says, shaking his head.

"Jesus," I say under my breath.

"I didn't though," Mikhail tells me as he places his hand on my thigh. He rubs his thumb against my skin, his touch sending shocks of electricity through my body.

Why is my body reacting to a man as fucked-up as Mikhail?

"No, he didn't. But I'm not even supposed to be here right now. Giovanni would have my head."

Giovanni.

"Enough," Mikhail says, ending the conversation. He lifts my legs off him and gets out of the booth. He takes his phone out from his pocket and places it against his ear. His veiny hands make the phone look small.

"Dimitri," he addresses him, "yeah, bring her to the house. I'll be staying here with Max for a bit."

The house?

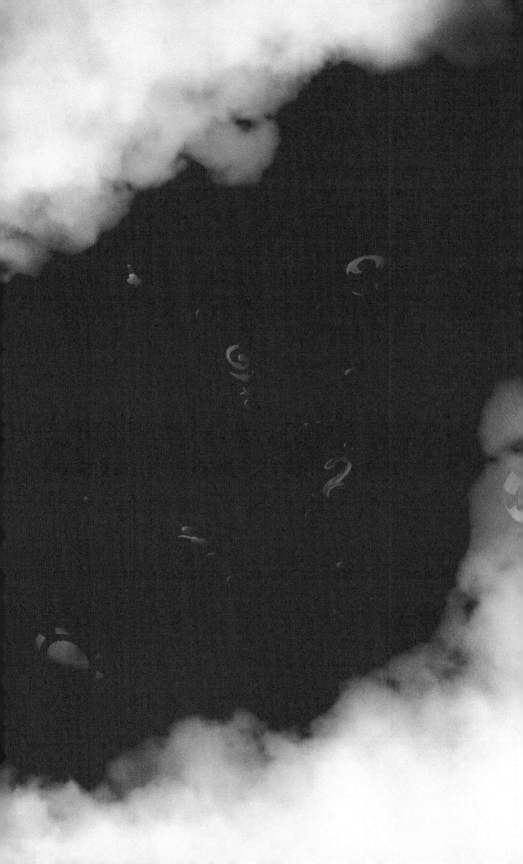

Chapter 12

Mikhail

Dimitri comes to get Sloane, and she doesn't look too happy about it. I'm glad she's able to enjoy my company.

Max and I walk up the couple of steps to the private bar. The bottles glow with the neon lights lining the shelves. I take a seat, and Max does the same.

He drinks alcohol as if it's water. That's how I know he's in a dark place.

Max has been like this for the two years I've known him. While I was on my way back to Russia after Giovanni tried to kill me, I saw him. He cornered me at the airport, demanding answers. Max was ready to kill me on the spot because he thought I was after Nina the entire time. I laughed in his face and explained everything to him. I'm not sure why I did. There's just something about him—I feel compelled to tell him everything about myself without any restraint.

And I did.

Many drinks later, he and I were fast friends.

I wish I could have him by my side at all times, but Giovanni would never allow it. As much as he loves Nina, he'd blow her brother's brains out if he knew Max were with me.

Or maybe he'd cut off his ear. I'm not sure if he still does that shit.

"Vodka," I tell the bartender.

Watching the man pour a shot, Max lifts his finger and orders one too.

"How's Nina?" I ask about his sister as I bring the sweaty glass to my lips. The burning taste of it in my throat wakes me up.

"She's good. I don't think she likes being pregnant very much. It's funny. Every time the baby kicks she calls our mom to ask if something's wrong."

I can't help but laugh. I never got to know Nina very much, but I didn't peg her as a damsel in distress. Maybe that's just a side effect of her wanting to protect her baby with her entire being.

"How does Giovanni manage living two different lives?" I ask, curious.

"Right now, he doesn't, but that's only because Mira isn't here yet. Until he has a son, I don't think he plans on bringing his work home. Don't ask me how the fuck he'll manage that, but it's what he wants."

"That couldn't be me. Son or daughter, their first toy will be a water gun so they understand how to aim and hold the trigger."

Max leans his weight on the bar and gives me a dirty look. "What a great father you'll be someday."

I chuckle and knock him on the head. "No kids, I'm just fucking around."

"Bratva would go to someone who isn't in your family—is that what you want?"

"No, but I don't want a wife or kids. It also won't be my problem when I'm six feet under."

Max tilts his head to the side and downs his shot. The muscles in his jaw tighten in reaction to the burn. "That's kind of dark, man, I'm not going to lie." His hand brushes down his hair. He used to have curly hair that dropped to his forehead, but he shaved it into a fade. It makes his facial features stand out a lot more: narrow nose, scruffy beard, and full eyebrows.

"What, like you can see yourself with a family? Didn't you just tell your father you refuse to marry?"

He cringes at my words, though they weren't meant to be insulting. "I wanted that. *Shit*, man, I had the start of it. I wanted the cookie-cutter future. A wife to come home to after a long day, three kids, maybe more, running around the yard playing games. But the moment I created all those plans in my head, everything vanished."

I watch him with wide eyes. He's never told me what happened to him; he just follows by my side. Maybe he bonded with me quickly because we were both dealt a shitty hand.

"You know, when you find that person, there's no one else in the world who can amount to them. From the way she laughs, the way she picks the tomatoes off her sandwiches, to the way she demands her clothes to be ironed before she wears them. And don't even get me started on her lifestyle. Everything had to be *Prada this, Prada that.* God, she was the most stuck-up woman I've ever met, and I loved her for it."

"Another, please," I tell the bartender as I listen to Max pour his heart out to me. This isn't exactly what I had in mind when I said I wanted to get a drink, but I'll listen because this is the first sign of emotion he's ever shown.

"She was so difficult to understand too. Her accent was so fucking strong it took me months to figure her out. It would've taken longer if she weren't manic as fuck. I knew everything about her because she didn't know how to shut up."

"I can relate. Sloane speaks before her mind catches up with her tongue."

He nods. "Listen while you still can," he says as if I could do anything else but listen to her. I try—I really do.

"It's hard to ignore her, trust me."

He laughs genuinely, adjusting the lapels of his jacket. "What is your plan with her?"

I allow a smug smile to pull at the corner of my lips. "I've got everything sorted out. If you can keep Giovanni off my ass, we'll be good."

"That's easier said than done," he says.

I lean further into the bar, allowing my head to fall between my shoulders. He's right. It's a risk bringing Sloane to the house this early, but I need to get a move on. I can stay dormant for as long as I'd like, but nothing would get accomplished. I've already waited long enough.

"Are you staying with us?" I ask.

He nods. "Yes and no. Your house is right across from mine, actually," he says, taking out a sheet of paper from his suit jacket. "You're looking at a proud new house owner."

My eyes widen and I nearly spit out my drink. "The fuck?" I ask.

His smile is wide—he's almost *too* proud. Why the hell would he think buying a house next to where I'm keeping Sloane is a good idea?

His hand hits my back, and he kneads my shoulder. "Relax. I'm restoring it, and the only other person who knew about it is dead."

I haven't been caught off-guard like this in a while. I would have expected his family to know about it, maybe even help him restore it, but I guess not. But nothing about this is smart.

"*Ya nenavizhu tebya*," I mutter. *I hate you.*

"I like the sound of that," Max says with a grin. "Say it in English, Stepanov."

Looking at him through my brows, I grimace. "Go fuck yourself."

He holds his hand over his heart. "Don't say such sweet things to me."

Digging into my pockets, I throw a bill on the table and lift myself out of the chair. "She should be there now. Will you be at the house later?" I ask before I head out.

He nods.

"Also, keep an eye out for Giovanni for me."

"You're going to owe me for this," he says.

"Why?" I ask.

He stands up from the chair and places more cash on the table. "Because we're fixing each other's problems." He smiles.

It'll be nice to have Max with me instead of him being with Giovanni.

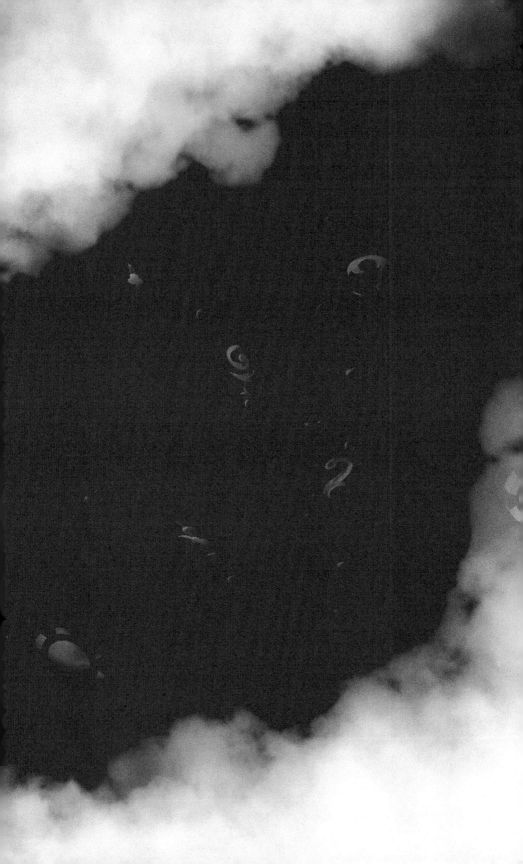

Chapter 13

Sloane

Shortly after Mikhail spoke with Dimitri, he was there to pick me up. We drove in silence for what felt like an eternity.

I stand in the foyer of the house, which has a modern touch, while Dimitri grabs my things from the car. He's different from what I'm familiar with. He almost looks irritated, but I'm not the kind of person to make his burdens mine as well.

"There are many rooms in the house. Pick one," he demands with a strong voice.

I give him a look and take my bag from his hands.

He lets out a huff when I turn my back and head up the stairs. Every wall in this house is painted white with no art. It's very bland ... It's very *Mikhail.*

The stairs are split into two levels with panels leading up the sides, and the floorboards are a light shade of wood in a patterned design.

The door handles and chandelier are black—they complement the white. Up the hallway, the lights are dimmed, and I walk on an aged red carpet.

I open the door at the end of the hallway and step into a dark room.

Flipping on the light, I see a large bed in the center of the room and two chairs by a curved wall filled with windows.

There's a large walk-in closet and a bathroom with a shower that's just as large.

I throw my bag on the bed and make my way back down the stairs. I wouldn't be able to sleep even if I tried. Adrenaline flows through my blood.

My mind runs in circles as I try to relive what happened tonight. It was the most fun I've ever had, even if it was with a man who probably wants me dead.

His friend, Max, seems like a genuine guy. He wears an expression of pain on his face like an accessory, but he smiles brightly with his eyes.

Stepping down the stairs, I walk into the living room. I turn on the TV, putting on Russian subtitles while I pull a blanket up to my chin and crumple a pillow under my head.

My eyes begin to feel scratchy from lack of sleep, but I open them wide when I see Mikhail leaning against the wall staring at me.

"You know ... that's a little creepy," I say, exhausted.

He looks down and shakes his head, trying to fight the smile that tugs on his lips. "What're you doing out here? It's one in the morning."

"Watching TV. You have eyes, don't you?"

"*Kroshka*," he warns.

I choose to ignore him because he isn't calling me by my name. He nods at the realization and pushes off the wall. He takes a seat next to me, lifting my legs onto his lap. Pushing the blanket off my feet, he takes his thumbs and kneads the bottom of my heel. I didn't realize how sore my feet were from dancing tonight, but why is he doing this? Mikhail isn't the sort of kind person who thinks about other people's pain before his own.

He doesn't give; he only takes. *So what is this?*

My arms lift above my head while I enjoy the massage for as long as it'll last. I don't want to take his kindness for granted.

"Sloane." He calls my name.

"Yeah?" I ask, keeping my eyes directed on him with purpose.

His jaw clenches and he looks over at me with his head tilted. "Was tonight your first night out?"

I think about all the times I've left the house before now, only to realize I've only left to go to my brother's matches. If it weren't for Ruslan, I never would have left the house. But I'm glad I did. While I might be here, I'm glad I don't feel claustrophobic anymore.

"Well, besides going to the ring with my brother, yes."

"And did you enjoy yourself?" His eyes glisten under the soft light.

"I think I did, yeah. What did we even go there for?"

He takes out a small orange envelope from his pocket and waves it in the air effortlessly. "Was it Max who gave you that?" I ask.

He nods. "When I first arrived."

A look of shock covers my face. "I don't even remember that. What's in it?"

It's as if my question offends him in a way. The smug smile that once spoke of his emotion is washed away as if it never existed. He reaches across the table and takes his drink into his hand. I become impatient when he ignores me for a while.

"Normally, when someone asks a question, you're supposed to answer them. Why aren't you answering me?"

His thumb traces circles on my thigh. "Why the hell are you talking so much?" he asks with a deep, alluring voice and leaves to go into the kitchen.

I flip him the bird. He deserves it.

Mikhail has no reason to be a dick about anything, but he is. If he wants to get angry about nothing, I can too.

"This house is made of reflections, Sloane. You'd be better off showing me the finger behind closed doors if you don't want to deal with the consequences of your actions," he says with his back to me.

The nerve this man has drives me insane. I sit up from the couch and inch my legs closer to my chest. "You know, some day you'll go far in life, and I hope you stay there."

His head falls back, and he sets his glass on the counter with a heavy hand. "Come over here and tell that to me again."

I bite my tongue and stand up from the couch to make my way over to him. *Does he think I won't do it?*

He turns to face me and lifts his chin. As I stand in front of him, I can't help but feel beneath him. He walks around with an aura that screams he is superior.

I straighten my back with my teeth clenched. He looks down at me as if I am nothing. "You want to say that again, *Kroshka*?" he asks while his lip lifts in amusement.

My mouth opens to repeat myself like he's telling me to, but he quickly puts his hand over my lips and leans in closer. My breathing picks up by the simple touch of his skin on mine.

"Jesus, how many times do you need to learn the same lesson, Sloane?" He steps even closer to me, bringing his mouth close to his hand. "I can teach it to you as many times as you'd like, but I don't think you'll keep up." Slowly, he takes his hand off my mouth, and I stumble forward when I feel his touch leave mine.

He turns on his heel to leave but stops when I mumble, "It's not like you've really even got far."

His head turns slightly. "If you expect to be heard, you shouldn't mumble."

I clear my throat and shove past him, knocking into his shoulder. "I don't need to be heard."

He grabs me from the back of my neck and pulls me against his body. The heat of his body warms mine. His hand snakes around the front of my neck and his arm holds my core still.

I try my hardest to get my breathing under control because I don't want him to know I'm nervous, but it's useless. As much as I want to, I can't ignore what my body does when he touches me. I hate that I react to him, but I hate that I like it even more.

His fingers dig into my hips, and he lifts me onto the counter. Warmth spreads through me, and I immediately stiffen at his touch.

What the hell is he doing?

"What are you doing?" I ask him. His eyes pierce mine with desire ... with need. His eyes don't leave mine. It's as if he enjoys seeing me weaken against his touch. My legs move apart when he steps between them.

His hands hold my face, and he pulls down on my bottom lip. "Something I shouldn't," he says on a worn-out breath of air, and I feel my heart in my throat.

Something flashes in his eyes as he looks down at my body pressed against his. His head falls back when he looks at me, and his Adam's apple rolls in his throat. His jaw hardens as he looks down at my lips. He's obviously conflicted about whether he should tell me what he's thinking.

"It's not real."

"What are you talking about, Mikhail?" My chest burns.

His fingers trail down my chest to my stomach. I chose a bad day to wear this silk robe—it doesn't hide anything. He can probably see my nipples hardening even though he's hardly touched me. He gathers my wet hair and pulls my head back. His lips touch my neck, and I let out a bitter noise.

The moment I feel his warm tongue trail my skin I lose control.

"*Na vkus ti takzhe sladka kak na zapah*," he breathes. *You taste as sweet as you smell.*

I want to melt into his touch, which is beyond me. Chills run through my skin, and my stomach feels like it's turning. I can't tell whether this is a good feeling or not.

His fingers untie the rope that holds my robe closed. My hands quickly move to his and I hold them still.

"No. Someone will see," I whisper in his ear. His men come and go all the time on the boat—what makes him think it'll be any different here?

He wraps my hair around his hand twice and curses under his breath. "Let them watch," he whispers back with lust marring his judgment. The strings fall open and my body becomes exposed in front of the man I've come to fear.

He grabs my chin and forces my attention to him. His eyes burn with lust as he looks at my lips. I feel my cheek burn from his glare, but this time it's in a good way.

Does he want to kiss me? Should I kiss him back?

He shakes his head while looking at my naked body against his, and his tongue rolls over his bottom lip as he takes in the sight.

"You lied to me," I insist with a small, cheeky grin.

His free hand cups my breast, his finger brushing over my nipple. "*Kak?*" he asks. *How?*

"You do want me," I admit hesitantly.

"*Glaza na menya,*" he demands. *Eyes on me.*

His fingers trail up the length of my arm and down my side, taking the robe off completely, and I watch him do it. I watch every move he makes because that's what he's asking of me, and I damn well enjoy doing it.

The only words he says to me are in Russian.

He takes my nipple in his mouth and bites down gently. I suck in a sharp breath while he sucks on it. I feel like I'm about to fall over the edge already and he's hardly touched me. My legs tighten around his waist, and I pull him closer to me. I've never had anyone touch me like this before. I never thought my body was capable of feeling this way from another person's touch. It's intense. Need flutters in my stomach as if there are two butterflies fighting inside.

His fingers snake down my body and push my underwear to the side. A part of me wants him to stop while another part begs for more.

His hand wraps around my thigh, gripping it tightly, and he moves my legs over his shoulders. I know exactly what he's about to do, and I'm nervous. I've never had anyone go down on me before. I've never had anyone *this* eager to taste me.

"*Smotri shto ti delayesh so mno.*" *Look at what you're doing to me.*

"Mikhail, this is wrong," I blurt.

But the moment his wet tongue touches my clit, I forget everything bothering me altogether. My back arches, and I'm unable to control my body's reaction to the way his tongue roams freely. He swears under his breath and groans, the mere sound turning me on even more, which I didn't think was possible.

I reach my hands down and place them on his head. I want to pull him closer to me. I want his body to smother mine.

What Mikhail and I are doing is too intimate. There's no way in hell my first of anything is going to be with my captor, but I've already let it happen. His lips are on my clit, and I couldn't stop him even if I wanted to.

Bringing my hand over my mouth, I try to cover my whimpers. He grabs them and holds them down to the sides of my body so I'm unable to move them.

"Let me know how I make you feel, *Kroshka*," he grumbles with eagerness in his voice.

"Oh my God," I moan.

Mikhail shoves a finger into me, and that's when I fall over the edge. My body throbs with pleasure, a sense of euphoria given to me from a man I never expected. He pushes my legs to the side, only furthering the feeling he's giving me.

Without a chance to gather myself, Mikhail pulls me up from the countertop and wraps the robe around me. He lifts his weight from me and licks his fingers. My head falls back at the sight of him.

He likes how I taste.

He ties the strings in a bow again as if I'm a present waiting to be unwrapped. His arms trail down mine, fingertips sliding gently over my soft skin. "Run along," he says lifting me down.

I gather up all my things and do as he says.

Chapter 14

Mikhail

shouldn't have done that. I don't know what the fuck I was thinking. She doesn't know anything. She's too innocent.

And that pisses me off.

I shouldn't have allowed myself to get caught up in the moment. They don't call her a witch for nothing. I don't understand how she was able to bring down my guard like that. The way she looked at me, I couldn't fucking help myself. I wanted to know how her eyes would look up at mine with purpose, with need. It was better than I could have imagined. The twinkle in her blue eyes dimmed with passion.

Nothing like that can happen again.

I readjust my focus on the papers I laid out across the coffee table. I need Sloane to get what I want, and I don't want to complicate things. She's getting in my fucking head, and it's not making this easier. I can't even focus on what's in front of me.

The way she tastes ... so fucking sweet. I can still taste her on my tongue. The way she searches for something to grab onto because she can't contain herself ...

"Mikhail!" Max's voice blares through the room, and I look to the main door.

He stands there with a man at his feet. Max clenches his fists and gives me a look with his eyes widened.

"Who the fuck is this?" I ask.

"I was hoping you'd know. He's been pacing around the house searching for a way in. Don't you have cameras here? Christ, Mikhail, you have Sloane—people are bound to be looking for her, and you need to keep her safe."

I forget everything I was doing and step toward the man. His hands are in front of him, his head angled down.

No one knows Sloane is here besides Adrian, Lev, Dimitri, and Max.

My eyes search Max's and we both give questioning glares in return. He doesn't know who this man is or how he found us.

"Who sent you?" I finally ask.

The man doesn't look up or even mutter a single word. I step on his fingers until I hear some kind of sound to show me he's alive. He thinks he can just creep around my house and take what's mine? He should swallow a bullet for the simple attempt. It doesn't take much for me to realize he's here for Sloane.

He seethes from the pain I'm inflicting on him, but that doesn't tell me what I want to know. His head falls between his scrawny shoulders and he continues to make useless sounds.

"Great," I tell him. I reach for my phone and order Lev to bring Sloane downstairs. "Max, why don't we share a drink? You can bring him."

We walk to the formal dining room and sit next to one another while we wait for Sloane. I can hear her struggling with the hold Lev has on her. She's shouting at him. I didn't want to wake her up, but I need to know if she knows this man. Lev isn't making this any easier. I don't like how he's grabbing her.

He pushes her into the room, and she stumbles forward. Once she lays eyes on the man Max caught, her eyes widen.

She knows him.

"Sloane, kind of you to join us. Why don't you take a seat?"

Her lips pout. It's as if she knows what's about to happen and she can't do a damn thing to stop it. Hesitantly, she pulls out the chair on the opposite side of the table and takes a seat. "This is unnecessary," she says in a steady voice.

"It's unfortunate we don't share the same opinion."

"He didn't do anything wrong."

I sit back in my chair and admire her. I haven't even told her a damn thing about what's going on—she's saying it all for me. She can be sexy when she tries to take control, but I need answers.

"I'd say trespassing on private property is wrong. I would know," Max says with a laugh.

I laugh with him because I understand his meaning. He used to get caught trespassing with a girl all the time. I've only heard stories, but it happened when he was younger.

"Sloane, are you all right?" the man asks, refusing to look at anyone but her.

The look on her face is hard to decipher. I can't tell if she feels sad or worried. Hell, she should be both.

"She's fine," I tell him, answering for her.

"I wasn't asking you."

"Anything that involves her involves me. Correct me if I'm wrong, but you're here to take her from me, aren't you?"

"She's not yours to have."

"That's where you're wrong. She is mine." I reach into my waistband and pull out my gun.

"Mikhail, please!" Sloane shouts, and a worried expression takes over her confusion.

I glare at her. If she didn't want any of this to happen, she shouldn't have gone against me. I set simple rules for her to follow, and she is the one who chose to defy me.

"Please don't kill him," she asks with a sweet voice. There's something about her tone that makes me want to listen to her, but I ignore it. Nothing pisses me off more than unwanted people coming to my house.

I laugh under my breath. "Oh, I'm not killing anyone," I say, reloading the gun and sliding it across the table. "You are."

The gun lands in front of her. Tears stream down her face, and her eyes flutter. "Mikhail," she says softly.

I lift a glass of rum and bring it to my lips. "Close your eyes if you must."

"I'm not doing this," she says with a halted breath.

She's weak. She doesn't understand her actions have consequences.

"Why not?"

She shakes her head. "You're fucking insane."

I get up from my chair and walk over to her. "You want him to live?" Brushing her hair out of her face, I stand behind her and put my hands on her small shoulders. "Just be honest, Sloane."

"Yes," she says.

"Then you will serve the punishment for him."

"Okay."

The commitment she has to her family amazes me. I admire the hell out of her for it. I wish my brother would have shown his love for me the way Sloane shows her love for others. But her love isn't the kind that gets things done. It's a pond full of still water; nothing changes. Nothing happens in still waters.

I nod my head slowly and click my tongue. "Lev, dump him on the side of the road."

"Sure thing." Lev stands up from his chair and drags the man out.

I don't need to know who he is in order to figure out Sloane's father sent him. He thinks if he doesn't come get her himself it won't be seen as a threat. But here's the thing: Ludis will do what I say. It's always been like that. He works for me until he doesn't. There isn't a life for him if he doesn't stick by my side. He's raised Sloane to listen to him, but that will change.

Sloane will do as I say, not what he says.

"Max," I call. "Take her out while I deal with this shit."

Sloane doesn't push me any further, and that's a smart decision of her part. I'm trying to be kind to her, but she's giving me a run for my money.

Clubs

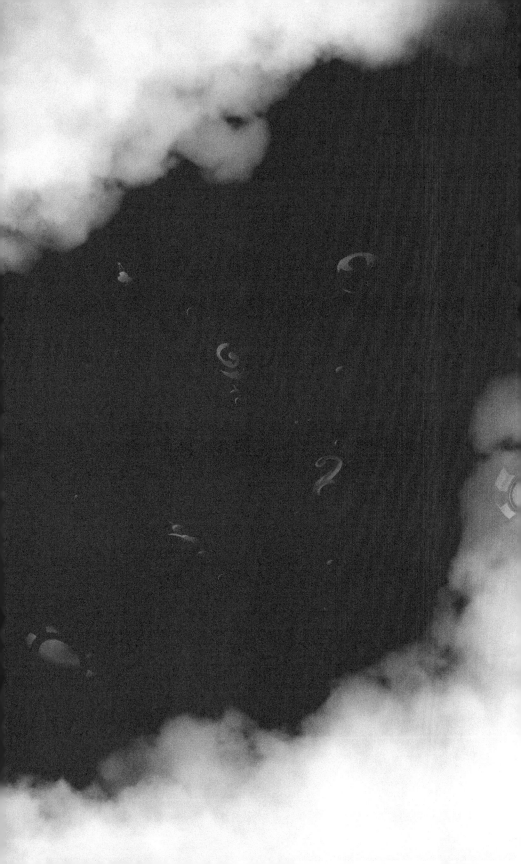

Chapter 15

Sloane

He said I would serve the consequences, but it's been two days and I'm in the clear. He avoids me like the plague, and for that I don't blame him. He lowered his guard with me, and it bit him in the ass.

I can't lie ... I'm not even upset with Mikhail for getting in the middle of my rescue. I still have a job to finish, and I know I'm getting somewhere with him because he showed mercy to the man who came here.

Being here isn't much different from the yacht. This house is fucking magical. I would expect a man like Mikhail to have a dark, gloomy mansion. Instead, he has a white brick beach house with a large pool and tennis court. Mikhail has too much money. He probably wipes his ass with hundred-dollar bills.

Still, I can't believe I let it get that far. I can't believe *he* let it get that far. *What the fuck was I thinking?*

The warm breeze spins around my body while I hold up the tennis racket and hit the ball against the stone wall.

"You've got a good arm," a voice says behind me.

Turning my head, I see Max standing beside the net in a pair of baggy blue jeans and an oversize green T-shirt. He doesn't wear what everyone else does, and he looks good this way. Max has the kind of face that makes people stop in their tracks to get a second glance. His smile could be famous. He's a handsome man.

"Thanks," I say on a worn-out breath of air.

"I'm sure you'd play better with a partner."

I laugh. "I'm sure I could."

He crosses his large arms as he steps closer to me. "Mm-hmm," he hums, grabbing onto my arm. I stumble back from his touch, ready to question him. That is until he takes my insulin pen from his pocket and holds it in front of my face. "What is this?" he asks in a deep voice.

"You went through my shit?" I ask, anger crawling over my skin.

"Bingo," he says with a snap of his fingers.

I pick at the skin that surrounds my fingernails as I grow nervous. I've never had anyone go through my things. This feels like an invasion of my privacy. Max will tell Mikhail—I don't doubt that.

He stands in front of me, becoming impatient for an answer. "Get on with it," he persists.

"It's just insulin," I mutter.

"*Just insulin*," he spits at me. "Sloane, this is dangerous. Are you even taking it correctly?" He speaks to me as if he's upset, but there's care in his words.

I shake my head. I know I'm not taking it accurately, but it's better than Mikhail knowing about it.

"Why?"

"Oh, please," I grit. "You and I both know how Mikhail is."

He's quick to shake his head and run his hands down his face in frustration. "Who gives a shit? This is your health we're talking about. Don't you dare let yourself run out. You come to me before that happens."

I stand there with my lips pressed together and the racket hanging in my hand. "Sure thing," I say, extending my hand out for my pen.

He gives me a glare before he passes it to me. "Do you think we could keep this between us?" I ask, hesitantly.

"Nah," he says, shaking his head. "Not a chance."

"Please?" I push the question.

He shakes his head and leaves me alone on the tennis court. I don't bother chasing after him because Max isn't the kind of man to change his mind, obviously.

With annoyance running in my mind on an endless track, I walk past the pool. There's a pathway that leads to the beach. The sand is a gentle hue of gold with a comforting warmth. The water that crashes onto the shore creates white noise like a lullaby. The marram grass sways with the wind, speaking to my soul. How can something sound so calming without even whispering a word?

I sit in the sand for the next hour before heading back inside. When Dimitri brought my things to the house, he also brought the books. I can tell he understands how I am because his wife has the same interests as me.

Looking at the stack of books, I feel defeated because I've already read all of them before. Sighing, I roll over on the bed. I guess there's still the notebook I could read. It feels a little personal going through someone's writing, but I can't help but feel intrigued.

The band that holds the book together is made of dark brown leather. It smells old and looks aged beyond repair. The pages are stained and wrinkled.

Expecting to see pages upon pages of someone's thoughts, I find the exact opposite. I turn the first page and find a list.

> One water bottle—one fingernail.
> Clean up living room—bruised face and a cracked rib.
> Protect Kirill—three back lashes.
> Come home late—broken finger.
> Run away—a back lashing for the number of hours I've been gone.
> Talk back—hot knife to the skin.

I shut the book and shove it away from me as if it holds dark magic. *What the fuck is this? Was this from someone else held hostage by Mikhail? Did he actually do this to people? That is fucking sick.* I knew Mikhail was messed up, but this is beyond what I thought he was capable of. I don't think his threats are empty, but if I stay here, there's a chance I could meet the same fate.

Oh my God.

I can't believe I let Mikhail touch me the way he did.

My stomach turns and I feel bile rising in my throat. Mikhail hasn't given any sign he'd do any of this to me, but I know he's capable of it. I won't endure any more time here. I need to get the fuck out of this house.

So much for enjoying my time here—how naïve I was.

I reach under my pillow and take my pen. Rushing over to the closet, I grab a jacket off the hanger and walk to the door. This isn't something I want to do, but I'd rather die trying to get out of here than suffer at the hands of Mikhail.

I take a deep breath and walk out of my room with a light foot. There isn't a single person in sight, which isn't unusual. Everyone here sneaks up on me all the time. I can only hope it doesn't happen in the next five minutes.

Food. I need to get some kind of food before I leave.

I make my way to the kitchen and grab a loaf of bread and a bunch of bananas. Grabbing a bag, I put everything I have into it. Then, looking around me to make sure no one is nearby, I step down the narrow stairs to the garage. In the corner farthest from the stairs, there's a door.

Four cars are parked in a row, and I sneak past each.

Just as I'm about to reach for the doorknob, the garage door opens, and I throw myself down by the nearest car. I crouch to the floor and hide behind the tire of a G-Class. The hair on the back of my neck rises when I hold my hands over my mouth.

My hands shake against my lips, and I slam my eyes shut as if that will help my situation.

Car doors open and slam shut. Dimitri's voice floods the room, and I hear Mikhail laugh at his words. They joke with one another before walking into the house.

The lights shut off, but I don't dare move. I can still feel the fear in my throat, leaving me incapable of walking out the door.

But I have to.

Throwing the bag of food over my shoulder, I take in a deep breath and ignore what my thoughts are telling me. This is right. This is what I need to do.

Anxiety washes over me when I open the door, but I'm yanked back by a hand on the back of my neck.

"Stop!" I screech at the top of my lungs.

I get pushed down to the ground and see Mikhail close the door and lock it. His eyes darken every second he stares at me.

One of his hands moves to my hair and the other lifts me up by my leg. His grip on my hair gives the painful sensation of needles being stabbed into my scalp. I pound on his back and kick my legs, but it's useless.

He carries me to the living room and throws me onto the ground. My bag spills open, revealing everything I took to survive on. I lift myself off the ground, but he steps on my toes, keeping me from standing up completely.

"How far did you think you'd be able to get?" He makes a *tsk* sound with his tongue and shakes his head.

I keep my mouth shut, pressing my lips together firmly.

"If the bread and bananas kept you alive long enough, the lack of water would have gotten to you soon enough."

I clench my teeth in frustration. "So what, do I get a back lashing?"

Something inside him flips. Anger washes over his face like I've never seen before. He lifts me off the ground by my shirt and continues to drag me further into the living room, where he takes a chair and pulls it into the center of the room so it's facing the kitchen.

"Mikhail," I start.

He throws me onto the chair, and I struggle to catch my breath. He walks past me with purpose and takes the rope that holds the curtains together. Standing in front of me, he stares at me as if looks could kill—and it feels like his is about to. My heart races and my lungs feel tight. I've never been so terrified in my life. Mikhail ties my arms to the chair and does the same with my legs. I try to move my hands even a little, but it's useless.

"Where'd you find it?" he demands while placing his hands on the arm of the chair.

He hovers above me with darkness clouding his judgment. I shake my head, frightened to say anything.

"Where the fuck did you find it?" he screams at me.

I shudder at his harsh voice. I wish I could hide from his anger, but I can't. I'm the one who caused it. I shake my head again.

"Okay, you can humiliate me all you want, *Koldunya*." He nods slowly. "Now it's your turn."

I can humiliate him? That doesn't make any sense. How does mentioning his torture tactics embarrass him?

My mouth drops when I realize.

That book wasn't written by someone who was held hostage here ...

It was *his* book.

I try to form the words of an apology, but they leave my mind when he takes a knife from his belt. "Mikhail, please!" I shout with tears filling my eyes. Worry snakes around my heart, tightening every second that passes.

"So she does have manners," he whispers to me.

He brings the knife to my chest. I stare at him, wondering if he'll actually hurt me. Instead, he tears through the thin shirt I'm wearing until my chest is bare in front of him. I want to slam my eyes shut, but I can't. If he wants to hurt me, I want him to watch. I want him to feel my eyes boring into his while he hurts me. If I'm going to feel nothing but pain, he will watch me struggle. Maybe then I'll see a shred of remorse.

I've never felt so exposed in my life. All Mikhail does is threaten and embarrass me.

"I have been kind to you, Sloane," he says, walking into the kitchen. "I've given you my trust. I've done a lot for you that I'd never do for anyone else." He lights the gas stove. From this distance, I can see him bringing the knife to the flame.

I crumble under the weight of my panic and try to gulp down my fear. I try to control my breathing, but it only comes out unsteady.

He's going to kill me.

"I'm not here for games, Sloane. I told you how it was going to be, and you chose to defy me. I'm not a man of useless words." He approaches me with a dark look. In a weak attempt to prepare myself for the endless pain I'm about to suffer, I clench my teeth together with a pressure so strong my teeth could shatter.

As I grip the arms of the chair, I feel the heat of the blade near my skin. "You won't do it," I mutter.

A wicked smile crosses his face. "You're making weak assumptions, little one."

"Am I though? If that was your notebook, you wouldn't hurt someone the same way you were hurt."

Something inside him flips. A look crosses his face, and I can't tell what it is. Guilt? Anger? Dread?

"Stop while you're ahead. Watch your fucking mouth."

"Or what? Hurt me. Do it!" I scream at him.

His anger wears off on me. It's toxic. I want to challenge him. I want to see if he's capable of following through on his word. I know if he were to hurt me, I'd never forgive him. It's hard enough to look at him now.

He brushes my hair out of my face with a calm look. "Yell at me again, Sloane," he says with a calm voice. My eyes search his. His anger is gone. Does yelling at him make him back off?

My face relaxes at his touch, and I fucking hate it. He's torturing me, and I'm welcoming it. *What the fuck?*

"You're sick," I tell him.

"What else am I?" His fingers trail down my thigh as he tugs at the bottom of my shorts.

"You're a psychopath."

"Hmm. That's quite the diagnosis, Sloane."

The blade is only an inch away from my skin. I feel the pain before he inflicts it on me.

"Mikhail!" A man's angry voice floods the room.

I take my eyes off him and look at the steps.

Max.

Mikhail turns to him with annoyance written all over his face. He argues something in Russian under his breath and shakes his head.

Max wears a black hoodie and a dark pair of pants. He doesn't seem to have a gun on him, or any weapon for that matter. He steps closer to me, looking me up and down, before he reaches his arms behind him and pulls the hoodie off his back. He walks up to Mikhail and takes the knife from him. His eyes fall with disappointment when he cuts me out of the ropes.

"You are being fucking ridiculous," he mutters. "You are better than this." He takes his attention off me and gives Mikhail a dirty look.

Mikhail keeps his eyes on mine. His hand brushes over his mouth, and his jaw hardens. He doesn't say a single thing to me, and I don't blame him. I don't want to say anything either.

Once I'm out of the ropes, Max lifts me up by my elbows. "Arms up, Sloane."

I do as he says, and he puts his hoodie on me. It falls to my knees.

Mikhail stands there dumbfounded, and I cross my arms.

Max leaves my side and walks over to Mikhail, grabbing him by the arm to take him away from me, but I can still hear them.

"I understand you. I do. Believe me. But if you want her to help you, this will get you nowhere."

"Max," he says with a saddened voice. A voice that sounds foreign to me.

"Don't you fucking dare 'Max' me. You disappoint me."

"I'm sorry."

I tilt my head and widen my eyes. Right in front of me is someone who's able to put him in his place. Not only did he do it, but he also did it as easily as if he just had to snap his fingers.

"Shit," I mutter.

He looks at me up and down while I stand by the couch with my arms crossed.

"Sloane," he says with a half-smile. "I'm really sorry about all this."

I look at Mikhail, and he throws his head back and runs both his hands down his face in frustration.

"Max," he starts, but he quickly shuts him up.

"No, Mikhail! God, what has gotten into you, man? He wouldn't want this. Neither of them would, and you know that. You *will* be kind to her. You *will* show her the little grace and decency you have left in your heart. You will have nothing if you don't. You'll lose yourself the same way Kirill did."

Kirill.

When Max says the name, Mikhail's eyes drill anger into his as if Max has no right to even speak about him. I watch them converse as if it's a movie playing right in front of me. Their dynamic is hard to understand, but I kind of love it.

Max saved me, and I love watching Mikhail get torn down.

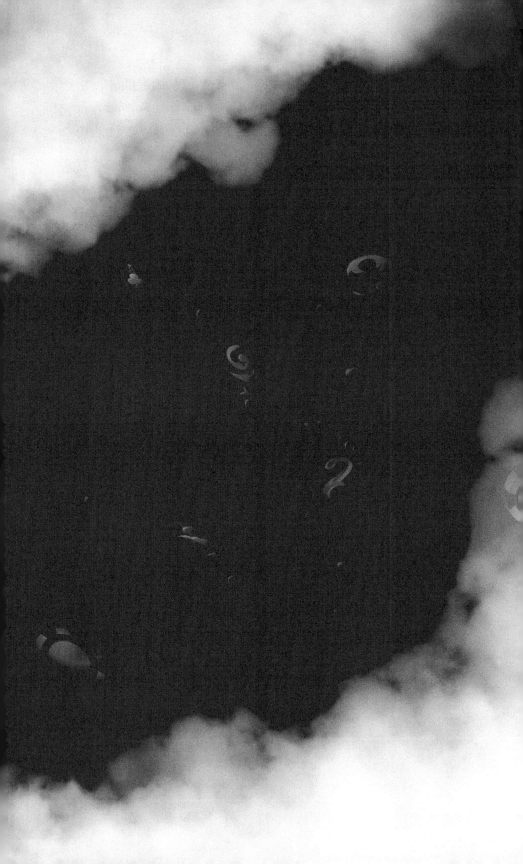

Chapter 16

Sloane

Max brought me back to my room that night, and I haven't left since. There's an awful taste in my mouth after everything that happened. Mikhail wants to show his authority, I get it. But it's gotten to the point where he needs to get on with whatever his plans are. If he wants to kill me, he needs to do it. If he wants my help, he needs to ask for it.

It's odd being here. One moment I'm enjoying my time like I never have before, and the next I'm left expecting the worst of my fate. *Is this what Stockholm syndrome is?*

Whatever it is, it doesn't excuse Mikhail's actions. He almost forced me to kill someone that night. He's threatened my life so many times I can't even count them on my fingers.

Mikhail's heart is cold. I don't understand him. I can't even stand the mere thought of him.

I didn't do anything wrong. Sure, I may have tried to escape, but what else would he expect from me when I found that notebook? Anyone with a brain would've run, just like I tried to.

He's making my life a living hell. "My worst fucking nightmare," as he once told me. He's scum. And to be honest, he terrifies me. Before, I thought I was scared of him because of his looks, but it's his actions and demands that make my skin crawl now.

So why can't I stop thinking about the way his touch feels against my skin? I shouldn't find anything about him attractive. What the hell am I doing? Leave it to me to be attracted to the psycho. I'm an idiot. I should be repulsed by him, but I'm not. I find him enticing. I want to push him to see how far he'll let this go.

While I can't see much of a human inside him, I know there must be one underneath all his hurt. No one is born a bad person. I truly believe Mikhail can be kind—he just doesn't have anything or anyone to live for. His heart is drowning in pain, and he survives through it somehow.

That notebook was his. He's suffered through everything on that list. I wish I still had it. I could read everything else he wrote in there and maybe get a better idea of what he's been through. Whoever caused him this much hurt deserves the same in return.

The bedroom door unlocks, and I turn my face away. If it's Mikhail, I don't want to see him. I need more time to get him out of my head. I need to remember how much I can't stand him.

"It's been two days, Sloane. You need to eat."

The second I hear Max's voice, I turn to look at him. He's come by six times each day, helping me with my shots and telling me to eat. But I can't. I don't have the stomach for it anymore. My body's begging for nutrition, but the mere thought of food in my mouth makes me sick. I'm just tired of fighting.

He walks to the end of the bed and places down a tray.

"I'm not hungry," I tell him for what feels like the hundredth time.

"Mikhail is getting frustrated with you."

"What's new?"

"What is your favorite food?" he asks.

"Max, I just don't want to eat right now." I take a deep breath. "I'm sorry, I don't mean to snap at you. I just can't seem to figure something out."

He smiles softly and sits on the edge of the bed. "Maybe I can help."

"I don't think you can," I tell him as I massage my neck. "I just don't understand why I'm here. I don't want to get you in trouble, but if you know anything, please tell me."

"Do you know a man named Giovanni?"

My eyes fly to his, and I hold back a smile. "I've heard the name, but I have no idea who he is."

He nods but doesn't give me an answer. "Have you heard of the Suits?"

"No."

He scratches his arm and leans in closer to me. He almost looks disappointed in me for not having a clue about his meaning. "What I can tell you is that Mikhail has been different since you arrived. He's less ... *cold*."

I laugh, unable to control myself. "Less cold? The man has it out for me."

"That's because of your smart mouth, doll. Mikhail is the most considerate man I know. You just haven't given him a chance to show that part of him." He pauses and shakes his head. "I'm not saying he's perfect. He is easily triggered due to the abuse of his blood father, I guess ... I guess you just have to warm up to him."

I watch him question his own words, but he nods once he's finished speaking. I can tell there's more he wanted to say, but he held back. Maybe he wants me to find out for myself. *But do I even want to give Mikhail a chance?*

"So you're telling me I need to be quiet around him?" I don't think I could be even if I tried. He says things that just piss me off.

He licks his lips. "Nah, I think he actually likes how you fight him. I'm not sure. You two have a strange dynamic, but maybe you could start with not trying to run away." His cheeks turn rosy and small dimples form in the centers. His deep chuckle fills the room, and I can't help but laugh with him. It's the first genuine smile I've felt in a while.

He clears his throat and says, "He asks about you every day. Lev calls him weak because of this. And don't take that lightly. It should mean a lot when his men talk about him like that and he doesn't mind."

Are we even talking about the same person? None of this sounds anything like Mikhail.

"Thank you for making me smile," I say, diverting the conversation.

"Don't mention it, sweetheart. Will you eat now? Mikhail has mentioned a feeding tube once or twice, and I'm starting to think it's not a joke anymore." He laughs faintly.

"I don't want a feeding tube, but I can't. I still don't feel great."

"I wish there was more I could do to help you, Sloane."

I shrug my shoulders before he slowly hands me a velvet box. "He wants you to wear this from now on."

Leaning my weight off the headboard, I open it to find a silver necklace that looks like the North Star. "Why?" I ask.

"Not sure, but he also wants you to join everyone for a dinner tonight. He's meeting with a couple of people—investors."

"Investors?"

"He's slowly taking over New York. His name is getting plastered all over the state."

"What does he even do?"

"Besides the obvious money laundering, he's been buying property all over the place. I think that's what his father would have wanted."

Hundreds of thoughts run though my head, and I decide to go along with his conversation. "I thought his father was crap."

He laughs and shakes his head. "I'm taking about his adoptive father. He was a great man."

My eyes wander around the room. "What happened to him?"

"Cancer took him. And his brother was taken from him as well. I played a part in that—which I regret, but I didn't have much of a choice. Everything changed after that. I'm sure there is so much more I'm not telling you, but I can only tell you so much, you know?"

"No, I understand, and you've really helped me."

"Mikhail will get you at seven. Don't piss him off tonight." He smiles as he heads toward the door.

"I'll try not to, but it's like walking in a minefield."

It feels like a weight has been lifted off my chest. I don't feel as angry.

I do believe there's another version of Mikhail I'm not as familiar with, but I'm not sure if I want to meet him.

For the first time in a while, I feel like I can lower my guard. I only hope I don't get too comfortable.

The energy in my room shifts instantly when I see Mikhail leaning against the doorframe. He makes the space look small.

I stand in front of the dresser messing with the jewelry in a weak attempt to bide my time.

He's dressed in an all-black suit with silver rings and a watch on his hand. Those sunken cheeks of his beg to stretch with a smile.

I watch him in the reflection of the mirror as I put on earrings. His eyes devour every part of me, not leaving a single inch of my body untouched by his vision. It's a shame a man as handsome as Mikhail gets rich from the suffering of others. No amount of money could be exchanged for his human decency.

"Mikhail?" I call, giving him a glare.

"Yes, ma'am?"

"You see that door?" I ask. "I want you on the other side of it."

He laughs darkly and walks inside the room, ignoring my demand. "Where do you find the strength, Sloane?"

Acting naïve, I ask, "For what?"

The room closes in on me when he places his hands on either side of the dresser, caging me in. His head lowers to mine. "Don't play coy with me."

I bite down on the inside of my cheek, ignoring him while I look down at his hands. The hands of a killer.

He lifts one arm and brushes my hair to the side, nuzzling his mouth close to my ear. "Find your words, love."

"I have nothing to say to you," I admit.

As if that was the magical phrase, he pushes off me and walks away. "Finally," he grits out.

My head turns to him and my mouth drops open slightly, ready to fight him with my words. It's like he always has to have the last word, but if I say something back then I'm no better than him.

"You know what would look great on you right now?" he asks as he crosses his arms.

My eyes flutter and my jaw stiffens. "What?" I ask hesitantly, knowing he's about to say something snide.

"That necklace you stole from me."

I shake my head. "You left it in plain sight—anyone could have taken it. Might I also mention you gave it to me?"

His eyes challenge mine. "That necklace you're wearing now? It's made from the one you stole. I made it to fit you better."

My hand lifts to the necklace around my neck. I fight the urge to process that it might have been a thoughtful gesture.

Rolling my eyes, I reach for the box of shoes Max brought over earlier. Yet another "gift" from Mikhail. My hands fall flat on the box.

"You know ... if you roll your eyes a little more, there's a chance you'll see the back of your head," he says with a smug smile.

"I have a question for you." I bite down on my lip. I want to laugh, but I don't want to give him the satisfaction of making me smile.

"By all means, Sloane, ask away. I'm sure you have many of them."

Look at that—he's right for once. What a shocker.

"Can you pick one personality and stick with it? You're giving me whiplash."

His eyes widen, but in the smallest way—shock that would go unnoticed if I didn't dissect every little thing about him. But I can't help it. I'm curious. He ignores my question, which doesn't shock me.

"I didn't ask for the attitude."

Reaching down on the bed for the shoes, I take them in my hands. "I know. It's on the house," I tell him with a bright, cheerful smile.

"Put your heels on," he says in an irritated voice.

I drop them and slowly stand back upright, folding my arms across my chest and forcing a smile. "You know ... I was going to, but now I don't want to."

"What are you doing?"

"Oh, I'm not doing anything," I say.

His tongue rolls over his cheek as he walks toward me with purpose. *"Bozhe, zhenshina. Ya hochu pocelavat tebya zamolchi." God, woman. I want to kiss you to shut you up.*

"I'm sorry, what was that?" I ask, looking up at him.

"I said put the shoes on."

"Is that what that was?" I tease.

I'm able to talk to him without being worried. His words don't scare me as much after what Max told me. He said Mikhail asks about me. I might be reading into that wrong, but I hope not.

"If you want the shoes on my feet, put them on," I say as I grab them off the floor and hold them up for him to take.

"You've got to be kidding me." His jaw clenches while I hold back a smile. He looks good when he listens.

He takes the shoes from my hands and kneels to the ground. I look down at him as he takes my foot in his hands and let out a small giggle.

"What's funny?" He slips my foot into the heel.

"I have you on your knees."

He looks up at me through his dark brows with an expression that makes my knees weak.

"You like me on my knees, *moya malenkaya koldunya?*"

It takes every atom in my body not to smile from ear to ear. I bite down on my lip and nod.

"Don't get used to it."

"Bummer." I frown.

I grab onto his shoulder as he puts the other heel on. He stands up, turns away from me, and walks toward the door.

"Let's go."

"Hmm, not just yet."

"Sloane, I don't have time for this."

"I do." I have all the time in the world right now.

"What do you need?"

I'm caught off-guard by his question. I think that's the first *kind* thing he's said to me since I've been trapped here. "I want you to apologize to me," I say.

"For what?" He looks confused.

He can't be serious.

"For the stunt you pulled in the living room."

His head falls back. "Forgive me, but which stunt are we talking about here exactly? When you came on my tongue or when you tried to leave me?"

He would bring that up, wouldn't he? "The third, actually. When you tied me to a chair and threatened me with a hot knife."

"I won't apologize for that," he says, shaking his head.

"Then I'm not going anywhere."

"Jesus Christ, woman." He walks up to me. "You madden me."

"I could say the same!"

"Well, we won't be going anywhere then. I'm not sorry for what happened. You pissed me off."

"That doesn't justify anything, Mikhail!"

He holds his finger up to me. "I never said my actions were justified."

I'm taken aback. He crosses his arms, and I cross mine. We look ridiculous bickering like children, both too stubborn to let this go.

"I—"

"Yeah? You what?" he mocks, stepping toward me and picking me up off the ground.

"Stop it!" I pound on his back.

"I need to get to the meeting, and this seems like the only way."

"Just apologize!"

"No. Unlike you ... I don't lie. I'm not going to tell you what you want to hear just to get my way."

He walks us to the door, and I hold onto the frame. But I can't hold on for too long because he overpowers me.

"You're impossible to like." My arms fall down the length of his back, where I feel his muscles tensing. I close my eyes to ignore the sensation my stomach makes when he touches me.

"That's all right," he says as he takes me to the dining room.

Three new faces stare at me. I'm already humiliated.

Mikhail pulls out a chair and sets me down. He takes a seat next to me. Many of the men surrounding me clear their throats.

"You must be Sloane Koziov," one of them says. Half his face is hidden by the bulk of his beard, but his bright green eyes pierce mine. "I'm Gabe. This is Mason and Oliver."

Oliver looks really young, maybe fifteen. His skin is light, and his face is round. His suit is too large for his body.

I smile. "It's nice to meet you all." Looking around, I find familiar faces. Adrian, Lev, and Dimitri sit across from me. Max sits on my other side.

"I went through the system and found three nearby buildings that can be taken over for the right price," Oliver says to Mikhail.

Mikhail takes the plate that was in front of me and switches it out with his own. His portions are nearly double the size of mine. He takes a container out of his pocket and puts a couple of pills on the napkin by my water. Then he pushes my hair to the side and pulls me closer to him.

"Eat," he demands.

I stare at the pills, wondering if they're drugs. Seems like something he'd give me.

Mikhail senses I'm hesitant. His fingers start to tap on the handles of his chair before he loses his patience with me. "I swear, Sloane, I will hand-feed you if I have to."

"I'm not taking those pills."

"Why?" he asks. "You need the vitamins because you decided starving yourself would be fun."

"I wasn't starving myself. I didn't have the stomach to eat. I'm sure you know why."

The arrogance of this man is sky-high. In a strange way, I can tell he's trying to take care of me, but it was his actions that made me feel the way I did.

He grabs my hand and puts the pills in my palm. "Swallow them."

I look around the table and notice everyone watching us argue. Not wanting the attention anymore, I take the pills and down them with water.

"You guys are having fun," Gabe mutters.

"Send it to me, Oliver. I'll talk to the owners about making a deal," Mikhail says, continuing the conversation and ignoring Gabe's comment.

"Sure thing. Also, Mom told me to tell you the charity event has doubled in guests who plan on attending."

Mom? Oh my God. How old is Mikhail? Is this his son?

"Tell her to double the catering then."

"Can't you tell her yourself? You never talk to her anymore."

He has a son ...

"Oliver, did Aaron ever get back that money he owes me?"

The men chuckle. "He got half. He's working on the rest."

"I told him twenty-four hours. It's long past due," Mikhail says.

I take a bite of the food. It feels good to be able to finally eat. I didn't think I'd be able to keep it down.

Gabe raises his hand. A burning cigar is placed between his fingers. "We're aware. He's caused a lot of trouble in the city to get only half. There's a reason you only give that kind of money to people you can trust to handle it."

"You don't tell me what to do with my money," Mikhail mutters.

"There are other ways to make it back. I'm sure Sloane could make you good money with her body."

The table goes silent.

"She's a pretty girl, worth fifty for a session."

"Jesus," I mutter, my jaw opening slightly. The man's trying to imply I'm a whore.

That's fantastic.

I turn to look a Mikhail. His eyes turn dark and his body tenses. If I thought he was terrifying before, that was nothing compared to how he looks right now. His head tilts back faintly and his hand brushes past his lips before he reaches behind his back.

"Don't—" Max starts, but he's interrupted.

In a flash of a moment, my body jolts with shock, my eyes slam shut, and my ears ring. I slowly open my eyes to find blood splattered across my body.

Not my blood.

"—do it ..." Max mutters, finishing his sentence.

I look back at Mikhail as he puts the gun down on the table. His hand reaches for mine and he grabs onto it firmly. My body's still shaking from the sound of the shot.

With his jaw clenched, he directs his eyes to me. "I'm sorry," he mutters before he clears his throat and pushes his chair back.

Sorry for what? Sorry for killing the man? Sorry for doing it in front of me? Sorry for Gabe's insult?

I don't watch him leave, but I can tell he's beyond pissed off.

Everyone follows him out of the room besides Max.

I finally let go of the air I've been holding onto. My breath is heavy and uneasy as I stare at the dead man. Blood falls down from the hole in the center of his forehead.

Drip, drip, drip.

I can't stop shaking. I've never seen anyone get killed before. And I never thought it would be to protect my honor.

"I told you," Max says, taking a sip of champagne, "very protective over you."

"I can see that." I reach for my glass and gulp down the entire flute. After the last sip, it feels as if my entire body is numb. It's not the alcohol; it's the dead man staring at me. Looking at me as if I can help him.

"And that's only the beginning, sweetheart," Max says proudly as he gets up out of his seat, leaving the room.

"Great," I say to myself, refusing to look away from the man's glassy eyes.

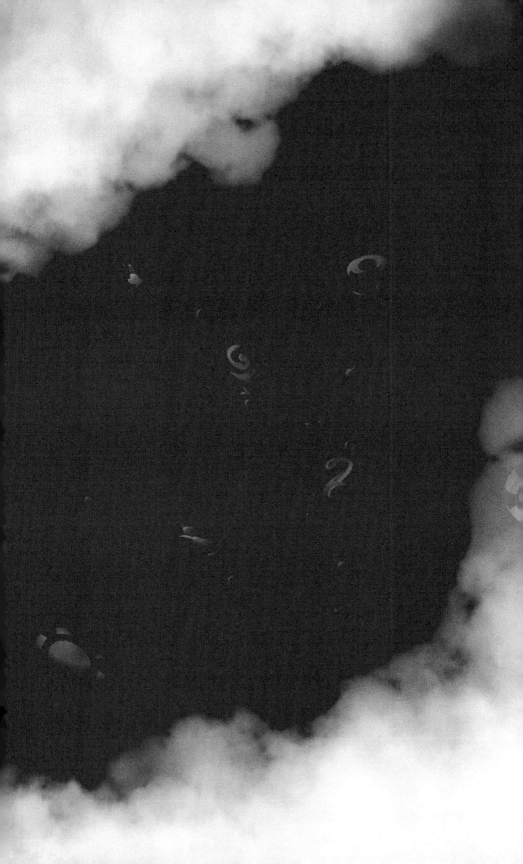

Chapter 17

Mikhail

’m fucking furious.

I never liked him, but that was the last straw. Sloane is more than just a body.

"Mikhail." Lev places his hand on my shoulder. "Take this." He hands me a glass of whiskey.

I turn toward all the men staring at me. "It would've happened eventually," I admit.

"I would've done it if you didn't," Dimitri grits. "What do you want to do with the body?" Dimitri never cares about the reason someone is killed; he just handles everything. Which is exactly what I need right now. I haven't been this pissed off in a while. I welcome the feeling. It reminds me of who I am. Sloane has been getting in my head way too much.

Fuck, I'm killing for her? What the hell is going on?

"Tie his feet to a cement block and drop him in the ocean. Nature will take care of him for me," I say as I sip the whiskey.

"Done deal," he answers proudly.

"I told you she'd be a problem," Lev mutters.

My grip around the glass tightens at Lev's comment. "I just got done killing a man for insulting her—do you not recognize the pattern here?" I say on a worn-out breath. "She's not the problem."

"She is. You feel the need to defend her honor."

I click my tongue. "Yeah, I fucking do. She doesn't deserve that disrespect."

"You disrespect her."

I clench my jaw in frustration and glare at him. I've never known Lev to have a mouth on him. The worst part is that he thinks he's accomplishing something. As if I'd listen to what he has to say. His smug fucking smile lifts more as the seconds pass.

It takes an immeasurable amount of control to keep myself from reminding Lev of his place beneath me. I'd gladly take a chair and bash his face in, but I'm feeling forgiving today.

Max shuffles his feet in the silence, breaking it by saying, "You made him mad ... That's not a good place to be." He laughs.

"Whipped," Oliver blurts, creating the sound effect of a whip. If he weren't so young, I'd teach him a lesson.

"What the fuck do you know? You're sixteen."

"Dad acts like that with Mom."

"Because your dad is smitten with your mom. They're in love. That's not what this is. This ... this is ... this is frustration," I say, stuttering over every word.

"Can I say something?" Max asks.

"What?"

"This could actually work out to your benefit. Investors might view you better if you have a lady by your side."

"Holy shit, that's a good point!" Dimitri says as he falls on the couch laughing. He's drunk off his ass. I can feel the heat of my anger boiling inside me like a kettle on a flame.

"I'll cross that bridge when I get to it," I tell him.

"We're kind of at the bridge—it's only a few days away," Adrian says with a dry, amused look.

"I'm going to bed," I tell them.

"Think about it!" Dimitri shouts.

At least someone's enjoying tonight. Leave it to Dimitri to make light of the situation.

All this started because I wanted to do something for my father. He wanted New York, and I want to give him New York, but it feels like the entire plan I've come up with over the past two fucking years is fading away from me. That's what Sloane is doing to me. She gets in my head and makes me forget my anger.

I wave him off and leave.

Stepping out of the room, I pass the dining room and see Sloane staring at the man I killed. His body is slowly falling out of the chair. I feel no pity for him. He should have known better than to say something like that.

Walking up to her, I crouch to the ground. Her chest is covered with specks of blood. I take my thumb and wipe the red spots off her face. Her lips move as if she wants to say something, but she isn't capable of forming words.

"Sloane," I say, trying to break her stare.

Her body doesn't react to the touch of my skin on hers. I didn't think she'd be left in a state of shock like this. Has she never seen a dead body before? She's the daughter of Ludis. There's no way he raised her for twenty years and she's never seen a dead body. And on the off chance she hasn't, I'll give him credit for keeping her so sheltered.

"Moya lubimaya." My love.

I force my mouth shut after the words suddenly slip through my lips. Her head turns slowly toward me, rocking as if she understands what I'm saying.

"You didn't have to do that," she says in a calm tone, the total opposite of her mouthy sass. Her words contradict the look on her face.

"But I did," I say in a soft voice I haven't used in ages. "Men don't get to talk to you like that, at least not when I'm around."

"I'm sorry you felt the need."

"Pokoinik. He was dead the moment he looked at you."

I've never seen her so ... composed. I prefer the sass she always shows me over this. I don't even know how to talk to her.

Her eyes slam shut for a moment before she reaches across the table and brings the bottle of champagne to her lips. She takes big gulps of it as if this is how she's choosing to cope. I'm glad I didn't find the same outlet after I took my first life. Sure, I drink every now and then, but I know I can handle my wrongdoings with a conscious brain. I had everything I needed after I placed that bullet in his skull. I knew I was capable of it.

I grab the bottle from Sloane's lips and put it back on the table. If she continues to drink the rest, I have no doubt she'll get alcohol poisoning.

"What can I do, Sloane?" I ask her.

She shakes her head back and forth.

"Kak ya mogu ubrat tvoyu bol?" *How can I take away your pain?*

We sit together for a while in silence as she processes everything. Then she lets out a sigh and stands up.

"I think I'm ... I think I'm going to take a shower."

I grab onto her hand to help her walk, but her skinny fingers slowly intertwine with mine, and I instantly want to back away. I don't do this shit. I don't hold hands with women. I never kiss them either. It carries too much emotion, and then they expect things from me. Things I'll never be able to give.

I don't commit to anything but my family and my job.

As much as I want to take my hand away from hers, I hold onto it. My stomach turns because I'm going against everything I believe in, but this is what she needs right now. She needs me to hold her steady and comfort her.

She's delicate. She's a wilting flower.

Her feet stumble onto mine. She lets out a laugh and leans her weight into my arm until I'm practically carrying her. "Why didn't you tell me you had a son?" she asks.

That's a first. My brow furrows. "Because I don't."

"Oliver. He was talking about his mom."

"How old do you think I am?"

"I—I don't know ..."

"I'm twenty-eight, Sloane. He's sixteen. There's no way he could be my son," I explain. "Oliver is my cousin."

"Oh, I'm sorry. It was wrong of me to assume ..." All of a sudden, she acts shy.

We make it to her room, and I open the door. "You should go clean up. I'm sorry you had to see that."

"You're right. I should shower."

I glare at her. She's acting different, like she's helpless. The witch I know doesn't ask for help. She figures out everything on her own because that's just who she is. A mouthy little brat who has to have everything go her way.

"Can you help me with the zipper?" she asks, turning her back toward me.

Hesitantly, I gather her hair and push it to the side. I unzip her dress down to the curve of her hips.

"Thank you," she says, turning to face me. She pulls her arms out of the dress, but she's slow to cover her chest with her hands.

My eyes stay on her body even though my brain tells me look away. Her breasts are small but perfectly round. She *wants* me to see her. She wants me to think about her body. The way her nipple fit perfectly in my mouth ...

It takes everything in me to turn and walk toward the door. Staring at her will only make my situation worse.

"I'll see you tomorrow," I say, closing the door behind me.

Getting involved with her will make me no better than Giovanni. I don't need a wrench in my plans. Everything is working out. Feelings don't need to be involved.

Chapter 18

Sloane

This is the second time I've walked into his room. Only, this time it's not because I'm looking for something of his. It's because I don't want to be alone.

There's a lot on my mind right now, and it's honestly terrifying to be left alone with my thoughts. Every time I close my eyes, I see the dead man staring at me. He could still be downstairs for all I know. His eyes could still be wide-open, staring at where I sat. Blood could be drying on his face slowly as the minutes pass. I was the last thing he saw before his soul left his body.

He'll never stop seeing me, and I'll never stop seeing him.

Opening the door softly, I look into the dark room. "Mikhail," I whisper, but I get nothing in return. I slowly inch toward the large bed he's resting on. What will he think if he wakes up and I'm in his bed? I tug on his arm. "Mikhail," I say in my regular voice, hoping he'll wake up, but he doesn't.

Taking a moment to look at him, I notice how handsome he is. His arms—the size of my head—should terrify me, but I almost welcome the fear. The man is fucking frightening. The tattoos covering his body don't help either. They trail all the way up to his hairline, covering his neck. Even his hands have ink on them.

Come to think of it, I've never met a man in the Bratva who doesn't have a tattoo, but I've never seen one have this many.

I step away from Mikhail and walk to the other side of the bed. My feet sink into the soft carpet as I stand there, hesitant to sleep in the same bed as him. Across the room are two black sofas. I couldn't sleep on them, but at least I wouldn't be alone.

Just get in the bed, Sloane.

I slowly slip under the covers and move to the edge of the mattress. The bed is huge, so this shouldn't be a problem.

That is until his arm snakes around my waist and pulls me closer.

"Does the night scare you more than I do, *Koldunya?*" he asks in a dark voice that makes me regret my decision to come here.

I choose not to answer him because I'm sure he doesn't want to hear the truth.

His face nuzzles into my neck, making my skin shiver and burn at the same time. Did I come in here because I was scared of being alone, or because I want more of him?

No, I can't want him.

But, *fuck*, I do. I don't even care what that says about me anymore.

"I asked you a question. Answer it."

It's hard to think about anything when his hand pulls on my waist, and he presses himself closer to me so I feel how hard he is. His fingers run up and down my body, tugging at the clothes that cling to my skin.

"Yes," I cry.

"Do I need to fix that?"

Oh Jesus, what am I doing right now? "Yes," I manage again.

He reaches his arm to the other side of my body and lifts me on top of him. Seeing him underneath me brings a feeling of power. Then he grabs my neck and pulls my face toward him, his lips only inches away from mine.

He hesitates.

I feel his warm, minty breath.

Mikhail's fingers dig into my hips, forcing me to ride on his. I feel every inch of him against me, and I've never been so turned on in my life. I'm welcoming a toxic lust into my life, and I don't see a problem with it right now.

I move away from him only slightly, and he takes the opportunity to grab onto my shirt and tug it off me. His lips land on my neck, then on my nipples. I want to collapse at the feeling of his lips wrapping around the center of my breast.

His hand cups the other aggressively as I lean into his body. Everything around me becomes nonexistent the moment he throws me off him. He pulls me toward him by my legs, then he pushes them aside and climbs between them. His fingers reach for my face, brushing my messy hair out of my eyes.

"*Ya lublu tvoyi volosi,*" he murmurs. "*Tvoyu kozhu, tvoi glaza, tvoi gubi, tvoi vesnushki.*" *I love your hair. Your skin, your eyes, your lips, your freckles.*

Mikhail lowers himself onto me and leaves a trail of kisses all over my body. He kisses every inch of my skin, but not my lips.

I can hardly see anything besides the shadow of him. I focus on where his hands touch my body instead.

He pulls on the waistband of my shorts, tugging them off my hips slowly. His arms land either side of my head while he hovers his lips over mine. I brush my fingers through his hair, tugging on the strands as an outlet. It feels as if my heart is racing to finish a marathon when he rubs my clit in gentle circular motions. I try to shove the sounds he's forcing out of me back down, but it's impossible. I want to scream with pleasure.

"You only get to make those sounds for me. Do you understand?" he asks firmly.

"Yes," I say.

"*Ti bistro uchishsa, Koldunya.*" *You learn fast, witch.*

My eyes roll when he pushes a finger inside me. It hasn't even been a day since the last time he touched me, but this all still feels brand-new, as if his hands were made for my body. He lowers himself down onto me and parts my legs.

Chills take over my skin when he licks me. He never demands anything of me when we share a moment like this. He never makes me do anything to him or even gives me the opportunity. He gets off by touching *me*.

His tongue moves over every sensitive part of my body, and when I grab onto the sheets beside my hips his fingers intertwine with mine.

"Oh, Mikhail," I moan.

He groans with the taste of me on his lips.

I never thought I'd be so easy to please. He's either done this far too many times to count or he knows how to work my body perfectly.

"*Ya hochu,*" he growls. *I want it all.* "*Kazhduyu posledniyu kaplu.*" *Every last drop.*

My breaths come out unsteady as I reach my climax. My stomach falls the moment I come on his tongue. He licks, sucks, and bites my skin. It's aggressive, and I love every second. I don't even know my own body as well as he knows it.

Mikhail stands up from the bed and opens his dresser drawer. He puts a shirt over me and tugs on the bottom. I already know it'll fit me like a dress. Then, walking over to my side of the bed, he fluffs a pillow for me. As if I'm incapable of moving myself, Mikhail lifts me up and places me in the center of his mattress, pulling the covers up over my body.

His shirt is baggy, beyond comfortable. I could melt in the scent of his cologne. It's a spice, but I can't put my finger on it.

"You should be able to sleep now," he says, walking out and closing the door.

I don't have the energy to run after him and apologize for taking over his room. Instead, my eyelids fall while I try to process what the hell just happened.

I'm woken up by the sound of Mikhail yelling at someone. The voices echo through the entire house.

I throw off the sheets and walk down the stairs to his office, cracking the door open just enough that I can see them. His voice is loud, so harsh I feel his anger within myself.

Why is he so pissed off?

My fingers curl around the fabric of Mikhail's shirt. Peering my head around the corner, I see him yelling at Lev, his fists slamming down on the table. Lev looks unfazed by his words, but he doesn't say anything back, which only fuels Mikhail's fire.

"You fucking did this," he says with his hands flat on the table, head falling between his shoulders.

"How the fuck was I supposed to know they'd follow me?"

Mikhail shakes his head slowly. "Two years. I spent two fucking years finding her, and now they know where she is."

My head feels heavy at this. *He spent two years looking for me?* What the fuck makes me so special?

"They're not here though. They don't have the balls to attack. They don't even have the men to attack," Lev bites back.

Attack? I don't want my family to attack. I don't want them to get hurt.

"They're trying to find the right angle."

"*Ona von tam*," Lev mutters under his breath. *She's right there.*

Mikhail turns his head toward me, and I throw myself against the wall, out of sight. Lev called me out for eavesdropping. It's what he'd do. He's never shared any ounce of pity for me. Not that I want his pity, but a little help in my position would go a long way.

"*Koldunya*," Mikhail says. "I thought you'd know better than that."

His cold voice sends chills down my skin. It's like frostbite all over my body.

"You woke me up. I just wanted to see if everything was all right," I say, trying to calm him down.

His gaze runs up and down my body as a soft smile tries to overtake his lips, but he bites it back.

A warm body presses into my back and pushes me into the room. "Wow, you really did have a rough night, didn't you? Mikhail finally break you in? Lev and I had a bet to see how long it'd take for him to crack."

Dimitri.

He pulls down on my curls, forcing my attention on him.

I shake my head quickly. I don't want them thinking *I'm* the one who cracked. I'm stronger than that. It was a moment of weakness. I didn't want to be alone, and it seemed Mikhail didn't either. It was as if he enjoyed my company.

"You can admit it, sunshine."

Dimitri is the last person I expected to irritate me. "I find it hard to believe Lev would stoop to your level of arrogance," I tell him. Dimitri is funny, sure, but he always makes things about himself. How is this any of his business?

He laughs. "Yeah, I thought the same thing. But he did."

"At least you admit you're arrogant."

"Arrogant, not ignorant." He glances at Mikhail suggestively, but Mikhail shakes his head.

"Take a seat," Lev tells us.

Dimitri throws himself on the couch facing the table Lev's sitting at. "If you're sleeping with him now—"

I stand frozen. "I'm not sleeping with him," I say.

"That's not what your neck is telling me. You've got a little bit of a red mark right there." He brings his fingers to his neck to show me where the mark is.

Mikhail lets out a huff of a laugh as he brings his hand up to his mouth.

The energy in the room shifts when Lev stands up and makes his way toward me. His fingers reach for my face, brushing my hair away so he can look at the mark on my neck. "I told you she'd be the one to ruin your plans," he tells Mikhail.

I try to pull away from his touch, but his other hand grabs onto my waist, dragging me into him.

"I am curious though ... Did he taste you?"

"Enough," Mikhail demands.

"It's enough when I get my answer." His eyes fall to my chest.

"My eyes are north, not south," I tell him, but I don't push him away. I can't help but think that if I were to push him away, his grip on me would only tighten.

"Oh, I'm aware. How does she taste, Mikhail?"

I look over at Mikhail. His knuckles turn white as he grips the edge of the table.

"I said that's enough."

Lev's mouth hovers over the mark on my neck. His warm touch makes my stomach twist.

Why isn't Mikhail telling Lev to stop? I stare at him the entire time. He doesn't want to watch this, but I can tell he's waiting to see how far Lev will go.

Lev's fingers lift the shirt to brush my inner thigh. My lips part, shocked by what he's doing. I grab onto his back to keep my balance. It's as if I can't move. I'm not allowed to. Lev isn't a kind person; pushing him off would only worsen my position.

"*Derzhi ruki proch ot neyo,*" Mikhail says huskily. *Keep your hands off of her.*

"If you don't tell me, I can find out for myself."

Dimitri walks up to us and pulls me away from him. Mikhail grabs Lev by the neck, shoving him up against the wall. He lets out a defeated sigh and smiles. Lev enjoys pissing Mikhail off.

Within a second, both men are yelling in Russian as Lev challenges Mikhail.

"Just let them fight it out," Dimitri tells me. "Lev won't stop until he admits it to him."

My entire body tenses. *What the fuck is happening?* "Admits what?" I ask.

"How you taste," Dimitri says.

"Why the fuck does that matter?"

"Because he's never been down on a woman before." Dimitri pours himself a drink. "We got drunk one night and Mikhail said it's too intimate for him. This is Lev's way of seeing how he feels about you."

The room goes silent as Mikhail grabs my hand and tugs me away from Dimitri. I stumble over my feet as I try to keep up with him. Looking back, I see Lev looks content, like he finally got his answer.

I don't know how to feel about anything right now. My thoughts are jumbled like they just went through a clothes dryer. Mikhail's hands venture to my waist and he walks me all the way to the north side of the house—a part I've never explored before. His hands still on my hips, he guides me up the stairs into a bedroom. His head drops as he walks to the bathroom.

The room is gorgeous. The rug on the dark oak floors is embroidered with a floral design. The bed is padded, and the paneled walls are cream. A crystal chandelier hangs from the ceiling. Mikhail flips the light on, and I follow the sound of water. The room has a feminine touch.

"What are you doing?" I ask.

"*Ti pozvolila yemu prikosnutsa k tebe.*" *You let him touch you.*

"I don't know what you just said, but I don't appreciate your tone," I muse.

"Get in the water, Sloane."

"Why? I took a shower last night."

"You allowed him to put his hands on you. Get in the water."

"I allowed him to put his hands on me? Are you fucking kidding me, Mikhail?"

He steps up to me and takes the shirt off my back, leaving me naked. I don't fight him because I want his hands on my skin.

"You hurt my feelings," he tells me, placing his hand on the small of my back with a gentle touch.

"Oh, really? How exactly did I do that?"

He doesn't have feelings. Mikhail has a difficult time letting out any sliver of emotion that isn't frustration or anger.

"Someone as beautiful as you shouldn't be touched by a man like Lev."

I look at the water pouring into the freestanding tub. He's not mad at me; he's mad another man touched me. "You make it sound as if I wanted him to touch me."

He brings his thumb to my cheek. "If you need anything, *Kroshka*, all you have to do is ask."

I shake my head and dip my toes in the water. He wants me to clean off Lev's touch. He thinks I'm dirty now. His mind works in such a strange way—a way I don't think I'll ever be able to understand.

"Let me," Mikhail says in a deep voice. There's something different about his eyes. They don't appear as dark as I once saw them. He's showing kindness in a way I've never known. It's different—a good different—and that's what's scary about it. I don't know how long it'll last. If I say one wrong thing, he'll go back to being heartless.

I allow him to wash my body. His fingers run through the ends of my hair, and I want to lean into his touch.

"I could sit here all day," I tell him.

He chuckles, the sound of chimes again. The most incredible sound I've ever heard. I turn to look at him and see his smile. The kind of smile that force his dimples to show.

"The water would go cold," he says.

"That's why you add new water."

He shakes his head and stands up, reaching his hand out for me to grab. I sigh and take it. Water falls off my body like raindrops.

"Mikhail."

"Yes, *Kroshka?*"

"This was kind of you," I tell him.

He ignores my compliment as if it's painful for him to hear. "Breakfast tomorrow—do you want to try again, or would you like to stay in your room?"

I take the towel to my face and pat away the drops of water. "I can join you guys."

He nods. "Good." After waiting a few seconds until my body is dry, he takes the shirt off his back and puts it over me. "A new one," he says in my ear.

I try to hide my smile, but it only widens when he pulls me in close. His arms wrap around my waist and his lips find the top of my head. He doesn't kiss me; he just immerses himself in the moment he created for us.

"Wear this in the morning," he whispers. "Run along now."

He lets me go, and I walk to the bathroom door, turning back to look at him before I leave. Dressing me in his clothes is his way of claiming me as his. I know it is. Mikhail wants me to show up at breakfast wearing his shirt for Lev to see.

What am I getting myself into?

When I get out of bed, the only thing I do is throw my hair in a bun and put on some ChapStick since my lips are beginning to crack. I walk downstairs to the sound of laughter in the breakfast room.

The second I walk in, everyone stops talking. Max looks at me and then directly at Mikhail.

"Anyway, you'll be leaving in a couple of days?" he asks.

Mikhail clears his throat, probably telling him stop talking, so I don't have a clue what they're talking about. It doesn't surprise me. Mikhail has shown me some kindness, but I can't forget I'm collateral damage. I have no idea what he wants from me or if I'll even make it out of this alive.

"Morning," Lev says, bright and cheery.

"Good morning." I shoot him a glare.

With a glance around the table, I see the only free seat is next to Mikhail. Moving one foot in front of the other to get there seems like a chore. My mind-splitting headache isn't helping matters either. Just as I'm walking over to the table, my vision begins to fade. I grab onto the chair for support.

"Sloane, what's wrong?" Mikhail asks with a concern that sounds foreign to me.

My ears ring and the world around me fades. I bring my free hand to my eyes and rub, trying to clear my vision. "I'm just dehydrated, that's all."

"Dimitri, call Knox," Mikhail says under his breath.

When I hear Max swear under his breath, I frown with guilt and shame. He told me to go to him for help, but I didn't.

When the black leaves my vision, I notice Mikhail standing right in front of me, holding me steady. My head is incredibly heavy. I feel myself falling into Mikhail's arms before everything in my mind drifts away.

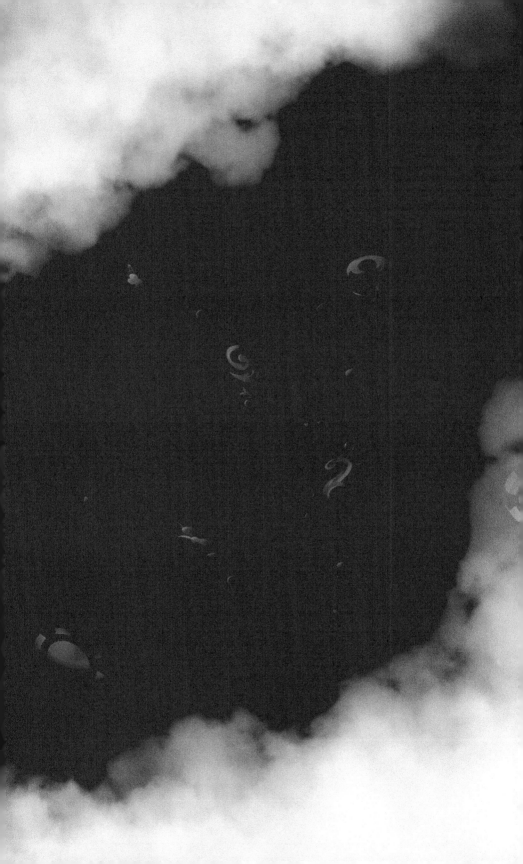

Chapter 19

Sloane

Loud, obnoxious beeps sound through one ear and out the other as my eyes flutter open. Tubes are taped to my arms, and I feel weak. I don't remember what happened. I was going to breakfast—that's all I can recall.

Mikhail sits in a chair pulled up to the edge of the bed. *His* bed. I'm in his room for some reason.

"Sloane," he whispers. It's not sweet. It's not angry. It's a dreadful sound.

I follow the cords attaching my body to an IV bag. I don't want to look at Mikhail.

"Why the fuck didn't you tell me?"

There it is. There's the anger. I take in a deep breath, trying to calm myself down.

"Tell you what?" I ask as if I'm clueless.

"Don't fucking do that. Why didn't you tell me you're diabetic?"

"You would have found some way to use it against me."

He clenches his jaw and stands up from his chair. His arms hold the back of his head while he paces the room. "Why the fuck would I do that?

You could have died," he says with fire in his lungs.

"Do you have any other swear words in your vocabulary?" I ask, genuinely curious. He says "fuck" in every sentence. "I'm a dead woman anyway—it doesn't matter."

He turns away from me and slams the door shut.

"Good talk," I mutter. I look down and notice my index finger has a plastic bit on it, weighing it down.

Moving my body up, I notice the blanket is warm. There's a cord at the bottom of it. *Did he get me a heated blanket?*

"Good. You're awake," a man says, entering the room. He looks older. My best bet would be that he's in his sixties. His mustache is gray, and his black hair has silver streaks in it.

"What is all this?" I ask, pulling on the tubes.

"Ah, yes. You're type one diabetic, Sloane. Why wouldn't you give yourself insulin?"

"I ran out," I admit.

"I can see that. The fluid in the bag is to rehydrate you, give your body some electrolytes. I'm also monitoring your heart. It's weak. You'll need supplements as well. You've starved your body of many things and it has no fat to break down."

I slouch back under the warm covers. "I see."

"I'll keep an eye on you and make sure you're getting everything you need. You also have this." He brings his hands to my stomach and lifts up my shirt, showing me a patch stuck to my skin. "It'll track your glucose levels day and night. It can last up to ten days. I've shown Mikhail how to change it. He will take care of you."

A part of me wants to laugh at the last bit of his sentence. *Mikhail will take care of me?*

I've never had anything this high tech on me before. My father always said it's good to use the pen so I remember my doses. He never wanted me to get too comfortable.

"This is great. Thank you."

"My name is Knox, by the way."

"Sloane, but you know that already," I say with a pitiful laugh.

"I do." He smiles. "You need to be careful with this—you can't just skip insulin. Your body literally cannot produce it."

"I know."

"Okay, I'll give you some time to rest."

I watch him turn to leave and spend the rest of my day in bed resting and flipping through channels on the flat-screen. Knox comes back in after a couple of hours to check in on me. He takes the cords off my skin and tells me to keep up my water intake.

Sitting here all day is great, but I slowly start to get bored.

I get out of bed and walk down the stairs. I don't mean to end up in front of Mikhail's office door, but here I am. I knock and walk in without waiting for a response.

He's sitting in his chair looking down at his phone. He doesn't acknowledge me. His thumbs scroll through the glass screen while he ignores me.

"I wanted to thank you for getting me help," I tell him as I walk closer.

His jaw hardens, his attention still fixed on his phone. "I'm standing right here, aren't I?"

It's as if he's using every atom in his body to ignore me. *What the hell is his problem?*

"Did I do something to you? Because unless you plan on texting your response, you're being incredibly rude to me right now."

He stands up from his chair and walks toward me, his eyes still glued to his phone. I watch him stop right in front of me and take his eyes off the screen. "If you think for a goddamn second I don't listen to every last syllable that falls from your lips, you're mistaken."

"Then why did—?" I start to complain, but I'm quickly interrupted.

"Could you just be quiet?" He slides his phone into his pocket. "You will not keep things from me anymore. You will tell me if anything is wrong, and I will listen."

Stunned, I can't do anything but look at him. He looks hurt, but I can't figure out why.

His fingers brush my arm then down the side of my torso. "Tell me what you need," he says in a deep voice.

Normally, I could think of a million things I need, but his touch is the only thing going through my mind right now. The way his calloused fingers threaten to tear through my skin, his eyes filled with purpose and his lips begging to be touched by mine. I shake my head. I don't want to admit that what I need is him.

"I need to go home."

"Tough."

I roll my eyes. I knew this would happen. Around Mikhail, no one is able to make decisions for themselves. His temper is as sensitive as a grenade.

"Don't ask me questions you don't want the answer to," I tell him.

"Are you finished?"

"Finished with what?" I ask.

"Bothering me."

My mouth drops slightly as I stumble away from him. "That was rude."

"Sorry, I forgot your heart was fragile."

Stepping back up to him, I can't help but shove him, pushing on his muscular chest. "I'm not fragile!" I shout louder than I thought I could.

Mikhail's thumb brushes over his lips, which lift with amusement. "You are. You just tried to hit me, and I went nowhere. Extra credit for the effort though."

I roll my eyes and turn to walk out the room, but the sound of him clearing his throat stops me.

"You need to toughen up."

"You're right. How did it take me so long to realize that? I am *so* sorry I'm not checking all the boxes on your 'good little hostage' checklist."

"I bet you're a joy in bed," he says arrogantly.

I scoff. "Probably, 'cause you get off on violence."

This gets his attention. "I don't, but there are many other women you can ask if you'd like some reassurance."

I cross my arms. "Charming. Was this one of your many quick fucks?"

"They're not quick, but if you're willing to find out ..." he says glibly.

"God, you are insufferable!" I scream.

"And yet here you stand, talking to me."

My arms fall down to my sides and I let out a wearied breath, curling my fingers into a fist. "Ego is one hell of a drug, Mikhail."

"I'm sure it is. That's how I got so far in life. What do you have to show? Nothing."

He uses my lifestyle against me as if I could do anything to help it. "And what do you have to show, Mikhail? Dead bodies? Fake cash because you can't get the real stuff?"

"Stop," he demands. *Looks like I've hit an open wound.*

I don't stop. "You know, you fear success, but you really have nothing to worry about."

"Stop before I say something I can't take back."

"Aw, what? You want to wound me with your words?"

He grabs me by the shoulders and grips me tightly, but not in a way that could hurt me. "I have things to show for my success. I do it for my family. But you couldn't relate to that, could you? No, because you were adopted." He speaks the word "adopted" as if it carried darkness. He might have gotten too caught up in the argument and skipped the part where he was taken in as well. Does he think I don't know I was adopted?

I lift my chin up and say, "At least I was wanted, you dumb fuck."

His head tilts in disappointment. "See, now that's the issue with open-minded people like you. They just don't know when to keep their mouths shut."

Before I can stop myself, my hand lands across his face with a loud crack.

Mikhail bites down on his lip and nods slowly. Stunned by my own actions, I back away from him.

"You have five fucking seconds." He stares me down while my back finds the wall. "One."

My breathing quickens, and I bolt out of the room. Running down the hallway, I pass by the living room and take the stairs two at a time. I question if I should run to my room, but he knows that's the room I'd go for.

Instead, I go to his.

All my things are still in here. The sheets are bundled together, exactly how I left them only a half hour ago. My heart is pounding so fast I can hear it in my head. I turn to look at the door and then rush to lock it shut.

"Oh God," I mutter to myself. "What the fuck is wrong with me?"

I turn quickly, making myself lightheaded. *Where the hell am I supposed to hide?* Moving quickly to the bathroom, I search the drawers for something to protect myself with. Luckily enough, there's a knife. Leave it to Mikhail to have a weapon hidden in every square foot of the house.

When I hear the bedroom door unlock, I throw myself against the wall, forcing my hand over my mouth the keep my noise to a minimum. I can hear his footsteps getting closer.

"You should learn to hide better."

The bathroom lights are off, but I can see him in the reflection of the mirror. Right as he's about to walk away, he turns slowly in my direction.

"Stars can't hide in the dark."

I take the knife and hold it steady in my hand. He walks away, and I hear the door close shut.

Tearing my hand from my mouth, I let out the breaths of air I needed. *I thought he knew I was in here.* Or maybe he's all talk.

I allow myself to relax and step out of the bathroom, but I slam right into him. Clenching my teeth together, I hold out my knife.

"Do you honestly think that will save you?" he asks darkly.

My eyes widen as he walks right into the knife, drawing blood. I gasp, throwing it to the ground. "You're so—"

"Fucked-up?" His blood slowly begins to seep through his shirt.

"More than that."

"You push every ounce of fucking control that I have." He steps toward me until I feel the edge of the bed on the backs of my legs.

I lift my head to look him in the eyes. "You have no control."

"You only have your words."

"And you only have threats that don't surprise me."

Gritting his teeth, he grabs onto my elbow and pulls me close. "If you want to argue with me, take it to the bed."

My chest rises and falls quickly as I stand on my toes and try to level myself with his height. I don't know if it's his words or if I'm just as fucked-up as him, but this is becoming a turn-on.

My eyes fall to his lips.

"What are you doing, Sloane?" he asks, shocked I might be about to take him up on his offer.

Bringing my fingers to his mouth, I trail his bottom lip with the tip of my thumb. Then I lean into him and press my lips down on his. I kiss him a couple of times before he opens his mouth and allows his tongue to find mine.

Mikhail grabs the back of my head and whimpers into my mouth. He kisses me with anger. It's like he doesn't want to be kissing me at all.

I reach my hand to his waist and pull on his belt. He buries his head in my neck before throwing me onto the bed, where his hands move onto my thighs, inching up toward my waist. He grabs onto me and lifts me on top of him.

With my legs straddling him, I can't believe I'm about to do this. My arms rest on his shoulders as he moves his face to my neck. Shivers run through my body when his lips touch me there. I'm overwhelmed, but in a good way. My breathing shallows as his hands drag my body down to his, closing the distance, creating pressure that demands release.

He pulls at the bottom of my hair.

"Mikhail—"

"Mercy."

I swallow. "What?"

"You say 'mercy' if you want me to stop."

This very well may be the sexiest thing I've ever heard in my life.

He pulls away from me, holding my stare. "You understand?" he rasps.

I nod, wanting him to continue. My body aches for him. I can no longer deny what I've felt since that night. I knew I felt something toward him at the time. It was hard to decipher what it was because we were so full of hatred for one another, but it was physical and all-consuming.

Something inside me tightens as he throws me off him so I'm lying on my back. Goose bumps cover my skin as he moves his body between my thighs. His large hands cover my stomach, and he places wet kisses all over my skin.

My eyes shut as every nerve sets on fire at his touch. He lifts up my shirt slightly, and it crumples right underneath my breasts. He doesn't take off my thong—he rips it off. The sound of the lace ripping excites me, much as I don't want it to.

Pushing my shirt up, he brings his mouth over my nipple and bites down on it gently. I suck in a sharp breath as he brushes his thumb over the other. Mikhail sucks the skin underneath my breast, claiming what's his. A soft moan falls effortlessly from my mouth.

"You can't make those fucking sounds, Sloane," he demands.

His mouth turns me on even more. I'm eager to hear more of it. My body reacts to his dark, demanding commands in ways I've never known. His calloused grasp travels down to my thighs. I need to be closer to him. I need him inside me. He's teasing me, and I can't keep up.

He lowers his body down mine, nudging his face between my thighs. As his tongue slides over my clit, the feeling makes me throw my head back. My fingers run through his dark hair strands, tugging on them tightly as his tongue moves from side to side, then in circular motions, licking every drop.

I bite down on my lips, trying not to moan because he said not to, but, *fuck*, I can't. A shaky sigh falls from my chest, making Mikhail tighten his grip on my thighs, forcing them open wider for him.

Just when I thought he couldn't give me more satisfaction than he already is, he glides a finger inside me.

It's overwhelming. It hurts, but it feels too good for him to stop. My back arches off the bed, and he pushes another finger deep into me.

This is too much. My face burns as his tongue laps around my clit, licking and sucking on me. My body feels as if it's being dipped in a pool of molten lava as my legs begin to shake. He holds them steady, and my hips move as I reach close to the edge. "Mikhail ..." I shudder his name as my legs lock and an orgasm overcomes me.

A deep groan grumbles in his throat. He lets go of my legs and nips his way up my stomach till his mouth is hovering near my ear. I try to regain control of my breathing. "I love the way you taste," he breathes. "I love the way you feel coming on my tongue."

This is so wrong, but it feels so right. I want him to demand everything my body has to offer.

"I want more of you," I admit, wrapping my legs around his torso.

"You're maddening. Addicting, *Koldunya*."

I cringe at the name. I don't want to be called that while he holds me like this. "Call me something else," I tell him.

"I'm sorry." He pauses for a second to muse on an alternative. And then he says, "*Moya Koldunya*."

Chapter 20

Mikhail

I will have this moment. But once this moment passes, that's it.

I told myself I wouldn't get to this point with her, but I've denied the feeling for too long. Lust. Longing. She is the sexiest woman I've ever laid eyes upon, and now I've had a taste, I don't think I'll ever get enough.

She tastes so fucking good. Like strawberries and coconut.

I move my legs out from between hers and lift her body up so she's on her knees.

"No, Mikhail, not like that," she begs.

I halt. "How?" There's something strange about the way she's speaking to me.

"I want to see you."

Missionary. I don't care how I fuck her—I just need my dick inside her right now. This is the only time I plan on being with her, so it doesn't matter to me.

But it will to her. She's the first woman who's ever demanded to look at me while I fuck her.

She sits up from the bed and tugs on my belt like she did a moment ago. I take everything off and pull her close. Her eyes widen slightly as my dick springs out. She lowers herself down my body and her hands trail my chest. She wants to take me in her mouth, but she's hesitant.

"Take it," I demand, gathering her hair and wrapping it around my hand.

She looks up at me with bright doe eyes. "I've never—"

She's never gone down on a man before?

"Just start slow," I tell her.

Her full lips part as she licks the tip, slowly allowing more of me to enter her mouth. It takes every ounce of self-control not to fuck her right now. But she wants to do this her way, and I'll let her.

Her lips tighten around me, and I almost come. She has no idea what she does to me. If she did, she would have done this a while ago just to get under my skin.

"Fuck ..." I gape as my head falls slowly between my shoulders.

Her eyes start to water as she takes every inch of me in her throat. She's already got me close, and that's fucking embarrassing.

I pull her head back by her hair and push her back down on the bed. If she kept looking at me the way she was I wouldn't last.

I push her legs open and align my dick with her entrance.

"Condom," she blurts.

"I'm not using a fucking condom with you," I grit. "I want to feel every inch of you on me."

This is the most idiotic thing I've ever done. I always use a condom. But it's different with her. I don't want anything separating her body from mine.

She pulls me down onto her. Her small body could be crushed by my frame, but she's just as eager as me. Her pale skin feels softer than silk. Her fingers dig into my back as she pulls my lips down onto hers. I bite down on her bottom lip, drawing blood. Her tongue finds mine as our lips work one another's.

I push myself inside her, and her body tenses. I should have given her a warning.

"So fucking wet," I tell her, breaking the kiss.

Then I thrust my dick deep, but something isn't right. She's too tense. I pause and pull out.

Blood.

Sloane is a virgin.

"Shto eto?" What is this? "Why the fuck didn't you tell me, Sloane?"

Her eyes wander everywhere, refusing to look at me.

"Look at me," I demand, taking my hand to her jaw and forcing her to meet my eye.

"You wouldn't have done it if I told you," she stammers.

"Yeah, I wouldn't have." My brow furrows. "Not like this. I would have taken my time with you."

It makes sense and it doesn't. The way she spoke to me—she sounded experienced.

She rolls her eyes at me and grabs her shirt, getting off the bed.

"Where are you going?" I ask.

"To get water or something, I don't know."

"You walk out of that door and you'll be dealing with a different version of me."

She walks back over to the bed, and I pull her in by her arm.

"Arms up." I grab the bottom of her shirt and lift it off. "Lie down," I tell her. Then I climb on top of her, kissing her neck. "Just relax. You're too tense." I rub her clit gently, teasing her entrance. She's turned on—I can tell by how my fingers glide into her pussy without effort.

Her response to my touch is undeniable. Her soft whimpers make me eager. Once we're back to where we left off, I slowly watch my length disappear inside her. Her pussy grabs onto my dick with each small motion. It's as if she were made for me.

"Go faster," she pleads.

"You'll only hurt yourself."

"Please," she pleads.

My chest begins to pound as I dive into her faster. I bring my lips down to hers, and she crashes onto me. Her kisses are full of angst, need. She whimpers in my mouth and digs her nails into my back from my shoulders all the way down. She's inflicting pain on me now. "If you leave scratches on my back, I'll leave marks on your neck."

"Is that a threat or a challenge?" she asks as her nails dig in deeper, and I move to her neck, biting and sucking on her skin.

I've been waiting for her to feel something for me, and now she does, I can't hold back. I want my body scarred with marks from her nails. Her smell is fucking intoxicating. I'll never be able to forget it.

"Oh God." She brings her hand over her mouth to muffle her moans.

I can hardly control my breathing as I pound into her. I watch her breasts move with every thrust I take.

I tear her hand away from her lips and hold her hands above her head. "Let me fucking hear how I make you feel," I demand.

She cries out in pleasure, and that alone makes it hard to hold back.

I never look at women when I fuck them, but I look her right in the eyes and feel the need to never look away. This isn't the same girl who spent her days sulking in the room; this is a girl I can see by my side. She's finally matching my energy, and it's the sexiest thing I've ever known.

She tries to turn her face away from me, but I pull her back. She's fucking beautiful. Her cheeks are rosy, and her dark lashes reach up to her brows. I thrust in and out of her, trying to pace myself to make sure she isn't in pain. I slow down when I feel her pussy clenching around my dick.

Her hands find my back again, and I throw her legs to the side and push on her pelvis so she comes harder. She rolls her hips in reaction.

I hold onto her body, noticing we're in sync.

I've always been able to last, but she pushes me to the edge quickly. I dive deep and tighten my grip on her thighs as I spill inside of her.

Sloane moves her legs so they're wrapped around my body. I bring my lips to her neck and bite down gently.

This woman is mine, and only mine.

I pull out of her. My cum drips out of her pussy, and I use my fingers to shove it back inside.

She tries to get up, but I force her to lie back down. "I need to clean up," she says, trying to move.

"Not while my cum is inside you." I pull her closer to me so her head is laying on my chest.

In a matter of minutes, her breathing slows as she falls asleep. The tip of my fingers brush in small circles on her back, and I stop when I notice exactly what I'm doing.

I'm fucked.

I'm woken up by a gentle slap on my face, and my eyes widen when I see Max hovering above my body like he belongs in my fucking bedroom.

I don't bother looking back at Sloane. I know she's fast asleep by the quiet snore that falls from her lips. A sleeping beauty.

Instead, I throw off the covers and grab Max by the neck, pushing him out of the bedroom. There's a heavy stomp in my walk, and he has a smile the entire time my hands are on him. "The fuck is your issue?" I ask as I close the door behind me. "The woman lying in my bed is *mine*. Do you want to take one last good look before I pluck your eyes from their sockets?" I gesture to the doorknob.

"I think you could benefit from therapy," he mutters before handing me a box. "There might be two parts in your brain that just aren't connecting."

I watch him get lost his thoughts and make a face at him. "What is wrong with you?"

He pushes me in the shoulder. "Why do you have to be so hateful?" he asks, but he decides putting a smile on his face will soften his words.

"You're not her—the fuck do I need to be nice for?"

"Oh, I don't know, Mikhail. Maybe because I'm the best friend you'll ever have? Anyway, open the box. You'll love the surprise, you sick fuck."

I'd roll my eyes if I hadn't given Sloane a lecture about the action.

Lifting off the top, I'm hit with an overwhelming smell. Picking up the hand that rests on top of some tissue paper by the finger, I notice it belongs to one of my men. I know it's from one of my men because of the tattoo on the finger.

"Christ," I mutter, putting it back down.

"There's a note," Max says as if this is an easy conversation to have. He calls me the sick fuck, but I think that title belongs to him.

Written on the notepaper is an address. If I remember correctly, it's the address of a church. Very fitting.

This is all Lev's fault. He decided to handle shit in the open, and now we're left defenseless against Giovanni. He knows where I am now. Staying hidden was the only upper hand I had against the fucker.

I make an annoyed sound. Before I can speak up, Max does first. "I take it you want me to watch the woman lying in *your* bed?"

"If you try anything," I threaten him even though I know it's useless. He hasn't been able to look at another woman in years because he only wants one.

He rubs the top of my head, and I swat his arm away. "I'm going to get *so* cozy in your fancy Egyptian cotton sheets." He laughs. "Remember you can only win something if there are risks."

Leave it to Max to say some inspirational bullshit right after saying something dumb. "Good thinking," I say sarcastically and glare at him.

I open the door and head to the closet, ready to change into proper attire. Max follows me inside with his arms crossed. He flashes me a wicked smile as he stands at the end of the bed. He has a death wish.

"You're behaving like a fucking child," I whisper.

His brows rise and he glances at Sloane. "You keep doing her and you'll have one."

"Enough," I mutter.

I tuck my gun in the waistband of my pants and leave the room. Making my way down the halls, I bang on Lev and Dimitri's doors and yell for them to meet me downstairs. I decide not to bring Adrian because he's already had a bad experience with Giovanni. I don't need him and his grudge to ruin my plans.

Starting the car, I wait impatiently for them to get themselves together. My fingers tap on the steering wheel when Lev and Dimitri open the car doors.

"Why are we meeting at the butt crack of dawn?" Dimitri asks while he rubs sleep from his eyes.

"Look in the box," I say, shifting the car into drive.

I hear the box rustle, and they both make a gagging noise. "Yeah, Giovanni says 'hello.'"

"That's one hell of a greeting," Lev murmurs.

We drive for a while until we finally make it to the address on the card. At first I thought it was an odd place to meet up, but now I understand. The church is the one place men like us don't bring our guns.

It could be a trap, so I'll keep Dimitri outside just in case.

On top of the church, gold crosses are placed on marble pillars. Intricate details are engraved in the stone, leaving the landscape looking dull. Dead trees and shriveled bushes line the walls. Iron gates cage the church, making it difficult to escape.

I look at my men. "No guns inside the building. Lev stays with me."

They nod in agreement.

I walk past the gate and enter the church. Colors flood the walls, and large chandeliers hang from the ceiling. Giovanni's right there, sitting with his head bowed as if he's praying.

"Interesting," I say.

He stands from the seat, making his way over to me. "Where is she?"

I stand in the middle of the aisle and hold my hands in front of me. "Where is who?"

His men, Enzo and Carlo, walk a couple of steps behind him. "My sister. Where is she?" he asks in a rough tone.

Does he not know she's in the house? No. He assumed I'd move Sloane after I became aware he knew where I was residing. But really, all he had to do was have his men enter the house. Why the fuck is he in charge of his people? He can't even think his plans through correctly.

"What makes you think I have her?"

"Damn it, Mikhail. If you fucking hurt her—"

"If I hurt her, what?" I interrupt. "You don't even know her. Shit, Giovanni, you had all the resources to find her, but you didn't. You took your sweet time looking for her. If she's so important to you, how did I get her first?" A smug smile crosses my face, only frustrating him even more. Anger is getting the better of him—I can see it in his eyes.

"What do you want? You want money?"

I want my land.

"Money?" I laugh. "What makes you think I want your money?" I step toward him. "No, I don't want a goddamn thing from you."

His hand reaches behind him slowly.

"I wouldn't do that."

I can tell Giovanni is used to how Kirill handled things, but my brother and I are very different. Kirill would have taken the money and got on with his day, but I won't make a deal until I've made Giovanni sweat. I want to show up in his nightmares. I don't want him to feel a moment of peace. While he's lying awake at night wondering how he's going to get his sister, I'll be taking back what's mine. I will have my section of the city by the end of this.

"If you deliver another body part, expect one of your sister's in return."

He straightens his back. He's growing nervous. "You wouldn't hurt her. You need her as leverage."

"It's almost as if ... that's the whole point," I say with a smile. "That's why it's called leverage. As long as I have her, you can't really do anything, can you?"

My feelings for Sloane don't make any sense to me, but that doesn't mean my threats can't be empty. He needs to get the hell out of here and run back home to his precious wife. He came all the way here for nothing. There's no way in hell I'm giving him his sister.

"If Sloane is leverage, it means you want something. Just tell me what you want," he says, sounding annoyed.

"Jesus fucking Christ, do I really have to hear this shit again?" I ask as a cruel laugh slips past my lips. "Do you honestly think I came here to hear you out? See what it was that you had to offer me?"

He begins to talk, but I shut him up.

"You sorry shits have no idea how good this feels for my ego," I mutter to him and his men as I place my hand on his shoulder. "Get some sleep. You look like you need it."

I turn around on my heel. Just as I'm about to leave the building, I turn around slowly. "Oh, Giovanni," I mutter.

He stands with his hands by his sides. His jaw ticks as he challenges me with his eyes.

"Give Nina my best."

The second I set foot in the house, I see Sloane standing in all her glory, crazy hair bundled on top of her head. She's holding a bag in her hands, and she walks up to me and shoves everything into my arms.

"When you leave, you take me with you," she demands. "It's six in the morning and I woke up next to Max! Why?"

The bag is heavy, full of her things. I never expected Sloane to have a getaway bag ... I can't help but feel intrigued.

I look down at her and smile. The little devil is becoming more and more like me each day that passes. "I had a meeting," I tell her.

"And you couldn't tell me that?"

"Yes, I could've—" I start, but I'm quickly shut up by her argumentative voice. She starts to ramble on about how I can't just leave her alone because I'm the only connection she has to her family. I feel bad, but then I remember all the cruel things she's said to me. While some of them may have been deserved, I do feel she can take it too far at times.

I want to talk back to her and tell her I can do whatever I want, but then I remember what Max just told me. I have to listen while I still can.

Standing in front of her with my arms filled with her things, I listen to her completely shit on my existence and find it incredibly sexy of her. As she starts to run out of breath, I laugh loudly, the sound shocking both of us.

"You think this is funny?" she challenges.

"I never said it was funny." I lick my lips, trying to wipe the smile from my face.

"My family needs to know where I am, Mikhail. This has gone on for too long."

"All right," I tell her.

She crosses her arms and gives me a questioning glare. "All right then."

I step close to her and pull her bottom lip with my thumb. "And here I was thinking it's because you wanted to be by my side."

"It's embarrassing how much you care, truly," she says with an attitude.

"Did I say I care?" I question.

"You care enough to answer."

The corner of my lip rises more, becoming a wicked smirk. "You're right," I admit.

"Maybe sleeping with you wasn't the worst thing ever."

I stare up at the ceiling and swear under my breath.

"If you expect to be heard, you shouldn't mumble," she mocks.

"You should watch your tone with me, *Koldunya*, or your punishment will change, and I promise you won't be able to endure it."

"I'll be the judge of that." She straightens her posture and holds out her hand. "Phone," she says.

My tongue rolls over my teeth and I reach into my pocket for my phone. "You know his number? If not, it should be saved under 'the help.'"

Her eyes lift with anger as she snatches the phone from my hands. I don't blame her for wanting to keep her family updated.

I don't mind her talking to them, but she will stay with me for as long as I want.

She turns away from me as if that'll give her some privacy. "Hi!" she practically screeches, making my eardrums pound. "Well, actually."

I watch her lips lift with a gentle smile. I want to make her smile like that, but it'll never happen. Whatever she and I are will only last for a little while longer. We were doomed from the start, and I need to start pulling myself away. If I keep allowing her to dig past my walls, it'll be fucking difficult to build them back up.

Sighing, I walk over to the couch and take a seat.

"Yeah. He had someone named Knox come help," she explains to her father. She looks at me and back to the floor, then right back at me. "He wants to talk to you," she whispers, covering the phone.

I lean back in my chair and hold out my hand. "Give it."

Sloane does as she's told.

Lifting the phone to my ear, I hear Ludis arguing with one of Sloane's brothers in the background. "Ludis, how's life treating you?"

"What are you doing with my daughter? If you put a fucking hand on her, I swear to—"

I cut him off. "You'll see her again, don't worry. She's safe with me."

His voice is coated with anger and regret. He's angry with himself for letting Sloane out of his sight. He's treated her like a princess locked in a tower her entire life, and that's not the life she deserves. She needs to see the world. I can tell she craves experience.

"She is kind, Mikhail. She doesn't deserve to be under your cloud of fucking gloom."

"*Ouch,* my feelings," I say, standing up from the chair to walk away from Sloane so she won't hear our conversation. "She deserves many things, including knowing the truth about her family."

Quickly, the phone goes silent on his end.

"You know, Giovanni, Mirabella ... the whole reason the three families don't get along anymore ..."

"What did Pavel tell you before he passed?" he asks.

This time I go silent. He has no fucking right to talk about my father. "You will not speak of him."

"For how calculated you make yourself out to be, you really aren't, are you?"

Jesus, this man is shooting me through the phone. "You'll be seeing me soon. And it won't be to give your daughter back."

"What the fuck does that mean?" he asks warily.

"I fucked your daughter, Koziov. She's mine now."

He grunts through the phone. I can tell by the static sound he's trying to crush it in his hands.

"Oh, I'm sorry. We *made love.*"

"You touched my daughter?" he sneers.

"Maybe I didn't, but even if I did, it's not like you could do anything about it." I hang up and put the phone in my pocket. Turning back to the seating area, I find Sloane standing right by my side.

"Did you just end the call? I hardly got to talk to him."

"He misses you dearly."

Her feet grow roots, blocking my way. "I want to say some really not-nice things to you right now." Her lips press together, creating a fine line.

I knew the sass was coming soon enough. "Say them," I muse.

"I fucking hate you."

Stepping closer to her, I say, "That's not what you were saying when you came on my tongue." Grabbing onto her waist, I pull her into the bathroom and lock the door behind me. I'd be damned if one of my men walked in on us. Her back falls into the marbled wall and her hands grab my chest, pulling me closer. This whole "I hate you" thing is just one of her acts. I know she wants me; she just doesn't want to admit it. She'll press her lips to mine, dig her nails into my back, and come on my dick, but she will never bring those words into existence.

"I think I'm a bad influence on you," I mutter in her ear.

"I don't fucking care," she says strongly.

My lips drop but lift quickly when I smile. "You're even swearing like me now."

"You're my only social interaction. You're like my shadow, constantly following me."

"And you're my North Star, always pointing me in the right direction."

Her brow furrows. "Sappy isn't a cute look on you," she says, pulling on the necklace I made for her.

"Eager isn't a cute look on you," I bite back.

She leans off the wall and pushes me against the sink. "I can walk out that door easily."

"Do it then."

Her head falls to the side as if I insulted her. She walks to the door, and I pull her back, crashing my lips onto hers.

"Fuck you," I murmur.

My hands snake to the small of her back and I pull her onto the counter. Her tongue fights mine aggressively. She kisses me as if she's had all the practice in the world. She's a quick learner. Her lips find my neck, and she sucks on it.

"*Kroshka*, what are you doing?"

She bites down, gently nibbling my skin. Her small hands venture to my back, untucking my shirt and pulling it up. "Take it off," she says.

"You're demanding things of me that I can't resist."

"Take it off," she demands again.

Quickly taking off my shirt, I let it fall to the ground while I pull her sweatpants down from her waist. Before I can help her with her shirt, she pulls it off in one swift motion. I lift her off the ground and set her down on the counter. Wrapping her hair around my wrist, I pull her head back and trail my tongue down her chest.

"One question," I say roughly. "You want it?"

Her eyes widen, dark lashes fluttering, and her cheeks quickly turn pink. She nods, pressing her lips together.

Good.

Grabbing onto her, I turn her waist so she's facing the sink and kneel to the floor. Her pussy is dripping for me. I love that I hardly have to touch her and she's already craving me just as much as I crave her. My hands hold onto her hips, and I pull her down onto my face. She's hesitant, but she allows me to guide her body.

The moment my tongue touches her clit I feel her legs threatening to give out on her. I could lick her for hours on end and never tire of her taste. It's addicting.

She is addicting.

She struggles to keep herself up, but I kind of want her arms to give out. "I can't," she moans.

"You can."

She knows she can. Her body wants to crumble, and it's the sexiest thing I know.

A groan escapes my throat when I feel her pussy throbbing on my tongue.

"*Fuck*," she whimpers.

Standing up slowly, I lick her off my lips and unzip my pants. "Grab onto the counter," I demand.

She does as I say and pushes her ass closer to me impatiently.

"Are you still sore?" I ask.

She nods. "My body will work it out."

I line myself against her and push in slowly. It takes all of me to control my pace with her. I want to fuck her as if I'll never see her again. The way her pussy clings to me makes me want to come instantly.

"Look at yourself," I mumble while I push in and out of her.

Lifting her head up, she looks at herself in the mirror.

"You're everything," I say. I wrap my hand around her neck and bring her lips to mine.

"Harder, Mikhail."

"So fucking demanding."

Doing what she wants, I slam into her quickly. I bring my lips to her back, holding in the urge to kiss every part of her body. I want to claim her as mine in every possible way. I've never felt so infatuated with a person before—it takes over every thought I have. I don't even remember why the fuck I'm always mad at her.

A loud pounding on the door startles her, and her mouth drops open.

"I need to pee, Mikhail!" Dimitri's voice floods the room. There are ten other bathrooms in this fucking house—why does he need this one?

"Focus," I say, turning Sloane's face back to the mirror. "You're in here with me."

When she pushes her ass out further, I bite down on my bottom lip to keep myself from coming, but the moment I feel her pulsating on my dick, I pull out and let everything drip onto her ass.

"You feel so good," she says, turning to me and pulling my lips to hers. She kisses me eagerly, like she can't get enough.

I lift her chin and place a kiss on her forehead, but I don't bother to tell her how good she feels too.

Before I dress myself, I take a washcloth and wipe her down. I almost came inside of her again. I need to gain a bit of fucking control.

She glares at me, and I open the door for her. Dimitri's leaning against the wall with his arms crossed. Sloane slips past us, probably embarrassed.

"Are you kidding?" he asks.

"I plan to fuck her on every surface I can find."

"That'll take you a while," he laughs.

"I have all the time in the world."

"Move and let me fucking pee," he says, pushing me out of the doorway. "And look at your computer. I pulled up some documents for you to review."

"The documents never end."

Stepping out of the hallway, I find Sloane sitting in my seat with a romance book in her hands. She looks up at me and flips me the bird.

She's cute when she's mad—even if she has nothing to be mad about.

I step toward her and place a kiss on the tip of her middle finger. "That's cute," I say, turning to look at the things Dimitri was nagging me about.

I'm doing more than my father wanted. He'd be proud of me. Kirill is probably rolling in his grave, pissed at me for taking what was supposed to be his.

Then again, he's probably proud too.

I'm taking what Giovanni wants.

The day flew past me while I sorted through everything Dimitri gave to me. I stared at the screen for hours before everything started to look like it was copied and pasted. While I tried to focus, I could only think about what Ludis said to me. It almost sounded like a threat ... like I don't know what I'm doing. But I do, and I'll be damned if he's the one to make me question myself.

I asked Sloane if she wanted to share dinner with me, but she denied me. She's getting too comfortable in this house and with everyone in it. That pisses me off in a strange way. She found a way to weasel her way into my life without me even noticing.

Max loves her, and they've hardly fucking talked. Dimitri does too. The only person I can rely on is Lev. His head is so far up his ass he doesn't even care about what's going on around him. At times, I think he cares about my plan more than I do.

I've never had someone irritate me more than Sloane does. But I can't seem to get enough of the mouth she has. I want to hear more from her.

I stare at the ceiling trying to figure her out, but that's an impossible task. Leaning on my elbows, I look at the clock on the nightstand. Three in the morning and she hasn't left my thoughts.

I throw the sheets off my body and make my way to the kitchen for a glass of water and a sleeping pill. I don't normally need pills to put my mind and body to sleep, but I do tonight because of her. When I close my eyes, I can see her vividly. It pisses me off.

I step off the bottom of the stairs and I'm stopped by the sight of Sloane in the kitchen. She's wearing a large knit sweater and shorts that show every curve of her ass. Her head shakes as she looks back and forth in the fridge.

Fuck me, she's gorgeous.

What she's cooking smells good—I don't know how I didn't smell it before I got down here. I had no idea she knew how to cook like Mia does.

I take a couple of quiet steps into the kitchen until the island is the only thing separating us. Her body lifts up and down as she hums to a song that sounds familiar, but I can't remember the lyrics. It's a song my sister sings all the time.

A lover of music.

"You are all I long for," she sings so gently I almost can't hear her, but she sounds angelic. "No, she wouldn't add this," she says in her normal tone.

Is she talking to me, or is she slowly losing her mind?

"Yes, she would. She always uses garlic."

Why the hell is this woman cooking so early in the morning? Is eating a meal with me really that insufferable?

She turns her body in a small twirl, her eyes closed.

Seeing her in this moment is like a breath of fresh air. With everyone else, it's always business, but she is true to who she is. Sure, she's a lot to put up with, but there's something about this moment that makes me forget all her snide remarks. The way she moves her body—it's as if she doesn't care who's watching.

Koldunya.

I want my hands on her every hour of every day, and that's the most terrifying thought I've ever had. It's like I'm trying to justify my thoughts about her. I'm interested in her, but I can't stand her—as if that makes my thoughts any clearer.

I move closer to her, unable to stand the distance between us anymore, until her back is only a few inches from me. My hands find her waist and I dig my thumbs into her sides gently. My touch startles her, but she welcomes it.

"What are you doing, *Koldunya?*"

Her head falls to the side when my mouth comes near her neck. I can feel how warm her skin is even though my lips aren't even touching her.

"We're going to talk about what *I'm* doing?"

"I could get used to this," I admit.

Her left hand wraps around mine as I tighten my hold on her. She stirs the sauce with her free arm and ignores my comment—which doesn't shock me. She doesn't want to let go of her stubbornness as much as I don't want to let go of mine, but I will for tonight. For her. Tomorrow, things can go back to normal.

Talking to Sloane reminds me of gambling. You throw in cash and say, "I'm done after this one," but that's a lie. You can't help but want to see if *one* more try will increase your chances, but it never does. That's why it's an addiction.

If I try once more with Sloane, I'll stop. Things can go back to the way they were meant to be. But for tonight I just want to let go. I want to be in this moment with her.

I close my eyes when I smell the shampoo on her damp hair. "Who taught you how to cook this?"

"Ingret did. She's the closest thing I have to a mother."

Does she know my brother is the one who took her mother from her? A wave of unease battles in my stomach. Why am I suddenly feeling accountable for my brother's actions? "She raised you?" I ask.

Sloane doesn't answer right away, but she nods a moment later. I can tell it brings her pain to be away from her family, but I can't think about that.

Her hand leaves mine and reaches for a small spoon by the side of the stove. She dips the metal into the sauce and tastes it. "It's missing something, but I can't put my finger on what."

"Salt?" I ask even though I haven't tasted it. "Pepper? Onion powder?"

"No," she mumbles. She leaves my arms and opens the spice cabinet. "Can you try it? Maybe you'll figure it out if you taste it." She nods to herself as if she's answering for me.

Sloane brings the spoon to my lips, but I don't open my mouth. The memory of her throwing the soup I made all over my face washes over me. Her eyes search mine, probably coming up with a bunch of rude comments.

"Try it again," I tell her. "I want to taste it from your lips."

She looks at me as if I've committed the darkest crime imaginable. As she brings the spoon to her lips her eyes fall to mine. I grab the silverware from her hands and place it on the counter behind her. Then I bring my hand to her face, pushing down on her bottom lip.

"Mikhail," she says softly ... as if she's asking me if I'm sure.

I trail my fingers up her arm then down the side of her body so gently I see her skin creating goose bumps. "Don't talk," I say before I pull her face toward mine.

She opens her mouth for me, her tongue finding mine. Her kisses start off as gentle and cautious, but they begin to ask for more. My hands grab onto her waist, pulling her close, but not close enough. I want to bury myself in her warmth. I want to forget about all the ways I've wronged her. I want *her* to forget them. But only in this moment, and this moment alone.

Just one last taste.

"Let go," I tell her. "Let your guard down for me, just for tonight."

Her fingers thread through my hair, pulling on the strands gently. Is this her way of letting go? I want to know everything she has to give. All the best parts as much as the worst.

She moans into my mouth, and I nearly lose it. I hold onto her tighter even though that should be impossible. I can feel how hard she's breathing from the way her breasts press against my chest. Her sweater is the only thing parting her skin from mine.

Sloane lifts to her toes to reach me better. She deepens the kiss, her tongue fighting with mine. I never thought a kiss could say things words never could.

But then she pulls back from me and looks away. That look tells me too much.

It's a look of regret.

"I can't," she says.

I nod even though she can't see me. Without a second glance or thought, I turn away from her and make my way back to the stairs.

"Thyme," I tell her before I walk up the steps. "You're missing thyme."

Chapter 21

Sloane

Why did I tell him I can't?

I *can*.

God, I am so fucking stupid. He finally showed me kindness and I shot him down. In the moment it seemed far too good to be true. How can a man like him all of a sudden want to show me he cares?

How could he ask me to let go if he hadn't truly let go himself?

I eat dinner by myself, and the entire time I want to walk upstairs to get him. I think maybe we could watch a movie or even just have a civilized conversation without wanting to tear out each other's throats. But I ruined it.

Shocker.

I think about the moment where I'm standing in front of the bedroom door—what I'll do, what I'll say. But there's no time to think too hard because before I can second-guess myself that's exactly where I'm at.

My hand rests on the knob while I try to figure out whether this is a stupid idea or not. There's no chance in hell he'll welcome me with open arms. Knowing Mikhail, he'll hold this against me.

I force myself to open the door anyway and step inside the bedroom. I smile when I notice the small light shining from the corner of the room. He turned on a salt lamp. The warm orange light welcomes me as I lift up the sheets and climb into his bed.

Sharing a bed with Mikhail has proven to be far too comfortable. I hate to admit it, but I love being by his side the entire night.

Once under the covers, I turn on my side so I'm facing Mikhail. He doesn't look peaceful like he did before. The darkness he carries with him during the day catches up with him at night, not giving him a break. I lift my hand to his forehead and feel droplets of sweat.

"Let him go ..." he mumbles.

I sit up and crawl closer to him. I've never seen anyone have this bad of a dream. I don't know if I should wake him. Bad dreams are kind of similar to sleepwalking ... I think.

"Please," he pleads.

I can't stay here watching him and not do anything. It hurts to see him like this.

"Mikhail ..." I shake him.

He lets out heavy pants. "Mikhail, wake up. You're having a nightmare." I shake him harder this time.

His eyes fly open, seeing me but not seeing me. He reaches under his pillow, taking out a pistol, and his hand grabs my neck, slamming me down on the bed.

"Mikhail!" I gag. I can't fucking breathe. I claw at his wrists. "I can't ... brea—"

The gun is pointed at the center of my head. I squirm my legs trying to get out from under him, but his weight is crushing me down.

"Look at me," I stutter, wrapping my hands around his. My life is quite literally in his hands right now, and I don't fear him. "It's me," I say, trying to force the words out of my crushed windpipe.

My vision starts to blacken and my ears ring. Pressure builds in my head before his hold on me loosens.

"Sloane." He swallows, letting go of my neck and taking the gun away from me. "I'm so sorry. I—"

I hold my throat with both hands. "It's okay," I reassure him. "It was a dream."

He shakes his head continuously. I place my hand on his wet chest. His heart is beating a million miles a minute.

"Are you hurt?" He grows concerned.

"Don't worry about me."

"How can you say that? I could have shot you, Sloane."

"What happened?" I blinked. "In your dream." I ignore his concern. I don't want to talk about myself—not when he had a nightmare like that.

He sits up, pushing himself back against the headboard. He reaches his hand out to my neck and gently pulls me closer. I sit cross-legged at his side, my thigh resting on his stomach. He brushes the loose hair behind my ear. Looking deep into my eyes, he inches closer to my face and places his lips on the top of my head.

His demeanor shifted. His nightmare took complete control of him. I *knew* Mikhail would never hurt me. But whoever hurt him in the past haunts him. Even behind shut eyes, he's still troubled.

"In your dream ..." I don't want to pressure him to talk, but my curiosity only grows. If he doesn't want to share, then so be it. I wouldn't want someone to force me to open up.

"It was my father," he starts. "He was going after my older brother, and I tried to stop him."

I look down instantly. His father. "He wasn't a good person?" I ask, wanting to know more.

"No," he whispers. "He was abusive."

When the words fall from his lips, I instantly want him to confide. Keeping it to himself, he can push down the hurt and ignore the memories, but telling the story makes it true. And sometimes talking things through can help ease the pain.

"Did he ever hurt your sister?" I ask. I don't know why I'm pushing him so hard. I should stop, but I think a part of me wants to know the story so I can be there to comfort him. I want to be the strong one.

It's strange seeing Mikhail like this.

Defeated.

I remember Max telling me a little about why he's so hot-headed. His father is probably the root cause of his anger.

"No." He exhales. "Anya was never a part of that, thankfully. My real father had me and my brother, Kirill, but my adoptive father had Anya."

"What did he do to you?"

Mikhail looks at me with concern. He doesn't want to tell me. He shifts his body so his back is facing me.

I place my hand over the long scars on his back. I've seen them from a distance, but I've never paid attention to them when he's near me without a shirt. He doesn't want to talk about them, and he taught me a lesson for putting my nose somewhere it doesn't belong. But now I see the scars are ragged and uneven. Some of the rooted cuts are much deeper than others.

"It was with a belt. I was seven when it started. I was trying to protect my brother. I got many punishments for protecting him."

The notebook ...

Was that his way of keeping track of the consequences?

"Mikhail ..." I choke back tears.

"Hey, it's all right." He turns to face me, taking his thumb and wiping a tear off my cheek. "It made me strong."

That's why he's so protective.

I never knew there was so much hurt beneath his anger. I feel like a goddamn idiot for pushing him around for so long.

My fingers trail down his back. I notice he has tattoos all over his arms, neck, legs, and torso. I can see he has many scars too—are tattoos his way of covering them up?

"Mikhail ... what do tattoos mean to you?"

"They're milestones. Things I hold in my heart, and things I want to remember."

"You don't mean to cover the scars?"

"No. I don't need to cover them. I'll always remember them."

I look at his chest and try to understand the meaning behind them. "The wings?" I ask. He has two wings covering his upper chest.

"My father."

I assume he means his adoptive father. "The rose?" I ask. The rose is in the center of his torso.

"My sister. She used to come home from school every day with a rose. An elderly woman gave her them from her garden. It's a great story—maybe you'll hear it from her one day."

I smile. "You never talk about your family."

"I think you two get along really well," he tells me as if she's an old friend of mine.

"I'm sure we *could* get along well," I say with a laugh, worried he's been playing me this entire time. *He doesn't know, does he?*

I look at his shoulder to distract myself and find more ink. "A club?"

"That's the bottom of the chain."

Bottom of the chain? Does he mean the Suits? Is that what Max was talking about?

I nod my head, acting as if I understand. "Do you plan on ever getting any more? I mean, is there anything else that might have enough significance for you to carry forever?"

"Maybe," he tells me, staring at my lips.

Before I can say anything else, I take his face and bring his lips to mine. It might be wrong of me to start something when he's feeling so vulnerable, but I need it. I need him, and I think he needs me.

His tongue battles mine and his lips move against me. Mikhail pushes me down, caging me against the bed. I want to surrender myself to him.

"Sloane, I can't," he mumbles, bringing his eyes to mine.

I question him, but not with my words.

"I can't," he mumbles again. "I don't want to hurt you, and I will if we keep going."

He's angry. Not at me, but our connection. He doesn't want to keep this going between us. He hurts me, and I hurt him—it's an endless cycle I never want to leave. Shaking my head, I bring my hand to his cheek and watch his expression change from anger to fear.

"Fuck me like you need to, Mikhail."

A sound escapes his chest as he pulls down my shorts. He's quick with his actions; he doesn't want to overthink this. Neither of us wants to comprehend what's happening, but we'll both allow the pain.

He's poison in my bloodstream, and I don't care.

Mikhail slams his lips back onto mine while he takes off his pants. His kisses aren't kind. They're demanding—full of anger, lust, and maybe even hate.

I love it.

The hate fuels our connection. He doesn't want to feel anything close to love, but hate is just as strong.

Without warning, Mikhail pushes himself inside me. He doesn't look at me. He doesn't say a single word. My fingers claw at his back as he moves in and out of me quickly. I want more. I want to feel his anger.

I dig my nails into his back harder.

He lifts his head up slightly. I cry out from the pain he's putting on me, but it's the good kind of pain. The kind that brings me close to climax. When he fucks me like this, he's telling me things his voice would never be able to. I know how he feels about me, and he's showing me with passion—whether he wants to or not.

My heart rate spikes when he moves my legs to the side. He pulls my head back with my hair, forcing my attention onto him. I wrap my arm around and pull him closer, slamming my lips to his. His moan in my mouth throws me over the edge. My core throbs and I bite down on his bottom lip—hard.

Mikhail pulls out of me and comes over my stomach.

My clit burns from the friction. I know for a fact I'll be sore. I make a face when I move my legs slightly. I wanted this, and I'm happy it happened, but *fuck* does everything hurt now. I grab my shorts and wipe his come off my stomach, sitting up on the bed. Just as I'm about to leave to use the bathroom, he grabs my hand, stopping me.

"Forgive me," he mutters, looking at me with saddened eyes. "I know I hurt you."

A smile tugs on the corner of my lips. "You gave me what I needed." I hold his face in my hands and wipe the frown away with a kiss.

Chapter 22

Sloane

Sunlight breaks through the floor-to-ceiling windows, blinding me as I walk down the steps. I stop when I see a note taped to the wall.

I have things to take care of. Dimitri is here to watch over you.

—Mikhail

Leave it to Mikhail to abandon me after a night like that.

He wanted me to let go for one night. But why would I give him that? He walks around with his head held high, constantly telling me what to do.

I can't be with him more than I already am. I told him I couldn't because I know I won't be able to act as if nothing happened. The man I used to loathe is slowly creeping past the fine line between love and hate. It's as if he's making me choose between the two.

When it comes to Mikhail ... I'll gladly choose hate.

Through the glass that surrounds the main door, I see a bright yellow car with the word "Taxi" on the top. My hands cover my face as I hold in a laugh on the verge of hysterical.

I turn away from the door and stop when I see Dimitri passed out on the couch with his mouth open, snoring. His phone is slowly falling off his chest with each huff of air he takes. I could walk up to him, take the phone, and call Ruslan. Mikhail knows my family wants me back, but he wants them to sweat—I know it.

Being trapped in the arms of Mikhail isn't the worst thing. I'm not treated poorly—at least not anymore—but I don't like the idea of being stuck in here like a house cat. I want to have a life to live. I want to have priorities. I can't just sit on the couch all day and wait for Mikhail to come home and tell me all about his productive day. I don't want to rely on another person for my own stability, but he's forcing me to do that. I don't have the option to do much of anything while I'm here with him.

At least, that's what he wants me to think.

I walk past Dimitri, trying my hardest to be as quiet as possible. I wave my hand in front of his face just to make sure he's asleep. When I hear a large huff of air, my eyes widen, and I jump back. He's definitely asleep. I slowly back my way to the door and question if what I'm doing will bite me in the ass later. It probably will, but there's a loud voice screaming in the back of my mind, telling me to leave.

I'll come back to Mikhail—I just want to explore. I want to sit in a car for hours and see the world. I love my family, I do, but if I go back to them, I'll be on a lockdown worse than what I'm currently enduring.

On the table I see a wallet. I open it up to find Mikhail's name plastered everywhere. *Why would he leave without his wallet?* Without complaining, I take his card, put on shoes, and open the door slowly. I'll probably regret this, but I need to get out, even if it's just for a little while.

Stockholm syndrome is no joke.

I walk out the house like I've done it a million times before. Seagulls fly above me in the open, blue sky, forcing a smile from me. The street is surrounded by gorgeous trees and bushes that have bright blue flowers growing on them.

Skipping across the street, I tap on the car window.

The man inside looks at me brightly and rolls the glass down.

"Hi!" I say, cheerful so I don't draw attention, even though I'm most likely doing the opposite. "Could you give me a ride to the city?" I ask.

He nods.

My heart races as I get in the back of the car and look at the house.

This is such a mistake, but I feed off adrenaline. It's something so simple, but this is the first time I've been out by myself.

Mikhail has shown me what it feels like to live on the edge. I don't know how he managed to do that considering I've been held captive, but I won't question it.

My feet tap on the floor as time flies and I stare at the passing cars that drive next to us. Everyone has places to be. They may have jobs they hate, but at last they have control of their lives. I envy that. I want to have a purpose, but that's something I will never have.

Cars honk on repeat and the buildings grow taller the further we get into the city. So tall I can't see the tops of them from my window. What would the view be like?

The driver pulls the car to the curb, and my mouth opens to say something. I just want to keep driving. I'm too nervous to get out and explore. How ironic.

The door on the other side of the car opens quickly.

A black German shepherd jumps in the middle of the back seat and sits facing the front of the car. I scoot back as fast as I can.

"*Suigh síos!*" a chirpy voice commands.

I bend over to look at the woman who just entered the car. *Is this normal?* I didn't think strangers shared cabs.

"Hi!" she shouts, and I jump back. "I'm sorry, I didn't know you were in here, otherwise I would have gotten a different cab."

Her accent is strong. I think she's Irish. Her bright red hair and freckled face give her away. She speaks an entire novel's worth of words I don't understand before looking at me as if expecting me to answer a question.

I'm mesmerized by her. She's fucking tiny, probably five foot, her face perfectly rounded and her nose pointed upward slightly. Her lips are full—especially her bottom lip. It's red as if she's been picking at it with her teeth.

"I don't mean to be rude, but I didn't understand a thing you just said ... and you said a lot, so that's unfortunate."

She throws her hair down and puts it in a high bun. It's long and curly, just like mine. The woman looks me up and down and raises her eyebrows. "You Americans are always so blunt."

"Russian, actually, but thanks."

"Russian? I don't hear that in your voice, but I'll trust you're being honest with me."

I glare at her. I can't tell whether she's stuck-up or just very ... I'm not sure, but I can tell she's a lot. "What reason would I have to lie to you? Unless you're a Russian spy." I lean my head closer to her.

She laughs, the high-pitched giggle sending an instant warmth to my heart. "I like you already and I don't even know your name," she says as she places a hand on her dog.

"Sloane," I introduce myself and reach out my hand. The dog watches it as if my hand's a piece of meat it's waiting to take a bite out of.

"He won't bite unless I tell him to, don't worry. My name is Rosalie, but please, for the love of whatever you believe in, call me Rose."

"What's wrong with Rosalie?" I ask, curious. It's a beautiful name. I don't see what her problem is.

"It makes me sound like one of those girls from high school who would bully you for wearing the same color as they did—you know what I mean? I don't know, it just makes me sound like a girl I don't really relate to. But Rose? Now, I can relate to her any day of the week."

"Good God, okay, Rose, I get it."

"Great! So, where are you off to? I'm sure the driver is growing impatient." She looks in the rearview mirror, and the man rolls his eyes.

"Honestly, I'm not sure. I have a card with a lot of money on it though."

She widens her bright blue eyes and grins. "Is your boyfriend rich? Oh, please tell me he is. You're living the life. He's probably out killing people right now while you spend his money and grow ignorant of the dark work he does. That's what rich people do in this city, isn't it?"

"Uh ..." I begin, tongue-tied in utter shock.

"Oh my gosh, relax. I'm just kidding." She beams at me.

Rose is enchanting, but she doesn't know when to shut up.

"Where were you going?" I ask.

"To bury a body."

I have a feeling her dark jokes are something I'll have to get used to since I'm stuck in the cab with her. "Great. Me too."

"Seriously?"

My mouth drops, and I am quick to shake my head. "No."

"Mm-hmm. Okay, well, I need to go to the butchers to get food for my little guy. You want to come?"

Little guy? His paws are the size of my hands.

I shrug my shoulders. "Why not? I have nothing better to do."

She hands her phone to the driver, and he nods his head, shifting the car into drive. Drivers behind us honk their horns, but I assume that's normal because of how crazy the traffic is here.

"Do you like to shop?" she asks.

"Not really." I look down at my outfit. I can't help but compare myself to her. She's dressed in what looks like an outfit worth half a million dollars while I'm wearing sweatpants and a tank top.

"I thought so. You look as if you just got out of bed." She pulls on the dog until he's lying on her legs, covering her entire lower body. "What do you plan to do with the money?" she asks.

"I was thinking about donating a lot of it."

She smiles, her round cheeks forming dimples in the center. "I donate a lot too. Mainly to animal shelters."

"I'd love to do that!" I tell her.

"Yeah? We can stop there before we go to the butchers!"

"Please."

"Driver, let's go to a shelter."

"Yeah, yeah," he mumbles.

Rose and I share jokes back and forth as if our lives depend on it. I've never had the opportunity to meet many people in my life, but something about Rose makes me want to open up to her completely. She's funny, kind, maybe a little stuck-up, but that's okay because she has to have at least one flaw. I can tell by the way she dresses that she spends money as if it's just a number in her account. Her clothes look like they've been to the dry cleaners. Her heels are bright green, her toes painted white. *Who dresses like this on their way to an animal shelter?*

The car pulls up to a building that looks run-down, the brick walls close to crumbling. Rose gives the driver three hundred-dollar bills as if they're pieces of notebook paper. She didn't have to pay for my drive. I make a face and scratch my cheek as I get out the car. She calls her dog, and he zips through her legs with every step she takes. Some of her words I can't understand, but I think they're commands because he starts to walk in circles around her.

"Do you want a dog?" she asks with a grin I've already come to know far too well.

I scrunch my nose. "I would love one, but I can't."

She brings her well-manicured hand to my nose and taps on it. "That's what you think. Just wait. Once a dog chooses you, you'll never be able to leave it."

I gulp, nervous that she's right. Mikhail would literally kill me if he came home to a dog sitting on his couch. I've noticed he likes things to be completely spotless, not a single crumb in sight. When Lev touched me that night, he made me clean his touch off me. I don't think that had much to do with him wanting to make me feel more comfortable; I think he just didn't want another man to touch what he views as his.

And he might be right. I feel as if he is mine and I am his, but that's a nightmare to untangle.

"Are you coming, Sloane?" Rose asks, opening the door.

I hurry up and rush after her, my ears instantly flooded with the barks and howls of beautiful animals locked in cages. Rose stops by the front desk and talks to a younger woman. She nods at whatever she says and then makes her way over to me.

"What kind of dog are you looking for?" the woman asks. Her hair is pin-straight and dark black, and her eyes are so dark they look as black as her hair.

"I'm not getting a dog, but I wouldn't mind petting a few."

Rose grabs onto my arm with excitement and pulls me to walk faster as the younger woman guides us in. We spend the next couple of hours lying in the playpen with a bunch of dogs, and my serotonin levels skyrocket.

"I think I get it," I admit.

"I knew you would." Rose sends a wink in my direction. "It's the mama Golden Retriever, isn't it?"

"How did you know?"

"She picked you. She forgot about her puppies the moment she saw you."

I roll my eyes. "Her puppies aren't even puppies anymore. That doesn't mean anything."

We stare at each other for a moment before bursting into laughter. At what I'm not exactly sure, but I can feel we've become fast friends.

"You should take her home."

I frown. "I really can't, much as I want to."

Rose stands up and holds her hand out for me to grab onto. Lilly, the Golden Retriever, whines by my side when I get up. Her whines turn into sad howls as she realizes she can't follow after me. Tears spring into my eyes.

Fuck, this hurts.

"At least put your name down for her. Go home, think about it," Rose tells me, and I nod slowly.

I write my name down for Lilly and tell the woman I'd like to make a donation. She turns the screen to me, and I fill in the card information. Once finished, I type in the amount of the donation, accidently adding an extra zero, and press enter. My mouth drops when I realize I just donated one million dollars.

"Oh," I say with an embarrassed smile. I feel my face redden, but I shake my head. It's better that Mikhail's money goes to a good cause instead of into the pockets of murderers. Plus, my best guess is most of it is fake anyway.

The woman behind the desk almost cries with happiness, and that's when I decide to leave. I don't want her thanking me for donating money that was never mine to begin with. I look around for Rose, but she's nowhere.

"Rose?" I shout on the street, but I get nothing in return.

Rushing back inside, I ask the woman if she saw the girl who came in with me. "Red hair, really short, *strong* accent. You can't forget her."

"I'm sorry, I have no idea what you're talking about, honey," the woman tells me. "You came in here alone."

What?

It's as if Rose never existed. She vanished like a ghost, a figment of my imagination.

Suddenly, I'm overwhelmed by the creepy aura surrounding me.

Am I going crazy?

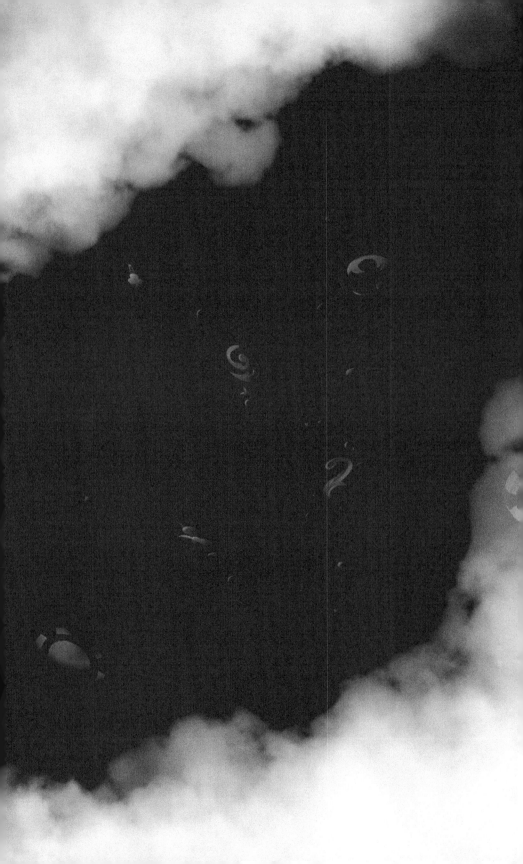

Chapter 23

Mikhail

The ticking of a clock fills the silent room as Adrian and Lev wait for me to sign the contract. I'm putting my money where my mouth is, but it's hard to focus. This property is in the Clarkes' territory. I told myself I wouldn't fuck with that family, but now I can't seem to help myself. It'll be the third lot I'm buying, which will put me on their radar.

Francesco runs his hand over his buzzed hair as he waits just like the rest of them. "It's either now or never," he says, gesturing to the pen in my hand.

I nod and sign my name next to the "X" on the bottom of the paper.

It's done.

Over the past two years, I've done what Kirill couldn't ever do. That alone is an accomplishment I'll take a shot for.

"Fuck yeah, brother." Adrian walks behind me, patting my back.

I nod, taking a cigarette from my pocket and lighting the end.

"One day till you got everything you need," Francesco muses.

I stand up from the chair and walk toward the cart stocked with alcohol in the corner of the room. I pour myself a glass and bring it to my lips. Then I reach into my pocket for my phone, which has been blowing up for the past half hour. I couldn't answer it because I was too focused on the paper in front of me.

I have six missed calls from Dimitri.

Shit.

I dial his number, and the phone doesn't even finish the first ring before he picks up.

"Mikhail, what that fuck, man? Answer your phone when I call!" he shouts.

"Sorry, I was busy," I tell him.

"Sloane is gone."

Everything in the room slows down as I hear those words come through the phone. Panic shoots through my bloodstream.

"What do you mean she's gone? Where the fuck is she, Dimitri?"

"I don't know. I fell asleep on the couch for a couple hours. When I woke up and saw it was past noon, I went to check on her, but she wasn't there. I looked through the house and found nothing. Her shoes are gone."

My grip strengthens around the edges of my phone. "You fell asleep."

"It's been a long couple of days, man."

"You. Fell. Asleep."

"I'll find her."

"You'd better fucking find her." I hang up and stride toward the door.

"What's going on?" Adrian asks.

I put the end of the cigarette out in an empty bottle of vodka. "She fucking left."

"Sloane?"

"Who the hell else?" I run my hands through my hair. She fucking left. Why would she leave? After last night, I thought things had gotten better between us—but of course, she has to defy me. It's in her nature to do the opposite of everything I say. She's a manipulative little brat.

"Okay, think," Lev says. "She'd go back to try to get in contact with her father, right?"

I shake my head. "She's careless, not stupid." Then I take the empty bottle and throw it at a wall, flustered. "Fuck!"

Hours pass by as I frantically tear apart the city looking for her.

She is a fucking witch. She used her body to gain my trust just to betray me.

My phone chimes, and I see an alert from my bank about a withdrawal. My head falls back and I let a laugh slip through my lips when I see the number. Without thinking, I approve the payment. Sloane will always get what she wants, and I hate her even more for it. She's got a magic wand that's able to demand anything of me and I'll simply oblige.

I update Dimitri on where she is and tell him to pick her up. I expected more of him, but I can't be mad. I've had them doing a lot for me. I should have stayed with Sloane or at least brought her with me today.

And now I don't know what I'm going to do with her.

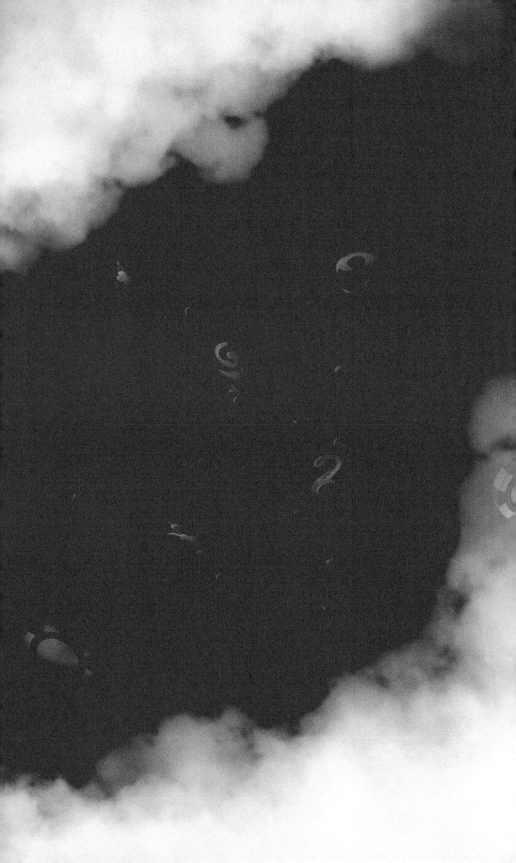

Chapter 24

Sloane

"If you think he's pissed at me, I'm nervous for you," Dimitri tells me as he opens the door to Mikhail's house.

I don't say anything because he's right. When the car pulled up to the side of the road and Dimitri threw himself out, I knew I'd fucked up. How did he find me? Not a fucking clue.

I step over the threshold from my freedom into imprisonment. The sun casts a shadow across Mikhail's face. He sits on the couch with his elbows resting on his knees.

Dimitri pushes my back, and I stumble closer to the man whose expression looks beyond pissed. He nods, and Dimitri slams the door behind me. Alone in the room with Mikhail, I shudder at the echo it sends through the apartment.

"Mikhail," I start.

"Don't." He runs a hand across his jaw. "You don't fucking talk."

Out of all the times I've pissed him off, I don't think I've ever seen him this mad. There are many things I'd like to say, but I have no idea how far his anger will take me. I know he's respectful to an extent, but there's no way to describe the shift in the room's atmosphere now. So instead I listen to him, not saying a word.

"Christ, Sloane." He pushes himself off the couch and walks toward me as he rolls up his sleeves. "You're the reason shampoo bottles have directions. How many fucking times do I need to remind you to stay put?" I back away from him slowly till I'm stopped by the wall against my back. Mikhail's eyes darken as he inches closer. I bite down on my tongue to refrain from saying something I'll regret.

Then he wraps his hand around my throat. Not tightly, but enough to bring my face close to his. His thumb traces the outline of my lips as he tilts my head to the side. "If you ever. Fucking. Leave. Again, there is not a person in this world who could save you from me."

I slam my eyes shut. His threats make my legs shake. "I won't—" I try to speak, but he shuts me up.

"I need your eyes and your ears, not your fucking mouth," he rasps.

My skin ignites at his touch. I should hate this feeling. I should hate how demanding he is of me, but I thrive on it.

It's toxic.

When I look up at him, he clenches his jaw, grabbing my face between his hands. He pulls my head closer to his and crashes his lips into mine, his kisses full of hate.

I kiss him back, moving my tongue past his lips and letting it glide against his. He groans into my mouth, picking me up off my feet. I wrap my legs around his back. His large hands touch me everywhere in an attempt to claim my body as his own.

"Fuck these clothes," he says, letting out his pent-up frustration.

With his lips still on mine, he walks over to the couch and throws me into the cloud of pillows. I sit up and reach for the hem of the top I'm wearing to pull it off, but he takes over and does it for me. He pulls my pants down my legs by the ankles, and in only a matter of minutes I'm stripped completely naked while he remains fully dressed.

Mikhail lowers himself down onto my body till his mouth is near my bare pussy. His hands grab my ass so hard I know there'll be marks left in their place.

The moment his tongue runs against my clit, I'm overwhelmed by everything that is Mikhail. I squirm under him, but he forces me back down.

"I could come from the taste of you alone." He puts a finger in me and then sticks it in his mouth.

His words are filthy. He can talk about how much he hates it when I do things he doesn't like, but I know he's lying. He gets off on it. He likes to teach me lessons, and I don't mind learning.

I need to feel him inside me again. "Fuck me," I plead.

"Ask me nicely," he demands.

"Please," I beg.

"Please what?"

"Please fuck me."

Once I tell him what he wants to hear, he unbuckles his belt and takes it out of the loops. "Gladly." His voice is dark. He pulls down his pants to below his waist.

I could look at his body all day and not get bored. I tug at the bottom of his shirt, and he takes it off quickly. Beneath all his tattoos he's built of muscle.

Mikhail grabs onto my hand to lift me up and flip me over so I'm on all fours with my back arched, leaving my ass in the air. He doesn't give me a warning before shoving his dick deep inside me in a single thrust. I grab onto a pillow and bite down. Mikhail is huge, and it takes some adjusting. His hands grab onto my hips as he slams into me fast.

He knows every inch of my body. I'm already close to my climax. It's everything about him. Every touch of his skin makes me wetter. His words elicit an eagerness I never knew it was possible to feel.

"You're doing so well," he praises in my ear.

Mikhail switches positions many times, throwing me around. He fucks me hard, panting as he stares down at me. It's rough, and at times I can't breathe, but I don't want him to stop. He isn't holding back, and I'm glad. I want him to fuck me with his anger.

My legs straddle him as he sits upright on the couch. His hands run down my back as I ride him. A burning sensation overpowers me, and I cry out. I don't even have to try to come with him—it's inevitable.

I press my forehead to his as he holds my hips still.

"Fuck," he says as his release drips out of me.

I can feel his heart racing against my bare chest. I want to hold him in my arms and make him forget why he's angry.

"I'm sorry I left," I say. My ears drown in the quiet that surrounds us.

He looks up at me, but that only lasts for a moment before his jaw hardens. I shouldn't have apologized; I just reminded him where his anger came from. Reaching my arms behind me, I put my clothes back on quickly.

Mikhail pulls his pants up so they're resting on his waist. Walking over to the kitchen, he picks out a bottle of water from the fridge. Screwing the cap off the bottle, he starts to take sips, his Adam's apple rolling with each one.

Walking back in, he leans into me so his chin is against the side of my head.

"Try that shit again and I'll lock you in that room."

His anger radiates through my blood, causing my skin to burn. I suck in a deep breath of air when he gathers my hair in his hands and pulls my neck back.

"If you think for a goddamn second I'm sharing you with the world, you're mistaken. You are mine now. If you decide to play nice, maybe I will too."

His arms pull away. His fingers brush his lips as he turns and walks toward the hallway, the darkness in his eyes telling me I crossed the line.

I spend the rest of the day rummaging through all of Mikhail's things. I know he'd be even more pissed if he found out I was doing this. He probably even has cameras hidden in random corners of the house, but I'm doing it anyway.

His computer is locked, and so is the safe shoved underneath his desk. There are stacks of papers with building layouts. None of that interests me—I just want to find something against him. I want a reason to fight him back, something that will get him to listen. He can't be the only one in charge.

If he didn't want me to be snooping, then he should be here to keep me from doing it.

The thing about Mikhail is that whenever he gets frustrated, he bolts. He just leaves me, and I become bored. It's an invitation for me to do things I shouldn't—like opening the briefcase next to his desk.

Undoing the thick strap that latches onto the middle of the bag, I see files upon files categorized alphabetically. My fingers brush past many of them until I see a file with my name on it.

I stare at it just as I once did with the diamond chain. I want to take it and read through everything in the file, but what good would that do?

I have to.

Letting out a scoff, I lift the file out and place it on the ground. Holding my breath, I open it but come to a stop when I see nothing inside.

"What?" I ask myself.

Grabbing the bag, I look for others. Dimitri, Lev, Max, Giovanni— they all have novels' worth of pages inside, but I don't have a single one. Here I thought Mikhail had an unhealthy obsession with knowing every single little thing about me ...

Unless he doesn't want anyone else to know what he has on me.

I scramble to put everything back, suddenly nervous Mikhail is aware of what I'm doing. Just as I'm about to put the bag where I found it, I see a small white envelope tucked inside the side pocket.

Is that what I think it is?

Reaching for it slowly, I see it's stamped for Mikhail. It even has his name on it in handwriting that looks familiar.

It's unopened. There are small marks on the surface that make the paper appear wrinkled. It's almost as if the marks were made by tear stains. Does Mikhail not know about anything because he wasn't ready to open the letter?

I hear the front door click closed and feel my heart pounding in my chest. Shoving the letter in the waistband of my pants, I rush over to the hallway as quickly as I can so whoever is here doesn't see I was in Mikhail's office.

As I walk down the hall, I see the man himself taking his suit jacket off and placing it on the counter. He doesn't care to acknowledge that I'm standing on the other side staring at him. His hands run down his face, though not in frustration. It's almost as if he's relaxed and happy to be home.

His elbows rest on the surface and his thumb brushes over his chin. "*Moya malenkaya koldunya*?" he calls for me.

"Yeah?" I ask, growing used to the small acts of affection he shows me.

"What have you been doing today?" he asks, sounding genuinely curious.

I walk over to him, placing my arms around his shoulders. He grabs onto my hand and kisses the top gently. "Spying on you," I answer honestly.

He turns around, pulling my body in between his legs. "Good," he says. I become hesitant as soon as I remember what lies in the waistband of my pants.

He smiles, reaching for his jacket. "Where are you going?" I ask, suddenly nervous of him leaving me here again.

"My niece has a ballet recital in the city."

"Can I come?" I ask.

"Absolutely not."

"Oh—" I begin to say, but I stop myself. "Why not?"

"Your erratic behavior."

My mouth falls open. "Are you joking?"

"Yes."

His hand lifts to the side of my face and he places his lips against mine. I kiss him back even though I'm slightly irritated with him. It's strange to see him so calm after what happened earlier today.

"Go get ready," he tells me, and I lean away from him with a smile on my face.

Once I'm changed, I place the letter in one of the dresser drawers. I meet him downstairs, and he leads me into the garage. When he opens the passenger door for me, I climb into the G-Class. He gets in and sits behind the wheel, turning on the engine. Turning his body to face mine, his hand moves behind the seat I'm sitting in and he backs out of the driveway.

Soft music plays through the speakers while Mikhail drives to the city. With his eyes focused on the road, he reaches his hand over and grabs onto my thigh. The veins in his hand stick out when he tightens his grip slightly.

I look over at him and notice he doesn't look as intimidating as he usually does. His thick brows aren't pinched, and his lips lift into a small smirk.

His long legs leave the space he sits in to appear small.

"Your niece—what's her name?" I ask, wanting to know more about his family.

"Alyna," he says with a smile. "This world isn't big enough for the spirit she has."

I lean in closer to him, wrapping my hand around his bicep. "She's energetic?" I ask.

He shakes his head. "She's like a carbon copy of my sister. She's got enough spirit to take over the world if she wanted to."

Hearing the way he speaks about his family brings a smile to my face. He isn't scared to admit how much he loves and cares for them. I think he would have been afraid to tell me anything about his family a few weeks ago—but now he feels comfortable enough to talk.

The calm aura that surrounds me and Mikhail has an expiration date— that I know for a fact. So, while the moment slips past me quickly, I grab onto everything and enjoy it while it lasts.

Seeing Mikhail content feels like a breath of fresh air.

Just as I thought, the drive is quick. Mikhail turns into a parking lot where hundreds of cars are lined up and drops me off at the main entrance. The building is large, much bigger than I expected it to be. While I wait at the steps, Max, Lev, and Dimitri walk up with a woman beside them.

"Sloane, thank you for coming," Dimitri says with a huge smile as he steps back, putting his arm around the woman. "This is my wife, Anya."

Anya.

She looks different from how she was described to me in the past. Not only is she beautiful, but she smiles with her eyes—a rare, undeniable look of happiness. She shines brightly from the outside just as much as she would from the inside.

Her hair is dark black, almost taking on the appearance of silk. The green in her eyes is subtle but stands out against her fair complexion. Her cheekbones are high—dominant even. She looks nothing like Mikhail, though I didn't expect her to since they're not related by blood.

She watches me and I see her lips purse. She wants to speak to me alone, I can tell by the way she scans her surroundings. "Hi," she says, throwing herself into my arms. "They're starting soon—we should get inside!"

Grabbing onto my arm, she places a small piece of paper in my hand and closes my fingers around it.

Feeling the paper in my hand makes me want to break out with sweat. I can't open it right now, and that drives me crazy.

With Anya still holding onto me, we walk through the double doors and enter a large room filled with red seats and dimmed lighting. As we walk down the path, I think about the things I've found that were hers. The books, the roses, the piano.

"Is there a story? Behind the flowers, I mean."

"Flowers?"

"Yeah. There were a bunch of them in a drawer on the boat. And Mikhail has a rose tattoo—I was just wondering if there's meaning behind them."

Anya is silent for a moment. "He got you flowers? What color are they?"

"Red?" I say like a question.

"*Shit.* Yeah. When I was little, I would walk home from school and there was this older woman who had *gorgeous* flowers in her garden. Every day without fail, she would give me one to take home. Her garden started to get bare because I took all of them. For years I wondered how I was still getting flowers every day when there were none in her yard. Then, one day, I got off school early and saw Mikhail giving her a bunch of flowers. I hid behind a wall because I didn't want him to find out that I knew. He didn't want me to know. But he saw me and acted as if he didn't. That went on for so long, but now he just gives them to me himself."

I can't help but smile the entire time she's talking. "That is a really nice story," I admit to Anya.

"It is. But he only ever got me white roses. He's never given anyone a red rose. Our dad told us red roses should be saved for someone you love deeply."

Her words eat at my bones. She's able to tell me how Mikhail feels for me without our whole story. What he feels for me won't last long.

"Here," Anya says as we walk to the front row and take a seat. Max takes a seat next to me, leaving the seat on the other side of me open for Mikhail.

Far in the back is the stage. Thick black curtains hang low, covering the entire stage.

The voices that surround me all sound muffled as everyone tries to keep their voices down. Mikhail comes around the corner and Anya springs into his arms. He holds her for a long hug before taking a seat next to me. He grabs my hand and holds onto it.

I look at him, wondering why he's all of a sudden being so affectionate. Just as I'm about to ask him what's going on, all the lights turn off except one: the stage light.

"Once Upon a Dream" by Invadable Harmony begins to play through the surround sound, and the curtains slowly open.

Leaning out of my chair slightly, I watch all four of the men almost shapeshift. The strong, muscular—and terrifying—men all sit back and watch the show with the grandest of smiles across their faces that normally lack all emotion.

My hand lifts to my mouth so I can hold back my laugh. It's extraordinary.

"That's her, the one on the right with the pink leotard," Mikhail whispers in my ear, pointing his finger. He doesn't notice they're all in pink leotards because he only sees her, but he's right. Anyone could pick her out in a crowd.

Alyna's arms are held above her body while she jumps on her toes. Her body sways with each musical chime as if it were as easy as breathing.

Her hair is blonde with hints of brown. Her expression changes from a focused look to a smile every few seconds. I can tell being on the stage is easy for her, not scary. The stage is full of many dancers, though everyone sitting near me is only watching her.

The little girl has all of them wrapped around her tiny finger, and I can't think of anything more ironic.

Alyna looks young, but I have a hunch she'll be growing up with ballet. The stage and her shoes will be the only things she'll want in life—I can tell by how elegant she is. The blisters, sores, and calloused feet will soon prove beauty is pain. But she doesn't show it—not even for a second—because she loves it.

Her arms link with others around her while they spin in a circle. When the music dies down, they all form a line and bow at the same time.

All four of the men stand from their chairs and scream for Alyna. Mikhail's hands cup his mouth when he cheers for her more.

She sees him and waves nonstop with a cheeky grin.

Mikhail tilts his head and blows her a kiss. Alyna catches the imaginary kiss with her hands and shapes a heart with her fingers.

Turning to the side so Mikhail can't see me, I unfold the note.

we need to talk

I quickly crumple the paper in my hands and turn to see Anya. She keeps her expressions to a minimum, but when her eyes lift slightly to the side of the aisle, I can tell this is her way of trying to talk to me in private.

"I'll just be a moment," I tell Mikhail as I rise from my seat. "I'm going to use the restroom."

His jaw clenches. "Be quick," he tells me, and I move past him.

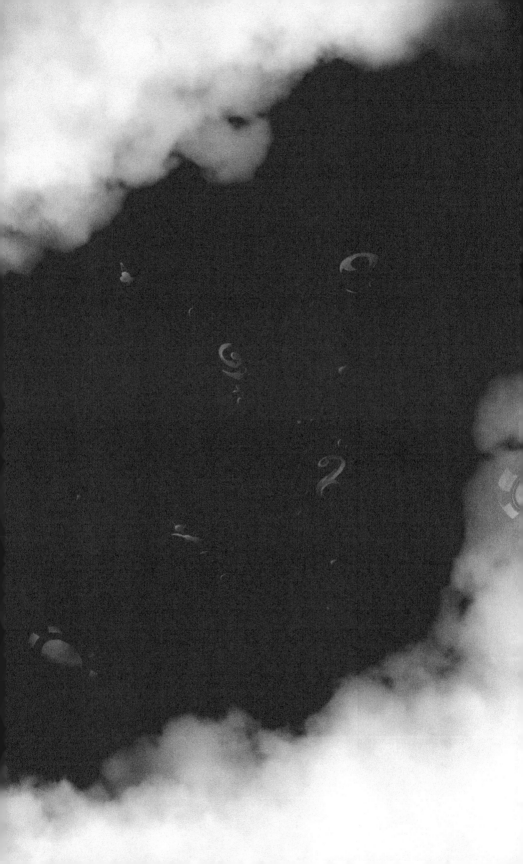

Chapter 25

Mikhail

Sloane walks past me, her arm carefully brushing against mine. There's a large part of me with an urge to grab onto her hand and pull her close to me. Turning around, I watch her walk up the dull pathway. Her black mid-length skirt hugs her beautiful curves while her long, almost white hair is tied in the back.

How is it that the woman is able to do as she pleases and still receive my decency? It's as if she challenges me constantly to see how far she'll get.

She must tire from trying to get under my skin. She is relentless about it. She had no reason to leave the house today, and yet she still chose to do so. I kind of enjoy how eager she is to get her way. It's a look not many can pass, but she can. She's a young woman who can take care of herself. She needs the space to learn about what spikes her curiosity. If it's the city she wants to see, she's lucky I'm able to understand.

I didn't plan on bringing her here tonight. It was never my intention to have her meet some of the most important people to me, but I'd rather have it this way than have her run away without my knowledge.

My only hope is that she won't take my humanity for granted.

There's something about Sloane I can't put my finger on. A part of me thinks she works well by my side. I can give her the adventure she craves, and she can give me a teammate in return. She has a boldness many men would fear. I can't tell if it's just a façade of hers or if she is strong at heart.

If it's all an illusion, that mask of hers is painted on seamlessly.

I know everything there is to know about masking. Sometimes it's a way to hide behind the fear that weighs down on my shoulders; other times it's a placeholder for emotions I don't particularly feel like sifting through. And yet even I know the longer the mask is on, the stronger the denial will be. It's a temporary fix and nothing more. You give up a moment of peace for a lifetime of ache.

I've had my mask on for years, and I know the moment I take it off, I'll be hit with years of building pain—the pain I've refused to look in the eye.

Turning, I see Anya staring at Sloane. She's quick to follow after her, which only spikes my curiosity. *Haven't they just met?*

"Dimitri," I call.

He turns toward me with a smile plastered on his face. His eyes crease in the corners. I lift my finger at Anya, who follows Sloane. Once at the top of the aisle, Anya grabs onto Sloane's shoulder and leads her away from the crowd.

"What's that about?" I ask.

His lips form a weird shape, and he shrugs his arms. "Fast friends?" he asks. Dimitri must've noticed my worry. He shakes his head. "Would you stop? Not everyone is out to get you. We're at my child's show, for fuck's sake."

I cross my arms and feel my lips lifting with amusement. "You just reminded yourself to watch your tongue. We are at your child's show, for *Christ's* sake."

"If children struggle to hear their fathers swear, I'm worried for our future."

I cover a laugh and pat his back. "You're right about that one," I tell him.

He turns away from me and continues his conversation with a man I don't recognize. Still sitting in the chairs, Max and Lev both argue. I take a seat next to them.

Music from "The Nutcracker" begins to play while the time passes.

"They can't dance to 'The Nutcracker' yet. It's only July," Max says in a nasty tone.

Lev lifts his weight off the back of the chair and turns to Max, staring at him intently. "Were you born under a rock, or have you not heard of Christmas in July, you dumb fuck?"

"If you put up a tree during July, I will personally press a knife in your chest," Max says, unamused.

"It sounds like you were neglected as a child if you don't enjoy Christmas," Lev says.

I cough, trying to break up their argument, but it does nothing.

"It sounds like you were coddled as a child if you enjoy it that much."

"Enough," I mutter, and they both shut up. While I get both viewpoints, I don't think this is the best place to hash it out.

"Well, what do you think?" Lev encourages me to answer, and I just look at him. "You enjoy Christmas, right?"

I smile and shake my head. "Neglected child here."

He looks away from me quickly and puts his head down. I hope I didn't make him uncomfortable, but what the fuck did he expect? Did he want me to say I love red and green thrown all around my house and twinkle lights? Oh, maybe I'll leave the fireplace off so Santa can make it down the chimney.

Can't forget about the fucking milk and cookies.

The kids regather on the stage and perform two more dances, all of them incredible. Alyna owns the stage. A woman stands next to them and begins to thank everyone for coming to the performance. They go behind the curtains for a while.

"Uncle Misha!" a kind, gentle voice calls from behind me. I turn to see Alyna walking with Sloane and Anya.

I kneel to the ground and open my arms for the little one. She jumps into my arms, her hair bow hitting me in the face, and I smile through the uncomfortable feeling. Alyna feels tiny in my arms, yet I want to hug her as tight as possible.

Her feet hang while I hold her on my side. She traces the ink on my neck and smiles. "Did you see me up there?" she asks.

"What kind of a question is that?" I ask. "You're all I saw."

Her giggle is high-pitched, just like Anya's was. I lift her over my shoulders. Lev, Max, and Dimitri talk to her about the show while I hold her up. Her small fingers wrap around my index fingers to keep herself steady.

It's moments like these that will be drilled into her mind forever. Having so many people care for her—people who would do anything for her—is priceless. This little girl obsessed with Disney movies, ballet, and feeding the fish will end up being the most incredible person I know. As time passes, the déjà vu she feels won't leave a bad taste in her mouth. She'll only have good memories to keep in her mental scrapbook. Memories like this—where we all cheer for her because she's all we see.

It's the happy memories that sustain us. Her heart won't be tainted with the devil's wrath—not if I have a say in it. I want her to imagine the world in her hands, because it is. Anything she wants, she'll get.

Sloane crosses her arms and gives me a weak smile while she looks at me and then Alyna. When she looks at me like that, I can't do anything but forget my anger. It's the gentle look in her eyes that makes them appear soft.

We all catch up for what feels like an hour. The entire auditorium clears out, and Alyna dances on the stage by herself. Dimitri tells me he plans on leaving me to go back to the house with Anya soon, and I don't blame him. I'm glad he's stayed with me as long as he has, but his family needs to come first.

As we say our goodbyes, Sloane grabs onto my arm and we make our way to the entrance of the building. Opening the door, a huge gust of wind blows past us. The lights make the pelting rain look like mist as it falls from the sky, splashing onto the concrete.

Before I can offer my jacket to Sloane, she looks up at me with a grin and runs outside. When I chase after her, she stops to grab my hand with a wide smile plastered across her face. Why the fuck does she enjoy this? Better yet, why is her smile making me enjoy getting drenched with water?

When we make it to the car, she looks at me but doesn't utter a word. It's the kind of look that gives me the ability to read her mind. For Sloane, I've come to understand it's the little things in life that mean the most to her. Running to the car was enough to give her the biggest smile. It's the kind of smile I'd like to give her with my words.

I shake my head and start the car, driving back onto the main road. She stays silent and picks at the skin surrounding her fingernails. Her head turns to face mine, but she's quick to turn away.

Wishing she'd just get on with it and say what she needs to say, I ask, "What's on your mind?"

"Can you pull over?"

I give her a worried look. "Are you sick?"

"Could you just pull over?"

I do as she says and move to the side of the road. "This isn't really a good place to stop," I tell her and shift the car into park.

Just as I turn to look at her, she reaches over and pulls my face close to hers. Her lips press against mine, biting on my bottom lip. In the split second that her skin touches mine, every nerve in my body is electrified with greed and anticipation.

The way her lips fit perfectly with mine should be a crime. She moans into my mouth, and I reach over to grab onto her waist, lifting her onto my lap.

Her smooth legs straddle either side of my lap as I kiss her neck.

Sloane is worse than a drug—worse than any addiction known to mankind. Addiction can be beat; this cannot. The more she gives to me, the more I want to take. It's the repetition that will cause my destruction. I've become familiar with how her tongue brushes against mine, challenging me. The way her hips lift and grind against me. Nothing about this can be cured despite my best efforts.

"I shouldn't want you," she mutters while her neck falls back.

My hands lift behind her head, and I undo the tie that holds her hair together. "Is that right, *Moya malenkaya koldunya*?" I whisper against her bare skin.

I take the thin strap of her shirt between my fingers. When I move them down, her breasts spill out of her top, and I brush my thumb over the nipple. There's something disarming about seeing her like this. Sloane will only show this version of herself to one person in this world, and it is me. I'll be dammed if any other pair of eyes is able to see the perfection that she is.

There's vulnerability in the look she gives me. The gleam in her eyes is pure. I tuck her hair behind her ear and grab onto her neck, bringing her lips back to mine—where they belong.

Her eyes search mine, and it's as if she can read my exact thoughts. She terrifies me. The woman straddling my lap has complete power over me, and there are no reservations in the back of my mind, only a million thoughts condensed into this single moment.

Her forehead rests against mine and her hand trails down my chest slowly. She calculates her next move, and her teeth sink into her bottom lip. Her hips rise and fall, pressing against me, teasing me for more.

I bury my face into her neck before I kiss my way down to her breasts. I suck, bite, and tug on her skin. My hands inch down to her hips, and I grab onto them with pressure, guiding her movements against me. She leans back, and I move my fingers over her clit.

"*Kroshka*," I begin. "Are you wearing anything beneath this skirt?"

She looks down at me with eyes that dominate. I lick my lips, and her hand grabs onto my jaw, her thumb pulling my bottom lips down as she slowly shakes her head. Her lips press against mine with aggression.

"Fuck," I whimper in her mouth.

Sloane continues to stimulate every part of my fucking body to the point where I'm longing for her. I want every part of me to be touched and caressed by the gentle tips of her fingers. She's teaching me a lesson on patience, and I'm about fucking finished with it.

"Stop," she says, grabbing my hands and putting them to the sides of my body. "Your greed is showing."

My teeth clench down in frustration. With patience comes power, and I am completely powerless against her. "I'm the greediest son of a bitch in the world when it comes to you."

Whatever attraction I feel for Sloane is the healthiest kind of toxicity I've come to know. It's everything I've craved, and yet it terrifies me. Sloane can see right through me, and there is no weapon to shield me from her. In fact, I'd give her the weapon to destroy me with if it meant I'd die at the hands of someone just as distraught as I am.

Sloane tugs on my belt and undoes the zipper, not wasting a minute before she lowers herself onto me. My head falls back when I watch her adjust to me being inside her. The thought of her body alone could ruin me. I've never known anyone more beautiful than Sloane. All rational thought and focus is washed away by desire and the pain of wanting her.

"Look at me," I tell her as I bunch up her skirt and hold it up. "Look at what you do to me."

She leans the upper part of her body closer to me and brushes her fingers through my hair, tugging on the ends. Her breasts press against my chest, and I hold my hand flat against her back, feeling myself sink into her over and over again. Holding her in my arms feels empowering. I'm a lucky fucking man to be able to have Sloane want me like this.

I watch her lift her body up and down on mine with awe. It takes an undeniable amount of control not to throw her in the back seat of the car and fuck her mindless, but I can tell she wants to be in charge this time. She feels delicate in my arms, and I feel powerful to be the man holding her.

She wants to see me at her full disposal, begging, craving more of her, and I'll let her do as she pleases. There's something so sexy about seeing her take control. She dominates me in a way I'll never admit. I want her to overpower me; bring me to my knees.

She overwhelms me in a way I'll cherish for years.

"Tell me what I do to you," she says with a soft pant.

I grab onto her ass, guiding her movements. "You make me weak, *Koldunya*," I admit.

"What else?" she demands.

"Jesus fuck, Sloane," I whimper. "You ruin me."

I've taught her everything she knows, and yet I feel as if I'm the one who's learning. She's learned the way my body works and exactly how to make me burn with desire.

She strips me of my strength, leaving me completely vulnerable. There's so much to admire about her, but in this moment it's her taking control. Never in my life have I let a woman dominate me the way Sloane is. It makes me feel defenseless, but there's beauty in that.

She latches onto every word I give her, making me want to recite a fucking novel of words for her to cling onto.

I want more of her.

My hands trail up her back. The smooth skin rises with goose bumps at the slightest touch of my fingertips. Even though she is in charge, I know I get under her skin just as much as she gets under mine.

She's able to break the endless pattern my mind runs on.

The windows are fogged, and orange streetlight floods the car, giving Sloane a soft glow. Everything about her is angelic. I gather her hair and pull her head back, kissing her neck.

She moans my name and rides me to my limit. Her hips thrust in a steady rhythm, edging herself close to her breaking point. I grab onto her ass and hold her tight against my body when I feel her throbbing against me. She puts her hands on top of mine and her breathing quickens.

I spill inside her, throwing my head back against the back of the seat. *"Ya nikogda ne smogu ustat ot tebya." I can never get tired of you.*

Her hair drops over her shoulders, and she presses her forehead against mine. Her skin is flushed and her breathing unsteady. "What is it about you?" she asks with a voice so careful it almost sounds worried.

My eyes search her for the meaning behind her words, but she doesn't expand on the thought. I lift her chin with the tip of my finger and give her a pained smile. "I wish I knew, *Kroshka*," I tell her in a soft voice.

Chapter 26

Sloane

Things with Mikhail keep progressing.

I'm in way over my head and I have no idea how I'm meant to save myself from the mess I've created. What Mikhail and I have is flawed, but it's perfect in its own way. I watch it all pass by me with regret in the back of my mind because I know I hold the detonator to the bomb that'll destroy him.

It's a constant game of push and pull—that's what makes this harder and easier at the same time. Everything contradicts everything at this point. It's moments like last night that make me believe things could look up—but what are the odds of that happening?

Slim to none.

Mikhail left early this morning and hasn't come back since. Once he feels something, he avoids me. It doesn't feel great.

Many of the reservations I feel toward him wash away when I remember how he was with his family. I've never seen him look so happy; so overwhelmed with joy. I could see his eyes glimmer when he looked at Alyna.

He didn't hold back; he allowed his emotions to consume him without regret. His dimples showed again ... That smile that could ruin me was shown over and over again. Every time I close my eyes I see him. He almost looked at peace.

If family is what makes him happy, why doesn't he keep them close?

Speaking with Anya felt like a fever dream. She reiterated everything to me, but it still felt unreal to know I'm not alone in this plan.

While it might not be happening the way it was supposed to, I have to make it work. Everything Anya told me last night made sense, but it doesn't make me like my situation any more.

A musical chime echoes through the entire house, and I open the door quickly.

A middle-aged man looks down at me with wide eyes. "Uh ... are you Sloane?"

I'm hesitant to tell him who I am because I have no idea what Mikhail's up to. "Yes," I say, choosing to answer anyway because curiosity always gets the better of me.

He hands me a bouquet of red roses and a box. "These are for you."

I take the roses and hold them in my arm as he hands me the box. I look at the man. "Who are these from?" I ask.

"There's a note attached. I'm just a delivery boy."

I can't help but laugh. He doesn't look like a delivery boy. He's in a suit and tie, just like the rest of Mikhail's men.

I slam the door in his face and turn toward the kitchen. Putting the roses down on the granite counter, I take the ribbon off the matte-black box.

A card sits on top of a white satin dress.

> 324 Parkway, 8 p.m. Wear this and put your hair up.
> Dimitri will drive you.
> —M

I throw the card down on the counter and hold up the dress. Much as I don't want to admit it, it's beautiful.

Draping the dress over my shoulders, I lean my weight into the counter.

It takes me a moment to realize I'm laughing uncontrollably now. I feel crazy in a way. *What the hell is even happening?* This has to be some kind of culture shock. Why am I doing everything a man says and acting at his beck and call?

A couple of hours later, Dimitri arrives to pick me up just like Mikhail said he would at eight on the dot. He opens the passenger door for me, and I get in the car. I glare at him as he closes the door and gets in on the other side.

Dimitri starts the engine and shifts the car into drive. "You look nice, Sloane," he says.

My head turns toward him. "Thank you," I tell him.

"So ... Mikhail told you to ... you know, to wear your hair up." He stumbles on his words, and a small smile forms in the corner of his lips.

I glare at him. "I don't have to do everything he tells me to do."

He shifts in his seat and clears his throat. "I see why he likes you."

"That's what you call it?"

"That's exactly what I call it. I've never seen him act this way before."

I scoff. "You say that as if it's a compliment."

"It should be."

I ignore him. My mind is already mush right now—I don't need to think about this situation any more. The more I think about it, the more confused I get, which doesn't even seem possible.

Eventually, we pull up to the side of the road. A man opens my door instantly, and I step out. Orange lights beam through the black-tinted windows of the skyscraper.

I walk toward the entrance, but I stop in my tracks once my eyes find Mikhail. He stands there in a black suit with a white shirt underneath. He looks so handsome in anything he's wearing, but especially this. I shake my head as I walk up to him. He watches me through his brows as his fingers adjust the cufflinks on his suit jacket.

"Your hair is down," he says.

I cross my arms over my chest and smile at him. His note asked—no, *told*—me to wear my hair up, so I did the opposite. "It is," I say.

"Good," he admits with a smile as his arm reaches around the small of my back. "I knew you'd do the opposite of what I said."

"What—?" I begin, but I'm interrupted by him.

"Let's get a drink."

I walk with him inside and head toward a bar in the corner of the room. There aren't many people in here. Those walking in through the main doors all make their way to the elevator.

Mikhail pulls out a bar stool for me, and I take it reluctantly.

"What am I doing here?" I ask.

He orders a drink before directing his attention back to me. Then he reaches into his suit jacket pocket and pulls out a velvet box. "You're my wife for tonight," he says, grabbing my hand and pulling it toward him.

He attempts to put a ring on my finger. I try to pull away, and he just smiles.

"I am not."

"Tell you what, Sloane, you've got a few more months with me, give or take. Do this for me, and I might let you go for good behavior."

"For *good behavior*?" I mock him. "Why should I believe you'd ever let me go after you threatened me?"

"I can't tell you what to believe, *Koldunya*. It's up to you how you act tonight."

I make a face at him. *Why the fuck is he gaslighting me right now?* I bite down on my cheek to hide my emotion.

"Why are you treating me like this?" I ask.

"Like what? Like how you treat me?" His jaw hardens.

I open my mouth to say something, but nothing comes out. I don't even know how to take that comment.

"Yeah, I thought so," he mutters.

"No, you don't get to do that," I say, my heel digging into the concrete floor. "I haven't done anything to you."

"You left me, Sloane. When I thought I could trust you." He sips on his drink, gripping the glass with force.

I'm at a loss for words. It feels like my brain is stuttering while I look at the man in front of me. How is this the same person? Was his anger delayed for an entire fucking day? I thought he and I sorted this out. Nothing makes sense.

I left his place with the intention of coming back because I *wanted* to. I mean, I didn't want to be trapped, but I wanted a little longer with Mikhail to see what kind of person he truly is. I was gone for only a couple of hours, and now he's acting as if I committed a serious crime.

"If I do this for you, you'll think about letting me go?" I ask before I'm even able to process exactly what I said. The more thought I give it, leaving Mikhail doesn't sound like something I want. I think ... I think I like being with him. Of course, not at times like this, but the good times with Mikhail make me feel as if I'm weightless. There's constant adventure when he's near, and I enjoy both the yacht and the house. If I were to leave him, Dad would keep me locked up.

I love my family, but I need to learn to put myself first.

"I'll think about it," he says.

"Okay, I'll do it," I say, contradicting my thoughts. "But why do I need to act as your wife?"

"I want this investment. Investors like to see commitment." He nods and places the glass on the bar top. "Ready, wife?" he asks, reaching out his hand toward mine.

"You say jump, I say where, right?" I say, annoyed with him.

He presses his lips together. "Something like that." Then he takes my hand and places the ring on my finger.

I look at the ring and try not to overthink everything.

Mikhail's hand rests on my lower back as we make our way to the elevator and ride to the top floor of the skyscraper. He's standing behind me, not letting go of my body. His possessiveness knows no bounds, especially not tonight.

I focus on my breathing, trying to get it under control. I've been nervous about tonight ever since the dress was delivered. I know a lot is riding on how I present myself. If I do a good job at his game, I could leave.

Tonight, I am Sloane Stepanov.

The name sounds beyond foreign to me.

It's taken me a while to understand my frustration. It has nothing to do with being trapped or kidnapped. It's because I felt as if I was finally understanding who Mikhail is, but now I don't know. I started to put my heart somewhere it had no business being. Mikhail is all about his game. His charisma is sky-fucking-high. He knows how to say things, and he knows the perfect times to say them. When things between us start to sink, he finds an escape route. It's admirable, really.

The elevator doors open slowly. I fiddle with the ring on my finger as we head down an open hallway toward a room where music is playing. "Feeling Good" by Michael Bublé trickles out through the surround sound. Mikhail looks down at me and smiles.

I smile back—not because I want to, but because I'm keeping my end of his bargain.

Everything about this building screams money. The artwork on the walls looks as if it came right from a museum. The ceiling looks two stories high. Glancing around, I see too many people to count. They're all dressed in elegant dresses and ironed suits.

We head to the bar in the center of the room. Bottles are stacked on shelves with bright lights behind them. Mikhail's hands rest on my shoulders. He moves my hair to the side and brings his mouth to my ear.

"You look like a goddess."

His deep, angsty voice sends chills down my spine. *It doesn't mean anything. He doesn't mean it. He's just fucking with your head.*

"Gin and Dubbonet, please. My wife will take a glass of champagne."

I could roll my eyes at what he orders for me. I would've loved a Dirty Martini, but I'll take whatever liquid confidence I can get.

"Mikhail?" a feminine voice calls out.

"Emily, it's so good to see you." Mikhail turns as the woman approaches us.

She kisses his cheek, and that pisses me off.

Emily. Slim figure, wearing a dress that looks absolutely amazing on her. She seems *nice*.

"I don't think you've met my wife before—Sloane." He grabs my hand, and I step down from the stool.

"Hi, it's so nice to meet you—Emily, is it?" I reach out my hand, but she doesn't shake it.

"Wife? Mr. Stepanov, you lead a very private life. I had no idea you were married."

I was wrong. She's not nice. She's completely ignoring me.

"A beauty such as hers doesn't deserve to be hidden, Mikhail."

Jesus Christ, I am so bad at reading people. I'm in such a foul mood right now I can only focus on the negatives. That's not who I am. That's Mikhail getting to my head.

"Sloane." She leans in toward me and hugs me quickly "I'm Emily. It's nice to meet you as well. Are you two bidding tonight?"

Mikhail smiles. "Yes. I intend to walk as the highest bidder."

"Good for you. I know you'd do great things for my husband's company."

Holy fuck. Okay, new plan. Act as if I'm not mad at him, or else my attitude will ruin all chances of him getting the investors to work with him. I roll my shoulders back in a weak attempt to relax. "Mikhail has great plans." I smile and grab onto his arm.

"I'm sure he does. We've kept up with the news on his renovations for West 90, and I have to admit, they're genius."

"Thank you, Emily. Your words don't go unnoticed."

"Of course. Do talk with Eric later. He won't shut up about how fine your ideas are, but don't let him talk your ear off!" She laughs as she leans in to kiss Mikhail on the cheek again.

She's so proper. I haven't had such a formal conversation in so long, possibly ever. She struts away, and Mikhail turns toward me, grabbing his drink off the counter. I discard mine because I don't want to be even the slightest bit drunk. If I'm talking to people like this, I need every brain cell I have.

"You did good. Just keep that up for the rest of the night." He brings the glass to his lips and takes a sip while the sides of his fingers brush against my cheek softly. "And don't lose this smile." He lifts my chin up with his thumb and brings his mouth to mine. A kiss that reminds me too much of how I felt before everything went to shit. "I'm going to greet a couple of people—would you like to come?"

I shake my head. "Maybe in a bit. I'm going to explore for a little while."

"Okay." He smiles and walks off.

I sigh as I walk in the opposite direction. Toward the back of the room, windows cover the entire wall. I exchange a couple of smiles as I make my way through the doors that lead to a large balcony. Dark ivy leaves wrap around the oak wood pergola covering the platform. Sleek electric fireplaces in the middle are surrounded by chairs that look like clouds. I walk up to the edge of the balcony and look down. I'm so high up I can barely make out the cars on the roads below. *How do they even make buildings this tall?*

"It's beautiful, isn't it?" a soft, tender voice asks, leaning against the railing like me.

The woman's hair is dark and silky. Her pregnant belly curves out of her figure-fitting dress.

"It's kind of terrifying." I laugh.

"Right? It's so far down. Sometimes I wonder how they even build things like this."

"I was just thinking the same thing!"

"I'm Nina." She extends her arm to offer me her hand.

I grab onto it and shake it gently. "Sloane."

Her face drops. "Sloane?"

Have I met her before? Does she know my father?

She clears her throat. "I'm sorry, that's a really beautiful name. How do you spell it?"

I spell my name for her, and her face lights up.

"I hope you don't think this is weird, but I'm going to write that down in my phone so I don't forget it."

I furrow my brow.

"I'm having a girl, sorry. Oh my gosh, I'm being so invasive right now, aren't I?"

I laugh. "No, no, you're fine. I'm glad you like the name." I don't mean to watch her so intently, but I can't help but notice she's texting it to someone instead of writing in the notes app. I guess she's probably telling her husband about the name.

"So ... are you bidding tonight, or are you just here to support?"

"My husband is bidding—I just came along with him."

"Oh, mine is bidding as well. Who's your husband?"

"Mikhail."

"Mikhail Stepanov?"

"Yes."

"Oh, wow. I didn't think he'd be here tonight."

"You know him?"

"Only by reputation," she says, taking her eyes off me. "His name has been everywhere."

"He's been expanding quite a bit." I smile.

A tall man walks up behind her and wraps his arms around her belly.

Turning to look up at the man, she smiles brightly. She turns back to me. "This is my husband."

He looks at me in a strange way. It's a look I can't figure out. "Sloane." He smiles. "My name is Ace."

"Ace? Like the card?" I half-smile.

"Exactly like the card."

My stance shifts when I notice an embroidered spade on his shirt. I force my eyes to look away. *The Suits? This is what Max was telling me about.* I don't think he's a good man. Max told me it was a good thing I didn't know the meaning behind the symbols.

Fuck. I should have asked him more questions while I had the chance.

"There you are." Lev grabs onto my wrist, trying to pull me away from Nina and Ace. I didn't know Mikhail's men would be here tonight, but I'm not shocked. They've been by his side the entire time.

I don't fight Lev because I know there's a reason he's pulling me away.

Nina wasn't writing my name down because she liked it; she was texting it to Ace. That's the only thing that makes sense. Lev exchanges death glares with Ace, his jaw tightening as he guides me to the opposite side of the patio.

"Warm up—you look freezing." Lev gestures to the couch.

I take a seat and warm my hands by the fire. It's cold at the top of this building. The wind is strong. "When I was younger, I used to toast marshmallows, but I always burned them."

He nods with a chuckle. "You're deflecting. What's wrong?"

Wow. I really do wear my heart on my sleeve.

"Who was that man?" I ask.

He takes a seat next to me. "That's the man who plans on walking away with the investors. Mikhail's competition."

I'm talking to people who are all sorts of wrong tonight. "That makes sense," I admit.

"What do you mean?"

"He was just looking at me funny. And then when I introduced myself to his wife, she got really weird when she heard my name. Do you think she would have tried to trap me into giving her information about Mikhail?"

"I'm not sure. Maybe. They both need this property."

"But Mikhail will get it, right? He has more money than Ace."

"Ace?"

"Yeah." I ponder. "That man?"

"He told you his name is Ace?" Lev's eyebrows pinch together, creating creases on his forehead.

"Yeah?"

He shakes his head. "It doesn't only come down to who has more money. It's about trust. It's about who will run the franchise more effectively."

Thank God I didn't drink. It would have only made this night more intense.

Chapter 27

Mikhail

I tell Eric all the plans I have for his business, and he couldn't be more pleased. Which is as I hoped. After all, Eric is the most important person to convince. Kevin and Jared are easily influenced by their brother's decisions, so this'll work out in my favor.

As I'm walking over to them, Adrian walks up to me, cutting me off. "Giovanni is here," he says quickly. "He spoke with Sloane. He knows who she is."

Well, shit.

I knew he'd be here tonight, but I didn't think he'd get to her this quickly. I wanted to be present when he saw her. I wanted to be able to see his eyes widen and his jaw drop as if it were playing out in slow motion. To see who his sister is and come to the realization he will never have the privilege of knowing her.

He'll never know how spirited she can be when she talks back. How much her words can mean to a person or even how her smile can make you feel like you've accomplished an impossible task.

I think about how their encounter must have gone. Sloane isn't stupid—

she's heard the name from Max before. But Giovanni wouldn't out himself to her off the bat. He wants to go about this the right way, just like I did.

Sloane didn't just fall right into my arms; I had Lev working with Sloane's father to get a better idea of the situation. Once he left her house, he told me where her brother would be taking her. While she was still asleep, I had Lev go back and get her clothes. Her father bombarded him with questions, but he knew not to take it too far—no matter how much he loves his daughter.

Seeing her in person for the first time felt like a breath of fresh air.

I could see the fear in her eyes, but that fear doesn't exist anymore. She looks more ... captivated now.

"She knows his name and didn't question anything?" I ask.

"Lev texted me. He told her his name was Ace."

"Ace?" I laugh. Of course he'd use that as his alias. He doesn't know if her father's told her about him yet.

"She's with Lev now," he tells me.

My eyes gaze across the room trying to find Giovanni, but instead I see Sloane talking with Kevin and Jared. "No, she's not."

She's making them laugh. Kevin even places a hand on his face to cover his burst of laughter. They seem to be swooning, which is good. This may even be the best part of the plan. She's a miracle worker.

"Um ..." Adrian pauses, and so do I, as Kevin reaches down to place his hand across Sloane's stomach. "You didn't ...?"

"I—no, she would have told me."

She would have told me if she were carrying my child. If she had a brain, *any* brain at all, she wouldn't keep something like that from me.

"Then she's a fucking genius," Adrian grits out. "She's making sure Giovanni has nothing above you."

The world around me moves in slow motion. The Valentino brothers are family men. Family means everything to them. I assume she found that out without me even needing to tell her.

"She is something else," I admit, gulping down a bitter taste of disappointment that I don't care to acknowledge. "I'm going over there." I brush past him and many other people as I approach Sloane.

"It's very early, so there isn't much to feel yet," she snickers, and I want to crumble under the weight of my panic.

"Well, if it isn't the man himself." Jared pulls me in and pats my back. "Congratulations, brother."

Brother. A term they don't use lightly.

"Thanks, man. It's a great feeling, it truly is."

"Hi, my love," Sloane says, standing on her tiptoes to reach my cheek. "Play along," she whispers softly in my ear.

There's a lump in my throat when I hear it was just a plan to deceive the people standing in front of me. *This is what I wanted. Why am I feeling upset right now?*

I've never wanted kids, but it feels like Sloane is taking away something I could have. A future where I'm not all alone. Someone to come home to and hold. The sound of pure joy from the ones who surround me. It's as if Sloane could show me the light at the end of the tunnel, but she'd never stick by my side. I've hurt her too much.

Or maybe she could forgive me.

I've never wanted anyone else by my side since Kirill died, but *damn* does it feel so fucking good to have Sloane by my side.

"Mikhail, you're creating one hell of a name for yourself," Kevin chimes in.

I roll up the sleeves of my shirt. "It's been a long time coming, but it's worth it. The assets have proven to be worth it as well," I explain.

"Eric told us before we got here what you've done. You turned a two-million-dollar revenue into eighty-five. I've never seen that done before, especially with a building like this."

He's talking about the club. I don't do much with it besides tell other people how to run it while I'm not here.

"It's the location. Many in the city thrive at night."

"It's not just the location—don't sell yourself short. You've turned it into something I've only seen in Vegas. It's a good thing a place such as yours is out there."

I smile. "Vegas was my inspiration. I made some pretty great memories there a couple years ago."

"Mikhail, could you turn this building into something like Sky Lounge?"

I run my hands through my hair as I think through my answer. Is it possible? "Those weren't the plans I had for this, but I could work with the idea. You'd have to tear out a lot of the walls. Apartments could be made from the office floors above as well. Rent those out for extra profit."

"See?" Kevin downs his glass. "This is exactly what I'm looking for. I'm tired of having this building empty. I want to do something risky with it. You've got to lose something to gain something, am I right?"

"Sounds like music to my ears." I nod.

"As for the cut, we'd like thirty percent of the club's income."

"Twenty," I bite back as Sloane grabs onto my hand tightly. She's trying to tell me to quit, but I won't. It'll take millions to get this place fixed up, and I'm not selling myself short.

"Twenty and we get a floor of apartments for our pesky teenagers. And you don't card them. They're nearly of age—there isn't much of an issue there."

"Liability is an issue, Kevin."

"A risk you'll have to take, just as we're taking a risk with you if we choose to make the deal."

"That's fair enough." I press my lips together.

"Good. We'll speak with you soon." Jared smiles as he and Kevin walk off toward Eric.

"Mikhail." Sloane pulls me close. "You didn't tell me you made *that* much money."

"It never came up," I admit. "You want to donate another million to puppies? If so, here." I take out my card and hand it to her. I admire her for going behind my back and doing what she wanted, but all she had to do was ask. Hell, I would have taken her there myself if she would have just told me what she wanted to do.

She puts her hands over mine and pushes the card down. "No. It's dangerous. The government won't just look past that much money."

"Raslabsya." Relax. I cup her face in my hands. "Every single penny I make comes from a reliable source. Well, some."

"What do you mean 'some'?"

"A couple million is washed."

"Okay, well, that ends now. You can't have anything traced back to illegal activity."

"Okay."

She looks up at me as if I might be lying to her, but I'm not. The washed money is child's play compared to what this place will end up making. "You're not going to fight me on it?"

"No." I press my lips to her forehead. "You've done so much for me. I trust you."

My own words send my mind into a spiral. I clear my throat to speak up about my mistakes, but I'm cut off by the sound of Emily's voice coming through the speakers.

"Hi, everyone! I just wanted to thank you all for coming tonight and showing your endless support. To those who donated, your kindness goes such a long way. Two of the highest-paying donors will be speaking up on behalf of 324 Parkway. Mr. Stepanov, everyone!"

Applause fills the room, and I look to Sloane. Her smile is bright for me.

"Go!" She shoves me in the arm, and I bend down to kiss her. I know I shouldn't, and I know she'll think it's part of my act, but it's not, and I can't help myself. I'll only be able to feel the softness of her lips on mine a couple more times before she leaves me to go back to her own life.

I make my way toward the small platform. Emily hands me the microphone, and I grab it.

"Thank you, Emily. There are so many things to be thankful for in this moment, but I owe so much to my wife. She taught me patience is a virtue and with time you'll get what your heart craves. She taught me love can be shown in many ways, and I have no doubt in my mind she'll teach that to our little one on the way. Hell, I hope they get all your qualities." I take in a deep breath.

It's all just a lie.

"My donation will be going to food banks and orphanages. Growing up in a low-income household, I understand the struggles life can throw at you. If my donation serves any purpose, I only hope it will be recognized as a small act of kindness toward many. Thank you all."

I hand the microphone back to Emily, who's wiping tears from her eyes. I flash her a gentle smile as I make my way back to my "wife."

"That was almost too good," Sloane says softly.

"Spoken from the heart." I wink.

"Spoken from lies."

Her words feel like a sharp stab right in the heart. But I can't be upset with her. She's emotionally checked out of whatever this is between us.

"Thank you, Mikhail! Now for Mr. Genovese, everyone!"

Everyone claps for Giovanni just as they did for me. I watch Sloane intently, noticing her eyes widen once she sees Giovanni. It's a look of familiarity.

I bite down on the inside of my cheek while I swallow a comment. I wrap my arm around Sloane and shake my head. I don't know why I'd even think something like that.

He steps up onto the platform and grabs the microphone out of Emily's hands.

"Wow. I won't lie to you all ... that'll be hard to beat," Giovanni begins.

Everyone laughs but me.

"When I was younger, I lost my mother to abuse. She never left because she didn't want to leave me with a man whose heart was tainted. Growing up in Sicily proved difficult. My mother didn't have the resources to help us break free of the many trials and tribulations the man threw at us. So my donation will be going toward shelters. Shelters for women, the homeless, the ill—I could go on. Life deals some real shitty cards, and we must use what we have. I want to help the people who feel they have no way out, as my mother did. But I have to tell you, nothing I do would ever come to life without my wife, Nina. My ideas are just that: ideas. But Nina breathes life to them. She's the reason I do anything. She's taken half my heart, and my child has the other half. Cheers, everyone. And to Mikhail. The bottom of the chain can be *fucking* brutal, but our love for our wives and children makes life worth living. As you implied, loving someone makes you anything but weak."

I bite down on my teeth in frustration. He's using my own words against me. Two years ago, I pointed a gun at his head while he was vulnerable. Thinking back on it, I have no idea how I managed to get out of that alive. His men ambushed mine. I told him I'd show him just how fucking brutal the bottom of the chain can be. That's why I took the clubs. I wanted to prove myself to yet another person who'd doubted me. I called him weak for falling in love. I called his wife his biggest mistake. But I didn't know what it would feel like to protect Sloane. If I knew that back then, I would have kept my words to myself.

Before Sloane, I never understood how Giovanni could risk everything to be with Nina. I still don't think I understand to the full extent I could. Nina's a walking target. Enemies of the Cosa Nostra would take Nina to get to his head.

But maybe that's why it works. He has something to fight for. He has someone to protect.

Falling in love isn't weak. Not admitting it is.

I look down at her. She'd be the most important thing to me, but I can't allow it. Not after what I've spent the past two years doing. The target is on my back, and that's where it needs to stay. If I were to somehow convince Sloane to stay with me, she'd never be safe—especially if I get this property. It's not the Romanos, Genoveses, or the Koziovs I'd have to worry about. They'd come after me, not her, because she's their blood. It's the Clarkes I'm worried about.

The Irish had an alliance with the Bratva and Cosa Nostra for years until word got out that Sloane's father was sleeping with the Capo dei Capi's wife. Sloane's mother betrayed the family. Then my fucking brother had to get involved. He caused all hell to break loose between the three families. The Irish cut ties with the Italians and Russians without looking back. We were deemed unreliable backstabbers. Honor is the one rule men aren't supposed to break.

Unfortunate for me.

They've been living under the radar ever since Kirill killed Sloane's mother. I know they're coming for me because I'm taking over parts of their land too. They don't work in the open like I do. They play with blood, waiting for someone to do the hard work for them.

That's another reason why this bid is dangerous. They'll kill me to take it. It's the easiest way, I'll give them that, not having to play nice with people they hardly know. I kind of admire them for it. They don't fool people just to get on their good side. They keep their eyes on the prize, guns drawn, and they're instantly rewarded.

I look away from Sloane and see Giovanni walking toward me, pulling on his tie. "Go see Lev," I tell her. "I need to talk to *Ace*."

Giovanni creeps in closer, and my heart picks up its pace. She needs to get the fuck out of here. I have no idea what she knows about Giovanni, and I don't need things to change right now.

"Go," I demand.

Her eyes flood with questions. "Kindly adjust that tone of yours," she mutters, her arm knocking into mine as she leaves me with Giovanni.

Giovanni watches his sister walk off in the distance before he comes to a halt in front of me. "Your idea of revenge is different from mine." He lifts his drink as his lips form a small curve.

My head falls back. Everyone around me is pushing every wrong button.

I shift my stance. "Killing her wouldn't serve any purpose. But I will admit, your sister has been a huge help."

"Couldn't have my wife, so you go after my sister? That's quite the obsession you have." He clicks his tongue. "Tell me, how does it feel to live in one person's shadow and then one day the sun breaks through, only for you to fall under another's?"

"I bet you thought of everything to say back to me after our conversation at the church, huh?" I say with a smug smile. "But I couldn't tell you. You took care of the only shadow I know, remember? Or do you need a recap?"

"No, I perfectly remember the way he begged for his life right before I scattered his brains across the wall."

"I'm glad you did." Giovanni killing Kirill was an act of mercy; the drugs would have been more painful. I lean my head slightly to the side. "Thanks to your act of *kindness*, I'm about to own the majority of this city. Towers so tall ... Come to think of it, you'll quite literally be in the shadows."

"Her father won't let you breathe once he finds you. I'd take the opportunity to end you right now, but if I let him, there'll be another alliance for my family. That's something you'll never have."

"Her father responds to me. And I think you're forgetting she's my wife."

"Is she though?" he says coldly. "Careful, Stepanov. The floor you're stomping on is made of thin fucking ice."

Rage boils my blood to see Giovanni stand proudly in front of me after everything he's done to my family. All the pain he's created. He wears confidence on his lips as if it were made only for him, and that pisses me off.

I mean, what the fuck? How would he feel if I took his cousin Carlo away from him? Fucking pussy would be up all night wishing his demons away, but they would cloud his vision. Sorrow would flood his eyes and he'd lie in bed for days on end. But me? I take back, and I refuse to let a man beat me when I'm already down.

Giovanni's threats don't mean shit to me. Half the crap he tells me is nothing compared to what I've heard from my brother. But he's not here to make me stronger anymore.

As I stare into Giovanni's eyes, which lack emotion, I realize that if Kirill worked with him, maybe I wouldn't be in this situation.

I back away from him to search for Sloane, making eye contact with many people until I finally see her. She's talking to Adrian, pulling on his tie. I stare at her, watching the way her body moves. She's trying to flirt with him, but she's failing miserably. I know how her body reacts to me. Her muscles turn to liquid at the slightest touch of my skin. But she's stiff with Adrian. She looks at me and then quickly away. Her head falls to the side, allowing her beautiful curls to flow with the turn of her head.

Adrian's a fool for falling for her words coated in innocence. He's had his eye on her since the very beginning of all this, and I don't blame him. Leaning against the wall, I cross my arms and watch them.

Dimitri walks up and nudges me in the shoulder. "Looks like he finally got her, huh?"

A smile overtakes my lips. "She's not his—it's just his turn."

He looks at me, searching for the meaning behind my words. But when he sees Giovanni, his mouth drops. "Oh," he says.

"Giovanni." He introduces himself, reaching his arm toward Dimitri.

Dimitri leans into me and whispers, "Can I shake his hand? Or would that be wrong?"

I give him a sideways glare.

"Right, okay," he says, leaving Giovanni's hand in the air.

"Mikhail," Giovanni says. "Why don't you meet me at the warehouse tonight? You remember where that is, right?" he challenges me.

The brief memory of him hovering above me with a weapon comes to my mind. I hold back my eye roll and agree to meet him. Giovanni turns around and finds his wife. He whispers something to her, and she turns to look at me with a smile. I smile back, but my smile isn't as genuine as hers.

Looking back at Adrian, I see Sloane is still with him. I watch her press her lips together in frustration. She's beyond pissed at me, but that only makes me hard.

I make my way toward the entrance and pay the valet. Sloane meets me in front of the car.

"Adrian, take her home for me and stay with her."

He nods and gets into the driver's seat, starting the ignition.

Sloane stands in front of me. We're only a few inches apart. It's as if she's trying to have a face-off.

"Get in the car," I say to her.

"What if I don't want to?" She tilts her head higher.

My eyes slowly rise to meet hers. "Well, that's all up to you, isn't it?"

Her chest falls as she shoves past me to get in the car. "You're not coming?" she asks through the open window.

"I'll see you in a couple hours. Try not to miss me too much."

"I don't have to try."

Yeah, right.

I watch the car drive off. I swear to fucking God, if Adrian ends up pulling some shit with Sloane, I'll castrate him myself.

I'm already dealing with Giovanni; I'd like to keep my enemies to a minimum.

Chapter 28

Sloane

"**S**ee you in a couple of hours."

That was complete and utter bullshit. It's been two days since I last saw him.

I walk downstairs to see what Dimitri is up to, only to find a body lying on the couch with blood covering the whole white seat. Rushing closer, I notice it's Mikhail. *Why the hell didn't he tell me he got back? Better yet, why the hell is he lying on the couch covered in blood?*

I flick his forehead hard, hoping he'll wake up, but he doesn't. Panic clouds my mind as I think about the possibility he could be dead.

"Mikhail!" I scream his name and dig my fingers into his shot wound.

He hunches over quickly, reaching to cover the hole in his body. "What the fuck is your problem, Sloane?"

"I was just making sure you were alive. Fuck, Mikhail! Who the hell passes out on their living room couch with a bullet in their body?" I scream at him. I'm *fuming*.

"I dug it out—I'm fine." His voice is different. He doesn't seem as if he cares about anything right now. He stands up from the couch and shakes his head.

"What's wrong?" I ask hesitantly. Was this Giovanni's doing? I was never able to put a face to the name, and now I have, things feel serious.

He shakes his head again and looks at the ground.

I step up to him and lift his head. "Hey, talk to me. Who did this to you?"

"You need to back the fuck up, *Koldunya*."

I'm taken aback by the anger he directs at me. I'm not the one who shot him—he has no reason to be pissed at me. If anything, he should be thanking me for being kind and worrying about him.

"No," I say, taking small steps toward him.

He brushes past me and stalks off to the kitchen.

"What happened to the version of you from a couple days ago? Why can't you just pick one mood?" I ask.

"That would be too easy."

I talk back to him, saying things I'm sure I'll regret, but my anger gets the better of me while he ignores me. Taking the flowers out of the vase I put them in the night I got back, I throw the whole bouquet at him, and Mikhail slowly turns toward me, his smile so bright it irritates me.

"You get it out of your system?" he asks.

I clench my jaw and walk toward him. "Did I get it out of my system!" I practically yell.

"That was my question, yes."

I push his chest, but he doesn't budge—not even an inch. I pound my fists against him until he wraps his fingers around my wrists. "I told you not to fucking leave me!"

"Is this your way of telling me you missed me?" he asks, bringing his lips close to mine.

"No."

"You're a terrible liar."

He steps away from me, taking containers out of a plastic bag on the counter.

"What's this?"

"I got you dinner," he says. "A movie and a board game. What we do tonight is up to you." He hands me a container of Thai food. It smells so good my mouth waters.

"Thank you," I say carefully, feeling the anger I just had wash away.

He nods his head and takes a phone out of his pocket.

"You didn't have to do all this," I tell him.

"I know."

Out of the corner of my eye, I see him walking away. "Where are you going?" I ask.

"I'm going to change."

"No, you need to call someone to stitch you up—you can't just walk around with a hole in your body."

He looks around, obviously trying to come up with something smart to reply with, but instead he sighs and mumbles, "All right." He tilts his head for me to follow him, and I do. We walk near the front door into a smaller bathroom.

Flipping on the light, I watch him lean to the ground and rummage through a bunch of things in a disorganized pile under the sink.

"What are you looking for?" I ask, growing curious.

"Medical kit," he answers. Then, looking back at me, his eyes suggest he's about to make me do something I *really don't* want to do. "You're going to stitch me up."

A white container falls out of the cabinet, and he picks it up. Reaching for my hand, he leads us back into the living room.

"I can't do this," I say while I shake my head and stumble over my feet.

He leans his weight on the arm of the couch and begins to unbutton his shirt. My teeth clench down when I watch him undress.

Now is not the time, Sloane.

Even though he has a gunshot wound, he still looks undefeated. "Just stick me with the sharp end and make sure the string holds my skin together."

I could full-on laugh right now. "This is unbelievably unsanitary. Why can't you just get someone like Knox to help you like you had him help me?"

"Because you needed the best care I could provide for you. This is just a simple fix."

His chest is bare, and blood is everywhere. The shot wound doesn't look bad, but I can see the tears in his skin where he most likely dug a knife into the wound to retrieve the bullet.

"How are you not bleeding out?" I ask, avoiding his sweet comment.

"A lot of it isn't mine. Do you take me for an amateur?"

"No," I admit. "I'm sure you've searched the top one hundred ways to die and you're testing out which one works the best."

"I can't lie to you, I've searched it more than once."

"You sound proud."

"I am." He smirks. "Next on my list is using an icicle as a weapon. No fingerprints to track."

My eyes flutter as I realize I'm sharing a bed with a psychopath. "You're the worst."

"Ah, well, I think you're the best. Now stitch me up, Slo."

I take the needle and thread from his hands and take a deep breath. I swallow, trying to gather myself. Feeling queasy, I ask, "Do you have any rubbing alcohol?"

He points to the table, where I see a bottle of vodka.

"Of course," I say and reach to grab it. Looking at him in anticipation, I bring the mouth of the bottle to my lips and take a couple of gulps before dumping the rest on him. I expect him to jump from the burn, but he lies on the couch perfectly still with a smile painted clearly on his face. Now I come to think of it, I didn't even see him flinch with pain when he got up from the couch—only when I pushed my finger into the hole.

It's strange how accustomed his body has become to pain—which only makes me think about all the terrible wounds he's endured.

Seeing blood makes me nervous. I don't know how he expects me to do this. A part of me wants to wait for the vodka to kick in, but this needs to be done.

"How many times have you been shot?" I ask, trying to distract him, just in case.

"Not my first rodeo."

"That's not what I asked."

I line the needle with his skin and begin to stitch him up as if I know what I'm doing. I've cross-stitched before, but that was with yarn, not on a body.

"This would be the tenth, I think."

I scoff. "You think?"

"That's what it means to be in my line of work. That's like me asking you how many books you've read."

Pulling the string through his skin, I direct my attention to him. "This year I've read a total of one hundred and twenty-six books. Twenty-seven if I count your journal."

"You can count it."

My face burns with heat for some reason. I'm not embarrassed or shy, but I feel happy in this moment. Him, sitting here with me—it's starting to be a comfort I could get used to.

I try to hurry up because I can feel the alcohol threatening to rise in my throat. "You're all done," I tell him a few seconds later while I gather the trash and clean up the mess he made. Once I'm finished, I begin walking up the stairs to call it a night, but his voice stops me.

"Where are you going?" he asks.

"To bed," I tell him. "I just assumed—"

"You do that a lot."

"I do. Is that a problem?" He didn't even let me finish my sentence. He interrupts me all the time, and it's the most frustrating thing.

"Did I say it was?"

"Mikhail, I'm trying my hardest not to fight you right now."

"Try harder." A smug smile tugs at the corner of his lips, and I want to smack it off. He's testing me. The mind games don't stop, and a part of me doesn't care. It's the toxicity I provoke.

My lips press together as I try to contain my comments. It's proving a lot more difficult than I hoped.

"When you get flustered, your nose scrunches. Do you know that?"

I make a face at him. I have no problem with keeping my attitude to a limit, but I didn't think that would give him an open invitation to push my buttons.

"Don't worry, it's cute."

I step down the couple of steps I just took and lean my arms on the back of the couch. "Mikhail."

"Yes, *moya lubimaya*?" *My love.*

Taken aback by his comment, I choose to look past it, because if I don't, I'll lie awake all night thinking about him and what we could be. "Can I ask you something?"

"Ask away," he says, motioning for me to take a seat next to him again.

"Why was the event so important to you?"

He reaches down and takes my legs in his lap. "I already told you. That property would change my career."

"Why just that one?" I ask as my fingers lift to his chest and trace the outlines of his tattoos. I stop the second I realize what I'm doing and take back my hand. He looks at me as if he wants to laugh, and that doesn't help my situation.

Mikhail clears his throat and says, "Because it'll connect my section of the city."

I nod slowly. "Why are you so greedy for so much property?"

"It's not that I'm greedy. I'm taking back what's mine."

"It's not yours, though, is it?"

His eyes darken, and he looks away from me. "It was my father's, and that means it's mine now. He wanted me to take back his section of the city, and that's exactly what I'm doing. Before he passed, he wrote down a list of properties he wanted me to take. I ran into a problem when I found out Giovanni wants the same one." He lays his head back and lets out a breath.

"What else did Pavel give you?" I ask.

His head turns to mine, though he doesn't give me a welcoming look. His fingers clench by his sides and the muscles in his jaw tick. "What else did ... *who* give me, Sloane?"

My mouth drops slightly when I suddenly realize what I've said. I just came clean without having to tell him a single thing.

I lay my hands down on the couch and begin to step away from him slowly. There's anger in his eyes like I've never seen before.

My breathing picks up to an uncontrollable speed as I panic. My mind overloads with feelings of regret. I try to swallow, but there's a lump in my throat.

He stands up from the couch, messing with his cufflinks. "Tell me what you know," he demands as I continue to back away from him.

Do not fear him; challenge him.

It's easier said than done when the man in front of you looks at you as if you are disposable. No matter how hard I try, I will always be beneath Mikhail. He carries the kind of power that isn't known to many, and I'm at his full disposal.

His eyes are dark, lacking the glimmer I once saw. Whatever it was that he felt for me vanished into oblivion the moment I uttered his father's name. The name I've had to swallow down hundreds of times since I've been near Mikhail.

My hands reach into my pocket until I find the pocketknife. I grab onto it, ready to defend myself at any given moment.

He watches my hands, already aware of what I'm doing. He laughs darkly and rolls his tongue over his bottom lip. Nodding, he takes a gun out of the waistband of his pants. Every limb on my body trembles with panic.

"You're scared," he says in a tone that almost sounds condescending. "I'd be more concerned if you weren't."

It's as if he blinked and just shut off all his emotions. His words are coated with anger, resentment … even betrayal.

I try to listen to my intuition, begging myself to give me an idea of what I should do, but nothing comes to mind when he walks toward me, reloading the chamber. "Please," I beg. My lip quivers and my legs threaten to give out on me. Tears spring into my eyes when I accept my defeat. At this point, I deserve it.

Mikhail felt like he could finally trust me—give himself to me—and I betrayed him.

He continues to stalk toward me, every emotion clear on his face. "I could fucking applaud you for the performance you've given."

When he lifts his gun at me, I slam my eyes shut.

"Sloane," my dad calls, and I follow the sound of his voice.

I grab onto the railing at the end of the staircase and swing my weight around it. Standing by the front door, my father holds his hands in front of his body while another man steps inside. I look up at both of the men, suddenly nervous to ask why Dad is letting me see someone who isn't a part of this family.

He has a difficult time even letting me go outside because he's nervous someone will see me.

"What's going on?" I ask hesitantly.

Dad doesn't say much—or anything for that matter. The stranger looks at me with a kind smile. It kind of contradicts the intimidating look he has. Even for an older man, I can tell many fear him. His body looks weak, but he still carries strength.

"Koldunya," he calls. Witch. *"That is what they call you."*

I nod. I'm aware of what members of the Bratva view me as.

Dad walks up behind me and places his hands on my shoulder. "This is Pavel," he tells me, and my mouth drops. The man standing in front of me is the boss of the outfit. The palms of my hands begin to sweat, and I suddenly grow nervous.

Am I presenting myself correctly? If I had known he'd be here, I would have worn something other than sweatpants, for Christ's sake.

I smile brightly and offer him my hand. He grabs onto me, but he doesn't shake my hand; he just holds it. All my life I've dreaded this moment. A part of me thought I'd never meet him. Another part of me thought he'd never want to meet me. I've caused him trouble just by being born—why would he ever even want to speak a word to me?

Regardless of the fact he is very close with my dad, I still feel like I don't deserve to stand in his presence.

"Why don't we take a seat?" Pavel says on a worn-out breath.

Dad leaves my side and helps him walk over to the couch.

I stand under the archway that separates the living room and foyer of the house. Dark leather couches surround the lit fireplace. Sheer white curtains are draped over the large windows. Outside, the snow falls softly. If it were quiet enough, you'd be able to hear the snow hitting the glass.

I read in this room all the time. It's calming.

"I'd say I have a few weeks left. A month at most," Pavel says while he grabs a glass of water from my dad's hands.

His hands are shaky, pale and veiny. His body is wearing him down, but his spirits are still high. I knew he wasn't doing well. Dad spoke about how cruel the world can be. From the stories Dad's told me about Pavel, the man has a heart of gold. while his work is dark, he never loses sight of what matters the most to him.

The outfit hates my father because of all the trouble he's caused. He fell in love with my mother, who was married to the Capo. If Pavel didn't have a genuine bone in his body, he would have killed my dad.

I let out the air from my lungs and walk over to the couch. "Can I get you anything?" I ask, only hoping to help.

"I came here to ask for your help, Sloane," Pavel says as he coughs into his hands.

Dad looks over at me through his dark brows. It's as if his looks are asking me what Pavel means, and I just shrug my shoulders. Does he expect me to understand what's going on? I've only just met the man.

"What can I do for you?" I ask, hoping he isn't going to propose a marriage to someone in his family. I like staying here. I mean, I want to go out and explore, but I don't want my hand to be forced into a marriage. To be trapped down by a man who couldn't give two shits about who I am as a person.

"I need you to watch over my son," he tells me in one breath. "He's going to break. I can feel it."

"Oh," I start, but I'm interrupted.

"Your brother killed my son, Kirill," Pavel says and waves off any incoming sympathies.

What made Giovanni kill Kirill?

"Mikhail is like a ticking time bomb, and once I'm gone, I feel he will go after Giovanni. Maybe it'll be for payback, or maybe it'll be to kill him—who the fuck knows with him? But when the time comes, I need you to be there for him. In a way that is not obvious. He will kill you before he allows you to help him." Pavel laughs, and the sound comes out cracked—painful almost.

"Why me? I've never even met him," I say.

"You are Koldunya. *You are capable of many things."*

I smile through my questions. Not to be a bitch or anything, but Pavel has no idea who I am, nor if I'm even capable of helping his son with whatever it is that he needs. "I don't know about this," I say.

"Sloane, I need you to challenge him. Beat him down if you must. But you will overpower him—I need you to. He needs to understand he has someone by his side, and I feel you're a perfect match to challenge him. But you cannot fear him."

"You make him sound terrifying," I say.

"He can be." He laughs again. "But you'll see past it."

Dad makes a sound and crosses his arms. "Pavel, I'm not comfortable with having my daughter leave."

A smug smile tugs at Pavel's lips. "Oh, I don't really care what you're comfortable with. I want the Stepanov name to continue, and that won't happen if Mikhail doesn't make an alliance with Giovanni. The Clarkes will be coming for them, and they need to be a team before that happens."

"The Clarkes haven't made their presence known in years. I'm sure they know about Sloane as well, and they still haven't made a move."

Pavel adjusts his suit jacket. "They'll be coming. The property Mikhail will take over is in their part of the city.

"You mean to wed Sloane to Mikhail?" my dad asks.

My mouth drops.

"Not quite," Pavel adds. "I just need Sloane to remind Mikhail that Giovanni is not the enemy. They will be strong by each other's side. Giovanni will be willing to hear him out because of Sloane. She is the glue of this fucking family."

"So, when am I supposed to go to him? How do I even go about this situation?"

"I've listed your information in an envelope for Mikhail. You'll work for him. I hope he opens the letter, otherwise you're all going down with me."

He tries to make light of the situation, and I admire him for it. How can such a powerful man have a gleaming personality?

My eyes fall, and I bite down on the inside of my cheek. "What happens if I can't convince him Giovanni isn't an enemy? I've never even met my brother."

"You can. But you need to make him believe it is his idea, otherwise he'll see

right through you. Mikhail is smart; he is calculated. That is why I want you to push him. Once his walls are down, you'll see who he truly is."

Mikhail's hand wraps around my throat tightly while I sob an ocean's worth of tears. My hands wrap around his wrists, and I feel the water rolling down my cheeks effortlessly.

"*Pozhalusta...* Misha, *eto ya*," I whimper. *Please ... Mikhail, it's me.*

He's caught off-guard by the language—just another indicator I've fooled him. "*Ty mne nikto*," he seethes. *You are nobody to me.*

His words hurt me more than any weapon ever could. I drown under his hurt.

"Tell me what you fucking know."

I shake my head as fast as I can. I can't tell him. Pavel wanted him to think it was his idea, and if I come clean, he'll never side with Giovanni.

Mikhail brings the eye of the gun to my temple. I struggle to breathe through the sobs that crawl their way out of my throat. My entire face is drenched, and I can hardly see Mikhail through the water in my eyes. I never wanted to hurt him.

"Stop it," I whimper with a shaky voice.

He brings his lips close to mine, but his face remains clear of any emotion. The sound of the gun clicking against my skull makes my entire body freeze up.

"I—" I choke back.

He just tried to shoot me.

"Tell me," he demands again.

My heart pounds inside my chest, and I place my hand on his neck. I acknowledge the pain I've caused him, but I wish he would still see me. I've been by his side the entire time. I've been here to help him, to guide him. I've been here to love him.

The gun lifts from my skull, and he places it against his. "Tell me what I need to know, Sloane."

My chest tightens as I stop breathing. "Mikhail!" I scream at him. I'd let him kill me before he found out, but now the gun is pointing at him, I can't help the words that will follow.

He stares at me, the veins in his neck sticking out when his head falls back slightly.

"Your father," I sob. "He wanted me to help you."

"Help me with what?" he demands. There is nothing familiar about the man I've come to know. The person standing in front of me is unrecognizable.

"He wanted me to help you and Giovanni team together. To protect you both from the Clarkes," I explain to him. There is so much more to say, yet I can't seem to find the best way to describe any of this situation. Weeks went by quickly with Mikhail, and I got comfortable.

What Pavel wanted me to do wasn't even my main thought or priority. I wanted to get to know Mikhail more. I found myself enjoying his company.

I take a step toward him, and he doesn't step away. Carefully, I stand on my toes and grab the gun from his hand.

Just as I go to empty the chamber, I see there are no bullets inside. My mouth drops, and I look up at him.

He tricked me.

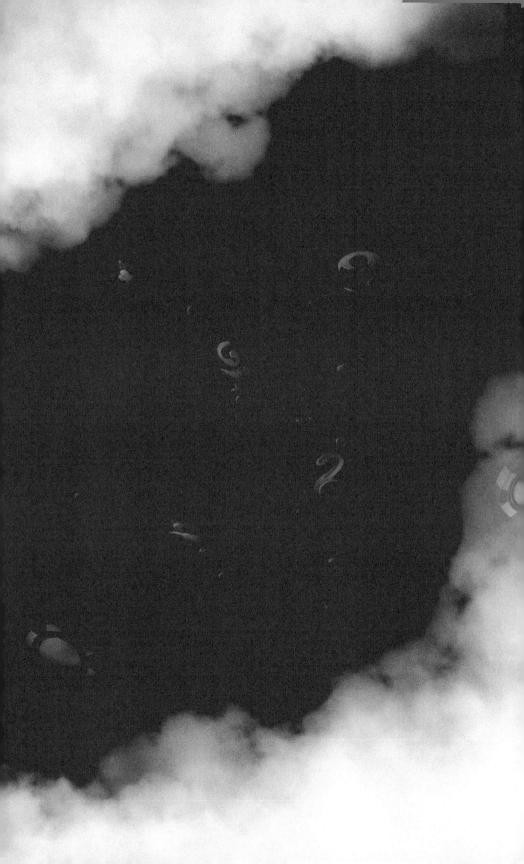

Chapter 29

Mikhail

I t's romantic homicide.

I once thought trust came before love, but now that both have been taken from me, I realize they happen at the same moment. Love is given within trust. It's not immediate, but there's no need for explanations. I didn't need to declare my trust in Sloane—I just gave it to her. I started to see something with her.

I could see her by my side. She was loyal even when she was aggressive. But loyalty always has strings attached.

She trembles under her fear. I once thought she was strong, even when I didn't want to admit it. How quickly the vision I had of her changed is beyond me.

I don't fight it. I should have seen the signs. She deserves a shiny fucking medal for the way she blindsided me. It feels like I've been drinking acid for weeks on end. The pain is hard to swallow, but I have to.

All this time she's been using my weaknesses against me, tearing me down until there was nothing left but bone. She accomplished what I intended to do to her before I was even capable of doing it.

I admire the brains behind her scheming.

From the moment my brother and father passed, I knew no one could ever amount to them. I'm all alone in this world, and it's on me for thinking things could be different.

"There are many things in life I wish I could forget, Sloane. But I've got to tell you ... " I pause and choke back my anger. "Meeting you is the only one I can think of."

Her face turns pink from the tears that stream down her face. I've never heard someone cry like this before.

"You met my sister. You met my niece. I let you in ..." I say, defeated. "You," I say with a laugh. "You did all this for Giovanni?"

She looks into my eyes, trying to find an emotion in mine to cling onto.

Lev was right from the beginning. It was fucking stupid of me to think I would have Sloane by my side. Of course, she'd do anything to protect Giovanni—just like everyone else on this fucking planet would.

"You're just like the rest of them," I tell her.

She walks up to me, placing her hands flat against my chest. Her lashes clump together, and she looks up at me with those doe eyes of hers.

I feel ashamed. The woman who grabs onto my shirt begs for my mercy. It's a strange concept to wrap my mind around. I think I might have loved her ... I would still do anything for her, but at the same time I can't even stand to look at her.

She betrayed me.

She went behind my back and played me like a fucking puppet on strings.

It was my father's doing, apparently. He wanted her by my side for some reason, but he would have told me. He would have told me what his fucking plan was.

Her head falls on my chest. A pained sound falls from her lips, but she knows not to say another word.

She took away my love for her. All because of Giovanni.

"Since you seem to care about him so much, you can cry at his funeral."

Looking back at me, her mouth parts slightly, and she shakes her head.

I take in a deep breath and grab onto her wrist. I lead her to the stairs, and she holds onto the railing with a strong arm.

"Mikhail, you need to listen to me," she says with a broken voice.

When I lift her off the ground, her hands lose their grip on the railing, and I bring her upstairs.

"Your father was thinking of the Clarkes," she tells me.

At this point, I don't give a fuck what my father had planned. There is nothing but anger running through my mind.

Giovanni took absolutely everything from me. Even Sloane.

I throw her to the ground and stare at her. "I didn't ask for much. I just wanted you," I tell her, and I turn my back. "I hope he was worth it."

Closing the door behind me, not taking a last look at her, I lock it.

I walk down the hall and hear her fists banging against the door. As I step down the stairs, Lev looks up at me and nods.

"You were right," I tell him.

He shrugs. "No, I wasn't. It was meant to happen this way."

My eyes slam shut, and I chew on the inside of my lip. "You knew?"

He nods slowly. "I had to follow Pavel's orders before yours, whether he was alive or dead. Her father was in on it too."

Everything hits me at one. It makes sense now. That's why her father asked what Pavel told me before he passed. That's how Lev was able to get her clothes without her father complaining about me taking his daughter. He's protected Sloane for her entire life—I should have known he wouldn't lie low if I took her. Everything was in front of me the entire time.

My anger toward Sloane and Lev are different. I knew Lev was familiar with my father. There was room for understanding, and he would stick by my side through everything. But Sloane? All of this is because she wants to protect Giovanni.

My enemies should be her enemies, but they're not. She doesn't have my back like I have hers.

"Where are you going?" he asks as I open the front door.

"I'm going to make an agreement with the Clarkes, and then I'm going to Giovanni."

Lev follows behind me, almost stepping on my feet. "You're going to kill him?" he asks.

"Yup," I tell him as I unlock the car and jump behind the wheel. "Pavel thought I needed him to keep the Clarkes at bay, but I don't think I do. Giovanni isn't worth any more thought than I'm already giving him.

Lev kicks his feet up on the dash and mutters, "Let's do it."

I step out the car, and he does the same.

I make sure my gun is tucked away in the waistband of my pants before walking inside. I could be stepping into a death trap, but I'll take my chances.

A young woman with bright purple hair sits at the reception desk, and her eyes widen when she sees me walk in. I shoot her a smile in the hope she won't ask any questions. The marble floor wraps around a corner, where I find four men. Exactly who I wanted to see.

"If it isn't the most well-known man in New York," Liam says, grabbing a cigar off the table in front of him. His hair is flame-red and his face lacks emotion.

"If it isn't the man who lurks in the shadows," I bite back.

He shrugs as a smile pulls on his lips. "It needed to be done. I don't work with liars."

"I'm not the liar. My family's wrongs are not mine," I say and take a moment to realize I said exactly what Sloane said to me once.

"Arseways." He clicks his tongue. "You work in a different way, a better way. I like what you've done, lad."

"Speaking of, I want to offer you something."

"Let's share a drink before you try to convince me of something,"

I force a smile. "Sure." I grab two shot glasses from the table and pour a scotch.

Lev picks up a glass for himself.

"Nervous" isn't the most accurate term to describe how I'm feeling. "Confident" might be better. I like the way this is going, but that could also be a scary thing. The Clarkes are unpredictable. Contracts don't mean shit to them considering my side of the family and the Genoveses ruined one before. They probably feel they have the right to break another. Which is a valid point, but that doesn't mean I like it.

I hold up my glass and knock it against his.

"Cheers," he says, downing the entire thing as I do the same. "I'm going to assume this is about Sloane."

I nearly cough up my drink. I feel it burning in my throat. I only guessed he knew about her, but I wasn't sure. In fact, I was hoping I was only assuming the worst, but now ... hearing her name come from his mouth just confirms my suspicions.

"Yes," I admit. "I want to offer you a large sum of my profits."

"Ah, the 324 Parkway property."

I knew he's been watching us. "Right. I believe the Valentino brothers want me to work with them. They liked my ideas."

"And why do you think I want any kind of profit you make?"

"Come on," I mutter. "We both know you'd take it with or without my help."

He laughs. "How is it you know me so well but don't know me at all?"

"I know enough," I demand.

I know for a fact he'll come for Sloane—she connects all the families. They feel she's a threat, and she is. I can only hope this will push off his attack.

"What percentage would we get?"

"Twenty."

"I want more."

"Twenty-five. I won't go higher," I lie. I'd give the entire profit if it meant he'd stick to his word, but I know he won't.

Why am I still willing to do all this for Sloane?

"Done."

"You put a hand on Sloane, the deal is off," I say despite my thoughts.

"I understand that."

I nod. "I'll have the information delivered to you soon. Thank you for meeting with me." I stand up from the chair and straighten my suit.

"Mikhail." Liam catches my attention. "I can't promise my men won't go after her. Just know that."

"As I've said, you put a hand on her then the deal is off. I think it'd be in your best interests to control your men." Without giving him a chance to say another word, I leave the building.

When I get back into the small car, Lev offers to drive. "Where to now?" he asks.

"They've got a ball tonight. I say we go."

Because after escaping one death trap, of course I'm about to walk right into another ...

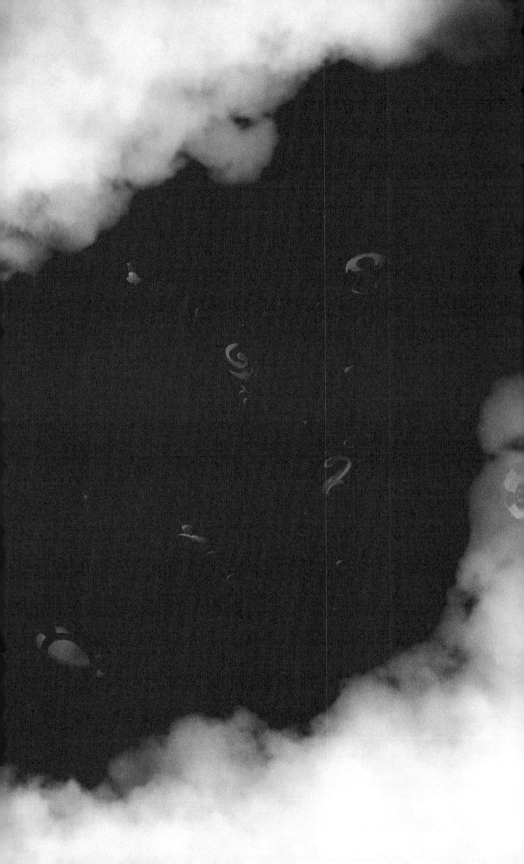

Chapter 30

Sloane

The house creaks through its silence.

I fall to the ground with defeat and rub my swollen eyes.

I couldn't manage to accomplish the one thing Pavel asked me to do. He wanted me to help Mikhail, and instead I ruined him. I betrayed his hard-earned trust, and he won't forgive that.

Did I betray him?

Mikhail respected his father to an undying level; he should be able to understand my reasoning, but he doesn't. His hate toward me blindsides the reality of this situation. Mikhail wanted someone by his side, and I was there. I have been here the entire fucking time.

I didn't mean for emotion to play a role in any of this, but nothing about this is going according to plan.

My head turns when I see the lights of a car shine through my window. I race over and see Max getting into his car. He's not wearing his regular outfit—he's in a suit and tie.

I push open the window and scream his name, but he doesn't hear me.

"Max!" I scream.

Again, nothing.

Peering my head out the window I look at the drop. "Fuck," I mutter as I lift my legs over the edge.

The brick exterior of the house digs into the palms of my hands. My legs dangle over the edge before I take in a deep breath, letting go of the ledge.

I tumble onto the grass and race to the street. My hands hit the car, and I see blood on the window. Max stops and gets out quickly, holding a gun to me.

"Stop," I shout. "Fuck, why do all of you want to kill me?"

Looking down at my hands, I notice cuts that are deep. My adrenaline is at a high, so I didn't even notice the pain before I saw the marks.

"Yeah, I wouldn't mind shooting you. I fucking told you to come to me when you needed insulin, and you didn't," Max says, lowering his gun.

I stare at him. "Are you kidding me? That's the least of our concerns." Out of breath, I say, "I need to find Giovanni and Mikhail."

His eyes widen, and I wave him off as I walk to the other side of the car. He gets in and tells me to buckle my seat belt. "How do you know Giovanni?" he asks.

"I've only heard of his name before the fundraiser," I begin.

For the entire ride, I tell him everything that Pavel told me to do, and how I've failed.

"I don't know what to do."

He pulls the car into a large parking lot flooded with people wearing elegant dresses and masks on their faces. Digging through the center console, he pulls out two masks. "We're going to go find him. Giovanni will be here tonight, and my guess is that he will be too."

I grab the mask from his hands. "Why do you have a spare?" I ask.

"I was going to pick up my friend, Maddy, but she'll just have to miss out. You're more important."

Hiding my smile, I look down at my clothes. "I can't go in like this," I admit.

He brings his hand to the back of the seat and pulls up a dress on a hanger. "This was for Maddy, but you two are roughly the same size. She's taller than you, so you'll have to hold up the dress. There should be heels in the back too."

I nod, thankful he even has something for me to wear. "Thank you," I tell him, and I scoot into the back seat of his car. Before changing, I push up the rearview mirror and get an eye roll in return. "What? You're not getting a free show."

"I'm the last man you have to worry about. My eyes are meant for only one woman."

"Who?" I ask quickly. "Maddy?"

He laughs. "Nah, but it doesn't matter," he says, dismissing me.

I shrug my shoulders and change as fast as I can.

Looking out through the window, I see many people walking up a long staircase. There are small lights lining the bottom of each step. Potted trees stand either side of the steps with decorations on the branches.

Opening the door, Max offers me his arm, and I take it.

Turning around, my heels dig into the sidewalk, and I stabilize myself. "Sway" by Michael Bublé plays through the speakers. I grab onto the stone railing and step up the stairs, exchanging smiles with many others as I walk through the doors into the building. Blue lights fill the room. They shine through the white curtains.

I have no idea what tonight will bring, but that's what excites me.

"Miss?" A stranger stops me. "You forgot your card."

I take it from him. "Thank you."

Max grabs one too, and I follow by his side. My stride slows as I notice the intricate detail in the room. The outside looked like an old museum, but the inside looks like a castle. Small designs are chiseled into the ceiling. The drapes cover most of it, but it's stunning.

"What's the plan?" I whisper to Max.

"Well, I'm going to eat," he says with a grin. He grabs a plate of fruit from the table next to the bar. I hate how he isn't taking this seriously. Giovanni is married to his sister—he should care more, right? If he doesn't, Mikhail is still involved, and I know he cares for him.

I stare at the table of food. It's strange how fruit reminds me of Mikhail.

I never thought I'd associate something as simple as fruit with a person, but I can't help but think about all the breakfasts we shared together. "Now we wait. I think Mikhail will play the game tonight."

I make a face and step in front of him. "What game?"

"The murder mystery. I guess we'll see if he makes the game realistic or not."

I hit him in the arm. "Max, this isn't a game!"

"Everything is a game."

After nearly half an hour, more people show up. It's going to be one hell of a night if there are this many people playing the game.

A man with a mask covering half his face comes over to me and hands me a flute of champagne. I take it from him and lift it up as a thank-you, taking small sips as the music fades and someone clears their throat in the mic.

"Hello, everyone!"

It sounds like Giovanni. He's wearing a mask too. That means Mikhail hasn't gotten to him just yet. He should be here.

I scan the room, but everyone looks the same.

"I know I'm not the person who normally speaks up about the rules of the game, but tonight is to celebrate my wife, Nina, and me. We're going to carry on the tradition as we found our love through a night like this. The beauty of love is much deeper than one's appearance. It's who the person is at their core that we fall in love with." He takes a moment to glance around the room. "We have two murderers tonight, and it's our job to catch them before they kill other people. Please take a moment to open your envelopes."

I take the card out and rip the top of it open.

I'm innocent.

Thank God.

"Be careful out there. As Nina's father would say, 'Be wary, watch your back, learn who to trust.'"

Laughter fills the room.

"To Nina!"

Everyone lifts their glasses in the air in a toast. I do the same.

Max smiles and leans into me. "I'll tell you what I am if you tell me what you are." He squints his eyes at me.

"Max, please. This is serious."

"Sloane, he's not going to kill Giovanni. That would declare war. Mikhail's not stupid."

"We need to find him."

"We will. Once you tell me what you are."

I roll my eyes and hold my card out to him, and he does the same. We're both innocent.

He sighs with relief. "Oh, good."

"Ready?" I ask him.

"Wait—I want to get a drink first."

I nod in frustration. "Would you relax, Doll? If you don't want to out yourself, you need to make it look like you're here for the game."

"But I'm not. I'm here for Mikhail."

"And as soon as he sees you, he could act out. What do you even plan on saying to him anyway?"

I shrug. "I don't know. Just explain the situation more, I guess."

"Why don't you tell him what you want rather than what Pavel would want you to?"

I hadn't even realized that. I feel as if I failed Pavel. Explaining myself was my way of making amends for fucking up the situation. But Pavel isn't here. Mikhail is—and I want Mikhail to understand me.

We reach the bar and look at the menu. "They must like Moscow mules—that's like the only thing on the menu," I say.

"That's Nina's favorite for this kind of game," the bartender tells us. He's about my height with short blond hair.

"Why is that?" I ask.

"She says it masks the alcohol taste, and it makes it more fun when people don't know how drunk they're getting," Max adds.

That's funny. I never thought of it like that. I'm beginning to think Nina and I will get along better than I thought we would.

"We'll take two of whatever flavor—surprise us," Max says.

"How many times have you come to this event?"

He leans his weight on the bar top and turns his head toward me. "Many times. When Nina and I were young, we would tear apart the dessert table."

"And now it's the bar."

"Well, not for her. She and Mira can enjoy the dessert table this year."

I laugh as we tap our copper glasses together and drink the entire thing. "Nina would be proud," he tells the bartender.

He grins as he mixes more drinks.

I put the empty cup down on the bar and look at Max. "You ready now?"

"Ready as I'll ever be."

We run out of the room, my dress weighing me down. I take my heels off as I race up the marble stairs. Looking around, I see the walls are covered in art. I feel as if I'm in Europe right now. The style of this building is insane.

"Come on!" I shout to Max as he takes his sweet time walking up the stairs. I rush back down to him and grab onto his hand, pulling his arm to get him to walk faster. Am I delusional for thinking Mikhail is capable of killing Giovanni? Max doesn't seem to be worried at all.

When he meets me at the top, we look around the corner to see if anyone else is up here. There are a couple of people running out of a room.

"Why don't we—?"

"Shh!" I interrupt. I duck behind the wall quickly when I see a man with red in his hand step out of the room.

Max stands on the opposite side of the wall, the archway separating us.

"Do you still see him?" I whisper.

He nods his head slowly as he backs up more.

We should go back downstairs, but I don't want to. This feeling is incredible. I can understand why they made this a tradition.

"Shit. He's coming," he tells me as he runs across the opening quickly. I begin to laugh, but he covers my mouth with his hand. "You have to be quiet."

I hold my breath when I see the back of the man walking toward the stairs. If he were to turn around, we'd be screwed.

He stops and turns slowly. We lock eyes, and he smiles wide.

"Okay, okay, go!" Max says with enthusiasm.

I rush back to the stairs and run for it without looking back. Once I'm in the main room, I stop and look around me.

"Where to now?" I ask, but I get nothing in return. "Max?" I ask and turn around.

He's gone.

Chapter 31

Sloane

I run past so many empty halls I lose count of how many closed doors I've seen. They could be anywhere.

A group of women rush past me giggling under their breath. They have no idea what's happening tonight. They're enjoying their night without having anxiety gnaw at their insides.

I'm the one who caused all this. I should have told him the truth from the beginning. I should have asked if he knew Pavel meant to put me into his life.

He would have been able to understand everything better if he'd read the fucking letter his father wrote for him.

I understand—I do. If my dad passed away, I'd want to cling to his last words forever. Having an unopened letter means he can always hear something more from him ... but it's ruining everything.

Lifting my dress, I turn to look behind me and see the group of girls rushing past me again. When they move in front of me, I ram into a muscular chest.

"Fuck, Sloane. You need to stick with me next time," Max says as he holds me steady by my elbows.

"Oh, so this is my fault?"

He grabs onto my hand and rushes us down the end of the hallway. The walls are covered in a dark orange wallpaper, and the lights are sporadically placed through the walkway. At the end of the hall is a steel door.

"You stay here," he says, and I pull him back just before he can open the door.

"No," I seethe. "Mikhail needs me right now. You can't tell him what he needs to know. You're not even taking this seriously right now, Max!"

His head falls back. "Both of them mean everything to me, and they hate each other. If you think for a fucking second I'm going to let you walk into the middle of their argument, you're out of your goddamn mind."

"You won't be able to solve their problems."

"And you will?" he challenges me.

I've never felt anger toward Max, but I do right now. It's running its full course through my veins. "Move," I say.

He makes a sound of irritation and opens the door softly. He grabs onto my hand and keeps my body next to his.

Stepping outside, I notice the door leads to a courtyard. Red bricks cover the entire ground and walls surrounding them. The sky is dark, but the two lights clinging to the metal poles light the area enough for me to see a man kneeling on the floor with a gun pressed to his head.

"You had it wrong." Mikhail's voice echoes through the courtyard. "I think you have quite the obsession. First my brother, Adrian, and now Sloane?"

Giovanni's hand clings to his rib cage, and I clench my teeth as panic courses through my mind.

"This is—" Giovanni starts to speak, but Mikhail interrupts him.

"Fitting?" Mikhail asks as he kneels to the floor so he's eye to eye with Giovanni. "Just two years ago I was in your exact same position. Tell me, Giovanni, how does it feel to be taken down by the grit and scum of the chain?"

Another groan slips past Giovanni, and he holds his ribs when he laughs. "It doesn't have to be like this," he says.

Mikhail's dark chuckle floods the air. "You have no fucking idea how much your shit voice pisses me off."

"I did what I had to do. You came after my wife."

"I never even touched her," Mikhail says. "I'm done letting you take everything I care about. Sloane was my last straw."

Max's grip around me loosens when he watches this play out. But he's making a mistake. He doesn't know Mikhail like I do.

He's angry at everything right now; there's no rational thought going through his mind.

"I said a few colorful words that pissed you off," Mikhail says, "and you take everyone I care about? How is that fair?" he asks as he points the gun at Giovanni again.

Giovanni holds his hand up as if it'll shield him from the bullet in the chamber of Mikhail's gun. He gives it no second thought and shows no sign of remorse as he shoots Giovanni in the thigh.

Giovanni's hands go straight to the bullet wound, and he swears under his breath.

At this point, I can't even say I'm shocked. I didn't flinch at the sound of the gun blaring though the air—I just watched it play out.

"I'm going to—" Giovanni starts to say to Mikhail, but he gets interrupted.

"You're not going to do shit. You've shot me three times—"

Mikhail kicks him in the head, and he falls onto his back, a pained groan slipping from his lips. "Mikhail," he says.

"You can't even mask your pain. Is that what special treatment will get you?" Mikhail grits out. "Let me be the first to say that I love watching you choke on your own mistakes."

"Max," I whisper, wanting to get in the middle of them. He ducks down and lifts me onto his knee, wrapping his arms around my stomach. "What are you doing?" I ask.

"Making sure you don't do something stupid. You have to let Mikhail work this out on his own."

My mouth falls when I see something silver rise in Giovanni's hand.

A gun.

Chapter 32

Mikhail

Giovanni crouches to the ground like a pussy, unable to serve for his own actions.

He pleads something, but I ignore him and grab him by the back of his jacket. Giovanni didn't even try to hide, let alone run. What happened to the confidence he had before?

There's a struggle in his arms to hold himself up, and I've hardly wounded him. He shot me last night and I'm still standing. The sound of his gun still echoes in my mind.

Mr. Gray takes a gun out of his waistband and places a bullet in the center of the man's forehead. He gives it no second thought, shows no sign of mercy. He shows no emotion at all.

My heart drops, and I shudder at the loud gunfire. A high-pitched ringing fills my ears and makes everything around me sound muffled. I had no idea they could be so loud.

The man falls to the ground, and I watch the endless stream of blood flow from his skull. I stare at the dead man as if I've seen many bodies drop to the floor. It doesn't shock me as much as I thought it would. Seeing the man fall to the ground isn't what scares me—it's the sound of him choking on his own blood. It gurgles through his closing throat while he fights for his final breath of air.

Mr. Gray walks up to the dead man and mutters something under his breath. He's calm and collected. That should terrify me, but it doesn't. In fact, I admire it. Even at the age of thirteen, I'm not ignorant to the idea the man who hit me deserved to die.

"Never speak empty threats. If you have a purpose, you stay true to it." He looks directly at me.

Looking down at the wound, I notice the stitches are ripped open.

"How's that healing up?" he asks smugly.

"Just fine," I tell him. I step on the fingers of his exposed hand, and he turns his head away from me, but I direct it back to me and take in a deep breath. "Are you going to piss yourself?" I ask him.

He smiles, almost encouraging me to continue. I grow tired of his repetitive actions. I reach for my gun and reload it. Pavel would have done this. I place the eye of the pistol in the center of his mouth, *dying* to press the trigger—how ironic is that?

Out of the corner of my eye, I see him lift something in his other hand. Before I have a moment to react, Sloane runs in front of me, grabbing onto my hand.

Why the fuck is she here? How did she even get out?

Her eyes search mine, but I look away. I can't even look her in the eyes anymore.

"Giovanni, are you fucking kidding me?" Max says, kicking the gun out of his hands. He lifts Giovanni up, holding his weight over his shoulder. He walks him out of the courtyard, and I watch him limp away.

"Mikhail, look at me," Sloane demands. My teeth grind and my jaw tightens. *"Est tolko ti i ya."* There is only you and me.

I turn my head away from her again, but her hands find my cheek, and she brushes her smooth skin against mine. *"Eto moya ochered bit sylnim dlya tebya."* It's my turn to be strong for you.

"Vi nichego ne znayete," I mutter. You know nothing.

This is what I get for trusting someone again. Maybe I just got too comfortable or I missed having that special person. What I felt seemed so unique, something that could forever be mine. I wasn't forced to deal with the feeling of being alone anymore.

Before Sloane, I was fine. I was comfortable with staying by myself no matter how much the thought of being like this forever terrified me deep down.

All I wanted was that one person. The one I could go to no matter what, knowing they'd support me for once.

I would've been a lot further ahead in life if I'd put myself first. If I hadn't worried about what others needed of me. I should have left Sloane alone.

Her thumb presses against my lips, and she brings her face in close to mine. I couldn't pull away from her even if I wanted to. It feels as if my heart is tied to hers.

"*Ya znayu tebya. Prosti menya,*" she whispers. *I know you. Forgive me.*

All my life I've been taught the same lesson over and over again: never trust or rely on anyone. But this is different somehow ... "It's my turn to be strong," she told me. Those are the words I saved for Kirill. I made sure to protect him even when I didn't feel like he deserved me. I gave everything I was to my brother, and I got nothing in return.

"You hurt me," I tell her. "You used my trust like it meant nothing to you."

Her mouth drops. "It meant everything to me. It might not seem like it, but I have been by your side for years, Mikhail. Pavel came to me because he thought you'd need someone like me. If you opened that fucking letter, maybe you'd know."

My eyes fall. The letter. I was saving that. "How do you know about the letter?" I ask.

"Because it's about me. Pavel told me he'd write down my information. I was supposed to work for you—then you kidnapped me and ruined everything."

"*I* ruined everything? You just had to tell me, Sloane!" I yell at her.

"I couldn't! He didn't want me to!"

I rub my forehead in frustration as I try to understand everything. Now I'm pissed at her for two things: betraying me and then not fucking communicating correctly.

"He said I was the glue. That the both of you needed me because the Clarkes are going to come."

I nod slowly. "Because of the property."

Her eyes roam over my body, taking in every look she can get. "You stayed because of Pavel?" I ask.

"No. I stayed because I wanted to be by your side. I wasn't really thinking much about Pavel when I was with you."

"Now ... excuse the fuck out of my French, but why the fuck should I trust you?"

Her head falls back with annoyance. "Mikhail, everything was real. I just had to do what Pavel asked of me. You would've done the same thing!" she shouts.

I've never had someone want to be by my side, and yet Sloane wants to. For years I have denied my heart from feeling anything other than hate, only to find something stronger in Sloane.

Commitment.

She is just like me.

I don't want the sappy shit that a child defines as love, and neither does she. Everyone who thinks love is created by two souls adoring one another unconditionally can go fuck themselves. All love is conditional. It is *my* choice to give myself to another person. This fifty-fifty crap is worth nothing more than roadkill. It should always be one hundred-one hundred. I want to see an effort. I want to see the passion behind her anger. Her anger should be blinding to the point where I only see *her.* At the end of the day, I want her to fall asleep in my arms because she fucking *wants* to—because she chose me too.

She let me shoot Giovanni, but she must've seen his gun. She chose to shield me ... not him.

"Mikhail!" Max's voice calls through the courtyard. "You shot him, so you drive."

Sloane looks at me, the shine in her eyes bright. "*Prosti menya*," she tells me. *I'm sorry.*

My arm wraps around her and I rest my chin on her forehead, soaking up the feeling of having her in my arms. "You are in severe debt, *Kroshka*."

Letting go of her, I follow behind Max. Sloane struggles to keep up with our long strides. Once we make it outside, Max throws me his keys and gets in the back seat with Giovanni.

"All of this shit was pointless, Mikhail," Giovanni grits from the back seat.

"Oh, you'd better be joking," I say with laugh. "I'm real close to shoving a gag in your throat so you shut the fuck up."

He groans but stays silent. *Fucking finally.* I take my time with the drive. I turn down wrong exits just so Giovanni will suffer longer. Max gives me directions as if I don't know who they go to for medical help.

Eventually, we make it to the run-down building, and I shift the car into park. Max opens the car door and helps Giovanni out.

"I can walk by myself," he tells him.

"It didn't seem like that a minute ago," Max says with his smart mouth.

Max stops walking once we reach the steps. He bangs on the door over and over again until a man swings it open.

"Are you kidding me?"

"I wish I were," Giovanni admits.

The man looks behind us to see if anyone followed and then lets the four of us walk inside. His home looks normal until we go into the basement. Here it looks exactly like an operating room in a hospital.

"What's the doc's name?" I ask.

"Jacob, and this is Mikhail," Max says.

"Nice to meet you," I offer him my hand, and he takes it.

"You as well," he says with a smile. "Lay him down," the doc orders. "Giovanni, I don't have anesthesia, so you'll have to go without it."

He lies down on the table and swears under his breath.

"You know," I start, "for the Boss, you're one weak motherfucker."

"Mikhail," Max warns, and I smile.

"You have an exit wound, so whatever it was laced with shouldn't be an issue."

"Fantastic. Now stitch me up," Giovanni orders.

"I said there was an exit wound, not that there aren't any fragments in your organs. I'll have to take a look."

"Get on with it," he tells him.

He brings a white cloth to his face. "You'll need this." He lifts the scalpel to his shoulder and digs through it. He clenches his teeth around the cloth with pressure to stop himself from yelling out in pain.

"I'm going to fucking kill him. I don't know why yet, but it doesn't feel like he's helping me. He's making my pain worse," Giovanni grunts.

Max laughs, and I do too. Sloane watches us as if we're insane, and I don't blame her.

"Giovanni, what blood type are you?"

"Something B."

"Any of you have O negative blood?"

Fuck. The room goes silent. I could laugh my ass off. Knox would have had his blood type. This guy doesn't know what he's doing.

"No one?" he asks once more.

Double fuck.

"I do," I grit through my teeth.

"You can laugh, Stepanov. This is funny," Giovanni says with a laugh.

I take a step closer to him and dig my thumb into his wound, just like Sloane did to me. I had no idea the pressure hurts more than the actual wound itself, and I'm not sure if Giovanni does yet.

"What the fuck!" Giovanni screams, and I can't help but smile. He seethes in pain before he says, "How do you sleep at night knowing you're scum?"

"Like a baby."

The doc brings equipment to the table and puts on gloves. "I'll need your arm," he tells me.

I shake my head and roll up my sleeve. "Just do it," I mumble to Jacob.

The irony of giving blood to the man I intended to kill is beyond me.

Clubs

Chapter 33

Mikhail

Holding the envelope in my hands, I stare at it. I'm almost scared to open it. I wanted to save it in case I needed to hear his voice again. To see the marks on the paper where his hands once were. To hold a part of him close to me.

Apparently, not opening this was one of my biggest mistakes.

I rest my elbows on my knees and pinch the bridge of my nose. "Fuck," I mutter to myself.

Ripping the paper open, I unfold the letter.

Misha,

I know how stubborn you can be, and I hope that you take this note from Mia. It's the least you can do for your old man.

As I'm sure you're aware, you need to take back control of the city. Start with 324 Parkway. The men who own it are looking for investors, and they'd be idiots not to invest in you. They are family men. Use that to your advantage.

you have everything you need in order to take over,
I just wish you wouldn't let your hate overwhelm you.
Kirill will be missed, and I'm sure you'll miss me as
well. But do not let it defeat you. If you're weak,
others will attack you.
Rebuild the Stepanov name. Mia will need help around
the new house. The deed has already been registered
in your name. A woman named Sloane Kozlov will be
able to help Mia. Reach out to Ludis to get her
information.
If you use her to get back at Giovanni, I will
come back from this grave and kill you myself. Not
everything needs to result in a bloodbath.

I stop reading to clear my eyes of the liquid that fills them. *Am I fucking crying right now?* Taking in a deep breath, I pick up where I left off.

See your sister often and stop making Dimitri feel
bad about loving her. Anya has a great man who
watches over her now, and you should be thankful.
Go to the ballet recitals for me and blow Alyna
kisses like I normally do. Anya and Alyna are your
strength. Don't push them away. They're going
through losses too.
Give me fresh flowers and don't let my tombstone
rot.

Don't forget about me, son.
Pavel Stepanov

I throw the paper on the coffee table and stare at it. If I had read that sooner, so much would be different. But I don't think I would have connected with Sloane the way I have. She wouldn't have been able to push me the way she has if she worked for me.

Speaking of Sloane, she steps down the stairs with her long hair hanging freely around her face. She's wearing one of my white button-down shirts like a dress. She twirls in a circle and steps outside, leaving the patio door wide-open.

She's trying to kill me.

Standing from my seat, I walk out the door and follow her. Stepping down the cobbled stone stairs, I see her standing by the pool. It's nearly midnight—what the hell is she doing?

I approach her with a gentle smile. Seeing her happy makes me want to smile like a little kid. It makes me want to show her how I feel—no matter how foreign it might feel.

Her arms cross and her head falls back as she looks at me.

"*Shto ti delayesh malenkaya zvyozdochka?*" I ask her. *What are you doing, little star?*

"*Pochemu vi menya tak nazivayete?*" *Why do you call me that?*

"*Malenkaya zvyozdochka?*" *Little star?*

"*Da.*" *Yes.*

I smile. I love when she speaks Russian. It feels like home.

Grabbing onto her arms, I turn her to face the sea. There's an open view of the ocean since the house is built on a small hill.

"Sloane, what do you see?" I ask.

She leans her weight onto my chest and takes in a deep breath. She overthinks the question for a moment before she answers. "I see the ocean."

"What does the ocean make you feel?" I ask.

Another pause. "At ease. But terrified at times," she admits.

My chin rests on the top of her head, and I wrap my arms around the tops of her shoulders, holding her neck gently in my arms. "I see the stars," I whisper so gently goose bumps take over her skin. "But the ocean holds the reflection of the sky. Like you and me, *Moya Zvezda.*"

She lifts off me and turns slowly. Lifting her chin with the tip of my finger, I direct her attention to the sky.

"Now, what stands out in the sky?"

She looks up to see thousands, if not millions, of stars, but only one stands out.

"The North Star," she answers.

"Do you understand now?" I ask, but I don't give her the chance to respond. "You are all that I see."

"Mikhail ..." she starts.

"If something were to happen to you, you'd be leaving me, and the sky would become dull."

I'm sure my words feel like a shock to her. She stands on her toes and wraps her arms around my neck, placing a gentle kiss on my lips. It's unlike the kisses we've shared before: angry, passionate, full of lust. This one is full of admiration and trust.

She feels safe enough with me to trust me in her most vulnerable state of mind.

"When you think of me, what do you see?" I ask.

"I see you—all of you," she responds.

Relief floods my eyes. "Can you see yourself here with me?"

"What are you asking?"

"I can't express my feelings well ... but I admire you, Sloane. I can have a meeting arranged with your father."

"Are you talking about—?"

Marriage.

"I am. Think about it, Slo." I lift my hand to her cheek. Her face fits perfectly in my hands. Her lips were created to touch mine. I press my thumb on her bottom lip and pull it down. She doesn't try to move from my touch. She wants this as much as I do. Could she see herself with me?

"Tell me what you want."

She reaches up, wrapping her arms around my shoulders. Her eyes fall to my lips then back up to my eyes. "I want someone who prioritizes me." She turns around slowly. "I want someone who is kind," she says while turning toward me again. "I want someone who doesn't kill people like it's their hobby. And most importantly, I want a man with a normal job. I can't have a future with someone like you. God, if we had kids, you'd teach them to murder!" She laughs hysterically, and I bite back a smile. "That's not what I want. I want a nice man who'll think of me the moment he wakes up and

314

the moment he goes to bed."

I grab her face and run my thumb down her cheek. "You crave adventure and darkness—admit it." My jaw clenches. "You'd get bored with a nice boy. You and I both know that."

I shake my head, suddenly not able to speak any more of my thoughts into existence. Though, none of them are appropriate.

She stomps her feet, and I swear it's the most adorable thing I've ever seen. When Sloane steps back from me, I step forward, grabbing her hands.

"I am truthful. I will learn to be kind even though it serves no purpose to anyone who isn't you. I kill people, yes. That's something I can't change. If we have kids, I'll teach them how to defend themselves—why the fuck wouldn't I? Why the hell would you want someone to think of you only twice a day when you have me who thinks about you every second, Sloane? Fuck, you say you want all these things, but I'm right here."

"No, stop it. Stop telling me all these things!" she shouts.

I don't.

"What you do to a room is beyond my understanding. The moment I was able to bring a smile to your face, it filled me with a feeling I've pushed away for years. Making you smile is my high. Every single word you say brings me happiness, and I fucking take that feeling. I take and take because I am greedy and fucking selfish for your love. I want to give it back to you because you deserve the fucking world."

"Misha," she says my name.

"Stop denying what you crave, *Kroshka*," I whisper in a tone of voice I've never used before.

She doesn't have to say a single word to me. A single glance says things her voice couldn't.

Her eyes fall down the length of my torso, and her breathing slowly quickens when she leans in closer to me, placing her delicate hand against my chest.

"Fuck, Sloane," I mutter. "You can't look at me like that."

She smiles ... almost manipulatively. "Why?" she asks smoothly. "Are you weak?"

I nod, fully ready to admit my defeat. "You've ruined me."

She bites down on her bottom lip and bats her full lashes at me. "Finally," she mocks.

My hand wraps gently around her throat, and I pull her over to the rattan daybed. Her smooth legs wrap around my waist as both my arms fall to either side of her body, holding my weight up.

My knuckles brush against her stomach, and I trail my tongue over her collar bone. Goose bumps take over her skin when she feels me making my way down her chest. Her nails dig into my neck, begging for me to continue.

Her breathing picks up when I suck the skin that surrounds her breast. I gather the bottom of her shirt and pull it up past her waist, noticing she's not wearing anything underneath it. My eyes lift to hers when the tips of my fingers brush her clit.

"You're ready for me, and I've hardly touched you," I whisper in her ear.

A whimper escapes her, and the second I hear it, I know I've got her worked up. She can't deny that our anger fuels our sex.

My teeth sink into her skin and I soothe out the marks with the pressure of my thumb. Her legs part further for me. When she looks at me with those eyes of hers, I forget that she wounds me.

How is it that the person capable of shattering your heart is the only one who can mend it back together?

She's my vice, and I'll go down longing for her.

My hand covers the majority of her stomach while the tips of my fingers trail down the center. She moves relentlessly, impatient for me.

I rub her clit and watch her face crumple with need that takes over her reasoning. My fingers move slowly as I watch her unfold beneath me. She tries to lean up to take over, but I hold her down.

"Some things are meant to be savored, *Kroshka*," I tell her in a low whisper.

Her bottom lip parts from her top when I push a finger inside of her. Her back arches to my touch, and I place a trail of kisses all the way up to her neck until I find her lips.

She wraps her arms around me, pulling me close as she places her lips against mine. Her kisses start off soft but begin to feel demanding. My bottom lip gets caught in between her teeth, and she bites down.

I push her legs to the side and feel her coming around my fingers. It takes an undeniable amount of control not to come with her.

"I want two more from you," I tell her.

She escapes my hold on her and pushes me down onto the cushions. Her hair falls over her shoulder, covering her breasts slightly.

"Someone likes control," I tell her.

Her body grinds on mine when she leans down, grabbing onto my hands and pinning them above my head.

"I like seeing you look up at me," she says while she bites on my neck. I planned on edging her, but the second she begins to unbutton my pants, I forget why I even planned on taking my time.

Before she continues, I wrap my arm around her, flipping her onto her back. I toy with her until her breaking point, continuing to place kisses everywhere on her body.

"Please," she begs with a heavy breath.

I pull down her lip with my thumb. "You need to breathe first, *Kroshka*."

Her legs wrap around my hips, and she pulls me close to her. She undoes my pants eagerly. I place my hand over her chest.

"Fuck me, Mikhail," she demands.

I bite down on the inside of my cheek and align myself with her entrance. She whimpers and spreads her legs for me.

Her nails find their place on my back, and I lean down to her. "I want to hear those sounds you make for me, Sloane."

I don't resist when I push myself in and out of her. She covers her mouth, and I pull it away, guiding her hand to my back.

"Keep your hands on me," I demand.

Pushing myself further into her, I give her every inch. She cries out, but it's not from pain—these are cries of pleasure. Cries that beg for more attention.

I glide in and out of her effortlessly, and I reach down, putting pressure over her clit with my thumb. I can feel her clenching on me, and I about fucking lose it. I pull out of her to give myself strength to continue.

"Mikhail," she calls.

"One more," I whisper as I dive back into her with a thrust. She cries with pleasure while I fuck her as if I'm never going to see her again.

I put pressure on her pelvis with one hand while the other grabs onto her ass, guiding her body to mine. With marks on her skin, her body begins to work mine. I lift her up and place her on top of me. Her arms hang over my neck and her forehead presses against mine. Her fingers thread through my hair, and she pulls my head back.

"*Ti moya,*" she says as she rides me. *You are mine.*

"*Ya ves vash,*" I whimper when I feel her throbbing. *I'm all yours.*

I'm dying to spill inside of her, and I do. Fuck control—I don't have any.

I hold onto her with my hands on her back. She places a kiss on my forehead, and I lean into her touch.

All this time I've had her by my side. Having Sloane is fucking terrifying, and I love it.

As I step out of the shower, I hear pounding on my front door. Sloane watches me from the bed as I quickly throw on a pair of sweatpants and rush to see who it is.

Max's voice comes through the door. I lied to him and said I needed to get up early because I wanted time with Sloane, but I don't think he understood correctly.

"All right, I know you said you didn't want to talk and that you have to go to sleep early, but guess what, Mikhail? I simply don't give a fuck. You are my best friend. You don't get to decide when we can and can't hang out. *I do.* I'm bored. I want a shot. I couldn't give two shits about the bodies you have to bury tomorrow. Let. Me. In."

I laugh despite how frustrated I am with Sloane and Giovanni. Opening the door, I find Max looking at me, both arms holding his weight against the doorframe.

"Mikhail?" he asks.

"Yeah?"

"You actually answered."

"Are you going to cry about it?"

"No."

"Okay, then get in."

He stumbles over his feet and finds his way to the couch. "I can't be by myself," he says, lifting the bottle to his lips.

"Put the beer down, Max."

He rolls his eyes and puts it on the table, and I shuffle the cards. He takes the cards from me and deals them. While he looks at the seven cards he has, I just look at him.

"Are we seriously going to play Go Fish right now?"

"What's wrong with Go Fish? You scared to lose or something?"

"Nothing's wrong with Go Fish. You start."

We take our turns asking each other for cards. Max puts all his might into the game, and it makes me want to laugh my ass off.

"I miss her," he tells me.

"I know, but you can't do anything about it."

Max likes that I never ask him questions or force him to do anything. Giovanni thinks he spends his time running a club his father gave him, but instead he's been trying to figure out what the Clarkes are up to. I don't understand his obsession with them. He isn't the kind of person to pick a side but his own.

"I saw her," he says. "I told her she was fucking dead to me."

My gaze lifts to his, and I see a familiar pain. His eyes try to hold back the tears, but they flow down his face effortlessly.

"Some days are just ... heavy, Max. Eventually, you'll make peace with who she is in your head."

We play for a little while longer until his eyes begin to flutter and his drink falls from his hands. I shake my head even though he can't see me. Grabbing a blanket off the arm of the couch, I throw it over him.

"Sleep tight, man."

Chapter 34

Sloane

A FEW WEEKS LATER ...

Mikhail's acting as if nothing happened while Max runs around like a headless chicken. The two couldn't be any more different. Mikhail doesn't seem to be worried about the Clarkes, but Max is eager to put an end to them.

I sit at the table in a restaurant that has smooth jazz playing in the background. Nina pulls Giovanni in and whispers something in his ear to make him shake his head. I understand that technically they're my family now, but it will take some time to warm up to them.

"They're smoking outside," he tells her.

"No, that's not what I asked."

Standing up from the table, I tell them I'll go check on Max and Mikhail. I've grown even more curious than Nina while they've been bickering about what the guys are doing outside.

I walk through a sea of tables until I reach the door and swing it open.

"He wants me to put an end to this Clarke shit," Max says, flicking the ash off his cigarette.

"Just tell me when," Mikhail mutters. His back fills his suit the same way it did the first time I saw him. This moment reminds me so much of that time. I remember crashing right into his chest and falling to the ground. I thought he was beautiful in a sickening way. Now, he's beautiful in a way that nothing can compare to. His flaws make him worth so much.

"Please stop putting yourselves at war," I demand. Mikhail has been through enough. He's risked his life for so long, and there needs to be an end to this. I'm exhausted, so I can only imagine how he must feel. Actually, I'm sure he loves this. *What the hell am I thinking?*

Max shakes his head, the breeze flowing through his dark, curly locks of hair. "Nah, they're asking for it."

Max has made it his mission to tear apart the Clarkes. He's got a vendetta against them for some reason. I've tried to talk to him about it, but Max is a very closed-off person.

My arms fall to my sides. "This is ridiculous."

"They won't stick to their end of the deal. They agreed, but they'll break it," Mikhail says to me. Max got in his head.

I roll my eyes and shove him in the shoulder. He grabs me and wraps his arms around my waist. His head rests on mine while we look at Max.

Behind him, I see someone who looks familiar. A black German shepherd walks behind her, scoping out the surroundings so she doesn't have to. She walks elegantly, but with purpose. Her stride slows the further she walks away.

I knew for a fact I wasn't seeing things before. That's Rosalie—it has to be.

"Rose!" I shout.

Max's head turns quickly while he gives me a death glare. "What the fuck did you just say?" he asks with a tone of voice I've never heard before. His face turns white and his lips part slightly. He looks as if he's seen a ghost.

I'm taken aback by his attitude, but there's no time to ask questions. "That's my friend. I'll be right back," I say, moving off swiftly. "Rosalie!" I shout again.

She turns her head slowly and smiles when she sees me. All this time

I thought I was crazy, but now I'm seeing her again, I knew I was wrong. "Sloane," she says, making her way over, but she looks at me strangely.

Not at me ...

At Max.

Max grabs onto my arm, pulling me away from her. His grip is tight against my wrist as if he's trying to protect me in a strange way. I look down at my wrist and back at him. His eyes are filled with dread. They fall with defeat.

He refuses to look anywhere but in the direction of Rosalie.

She's running away fast. Her dog looks back before he races to catch up with her.

"Do you know her?" I ask.

"Do I know who?"

"That girl."

Max moves past me, walking back over to Mikhail. "I don't see anyone," he mumbles, shrugging me off.

"But you reacted when I said her name!"

"You're seeing ghosts."

My brow furrows. "No, I'm not. I literally just saw her."

He ignores me and walks back inside after he throws his cigarette to the floor, stomping out the butt.

My mouth hangs open while I process what the hell is happening. "You saw her, right?" I ask, turning back to Mikhail.

He doesn't say anything; his eyes just fall.

"Mikhail," I demand.

"I think it's best if we go inside."

First Max, now Mikhail? It's like they're both refusing to admit they saw her too for some reason.

Mikhail's hand holds the small of my back while he leads me back inside. How is he able to act as if nothing happened before we came back inside? Are we both just going to ignore what we saw?

Laughter fills the room when we enter, but I don't feel happiness. I feel like I'm dying with questions. Rosalie is quick to appear but disappears like nothing ever happened. That's not normal—I know that much.

I take a seat on the bench with Mikhail. Max takes Mira from Nina's arms and sways her in his large arms. I watch him in awe.

Nina's baby, Mira, was born about a week ago, right after the ball where Giovanni was shot by Mikhail. The two of them act as if it never happened. I can't tell if they don't have the energy to hash out their differences or if they're putting their differences aside for me and Nina.

The second Max grabs Mira, it's as if he forgets all his worries. He only sees her. When I look at Max, I don't usually see a family guy in him, but I do now.

"You look just like her, you know?" Giovanni says to me, finally breaking the awkward feeling. I've always wanted to know more about my mother, but Dad told me it hurt to talk about her.

"Do you have a picture?" I ask.

Giovanni reaches into his pocket and pulls out a picture of our mother.

"Wow," I say. I really do look just like her. "It's the hair," I tell him with a laugh.

"Different colors, but ..."—he pauses as the corner of his mouth tugs up—"very curly."

I take the picture in my hands and see another behind it. The second one is a photo of me at the house in Russia. I think I'm fifteen in the picture. So many things have changed since then.

"How did you get this picture of me?" I ask.

"Kirill."

Finally, I ask the question I've been dying to know. "Are you the Suits?"

Everyone directs their attention to me.

I'm not asking this out of nowhere—Max is wearing an embroidered heart. I can't even begin to understand the meaning behind it.

"Yes," Max admits with a grumble.

The only reason I'm not completely intimidated by Max is because he has a gentle face. His jaw is sharp, but there's something about his eyes.

"Do you mind if I ask the meaning behind the group?"

"Not at all," Giovanni chimes in. "It started with Max. It was a way for people to decipher business deals between him and his father. Since they shared the same last name, he didn't want people thinking the business transactions would benefit him. While Max's father is still alive, it's a way for him to take over profits under a different name. I followed the idea while my father was still alive. Max's friend Marco was by his side through everything, and he decided to follow his idea. He has diamonds."

It's getting kind of difficult to keep up with all the information being thrown at me. It makes sense, but it's a lot. "And Mikhail took over clubs," I say.

"He did. Probably because of Kirill, but I'm not sure if he knew the meaning behind it at the time. He was trying to get under my skin when he took the name."

"Bottom of the chain," I mutter.

"I wanted to join in the fun," Mikhail says with a half-smile.

"It's not something you should concern yourself with. We've made a lot of enemies doing this. Many think we're creating separate families this way. It makes the threats higher if there are more families involved. I can't really say I blame them for it either."

I nod in response. It's going to take a while to warm up to Giovanni and Nina.

Everyone besides Max lowers their voices when they see a man approach the table.

"Marco," Max calls.

Not a thing about him is approachable. "Are we not going to talk about it?" he demands while pulling up a chair. He gives me a strange smile. His eyes are brooding, and his nose lines up perfectly with his full lips. His dark complexion makes his hazel eyes stand out. The dark lashes that lift from his eyes are long and curl effortlessly.

His attention drifts across the room, and I feel myself beginning to question everything about myself. His eyes are not kind; they're judgmental, as if nothing around him is even worth a second glance.

We all stare at him, wondering what he means. "Talk about what?" Giovanni asks, not seeming interested in Marco at all.

"Where the fuck is my money?"

I look at Mikhail. He's just as confused as I am. "What do you mean?" Max asks.

Marco's tongue rolls over his cheek. "You've got to be fucking kidding me. So it's just me then?"

Mira coos, breaking the awkward silence between us all. "Check your accounts. Right now," he throws out, and the men oblige.

I scoot closer to Mikhail, growing nervous. I don't care for money, but I know it means a lot to the people surrounding me.

Max's face falls flat.

Marco leans back in his chair as if he's content to know it's not just him.

"I still have everything," Mikhail admits.

"As do I," Giovanni adds.

I take in a deep breath, glad I won't have to see Mikhail lose his shit.

"What the fuck is happening?" Max asks.

Marco laughs, but it's not the kind sprouted from joy. "Come on, Max. You're a big boy. Figure it out."

Max clenches his jaw, irritated by how Marco is talking to him. He shakes his head and puts his phone down on the table. He stands up and hands Mira to Giovanni. He places his hand on my shoulder as he passes behind me, making his way over to Marco.

"What did you do?" Max demands.

Marco smiles, not hiding his emotion. "You're joking. Please tell me you're joking," he says as he stands up from his chair. He presses a finger against Max's chest. "*You* are the one who decided to get involved with the Clarkes. You just don't know when to quit. Because of you, we have a fucking joker on our hands."

"I'll deal with it," Max seethes.

I hold my tongue and watch them hash it out.

"If you want to deal with it, you need to fucking end it. Stop toying with that fucking family, Max. I'm over it."

Max folds his arms and his head falls back. "Remember who you're talking to."

My glare turns into a worried expression. I've heard Max and Marco are really close friends, and to see them fighting like this concerns me. I can only assume they're talking about the Clarkes.

I turn to look at Mikhail, and he simply shakes his head. He grabs onto my hand and stands up from his chair. "Let's go. We're leaving."

Clearing my throat, I tell Nina and Giovanni I'll have to catch up with them another time. It's clear to me Mikhail doesn't want me involved in Max's argument, but at the end of the day I want to be involved. He was there for me when I needed him the night Mikhail found out everything. If he hadn't stuck by my side, I wouldn't be surrounded by everyone tonight. Giovanni wouldn't be here. I could see the hatred Mikhail has for Giovanni as clear as day when he held the gun up to his head.

I want to help Max the way he helped me. He is a kind man suffering from a heartbreak—I think. I'm not entirely sure because he refuses to even talk about it.

Chapter 35

Mikhail

I tap on the hood of the car and turn to walk back inside when Sloane steps next to me. "I think you should help Max," she tells me with tenderness.

Opening the door for her, I nod. "You can't force someone to take help they don't want."

She lets out a huff of air. "I know, but he's changing, and not for the better."

I walk down the steps from the foyer that lead into the living room. "Max is smart. He knows what he's doing." I try to reassure her as much as I can, but when Sloane cares for someone, she will dig. I'm not even sure how she and Max were able to connect, but I kind of admire her for it.

Max can be a difficult person to care for since he's so disconnected from reality, and Sloane is exactly who he needs.

"*Kroshka,*" I call for her just as she's about to walk up the stairs.

Turning back around, her eyes slowly find mine, and the second they do ... I crumble. I could stare at her for hours on end and never tire of her beauty.

God, I want to hold her.

She steps toward me with a pained smile. A smile that begs to be kissed. I would do so much for that smile.

Her hair is in a tight bun, the kind ballerinas wear. Her button nose is covered with freckles. Her dress is white linen. Everything about her is heaven.

I cup my hands around her face. Her hand falls to the back of my head, and she runs her fingers through my hair in the way only she can.

Her arms wrap around my shoulders, and she places her lips on mine. Her kiss is eager, begging more of me. My arms wrap around the small of her back, pulling her close to me. Then I lift her by her legs and move her onto the counter. I tug her hair out of the bun and watch it fall over her body.

I've never seen anything more stunning than her.

She pulls me into her by the collar of my shirt and unbuttons it slowly. As eager as I am, I want her to take her time. I want to absorb every second she gives me because I'll never get enough of her. "You're not good for me," she tells me, though I know it's a lie.

"You're not good for me either, but guess what, *Koldunya?*" I whisper in her ear. "We're a match made in hell."

Sloane's kisses are deadly. They hurt me in the best possible way. Nothing in this world could ever compare to her.

"*Ya lublyu tebya,*" I whisper in her ear. *I love you.*

Her body stills in my arms, and I swear I feel her heart begin to race. "How long will your love last?" she asks.

I hesitate at her question, but only for a moment. "Until long after my last breath."

She looks deep into my eyes. "*Ya tebya tozhe lublyu,*" she finally admits. *I love you too.*

I grab onto her waist and lead her into the living room. "Right there," I say and point to the corner of the room. "That is where your bookshelves will go." I turn her body toward the kitchen. "That is where you'll dance your heart out cooking to classics. Or it's where you'll brew your potions—hell if I know."

She turns around laughing and slaps me on the arm. I wrap my arms around her waist and place my chin on top of her head.

"I'm not a witch."

Sounds like something a witch would say.

I smile as I turn her toward the fireplace. "This is where you'll watch all your favorite movies while I rub your back."

She moves her hands to grip mine. I hover my lips above her neck. She melts into my touch as she moves her head to the side, welcoming my kiss.

I smile and turn her toward the stairs. "Up there is where you'll lie with me each night. It's where you'll help me decorate a nursery when the time comes."

She lets go and turns to me. Her eyes bore into mine, challenging me.

"Don't say anything," I beg. I don't need her mouth to ruin the one moment I'm trying to be a romantic. I know she'd call me out for even bringing up the idea of having children, and she can save it because I don't want to hear it.

She tries to wrap her arms around my neck, but I stop her. *She's an eager one.* Holding her face in my hands, I brush her skin.

"And right here is where you bring me to my knees and I ask you to love me forever." I grab onto her hand and kneel to the ground. The look on her face is priceless. It means everything to me and more.

"Mikhail," she starts.

Her love chains me down in the best way possible. I never thought love could have different meanings, but it does. The love I have for Sloane is the kind I'd burn the entire fucking world for.

The simple look in her eyes could bring me to my knees.

"I've never had anyone to call home before. You are my home," I say. "Take my name. Take all my time. Take my heart in your hands. Take me as your husband."

She drops to the floor and holds onto my hands, wiping away the tears before she places her forehead against mine. "You and me?"

I nod. "You and me, *Koldunya.*"

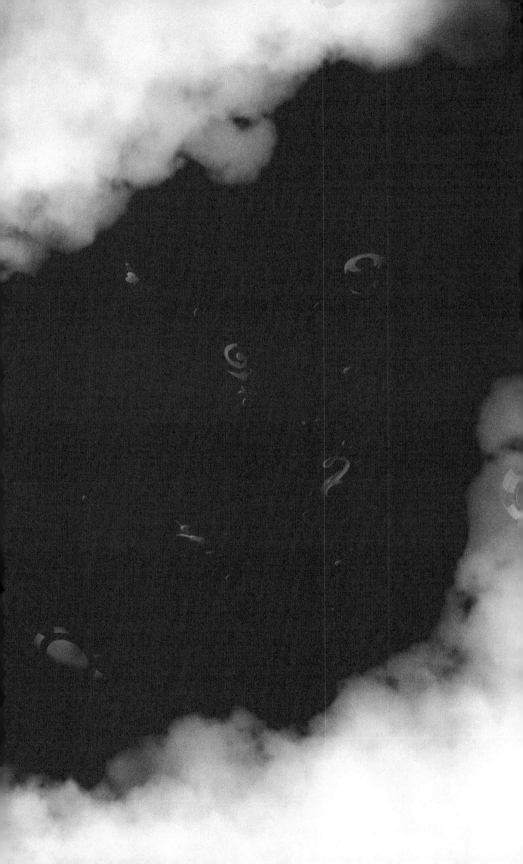

Chapter 36

Mikhail

Sloane grumbles while she climbs on top of me, grabbing my phone off the nightstand. It rings with an obnoxious tone. It's the only one that ever wakes me up, but it didn't this time. Sloane—a very heavy sleeper—heard it before me.

"What do you want?" she demands of the other person on the line.

Her legs straddle my hips, and it takes everything in me not to act on my impulsive thoughts. She's so sexy when she's angry.

"She's alive." I hear Max's voice through the phone. It sounds broken and hopeful at the same time. I'm not sure if that's a good thing or not.

Probably not.

Sloane brings her attention to me with a look of curiosity. "Who?" she asks hesitantly.

"Rosalie ... the woman you saw. I saw her too, and she's not where I thought she was."

My eyes slam shut when I think about what he's doing. He wouldn't do that ... *would he?*

Sloane mumbles something to me that I can't understand, but she shares my shock. "Where did you think she was?" she asks.

Max pauses. When it takes him some time to answer, my suspicions are confirmed. "Uh, in the ..." He stutters. "I thought she was in her grave."

I snatch the phone from Sloane and bring it to my ear. "What the fuck are you doing?" I ask with anger.

"Doing what I should have done years ago."

I take in a deep breath. "Where are you?"

"Glenwood Cemetery."

Sloane watches me intently, wondering what's going on, and I explain to her that Max is in the Clarkes' territory. I thought Max and Marco hashed it out, but I guess not.

"I'll be there in half an hour. Stay put."

As I get ready I can feel the steam blowing from my ears. I fucking try, I really do. I wanted to take Sloane out to see the world and explore places she's always dreamed of seeing, but that'll have to wait since Max is starting something instead of ending it.

She looks at me and pulls the sheets back over her body, falling back onto the mattress. "I take it you don't want to tag along?" I say with a smile while I get ready.

"No. It's like four in the morning."

Once my jacket is on, I climb back into the bed with her and hover my head over hers. "I want a kiss," I tell her.

She smiles, wrapping her arms around my shoulders, and I place my lips on hers. Being in her arms makes me want to forget about everything I need to do and just stay here with her.

"I want more when I get back."

I lean off her and walk out the door, hearing her mumble, "Your wish is my command."

Getting to the car, I drive to the part of the city where Max is at. When I pull the car up to the curb, I shut it off and get out. Rain pelts my forehead, and I brush it away. Stepping onto the sidewalk, I see Max sitting on a bench with dirt covering his suit—the same suit he wore to the dinner.

What happened when we left? I'm sure Marco said something offensive to

Max, otherwise he wouldn't have dug up a fucking grave to prove himself.

My hands fly in the air.

"I had to," he tells me as if he needs to defend himself.

Honestly, I don't care much about the reason behind his pain. Whoever hurt Max hurt me as well.

"You could've called me, you fucking idiot," I tell him.

He walks past me. "I did call you."

My head falls back. "I meant before you dug up a grave."

He smiles. "Well, you're here now."

I follow him up the hill. We pass hundreds of graves that appear black from years of being left alone. He stops at her grave. Mounds of dirt surround the hole, and I stare at him.

"You can't just leave this open."

Taking a closer look, I see the open casket with white padding surrounding the walls. I make a face of approval.

I guess he was right.

Jumping down, I close the casket and shake my head again. I can't believe I'm doing this right now.

My hands reach the top, and I lift myself out.

"There's nothing in it. There's no point," he says.

I shake my head and scowl at him, taking the shovel leaning against a tree. "People would notice wet dirt, let alone an open fucking grave."

I start digging the dirt back into the grave when Max clears his throat.

"Say 'fuck' one more time," he muses.

I pause and give him a look. He watches me for a while until I throw the shovel at him. The rain worsens, and Max starts to grunt while he gets exhausted.

My phone rings in my pocket, and I can't help but look at my hands—they're covered in dirt, and so is my suit. "You're buying me a new one," I tell him before I wipe my hands on my chest.

Taking my phone out of my pocket, I answer. "Stepanov."

"You think you can come to my land in the night and I won't see you?"

Liam.

335

My mouth lifts as a wicked grin takes over my lips. I shouldn't be excited to hear from him, but I am. In a strange way, I kind of understand why Max is so obsessed with this family. It's a constant game of tag, and I *love* it.

I step toward Max and put the call on speaker. Max doesn't look as thrilled as I am, but he brought me into this shit, so I may as well have my fun.

"What are you doing?" Liam asks, demanding an answer.

"Digging a grave on this fine morning," I answer.

"That's my daughter's grave you're destroying."

I'm aware.

Max digs the shovel into the ground and grabs the phone from me. "It's not like her grave serves a fucking purpose."

"You had no right, Romano."

Max smiles. *There it is.* He's just as sick as I am. "I have all the right."

He turns and searches around us, and I do too. A couple of men are hiding behind the trees on the top of the hill. Their dark clothing doesn't hide them very well since the sun is starting to illuminate the sky slowly.

"You move a fucking inch, and I will put a bullet in the back of your head."

My brows rise, and I laugh. "Look at this badass," I say sarcastically.

"You plan to marry Sloane, right?" he asks.

"Of course."

"Good. We'll need that alliance."

My eyes lift to Max's, and we both grin.

We're only just getting started.

To be continued ...

Acknowledgments

First—to all of you. Thank you all for reading Mikhail and Sloane's story. I know I'm hard to keep up with sometimes, but blame Sloane and Mikhail, not me. (They're the ones who keep changing things.) Okay, being serious now, so many of you have been right by my side cheering for this series. I wish I could give you the world. Writing "to be continued" felt strange to me, but I felt as if Sloane and Mikhail didn't need an epilogue. It wasn't them. They both crave adventure, and they wouldn't want a "the end." Their story will continue through this series, and I'm sure you'll be seeing a lot of them in the next book! Writing this story meant everything to me because I was able to depict that love has a million definitions. It's unique to every couple and will never mean the same thing. Max's story will be a roller coaster. I'm nervous, and I've already cried about it, but you'll find his love in one of the million ways there are.

Bryony—you *might* want to edit this page too. No, I'm *sure* of it. Thank you for being the best at what you do and going through this manuscript with a fine-tooth comb. Without your help and suggestions, this book would be very different. You've helped me flesh out the characters in a way I can't even begin to explain. You're the best! I wouldn't want to work on this series with anyone else. <3

Anastasia—@nastusha.vayner—this manuscript would have been a mess without your help. You helped me with the translations and went above and beyond so that I could accurately portray the Russian language. I wouldn't have been able to do this without you! <3

To my beta/alpha readers—@abbies.reads, @mackenzies_library, @_onlypages_, @zainabslibrary, Natalie, and Jordan, you guys are so lovely. There truly are no words to describe how much I appreciate everything that you do. All the comments, suggestions, and excitement brought a *huge* smile to my face. Without your help, I never would have noticed that I lost sight of the plot halfway through, haha! Thank you for being a part of this story.

I couldn't do this without you. <3

To all the bloggers—you post about the book, but I only see you. I'm in awe of all of you. Nothing makes me happier than seeing you all on my timeline. <3

Ana—this book is dedicated to you, so I hope you read it. (I know you will, I don't know why I'm saying that.) Anyway, during hours and hours spent by the pool in the summer getting our tans, you helped me bring this book to life. You'd come up with such crazy ideas at night that some of them kind of shocked me, but I was completely amazed. You once told me something along the lines of, "I can't write it, but how fun is it to imagine that story?" I wrote that kitchen scene for you. It's real now. When you make something with thyme, I hope you think of me. (:

To my family—thank you for cheering me on even if you can't keep up with my ideas. I'm sorry for changing the plot so many times. But I can't help myself; the characters write themselves, not me.

Mackenzie—"I already want to reread Clubs." You crack me up. Thank you for always being my number one speed dial. I know you're anxious to read about Max, but don't worry: he is next, and you will *love* him.

Lauren Asher and Sophie Lark—you guys have helped me with so much I can't thank you enough.

To all of you who want to be an author—write the damn book. I want to read it.

Want to keep in touch?
I post updates here:

Instagram
@Kyrairene__

TikTok
@Kyrairene_

Made in United States
Orlando, FL
28 December 2023

41779982R00211